PRAISE for

THE DAY TRIPPER
BY JAMES GOODHAND

'An essential, profound read.' —*THE WASHINGTON POST*

'It takes tremendous skill to transform a sci-fi trope into an emotional tear-jerker, which James Goodhand does.'
—*SHELF AWARENESS* (STARRED REVIEW)

'Witty and wise, *The Day Tripper* had me pulling for Alex through all of his mixed-up days. James Goodhand brings a fun, fresh voice to the time travel genre in this gem of a novel. I loved it!'
—SHELBY VAN PELT, *NEW YORK TIMES* BESTSELLING AUTHOR OF *REMARKABLY BRIGHT CREATURES*

'*The Day Tripper* is absolutely astonishing, from first page to last. Warm, clever, hopeful, and superbly written. James Goodhand is a brilliant storyteller at the top of his game. I adored it.'
—STUART TURTON, *SUNDAY TIMES* BESTSELLING AUTHOR OF *THE 7 ½ DEATHS OF EVELYN HARDCASTLE*

'*The Day Tripper* is a brilliantly-written exploration of the choices we make every day, and how those choices shape the people we become. It blew my mind and broke my heart, and I haven't stopped thinking about it since I finished it!'
—GARETH BROWN, *SUNDAY TIMES* BESTSELLING AUTHOR OF *THE BOOK OF DOORS*

'*The Day Tripper* is a page-turner.' —*BOOKLIST*

'Goodhand's debut is a compelling look at the way decisions, good and bad, build up over time to create a life.'
—*LIBRARY JOURNAL*

REPORTS OF HIS DEATH HAVE BEEN GREATLY EXAGGERATED

JAMES GOODHAND

/||MIRA

If you purchased this book without a cover you should be aware that this book is stolen property. It was reported as "unsold and destroyed" to the publisher, and neither the author nor the publisher has received any payment for this "stripped book."

///MIRA™

ISBN-13: 978-0-7783-8746-6

Reports of His Death Have Been Greatly Exaggerated

Copyright © 2025 by James Goodhand

All rights reserved. No part of this book may be used or reproduced in any manner whatsoever without written permission.

Without limiting the author's and publisher's exclusive rights, any unauthorized use of this publication to train generative artificial intelligence (AI) technologies is expressly prohibited.

This is a work of fiction. Names, characters, places and incidents are either the product of the author's imagination or are used fictitiously. Any resemblance to actual persons, living or dead, businesses, companies, events or locales is entirely coincidental.

For questions and comments about the quality of this book, please contact us at CustomerService@Harlequin.com.

TM is a trademark of Harlequin Enterprises ULC.

MIRA
22 Adelaide St. West, 41st Floor
Toronto, Ontario M5H 4E3, Canada
MIRABooks.com

HarperCollins Publishers
Macken House, 39/40 Mayor Street Upper,
Dublin 1, D01 C9W8, Ireland
www.HarperCollins.com

Printed in U.S.A.

For Janet & Adrian

REPORTS OF HIS DEATH HAVE BEEN GREATLY EXAGGERATED

1

TUESDAY

THERE WAS NOTHING OF NOTE ABOUT THE GENTLEMAN AT MY FRONT DOOR that evening to suggest he would drop dead in little over an hour.

My instinct had been to ignore the doorbell altogether. All I really wanted was to be left to my own devices.

'Be a pal, would you, Ron?' the gentleman said. In one hand he rocked a tartan Thermos side to side. With the other he pinched the collar of his mackintosh tight as an icy wind whipped along the street, sweeping newly spread salt to the kerb. Late March, but not yet a whiff of spring. 'Been three days without the electric,' he told me. 'Would you believe it? If you'd be so kind, Ron?'

I held the door open no more than was necessary, my head sandwiched between it and the jamb. 'Some hot water?' I asked. I should have taken this opportunity to mention that my name is in fact Ray, not *Ron*, but I let the matter lie, accepting that— chance missed—I'd be misnamed for the duration. He and I had known each other, in passing, for twenty years or more. His name was Barry Detmer. He lived not-quite-opposite in the ground-floor flat with the gaffer-taped letterbox and the budgerigar cage in the window. We exchanged pleasantries here and there and had spoken a couple of times at greater length: once about an abandoned van, on another occasion about the proliferation of smaller dog breeds. These conversations all felt as though they'd happened within the last year or two, but on closer scrutiny of my memory were more than a decade ago.

'Council said it'd be fixed yesterday,' Barry told me. 'Then it was this morning. Then it was by the end of today. Drive you mad, don't they, Ron?'

'Let me guess, electronic ignition boiler?'

'You got it. No leccy, no heating neither.' We shared an ironic chuckle at *progress*.

'Three days? You must be bloody frozen.'

Barry searched the ground at his feet, as people tend to, for the point to which my stare kept returning. I've never been a natural eye contactor; when I *do* try I feel invasive and find my gaze wandering south entirely of its own accord, causing unease and a shifting of clothing, most especially when addressing a female.

'I'm sure I've a Primus stove *somewhere*,' I said. 'Whether I have a gas bottle, well that's another matter.'

'Just a kettle full, Ron—that'll do me. Enough for a brew and a wash.'

'I think I should probably have you in, really,' I said, slackening my hold on the front door.

'I don't want to be a nuisance.' He gritted his teeth as another gust snapped his trousers round narrow legs.

'No. I really should.'

'You're a pal, Ron,' he said as I led us down the one-person-wide path along the hallway, between the books and boxes stacked to one side, the many local papers and periodicals that I've not yet got around to, on the other. The topmost was a garish red promotion from an appliance store, emblazoned *Special Offers for Ray Thorns*. I turned it over to spare Barry's blushes at misremembering my name.

'Steady on. Steady on,' I said as we squeezed into the darkened lounge, where we stood too close in the square of available floor.

'My word,' Barry said. 'You have some bits and pieces.'

'You know how it is. One tends to . . . accrue.'

'Well, you have *accrued* all right, old pal,' he chuckled.

It was odd how the house looked so suddenly different, knowing it was being viewed for the first time by someone. The slack woodchip, the blues records stacked haphazardly to waist height, the many binbags stuffed full of unsorted charity shop purchases, the sheer weight of the shelving leaving the television set somewhat askew: things I've barely ever noticed, far less *thought about*, in years. I switched on the second and third bars of the fire. The stench of burnt dust rose from the glow.

Barry warmed his palms. 'For the grandkids?' he asked, eyeing the model Mercedes–Benz racing car lying stripped to every last screw and rivet on a tea tray.

'Yes. Yes, of course. Ready for paint, now. And a little chrome plating here and there.'

'That's some collection you've got, Ron,' he said, looking at the many completed projects parked around the room and on the furniture. He studied a couple up close: a desert pink de Havilland bomber I restored from a car boot sale, a somewhat unloved mobile cinema truck now gleaming in its white and blue livery and with all new glass.

'Something to keep me out of trouble. It's not so much about the finished products, it's the search and rescue that I rather like.'

'How old?' Barry asked.

'Oh, quite varied. 1950s are something of a golden age. Some much newer, eighties and even nineties. I've a few pre-war Schuco models about too.'

'No,' Barry laughed. 'The grandkids! How old?'

'Yes, right. Twelve and . . . nine.'

'Nice ages.' He didn't ask for names or genders.

'And yours?'

He looked a little warmer at the thought. 'In their twenties now. All five of them.'

'Blimey.'

'Just the two for you?'

'That's right.' I busied myself clearing an armchair of dinner plates (unused) and folded clothes. 'I should make that tea. You must be gasping.'

'Been doing me in, I don't mind telling you. That new family two doors up—you think *they'd* have to wait three days?'

I smiled at the floor. I'd no wish to encourage him, nor seem impolite. I was quite aware which family he meant. They've certainly caused *me* no bother.

'What are they, Ron? Albanians?'

'Ukrainian I believe.'

'Should've given some foreign name, shouldn't I? Council be right around, make sure I'm in the lap of luxury.'

'Perhaps so,' I mumbled.

'Always us last in the queue, isn't it, Ron?'

'Go a little easy on this old thing,' I said, dusting down the cushion. 'It's of quite some age. Would you believe that my own mother was breast fed on this very chair? I turned some new bun feet for it a while back from a little salvaged walnut, though. Good for another century of service.'

'Yes. Right. Thanks,' he said, looking a touch jarred but taking the weight off his feet all the same.

'I don't imagine you've eaten?' I called from the kitchen over the roaring kettle. It had taken some minutes but I'd dug out my favourite of the larger teapots (stout steel, charity shop, five cups with ease).

'Had something at lunch. Cold, needless to say.'

I felt a faint dread at his answer. Of course, the right thing was to provide the man a hot meal. I'd eaten alone, almost exclusively, in the twenty-something years since my earlier-than-planned retirement. Should I not be glad of the company? I took the menu from the drawer. I usually only treat myself on Christmas Eve; the thought of another takeaway in barely three months sweetened the deal. 'You eat Chinese, Barry?'

'Damn right I do!' He was moseying in the hallway, examining the pictures on the walls, hands clasped behind his back, expression of mild interest on his face, the way a royal surveys a foreign custom. 'But honestly, Ron, don't worry yourself.'

'My treat. Please. They're very efficient. We'll have you back home inside an hour, lickety-split, warm and fed.'

'You're a true gent.' He took his tea mug from me with two grey hands.

'The set menu for two has always stoked my fancy.'

'Allonby House?' he said, peering closely at a school photograph hung by the kitchen door. 'Your kids went there?' He didn't disguise his amazement that someone of our standing might educate their children at such a place.

'No. Not *mine*.' I replied.

'The fees must be *frightening*.'

'I believe they are. No, I was on the staff. Gave thirty-nine years of my life to that school.'

'Get less for murder,' Barry said, gulping his tea.

'I was the caretaker, officially speaking.'

'Unofficially?'

'Well, I did all sorts. Built props for plays, coached the chess team. And I taught some classes too, as time went on. Science mostly. English. History sometimes for the older boys—eleven, twelve, thirteen in some cases. I even had my own tutor group for a while—a scholarship class.' My tone was braggy. I tamed it before continuing. 'Things weren't so *regimented* back then, I suppose.'

'They must've thought very highly of you, Ron.'

'The boys used to call me Spike. You know, instead of Mr Thorns. You get it? Instead of . . . Thorns.' I stopped myself saying *Ray* just in time.

'Spike. I see.' The nickname didn't amuse him like it does me. 'Who's this bloke with the bright green hair?' He tapped a shaky finger on the glass over where the masters were seated.

'Well now that, would you believe, is in fact yours truly.'

'No!'

'As God is my witness.'

'You're telling me punk made it as far as London's poshest prep schools?'

I laughed. 'Something like that.' I must have in my possession twenty school photographs from my life at Allonby House, but it was this—1982, year of the green hair incident—that I'd given wall space to, hanging there long enough for the fleeting sweep of morning sun to begin washing the colours away.

'That *is* you,' Barry said. 'I can see it now.'

I smiled at those stacked rows of young men, each of whom would be something around fifty now. 'Yes. I suppose it was.'

'So you couldn't have sent yours there, then?' he asked, as I refilled his mug. He was still wearing his coat, still looking every bit as cold and pale.

'Sorry, my . . . ?'

'Your own children.'

'Yes, right.'

'Don't they usually do a deal for teachers? Cheaper fees?'

'I wasn't a *teacher* in the strictest sense. Perhaps there was an arrangement in place, I forget. But no, I didn't . . . take it up.'

'Don't suppose it did them any harm.'

'Tell me about yours,' I said quickly. He was only too keen—gabbing for some minutes about his son and daughter-in-law's emigration to the Costa Blanca, their many successful businesses, the achievements and fledgling careers of the grandchildren.

It's not that I'm in the habit of *inventing* children and grandchildren for myself. More that people assume, and I don't go out of my way to correct them. This was not the first time I'd found myself head of a fictitious family, through no real fault of my own. The trouble is, people do love to talk about these things. There seems no harm in letting it be imagined that I had a wife, be her dead or divorced, and my quota of two-point-four children; not if that belief leaves someone free to enthuse about them and theirs.

Easier, certainly, than trying to convince someone that I am perfectly content to be a bachelor. It does afford one so many freedoms, after all.

I have, on a few occasions in the past, dared to confess to the fact that I almost *did* marry someone, once upon a time. But it's a statement that invariably leads to all sorts of questions that I'd, frankly, prefer not to entertain.

'You're shivering, Barry,' I said. His monologue had run its course, during which he had sunk onto the only stool in the kitchen.

'Yes, I'm not quite feeling a hundred per cent.' There was a stubble of sweat on his top lip.

'I think these few days have taken their toll on you, young man,' I said. My voice was suddenly different, a sound that echoed back to decades ago.

'Think so,' he huffed.

'A nice warm bath? Would that be the thing?' And still there was, I'm sure of it, no indication that he was seriously unwell.

'That's a fine idea,' Barry said.

I cleared a path up the stairs in order that a foot could be landed on every step. Thankfully, there was a clean towel, one of the good ones, resting against the cylinder in the airing cupboard and piping hot, perfect for when he was done. I filled the tub to within a whisker of the overflow with a decent glug of bubble bath (used not as an indulgence, but it works wonders in preventing a tidemark after draining). With the towel, I left a choice of talcs, and a good pair of slippers I've yet to wear.

'You go and relax, Barry,' I told him in the hallway as I slipped on my overcoat to go and grab the takeaway, figuring the privacy would be appreciated in addition to the warmth. Finding little cash in my wallet, I left it on the telephone shelf, instead retrieving a couple of twenties from one of my hiding spots inside the 2007 Yellow Pages. 'I'll be back in half an hour or so, armed with a feast!'

'You're a pal, Ron,' he said once more.

2

I WAS GONE LONGER THAN I EXPECTED. THERE'D BEEN A GENTLEMAN AHEAD of me in the queue with a large order and few manners. He wore *designer* white Wellingtons, which put me in mind of an abattoir. When eventually I was served, I had no wish to cause further nuisance by mentioning that I'd been given pineapple chicken and beef with onions instead of the spareribs and crispy duck I'd ordered. No matter: the warm and weighty carrier bag that swung against my leg as I strode home pumped divine-smelling steam against my knuckles.

I'm ashamed to admit that I was not especially concerned at first by the presence of the ambulance; ours is a well-populated street with a handful of residents who have drop-in carers and a propensity for *falls*.

I stopped dead in my tracks at the sight of my own front door, wide open. Of Barry, being fastened to a stretcher just within the hallway. A paramedic tucked his bare, pale arms beneath the red blanket; it appeared he was nearly, if not completely, naked. I stood at the roadside and watched. Barry was most severely grey in the face.

'Thank you, sir,' one of the paramedics said as I stepped clear of the stretcher.

'Steady on, steady on,' I said at a safe distance as she hustled it across the rutted pavement. I attempted a reassuring smile at Barry as he was whisked into the fluorescent light of the ambulance.

His eyes flickered open but found no focus. He mumbled and strained at the belts retaining him.

'Sorry, I don't want to interfere,' I said to the paramedic as she slung her kit bag through the doors. Her colleague meanwhile was inside with Barry, stretching an oxygen mask around his head.

'You know him?' she asked hurriedly.

'Yes. Indeed. He lives opposite me. We're neighbours. Well, friends I suppose.' I glanced at my takeaway. 'We were about to eat.'

She held up a palm and took a step backwards. 'He's having pains in his chest,' she said. 'We need to get things moving along. He needs to be fully assessed. Hospital's the best place for him.'

'Oh. Chest pain. Christ. Yes, of course. Don't let me . . .'

'Saint Helen's,' she said, half in the driving seat already. 'If you want to follow along?'

'Yes, I may do that.'

Blue light splashed across the fronts of the houses and flats. 'We've spoken to next door,' she said, pointing to *my* next door neighbour's house. 'They're aware.'

'Right. He's okay though, would you say?'

'We'll be taking good care of him.'

'Of course. Jolly good.' I raised my bag of Chinese. 'Would you and your colleague like this?' I asked through her open window. 'For the road, so to speak.'

'That's kind, but we're all right,' she said with a quick smile.

'God alone knows how you good people find the time for a meal break,' I said, inspecting the contents of the bag. I was rather making a fool of myself; I realise that. Not in *shock* perhaps, but I was a trifle flustered. 'It's really no bother. I don't imagine I'll be eating.'

But she was already on the move, wheels scratching at the gritted road. A siren tore through the frozen night, and faded away down the road, till it was just one more in the chorus that hovers always over London.

THE HALLWAY WAS A DREADFUL MESS. ON HANDS AND KNEES I REASSEMBLED the pile of local papers scattered about the floor. Barry's mackintosh, together with several of my own coats lay across the stairs; their wall peg had been sheared off. *Poor old chap*, I kept mumbling as I restored some order from the carnage of his staggering about. *Poor, poor chap.* If only I'd been here at the critical moment.

A duotone whistled at me from the telephone receiver, dangling on its coiled cord. It occurred to me that my wallet wasn't where I'd left it on the shelf by the door, nor was it anywhere obvious nearby. I fretted for a time, checking beneath and behind things, but after a time it didn't seem such a pressing matter.

The bath water was tepid but unused. Barry's clothes and shoes were heaped on the lavatory seat. I folded them into a neat pile and took his bunch of keys from the pocket for safekeeping. I smoothed his pale green shirt beneath my palms. It was worn through at the fold in the collar. There was a mustiness about it and layers of days-old cologne.

I was struck by sudden concern for Barry's well-being, not to mention a private embarrassment that putting the house in order had seemed such a priority this past half hour. He'd be needing his clothes. Perhaps other things from home too. Casual acquaintance or not, who else was there to help the poor old chap out?

3

'BARRY?' THE GENTLEMAN AT THE CASUALTY RECEPTION ASKED FOR A SEC-ond time, dragging a computer mouse agitatedly about his desk.

'Detmer,' I said, forced to raise my voice above the mêlée in the waiting room, where there were at least twice as many people as there were seats. 'It's like rush hour at King's Cross in here.'

'I've got nothing,' he said, giving a comic show of Godzilla-esque rage at two bleating phones competing for his attention.

'Steady on, steady on,' I said. 'Don't fret, it's bad for the constitution. I'll wait over . . . somewhere. You get me when you have a chance to look into it.' I unwound my scarf; I'd walked briskly to make the journey in forty minutes and my cheeks still burned. They could certainly afford to turn their thermostat down a degree or two, although I thought better of sharing this money-saving tip.

'When did you say he came in?' the man said. A young lady wearing green scrubs joined him behind the desk and rifled through a stack of forms.

'This evening. Not so long ago,' I said.

'By ambulance, yes?'

'He was suffering with chest pain. He didn't have any clothes on, in case that helps jog anyone's memory. That's partly what brings me here.' I hoisted the bag onto the counter, the handle of which had carved purple grooves into my fingers.

The woman next to him stopped what she was doing and jabbed the man's arm. 'Bay three, resus,' she mumbled. She stared at him and did something with her eyes that had the look of a secret code amongst those *in the trade* about it.

'Are you a relative, my darling?' the woman asked me.

'No. No.'

She glanced behind her for what I was staring at, as people do. 'Just a friend, yes?'

'In a manner of speaking. Well, yes, actually.'

'There's nothing I can tell you just now, I'm afraid.'

'Would you like to take him his things at least?' From the bag I pulled the flask that Barry had been holding when he arrived at my front door. 'I've made him some hot tea. In case . . . well, I can see things are jolly busy.'

The woman set her paperwork down. Her face softened. 'You hang on to those for the minute, my love.'

'Of course. No problem.'

'Are you all right waiting? I'll try and be over for a chat in a little while.'

'Fine. Take your time. As much as you need.'

I propped myself against the vending machine and watched the *News at Ten* on the silent television set. No sooner had the backlog of hacking coughers been cleared did the holding pen refill with the aftermath of some punch-up: three men, one with a crimson-soaked tea towel wrapped round one hand and a piece of ear missing.

'What total chaos you have to contend with,' I said to the green-scrubbed lady when she eventually returned to me. It was close to midnight and the lights had been dimmed in this now more peaceful waiting room. 'You deserve medals. Every one of you.' I managed some eye contact for sincerity's sake. She folded her arms across her chest.

'You should get yourself off home,' she said, taking the seat next to mine.

'I suppose I should. How's the patient faring?'

'With you not being a relative, it's a tricky situation. We will need to speak with your friend's next of kin first.'

'Understood. He has a son in Spain, he was saying. Five grandchildren, would you believe?'

'In a situation *like this*.' She looked intently at me. 'We are duty-bound to notify his next of kin. Before discussing with anybody else.'

'I'm not sure I can be of help with that.'

She put her hand on mine. It felt very pleasant. I'm not sure I could recall the last time I'd been touched intentionally. Certainly months. Could it have been years?

'We'll contact his GP practice first thing in the morning for the information we need,' the lady went on. 'We'll take it from there.'

It was, I realise, unforgivably slow of me to have taken this long to catch her drift.

'Are you okay, my love?' she asked.

'Yes. Yes.' It wasn't strictly true. The wind had come out of me.

'You understand me?'

I nodded slowly. 'I . . . fear I may.'

'I'm so sorry. He was your friend.'

'When did he . . . ?'

'Look, I really am not supposed to discuss this when next of kin are unaware.'

'No, of course.'

'It was very quick. No suffering.'

'That's something. Thank you. All of you. You'll have done your damnedest, of that I'm certain.'

'Are you going to be all right getting home?'

'Don't you worry about that.' In the absence of my wallet, it would be a below-zero walk. Although perhaps that was what I needed. 'Please, you must get back to work.'

She told me again how sorry she was, and that I could stay in the warm as long as I wished.

OUTSIDE IN THE HOSPITAL GROUNDS, I SAT FOR A FEW MINUTES. THE STEEL bench glittered with frost. It was the sort of cold one feels first in the eyes. Orange perimeter lights glowed in the mist. I inhaled through my nostrils and felt the cold in the far reaches of my lungs. Sadness had sucked the energy from me. Inevitably, I thought about death. Up close like this, it has no mystique; just another part of life. I remember that from when Mum passed. It really was like she had simply slipped away to another room, somewhere very near—just like that old poem says. But time passes and the whole thing becomes unknowable, terrifying again.

It's something I generally try to avoid thinking about—death, *dying*. But with the advancing years such thoughts have become rather like a ghost stalking the house: they appear almost nightly in the blackness of the small hours; I can switch on the lights, I can busy myself by making tea or listening to the radio, but they linger, waiting to catch me sleepless, ready to scare the wits out of me.

There's something the wisest man I ever knew said to me. His name was Charles Sethi. He was headmaster during my best years at Allonby House. 'Retirement is the first death,' he told me, as we shared a brandy and a smoke in his study on his last day. 'It's the death of being useful.' Some years later, when I myself was also forced to end my career, I refused to let it be such a first death. If one is always surrounded by things unread, items to fix, information still to know, then is one not still *useful*?

A distant wail of pain tore through the night. I sat bolt upright and watched the hospital building. It was dozing; most of its arched windows dark, just a glimmer of light here and there. The noise came again. It was an almost animal cry. My instincts said this wasn't the resetting of a dislocated shoulder, nor the keening of the just bereaved.

And again. Louder, drawn-out. *Guttural.* But there was a finality about it this time. Certainly no chance the sound of new tiny lungs could be audible at such a distance. I couldn't help but think of poor old Barry, laid out somewhere within those red brick walls or in one of the many grey *wings* appended to them. My gaze followed the giant round chimney as it climbed heavenward, disappearing into the mist. Touched by that unsettling magic of the otherworldly, my natural cynicism was silenced. I let myself enjoy the sense of balance: one life over, and another that had just begun.

4

IT WAS AT THIS VERY PLACE (SAINT HELEN'S INFIRMARY, EASTGATE ROAD, Streatham, South London) that I came into the world. 8th May 1945—the first dawn in nearly six years to break over a Europe not at war. Reports would have you believe it was a day of universal revelry and the rolling out of barrels, but Mum said it was nothing of the sort. Instead, it was a sense of loss that was the mood of the day, she reckoned. Beneath the clear blue sky and surety of peace, the wrecked streets and pictures of absent friends came into a new sort of focus, begging the question *What was it all for?* News reels record an ecstatic Trafalgar Square, but Mum would say she was the only person smiling in our street when she returned home after a tricky labour.

Dad could tell a war story or two. The combination of a knee injury which occasionally played him up, and a couple of unexplained fits at critical moments meant he'd not been permitted to serve, but he'd regale my brother, Dennis, and me with tales of exactly what he would have done if only the bastards had let him fight.

He was an immaculately spoken man (he would, by way of example, pronounce that most famous London street as *Pell Mell*), and he knew exactly how to wear a suit. In later years, Mum could be heard referring to him as a *tailor's dummy*. When Denny and I were very small, Dad was doing well. He traded cars on Warren Street and he was good at it. With no cars being built, and a glut of second-hand vehicles parked up since 1939 never to be reunited with their driver, there was money to be made by someone who could talk.

I wasn't yet a year old when we left London and moved to a house in Kent with a fireplace big enough to sit in and no less than three lavatories. There was an orchard, a pond we once skated on, flowers in hedgerows I could pick for Mum, a Wolseley family car. By the time I was six, Dad's work was keeping him away later and later into the evening. Denny and I would feign sleep just to catch a glimpse of him drawing up onto the drive. Midnight or later became the norm. Until one night, when he simply never returned. There'd been a wife before Mum, she later told me. He swore on his heart he'd never do the same to her. What a fool he must've been to imagine he could do better.

And so, South London again.

'Are you scared, Raymond?' Mum said at the school gates. Her hand clasped mine so tightly it hurt.

'I don't know. Maybe.' Children my age but noisier tore around on the other side of the fence. I'd done my first year at a village school in Kent. This was nothing like it. Denny left us standing there without a word and involved himself. He was fourteen months my senior, and he was fearless.

Mum crouched level with me. She held her hand to my face. Around her middle finger was a narrow gold ring with a tiny twinkling diamond and an even smaller ruby. It was the one thing from Dad she'd clung to when we lost damned near everything else. Sometimes she'd mumble about pawning it but I'd talk sense into her. It was beautiful.

She wiped her thumb beneath my eye, though the tear was in fact running from hers. 'You are everything in the world,' she said to me. 'Even when you can't see me, I'm there with you. Because I'm thinking about you *all* the time.'

She glanced sideways at a group of mothers near the gate. I imagine they already knew Mum. A poker-faced look was exchanged between her and a couple of their number. 'Head up high, my perfect boy,' she said smiling at me. 'Cream always rises to the top. You'll be just fine, you'll see.'

I wasn't scared actually, but I did cry in prayers that morning. All because I was thinking about Mum at home, alone, thinking about me.

The school wasn't so bad, though. I was good at reading and history. There was a spelling cup and I won it once. I made no enemies. And no friends.

The fun to be had by Denny and me in this new place was different to how it'd been out in the sticks. We had a fixation with the Thames and would cycle out on the weekend till we reached the banks. The marshes out East enthralled us. There were dilapidated caravans there, and shacks cobbled together from tea chests. I've never seen men like the ones we encountered, who called the lowlands home—not before, not since. They were army deserters, or otherwise ruined by war. Black-handed men with filth in their beards and the devil in their eyes. When they caught sight of us on our bikes they shouted unrepeatable things. But Denny being Denny, after a while that alone lost its thrill.

We nicknamed the man Bernie, because he slobbered like a Saint Bernard. He was the wildest of the lot. Having set out at the crack of a spring dawn, when we got there the whole godforsaken place was yet to stir. Embers smouldered in a makeshift grate on the ground. There was the usual smell: charred timber and human waste. Bernie's caravan probably dated back to the twenties and it looked like a dilapidated mock-Tudor house in miniature; it even had lattice-leaded glass.

Denny tried the door but it was bolted. 'I think we could kick clean through this,' he said, picking at the onion layers of the exposed plywood. 'Give the dirty old bugger a proper fright.'

'Let's ride down the river a bit,' I said, five paces behind him.

'Why do you never want an adventure, Ray?'

'I do,' I mumbled.

The window squawked as Denny hinged it upwards. 'Blimey!' he said, waving a hand under his nose.

After some minutes, I gave in to his furious beckoning and joined him, poking my head inside. It is a smell that would sometimes come back to me, even decades later. If that hadn't made me want to vomit, the pornographic images stuck to the walls certainly did. The floor was filled to the depth of Bernie's mattress with dog-ends and bottles. At his feet was a length of two-by-two, with six-inch nails poking out from the top half at all angles. He was curled up like a dog, sleeping in the same suit he always wore: once black but stained like a map of the night sky. He looked peaceful. I felt suddenly and terribly sorry for him.

Denny had a stick in his hand. He waved it around inside the caravan and allowed it to hover a whisker away from Bernie's blue nose.

'I'm going home,' I told him, back on my saddle in one movement.

'You're such a fucking sissy, Ray,' he snapped, though he did follow me. 'Why are you scared of having fun?'

I didn't answer him. It was never *fun* that scared me, though he wasn't the last to throw that accusation at me. Who didn't want to have fun? I kept myself away from danger for the sake of Mum; what it would do to her if something happened to one of us didn't bear thinking about.

We never went back there. It was barely a fortnight later when there was a story in the paper about a child of ten being found dead in those marshes out East. Denny started playing football on Saturdays soon after, and that was the end of the two of us adventuring together.

'DO YOU WANT TO KNOW A SECRET?' MUM ASKED. HER EYES TWINKLED LIKE they always did when she asked that question. 'I'm so glad you can't *bear* playing sport.'

We were in the Viscount Café, a mile from home. It had become a regular haunt for Mum and me whilst Denny was at training. The place was run by a man called Tony who was a shy Italian, and a proud Brit. There were fresh-faced pictures of our new queen on the walls, and a Union Jack draped above the stove—a patriotic accident waiting to happen.

'I don't *hate* sport,' I said. 'I'm just not terribly *good* at it. Certainly footie, anyway.'

'Well you can't be brilliant at *everything*,' she said, jetting cigarette smoke into the blue cloud that floated eternally beneath the ceiling. 'No one can.'

'Maybe I've never really applied myself to it,' I said, scooping a track through the sugar bowl. 'I seem to always be picked last, and then no one passes me the ball, and well . . .'

'All that mud!' Mum said. 'How perfectly miserable!'

'Yes, that part's no fun.'

'Well I must say, I really look forward to our little dates.'

'Me too, Mum.'

Our regular order of a plate of homemade cakes was delivered to the table. The owner set a cup in front of each of us, head bowed and hands shaky.

'Half-and-half for both of us, please, Tony, my dear,' Mum said. She kicked my leg under the table and we both giggled. The majority of the steaming black coffee and hot milk landed on target, just a little in the saucers. It was no secret that Tony had taken something of a shine to Mum. He was never fully composed when up this close.

'My youngest connoisseur of the coffee,' he said as I thanked him.

'Why let the grown-ups have all the fun?' Mum said, winking at me. 'This one's an old head on young shoulders, mark you.'

I was nine. The coffee tasted bitter and sophisticated.

'I should change the music,' Tony said, as though guilty of a major oversight. He shot a look in the direction of his electric record player up at the counter.

'Well I never like to ask,' Mum said.

'How about Billie Holiday, Mrs Thorns? I have a new long-player.'

'Sounds like bliss, Tony. And how many times, it's *Lil*!'

There was a table across from us where four children grumbled when the scratch of a needle silenced the driving piano of Fats Domino. Mum closed her eyes and drew on her ciggie as the sweet sound of Billie Holiday drifted through the place ('Blue Moon' if memory serves). For a moment it felt a little like we were in a film.

'He's a sweetie,' Mum said, nibbling at a lemon drizzle cake that she'd sliced into perfect quarters. 'What do you think?'

'About what?'

'My admirer!'

'I think he bakes lovely cakes.'

'Perhaps that's what I need. A new man.' She said it with a dramatic flourish and we both laughed.

'Stop it, Mum.'

'I'm sure you've heard what they say about Italians. It's not just in the kitchen that they have special talents.'

I pretended not to understand what she meant and stuffed more fruitcake into my mouth. My earlobes felt hot.

'You think I'm better off staying single?' There was no pretense; it was a genuine request for advice.

I gave the question some thought for a minute. I'm sure some children would have found such discussions with their mother unsettling, but it never bothered me. We spoke about all manner of things. 'I suppose I couldn't blame you if that's what you wanted.'

'A girl's entitled to a little fun, wouldn't you say?'

'I'm sure. It's a matter of weighing up pros and cons.'

'Must it be so *practical*, Raymond? Sounds awfully dreary.'

'I'm just saying, if you think you'd be happier, well then you'd have to . . .'

Mum dabbed the crumbs from her lips with a napkin and lit a fresh smoke. 'I don't imagine I'd miss that wretched old typewriter.'

'But you like your job.' Since our return to London, Mum had been working half days at Fletcher & Co Solicitors. Her boss, though famously boring and older than Jesus, was good about her catching up on work at home so she could look after Denny and me.

'It's perfectly tolerable, darling. Not quite the same as enjoyable.'

'You enjoy the independence.'

She considered this for an instant. 'Yes. I absolutely do. Have I said that?'

'Maybe not in exactly those words.'

'You are remarkably wise for one so young.'

'You've definitely said *that* before.'

She playfully kicked me under the table. I tucked in to a piece of chocolate sponge. Mum slid the two remaining quarters of her cake onto my plate. I shook my head and pushed them back onto hers. She rolled her eyes. 'Don't you dare complain when you've got a fat mother,' she said.

'Don't be silly,' I whispered.

She crossed her eyes and stuck her tongue out sideways and we fell about laughing, both being kids for a moment.

'Are you worried about Denny at all?' she asked me once we'd pulled ourselves together, serious all of a sudden.

'Nothing springs to mind, I don't think.' I leaned forward and lowered my voice, intrigued. 'Are you?'

'He's so . . . oh, I don't know. Do you find him . . . different?'

'To what?'

She seemed a little disgruntled that I didn't immediately catch her drift. I mumbled some agreeing noises, annoyed with myself.

'He's not quite *with us*. Does that make sense?'

I wracked my brain, keen to bring something of substance to this very private chat we were having. 'He has some new friends, I know. He sees them at football. One or two go to Longrove Grammar.'

'Longrove Grammar indeed. Aren't they a little old for him?'

'You know Denny. He's always popular, isn't he?'

'Very, it seems,' Mum said, loaded. 'I wasn't snooping or anything, Raymond. I was just checking his school bag in case there was, I don't know, letters home or anything. I stumbled on something that took me quite aback.'

'What, Mum?' I whispered.

'I didn't go there looking.'

'No, of course.'

'Because I would never, really.'

'I know.'

'I was *very* surprised, actually. He hasn't mentioned, to you, a girlfriend, has he?'

'No. Nothing.' I felt a twinge of what I suppose was jealousy. Not at the suggestion of a girlfriend as such, but at the reminder of the ever-growing difference between my own experiences and my brother's.

'He's eleven, Raymond! And only *just* eleven.'

'What did you find?'

'Well I suppose you'd call it a *love letter*.' She looked disgusted, which surprised me. 'Pages and pages of the damned thing.'

'Did you ask him about it?'

'Let's just say, he wouldn't be drawn on the matter.'

'Probably embarrassed,' I said, upset that he'd confided nothing in me. Although, on reflection, it was perhaps a matter of insignificance to Denny. His effect on members of the opposite sex was set to become a thing of legend. How different, in that respect, two brothers could be: whilst he'd go on to treat female-kind as some sort of buffet to gorge himself on, I was set to pass up the one opportunity at love that fate would serve me.

'Even handholding seems a bit . . . *old*, don't you think?'

'I don't really know, Mum.'

'You *do* know, Raymond,' she said, a touch sharp. 'You know how much I value your opinion.'

'I suppose he's a bit young.'

'He's becoming so secretive too. I find it very upsetting.' She shook her head and drained her coffee. 'He's taken to locking the bathroom door! Have you noticed that?'

'I think so.' I had. That sound of the lock tumbling felt like a wall going up in the family home, for reasons I couldn't understand.

'Talk to him, will you, Raymond? He'll listen to you. Everyone does.'

'I don't know about that. I could try, though.'

'I'm not asking you to tell tales on your brother.'

'I know.'

'But if there is anything I should know . . .' She tapped her foot on top of my toes. 'Would it be terribly terrible to say how . . .' She pulled away. 'No I really mustn't . . .'

'Say what, Mum?'

She smirked. 'Is it awful of me that I wish he could be more like you?'

'Well I shan't tell *him* that.'

'You're just like me, is the thing.'

I smiled, though I always felt guilty for Denny when she said that to me.

'I think we need another coffee,' Mum said, sweeping the subject away. 'Wouldn't you say?'

I nodded.

'Tony, my dear man,' she called out. 'I think I need you.'

He had his back to us, clearing a table. Spinning to face us with a tray in his hand, a stack of ice cream coupes wobbled off balance. He performed an ungainly dance to right them, staggering left and right and articulating at the waist, narrowly keeping them from falling to the floor. When he left to fetch the coffee-pot Mum and I began to laugh. We were soon in fits—we just couldn't help ourselves. The family nearby were looking over at the pair of us.

I never once allowed myself to forget it: just how lucky I was, to have a mother like her.

5

WEDNESDAY

I MAY BE NEARLY A QUARTER OF A CENTURY INTO MY RETIREMENT, BUT I'M seldom at a loose end. Monday, Wednesday, and Friday mornings are for scouring the charity shops—Maime at the big Oxfam is especially good to me: she usually has an old model train or car, or perhaps a blues or rock 'n' roll record, set aside for my consideration from the weekend's influx. Tuesdays and Saturdays are for getting the bread—there's a bakery whose produce is a different grade to what you'll get in the supermarket, but it's three miles each way and I stop for tea and a sandwich, so I can kiss goodbye to a morning on that errand.

Then there's Mum, of course. Two afternoons a week in winter, three in summer. Would you believe that in peak season grass grows a quarter of an inch every day? It's a terror! And all those flowers to be kept watered too. She liked things neat and tidy. It's the very least I can do for her.

Sundays I run through all the checks on my car and give the old girl a wax. She's a 1951 MG TD open-top roadster and she's been by my side since she was eleven years old. Not that she's turned a wheel in three decades—hardly fit for modern traffic! But even tucked away, cosy and warm in the garage, she brings me untold joy.

And then there are my many repair projects about the house, not to mention the business of simply *keeping home*. I am, generally speaking, rather busy.

But this morning, it seemed appropriate to break with routine. Barry's flat was oppressively, stagnantly cold and smelt strongly of *bird*. A frantic rattle of chirping came from another room the moment I let myself in with the keys Barry left in my bathroom last night.

'Steady on, steady on!' I called back, my breath bellowing steam. I eased the front door closed, behaving every bit like an intruder, which I suppose I was. A red card had been shoved beneath the door. *We called but you weren't home!* it said in unforgivably jolly script. It was from the electricity board. 'A little late now, don't you fancy?' I muttered.

'Good morning, chatterbox!' I said in reply to the blue budgerigar who tweeted from his cage by the living room window. Creeping slowly, I raised my palms in surrender. 'Don't worry. No one's forgotten you. You'll not go hungry. Gosh, don't you have a lot to say?' I knelt and poked a finger through the mesh. It really was the most strikingly handsome bird: plumage of cobalt blue with fine pinstripes of black and white to the wings. 'May I call you Little Boy Blue?' I asked. The name had sprung naturally to mind, and he (or she, perhaps) chattered happily enough in reply.

The business of Barry's bird had been my first waking thought. Who knows how long it might be before the next of kin are roused by the good people from casualty and make their way over here, all the while a small animal goes unfed. No, I wouldn't have it.

I surveyed the surroundings again, and my word, how sparse the place was—so little to show for all those decades of life. Aside from the birdcage, the living room contained a television set (admittedly a rather natty *flat-screen*), a single armchair, a low coffee table, and few copies of the *Racing Post*. There was little else.

'Breakfast time, young man,' I told Little Boy Blue, opening a bag of fruit and nut mix I found in the kitchen. He chirped more insistently than ever. I unhitched his small door and retrieved an empty bowl. 'Steady on, steady on,' I said as his wings buzzed with excitement.

Animals, like children in my experience, have an instinct for sniffing out incompetence. For punishing the amateur. My attention was elsewhere for two seconds, and full advantage was taken. By the time I was up and giving chase, the blue bird had fluttered to the kitchen. He lapped the room at head height whilst I leapt in the air like a madman. I changed my approach after some minutes of this, instead keeping sentry cross-armed in the doorway. He perched on the cold tap across the room. I tired eventually of the silent standoff, but every grab I made resulted in him taking flight and settling in the very place I'd been standing a moment prior. This swapping of positions went on for some time. He responded to a heroic lunge by taking me on a complete tour of the flat, travelling only fast enough to evade me and no quicker.

'You win, Little Boy Blue,' I conceded after twenty minutes of a cartoon-like chase. I left him to his own devices in front of the bathroom mirror, seemingly in a trance of self-fascination. 'It's here when you're good and ready,' I said, placing some food in his open cage.

Then I made a more leisurely lap of Barry's home. With his family in mind, I made his bed and washed up his plates and glasses: *I'd* rather find a loved one's home in such a way. There was a poorly hidden pile of DVDs in the living room (blue movies, lurid and thoroughly indecent pictures on the cases). 'Enough to give anyone a heart attack,' I mumbled, permitting myself a little gallows humour as I double-bagged and taped them, now ready for the dustbin.

There were some photographs dotted about the bedroom. Evidently most were of his grandchildren. Only one picture featured Barry himself. It was old enough for the Spanish sea and sky to have turned a wishy-washy green. Pinned to one wall was a smattering of cards, all with a common sentiment: *Sorry we can't be there to celebrate with you!* Years of birthdays and Christmases had passed by with nothing but a good wish and an apology from his dearest loved ones.

He'd talked yesterday evening as if his was an inseparable family. Was Barry a fraud, like me? Granted, his brood did actually exist. But at such a remove as to make his enthusiasm a touch misleading, I felt now. 'Oh, Barry,' I said, pinning the cards back into place. 'Poor old chap.' Would this most recent development be a good enough reason for his relatives to put in an appearance? I wondered.

My sadness caught me off guard. Him feeling the need to exaggerate his family situation . . . How strange that the idea of someone doing just as I do should affect me so. I unfolded a sheet of kitchen roll from my pocket and dabbed my eyes.

More in hope than anticipation of anyone showing up, I left a note on the coffee table, explaining where I was if any help was needed, and that I had Barry's keys. I left his clothes and flask, and his mobile phone from his mackintosh pocket. A final attempt to reincarcerate Little Boy Blue failed, so I checked all the windows for security, closed the lavatory seat, and put a little water in the washbasin for him. He chirruped back when I bid him farewell as I slipped out. He was, I suspect, laughing at me.

WITH URGENT DESIRE TO RETURN TO MY SCHEDULE, MY AFTERNOON WAS spent on the common. I gathered six full bags of rubbish and delivered a teddy bear and three gloves to the unofficial lost property fencepost in the car park. The sky remained a pale grey and heavy with the promise of snow, which kept me working at a pace. It's not an *official* volunteer role, merely a job that needs doing. I've given a couple of afternoons a week to it for years.

I also happened upon a good comb (tortoiseshell, all teeth present) half buried in the brush and a quality dinner fork trodden into the earth. With slim chance of reuniting them with their owners, I brought both home. To think—they were mere hours away from being blanketed with snow, and perhaps lost forever, but with so much more life to give.

IT WAS A TOUCH BEFORE EIGHT WHEN I HEARD THE LETTERBOX GO. I WAS IN my *office*, a rather grand term for what was once a fitted wardrobe in my bedroom. I converted it some years ago, back in the days when I was still living here with Mum. The louvred doors remain, but inside is a small desk and filing cabinet, and—a later addition—my personal computer. I tore myself from my on-screen chess game and made it to the window in time to see a pair of taillights fading into the flurry of snow.

To the Family of Raymond Thorns, the envelope on the doormat read, *BY HAND*.

I admit, this didn't strike me as strange, in the way it surely should have.

The hallway was still in some disarray from poor Barry's stumbling, but I found my letter opener soon enough. With a fencer's flourish I scythed the envelope open.

Inside, a glossy greeting card. The photograph on the front could scarcely have been a more familiar sight. That luscious striped lawn was mowed by yours truly for thirty years or more. The yellow brick building beyond, with its ornate gables and stained glass windows, contained not a single room that I hadn't at one point or another repaired or improved or imparted some lesson in.

I studied it with a smile. Allonby House is five miles from here. I take a bus out there every now and then, just to take a walk around the perimeter and enjoy the sight of the place. I don't go in anymore. After all, it was a job I left under something of a cloud. There had been, some years ago, a couple of invitations to staff reunions which I'd been very surprised to receive but opted not to attend. This was the first thing from them in, what, over a decade?

To The Thorns Family, it read inside—

We all at Allonby House were very saddened to hear, earlier today, of Ray's passing. He is remembered most fondly by both the staff he served alongside during his long career, and by many of our former students by whom he was greatly respected. You are in our thoughts and prayers.
   Best,
   Dr H Plumpton MA Oxon, Head Teacher

It took me a moment to process what I had read. *Ray's passing?* They couldn't have meant, me, surely! I thought I should call them, set the record straight, explain that I am very much alive, that there'd been some mistake.

I studied the text again. The warmth I'd initially felt—at being *remembered*, remembered *fondly* and not thought ill of—faded. Handwritten as it may have been, these were stock phrases, doubtless used by this headmaster for all the deceased has-beens he knew little of. How foolish to imagine that I was anything other than long, long forgotten.

The making of a call seemed unurgent: perhaps I'd get around to it, in order that *Doctor Plumpton* could take a little more care and send off these same words to the family of the poor unfortunate who'd actually snuffed it. I did, however, find room for the card on the mantelpiece. The picture was a treat.

A strange nagging kept me returning to it all evening, though: re-reading it, over and over, in between dinner and doing the dishes, after my nightly routine was complete. Of course, I should've put two and two together long before.

It was as I was drifting off to sleep that the whole thing assembled itself in my mind. There was no sudden eureka moment, merely creeping realisation. My missing wallet. Barry unclothed in my house. My neighbours talking to the paramedics, giving the name of the man who lived here, to be further confirmed by my own bank cards et cetera.

I got out of bed and paced the bedroom in a panic.

Should I go now, to Saint Helen's? Tell them there'd been a mistake, alert them to the mix-up?

Or would this be a matter for the staff in casualty? Poor old Barry must be long gone, no longer a charge of the green-scrubbed nurse.

It was a familiar feeling, of trouble tumouring out of all proportion because the first opportunity to own up was not taken, echoing back to childhood misdeeds and mishaps.

With all thoughts of sleep abandoned, I fixed myself a brew and thought things over in the kitchen. Had the hospital contacted *my* next of kin? Who would that be? My brother, I supposed. Though I'd not seen Denny in many years. What would he think when he heard his only brother had died? My mind wandered to any feelings of grief that would come his way, or would it be annoyance at having to plan a funeral, take care of my things, of my remains?

My remains—surely there would be the identification of a body to come? Estranged or otherwise, brothers do not go forgetting what each other look like. Denny would know, know that it was not me. Maybe he'd even laugh. This realisation calmed me. Yes, they would see, figure out that this was all just a tiny mistake. Nothing worth fretting over now.

In any case, I'd be doing my own bit to make good first thing tomorrow. The hospital would be the place to start, I decided. They could direct me from there.

I retired to the living room and cleared myself a chair. But even with a plan, the whole thing left me feeling a tad unwell.

On occasion I found myself struck by a need to talk to another person. More a *hunger* than a need, perhaps. It invariably tended to strike at terribly impractical times. It's not that my life exists without human interaction; I chat with people daily. But it's what one might call *shop talk*: the sort of exchange enjoyed whilst waiting at the bakery, for example. Is it unusual to, every now and then, crave something more? A little *dissection*, perhaps?

A conversation to get a handle on why that card from the school needled me so. On why the idea of Denny being misinformed of my demise was so unsettling. To muse over why I was feeling so damned sorry for myself, despite being very much not dead.

I flicked through my LPs in the low light, finding without difficulty Howlin' Wolf's 'Moaning by Moonlight'—a blues masterpiece. The sound, as it always has, stirred memories of 1960 and the summers that followed. Of *newness*. Of a girl who, in different circumstances, I'd have married.

Thoughts of Denny, thoughts of next of kins, of the urge to really talk to someone, had inevitably led me there: to Junie.

In truth, the idea of her was rarely far away. Still, I'd catch myself thinking up a witticism, or a piece of satisfying wisdom, and I'd daydream that I was telling it to her, and her being . . . impressed by me, I suppose. Nothing more than that. It averagely happened a handful of times a day. The woman I pictured in these follies of imagination probably bore little resemblance to the real Junie, though; it had been fifty-seven years since we'd parted, nigh on forty since we'd last had any real cause to talk.

The music calmed me. 'Smokestack Lightning'—what a track! I closed my eyes. A tingling in my guts, some faint muscle memory of being very, very alive. Of those dangerous times of existing right at the leading edge of time as it unfolds.

6

WE WERE NOT QUITE FIFTEEN WHEN WE MET. I WAS OLDER THAN HER BY twenty-three days and twenty-three hours. It had begun with an old lady, wading fully clothed into the sea. Mum, Denny, and I were on holiday in Ferring (Sussex coast, a short hop from Worthing). Our prefab bungalow close to the beach belonged to Mum's boss, Fletcher; he was a decent fellow and gave us use of it in the off-season. It was a warm, windy, and golden day, like all the best May days are. I was flying a kite at low tide. With fifteen hundred feet of line wound out, the wretched thing corkscrewed to ground. It was quite the walk to recover it.

There the poor old dear was, up to her thighs in the drink. Her maroon skirt floated around her like an oil slick. Now, this was a time when it was commonplace for people to take a paddle fully clothed; men in suits rolled to the knee. But this was no splash in the shallows. I weighed down my bent kite with pebbles and went out to her. She was staring blankly to the horizon. Her face was fully made up, although up close she looked as though she'd been coloured in by a young child.

'Are you all right, miss?' I asked her.

She didn't look at me, merely smiled briefly. Her front teeth were painted crimson.

'The tide's already turned,' I told her. 'Afternoon low was four thirty-three.' I was quoting the fisherman's table Denny and I had checked earlier.

A faint hum from her, nothing more.

'Where do you live? I could get somebody.'

She glanced in my direction. There was a cloudiness about her eyes; she was no more than partially sighted, not that there was any suggestion she'd strode out to sea unintentionally.

'Where would you like to go?'

'I need to see the vicar,' she said, as though we were standing in the rectory.

Deepening water slopped against my thighs, reflecting flashes of sun in dazzling slices. 'I think I know where he is,' I said, gently taking her arm in mine. She fell into step effortlessly at my side, looking a great deal more comfortable than me.

I knew of only one church, a spire visible inland on the far side of the village. It looked closer than the two miles we surely walked with her shoes squawking and her drenched skirt slapping my bare calves.

The man at the church was very grateful to me, even if the old lady was adamant that he was not the vicar at all.

'I'm the curate,' he whispered to me with a smirk as he took her hand. 'Mrs Aylward lives just up the way. I shan't be a minute. Hold on here if you like?'

I was standing alone in the lobby. Beyond one door was the churchyard, mottled by the shade of new leaves and blossoms plastered thickly to the path.

A voice came from beyond the other door, within the church itself. 'She's as mad as throwing buns at an elephant, that one.' Female, amused.

'Hello?' I mumbled, taking a few paces inside and letting my eyes adjust to the dimness. The air was cool and waxy. I've always enjoyed a curious solace setting foot in church. Did I feel it at that moment, I wonder, or was it perhaps this very incident that led to every church thereafter feeling like a personal haven?

'That silly old trout,' the girl said. She was five feet off the ground, sitting in the corner of an arched aperture, behind which the many towering tubes of the pipe organ. She had a clipboard propped against her knees and pencils were scattered on the stone around her.

'You know her?' I asked.

'Everyone does. Roaming round people's gardens is a favourite of hers. Surprised she hasn't got herself shot yet.' She grinned wildly at me, raking her hand through her short blond hair. Sixty-five years on, and I can still conjure the image with absolute precision.

'What's . . . wrong with her?'

'Nuttier than a bucket of squirrel's shit.' She comedically tapped out a cross on her torso and whispered, 'Sorry, Lord of All,' into the rafters. 'You not from round here?'

'South London,' I said. 'Long weekend.'

'Wish I was from London. Want to put me in your suitcase?'

I chuckled for too long. Girls, at this point, were not merely a source of angst to me. I was terrified of them. They were completely unknowable, an alien species whose ways and motivations I had no comprehension of. I was convinced that any interaction with their kind was certain to lead to humiliation.

'What are you doing in here?' I asked.

'Praying,' she said.

'I see. Do you do a lot of . . .' I was silenced by her guffaws of laughter.

'Praying to get the bloody hell out of here,' she said. 'I'm doing my homework. Dad doesn't trust me to do it at home.'

'Why?'

'Because I don't do it at home. I get . . . *distracted*.'

'Your dad's the vicar?'

'Curate.'

'Right. What's the difference?'

'Vicars get nice big houses. Curates get a smelly old shoebox.'

'That doesn't sound fair.'

'A curate's like a *deputy* vicar,' she explained, swinging her legs off her high platform and letting herself drop to the ground. A cascade of pencils followed her down. 'Dad'll get his own place sometime. Maybe even in *London*!' She stood facing me. At most she was four ten. Her clothes—a rather tattered pair of trousers and a white tee—looked to belong in a boy's wardrobe.

'How's your differentiation?' she asked me.

'I'm second top in my maths class,' I told her. It was, I discovered, impossible to make such a statement sound nonchalant, despite the very great effort I put into making it so.

'Well isn't that *fortuitous*!' She took my clammy hand in hers and led me to the front of the church. 'So you're not just a pretty face, then?' There was a faint smell of cigarettes about her.

'I'm not an expert.'

'We'll see.' She manhandled the silverware from the altar, catching an empty jug before it rolled onto the floor. 'Now, is this the best desk you've ever worked at? Don't you feel a bit like . . . *God*?'

I smoothed out her question sheet; it was a Banda copy and the purple ink had begun to bleed. It was legible enough though and didn't pose me too great a challenge. We chit-chatted and established a little about each other as I worked. She looked over my shoulder and made approving noises, which kept me working at a fevered pace.

A delivery by a florist took her away from my side as I completed her homework. Junie handled it with the friendly efficiency of someone far older.

'You help your dad out a lot?' I asked.

'Slavery isn't dead, Ray.' She had begun attaching posies of flowers to the ends of pews. 'Two weddings tomorrow. There goes my Saturday.'

'What do you have to do?'

'*Everything.* Make the place look nice, put up the hymn numbers, sing in the choir.'

I sniggered. 'You're a choir girl?'

'So what? I get paid for it. If it's a wedding I do, anyway.'

'I wasn't laughing at you,' I said, reddening. 'You just don't really look like someone who'd . . . do that.'

'Want me to put my gown on for you?' She pressed her hands together. 'I'm quite the little angel when required.'

She was close to me again and I took a step backwards, my left hand flailing behind me for something to prop myself against.

'Did a great funeral today,' she told me.

'What makes a funeral *great*?'

'Circumstances of death. What else?'

'Of course,' I said.

'The old woman had been dead for a whole *month* before it was reported, they reckon.'

'Oh dear.'

Junie was more animated than ever. It was a demeanour of hers that I'd encounter a hundred times over the years that followed: the love of having a story to tell. 'Her husband, he'd kept her at home. In the *bed*. That's what I heard.'

'Blimey. Think it's true?'

''Course it's true, Ray.' She looked half offended. 'They say he didn't think she was dead.'

'He must've known.'

'Maybe she'd always been a bit of a quiet one,' Junie said, grinning.

'I guess he wasn't ready to . . . accept it?'

She shrugged away my rather mundane point. 'Reckon they were still, you know, having it away?'

'Oh God.'

'Bet the old man could do what he darn well pleased to his poor old wife.'

'Can't bear thinking about it,' I said through giggles.

'He looked all respectable, as well. In the front row today he was, belting out 'Cwm Rhondda' like a God-fearing pillar of the community. Imagine it, Ray! All these last few weeks he's been going about the town, acting like everything's normal, and no one's got the first clue he's about to go home and get all intimate with a . . . stiff!'

'You're nuts!'

'Want to see the grave?'

There was of course only one answer, and we were soon standing shoulder to shoulder in the churchyard, inches from a wooden cross. The warm evening breeze swept powdery chalk from the soil that mounded up from the plot.

'Decent age, though,' I said, noting that she'd been born in 1897. Sixty-three struck us both as good-going.

'She wasn't embalmed,' Junie told me. 'So should be about four years till it's only the bones left.'

'How do you know that?'

She shrugged. 'Want to hear a funny story?'

I nodded. I followed as she weaved between gravestones to a bench at the summit of the sloped churchyard. A little later, I'd reflect that this was shaping up to be the longest conversation I'd yet had with a girl my own age.

'I met a boy here a while back,' Junie told me.

'Okay,' I replied, a touch uneasily.

'He was a *man* really. And I scared him half to death. It was priceless. The things he's been telling everyone.'

'Go on.'

'I'm sitting out here, minding my own business, waiting for Dad. And this boy, he sits down and starts talking at me.'

'How old?' I asked, sounding too curious. My breathing was shallow. Something about the subject had caused my body to respond as if in danger.

'Eighteen, nineteen maybe. Swears his name's *Chet*. Real know-it-all. Bragging about how he's going places. Says he's getting himself a nice car any day, and he's getting out of here. Says he's looking for a sweetheart to take along for the ride.'

'You told him where to go?'

'He's one of those boys who work down at the Point, unloading the catch. You've never seen fingernails like it, Ray. And he's been sat there three minutes, and he's already getting a bit . . . *handsy*.'

'Cheeky little . . .'

'Says he knows how to show a girl a fine time.'

'Did you . . . erm?'

'No bloody chance! I'd bury him out here before he got halfway near. But he keeps wanting to know my name, Ray,' She grinned at me. 'So I gave him . . . a name.'

'What did you say?'

'Celia Bretton,' Junie said with a beaming flourish. 'I told him how much I love this church. How this is my very favourite place to sit.'

'You made the name up?'

'Not quite. I spun him some yarn about people missing me. I told him he could meet me here tomorrow, though.' Junie shuffled along the seat, inviting me to sit.

'He came back the next day?'

'Of course he did,' she said with a hint of pride. 'Only once, mind. Don't think we'll be seeing him in these parts again.' She tapped her well-bitten fingernails against the bench's backrest.

'Celia Bretton, 1882–1948,' I read aloud from the brass plaque on the bench. 'Who loved this church.' The penny dropped. 'Oh that's brilliant.'

'I was quite pleased with myself, I must say. I mean, if he was less of an idiot, perhaps he'd have cottoned on. I heard he's been telling everyone. Reckons the place is haunted halfway to hell!'

We were interrupted a moment later by the return of her father, minus the crazy old lady. He was puffing from the walk.

'Enjoying one of our Junie's tales, are we?' he said. He gave me a conspiring smile. 'She rather likes to add a little colour to things.'

Junie lay across the bench, feet up on the arm. She protested her father's point and told him how she, courtesy of my *fine influence*, had polished off all her schoolwork.

'In which case,' her father said, releasing the dog collar from the studs on his shirt and whipping it free, 'we might as well call it a day.'

I was suddenly a little heavier at the thought of turning my back, returning to the relative flatness of everywhere in the world other than this exact spot.

'Mrs Aylward was most thankful for your assistance,' her father told me. 'Nearly got herself into deep water there.'

'It's only a sixteen-foot tide today, sir, so she'd perhaps have been okay for another hour,' I explained.

'Well, *figuratively* deep water, at least,' laughed her father.

'Can we have Ray back for tea?' Junie asked.

'Let's see . . . he saved the infirm from certain death,' he said. 'And what's more, he does my dear daughter's homework! Have him for tea? I rather think we should recommend him for sainthood.' He bowed before me. 'Saint Ray . . . of . . .'

'Differentiation!' Junie shouted.

As we meandered across the churchyard he put his hand on my shoulder. It smelt of Imperial Leather. 'Saint Ray of Differential Calculus and . . . Damp Old Dears. Yes, that's it.' I'd not properly met a man of the clergy before, but any preconceptions I might have been fed along the way were proven wrong. In all the time I knew Reverend Rudolph Burnham, he was nothing other than a gentleman of great warmth and wit.

I'd kick myself for it for months to come, but I passed on their kind offer of tea. Mum would have been worried sick, wondering where I'd been all this time. I couldn't do that to her.

Instead, I had to make do with the last look Junie gave me as she walked away: over her right shoulder, a half smile and a gaze that swept up and down me twice. I floated, grinning like a maniac, all the way across the village to our bungalow.

BACK IN SOUTH LONDON, THE SUMMER OF 1960 DRAGGED BY IN A STICKY haze of reduced appetite, constant imaginings of Junie, and a new hobby to be enjoyed solo in the lavatory. On this latter point, I eventually rationed myself to once every four days. Like so many of life's joys, it was inevitably followed by a moral hangover, but without my self-imposed regulation I'd have been at it like a baboon.

It took me a month to muster the courage to write to her. I addressed it to the church and hoped for the best. I'd done the maths: sending it first class, allowing a day for her to read and respond, plus return postage, meant something could theoretically arrive back in four days. As it happened it took seven. A tense week.

So began our writing back and forth across the country, with thankfully shorter lengths of time in between as we went on. But viscerally alive as I felt that summer, I was also wracked with guilt. With our correspondence a regular thing, I was a boy with a secret. There was no question of telling Mum about Junie; the very thought of her knowing made me panic. What if it changed our relationship? Came between us in some way? But the lying to her (if only by *omission*, but lying nonetheless) was killing me, regularly, to the point of causing me to be physically sick.

But, as they say, no one knows you like your own mother. She seemed to have something of a clue what was going on. There'd be jokes made when I'd slick my hair back, about how I'd probably be disappearing for the night, how I was a heartbreaker in the making. Such things embarrassed me terribly. She was almost entirely silent once when we went for our weekly *date* at Tony's café, which had happened to coincide with the arrival of a letter from the coast. As time went on, Junie's post tended to have something of a crinkled appearance, seemingly having been shown a kettle's spout. I could only imagine that Junie was in the habit of thinking to add her many post scripts after having already sealed the envelope.

'I'M GOING TO THRASH YOU INSIDE TWENTY MOVES,' JUNIE TOLD ME. 'JUST you wait and see, baby boy.' She put the finishing touches to the chessboard she'd drawn in the sand with a broken pebble and set out the ivory pieces she'd borrowed from her father. It was late September of the same year and Mum had the bungalow again for a weekend.

'Shall we bet something on it?' I said, discretely correcting the relative positions of the white king and queen.

'Whatever could we have at stake?' Junie mused, lying on her front with her hands propping up her chin.

'Just having a joke.' As would always be the case, it took the first twenty minutes in her company to find my stride.

'Dad's been teaching me. You know I'd never played in my life till you mentioned chess in one of your letters?'

Junie and I had holed up on a section of beach that was not overlooked by holiday homes. Inland, the sky was turning pink, and we huddled close to the breakwater. Still, the breeze ruffled my hair and teased the hem of Junie's dress away from her tanned thighs.

'Well, I bought a blues record,' I told her, whilst sliding a pawn across the sand in response to her first move. 'Like you told me to.'

'What did you get?'

'It's called *Fresh Sounds from Chicago*. The shop had to order it in for me.'

'Isn't it just the greatest? It gets into your bones, doesn't it? All that . . . angst. And those bendy notes they do.' Her eyes swelled, like they always did when she spoke about something she was mad over.

'*Bendy!* I like it!'

'I'm so glad you love it, Ray. I knew you would.'

Of course I loved it. I'd bought the LP with all my birthday money. To avoid questions, I could only play it when Mum and Denny were out, but every time I heard those creamy, longing voices of Muddy Waters and Bo Diddley it was like a sound from another world.

'You know some people say it's the devil's music,' I said. 'I heard this man say it on the radio.'

'*Devil's music.* I think I'm even more taken with it now.'

'There's a surprise,' I said, taking one of her knights.

She blew a raspberry at me. 'I've started playing a bit. Just on my own.'

'The blues? You never said.'

'I'm not up to much,' Junie said, unusually shy.

'You got a guitar?'

'I wish! No, just playing a bit of harp.'

'A harp? That's crazy! I mean, you did tell me how angelic you could be. You know, when we met in the church.'

She smirked at me. 'That's a good memory you've got.'

I avoided her gaze and played my move. 'Not sure if I've heard any harp on my record.'

Junie laughed. 'Not *that* sort of harp, Ray. Imagine!'

'Right. I see.'

'One of these,' she said, rolling over on the sand and producing a small harmonica from her wicker bag. 'Blues players call them harps.'

'You take it everywhere with you?'

'No,' she snapped. 'Just, I don't know, thought you might . . .'

Feeling bad, I took it from her and studied it in my hand. 'It's neat.'

'Have a go.'

I puffed out a couple of notes, enjoying too much the knowledge that this thing had previously touched her lips. 'Where did you get it?'

'My dad had it in his sock drawer. Think he used to play "Amazing Grace" on it. Of course, a real harp player would have one in every key, and a chromatic one too. I'm saving up.'

'Feel like playing something?'

Sitting cross-legged on the sand, she put me into check with her rook. 'I don't know. You've got to promise you won't laugh at me.'

'Scout's honour.'

She checked all around us whilst moistening her lips. Gazing out to the horizon she blew a single note, then shook her head. 'Sorry.'

'It's only me,' I whispered.

Junie nodded and, tapping her foot, began. It was the first time I'd heard 'Smokestack Lightning'. She played the hook on her harmonica, clean and tight. With her eyes closed and a look of intense concentration, she began to sing. A choirgirl's soprano range married to the soul and grit of the blues was like nothing I'd ever heard. In between the vocals she played little wistful phrases, cupping her fingers around the harmonica and making it warble like a small bird in her hands.

'You're so talented,' I told her when she'd finished.

She was red in the face. 'You're just saying that.'

'I can't believe how good you are. I'd think you'd been playing . . . forever.'

'Come off it.' A smile seeped across her face. 'You know I've never played in front of anyone.'

'Wow.' I wanted to tell her how that felt like a very great privilege, but couldn't find the words, or the courage. 'You're such a natural. I mean it.'

'Reckon it's the devil? You think he's put his music in me?'

'Aha! That'll be it!'

The evening closed in around us as we finished our chess game. I'd managed to ignore the thought for hours, but I'd told Mum I was taking a walk into Worthing and knew I'd need to be heading back soon. Junie had missed the opportunity to checkmate me twice already, though I suspected it was no oversight. With foamy waves trickling towards us intent on dissolving our chessboard, she finally finished me.

'Loser takes a swim,' she said.

'That's not fair.'

'It's not even *that* cold.'

'I haven't got my bathers.'

'Come on, Ray. Who cares about *bathers*?'

I slackened my shirt. 'I suppose,' I said, steeling myself. 'What if the winner was to take a dip too?'

'It's all right. I lost at chess to a beginner. It's a fair forfeit.' I waded in, rolling up the legs of my shorts.

'So you don't want me to come too, is that it?' Junie said, scuffing a foot over the sand. For reasons I couldn't understand, she appeared put-out.

'I didn't mean that. Not at all. Come on, please. You're right, it really *isn't* that cold.' The water was deep grey now the sun had set.

Junie grabbed the hem of her dress and threw her arms upward. I turned my back.

'Let me know when you're decent,' I said.

'Who wants to be *decent*? Ugh!' Junie said, creeping up behind me. Fully submerged, she floated around where I stood. I could see the faint grooves on her shoulders where her bra straps had been and was glad of the water covering me to my waist.

We swam further out than I'd been before. The rich black of a coastal night settled fast. Just a stripe of pink light hung low over the land. Beyond the beach, I could make out the silhouetted spire of Junie's father's church.

'Doesn't it feel like we're the only two people in the world?' Junie said, treading water inches from me.

I had an inexplicable sense of having left every care back on the stones with my shirt and sandals. 'Sure it does.'

She put her hands on my shoulders. There was nothing awkward or shameful about her body against my bare torso. and however tight I held her, I found I wanted her closer still.

My first proper kiss was brief and a touch ungainly. Her lips were salty but warm.

For the remaining three days of my holiday, we were apart as seldom as possible. I kept telling Mum I was going fishing with some new friend in the village. In an attempt to assuage my guilt I'd spend the morning sprucing up the bungalow and making lunch for her and Denny, for all the good it did me. I kept telling myself I could make it up to Mum back home.

Junie and I cared little about where we were, as long as there was nothing to stop us being all over each other. She very much led the way, but I was a very willing if nervous follower. We didn't go *all the way* during those few short days, though we made it a good distance. I had no experience and there were gaps in the common knowledge I'd absorbed at school, but it caused us no hindrance. Like swallows knowing to fly south, we were at an age when things came naturally and without doubts.

'Should I have made you wait a while? Get desperate to get your hands all over me and start jumping through hoops?' Junie asked on our last evening together. We were sitting against a wall at the secluded western end of the churchyard. The gravestones surrounding us jutted like bad teeth. They bore nineteenth-century dates and thick lichen. Aside from my raincoat draped over our knees, we were both perfectly naked.

'I'd still jump through hoops,' I told her. 'Any time you like.' It was an opportunity to tell her I loved her, which I was too tame to take.

'I'm too impulsive, that's my trouble.' She shot a disdainful glance towards the church. 'Why should we all deny ourselves what we want, just because we might get something better later?' She passed me the ciggie she'd rolled from the dog-ends left after a mothers' meeting. I took a pretender's puff and passed it back.

'You'll probably get bored of me now,' she said.

'Never ever,' I replied. I kept myself under control, but knew I'd cry all night when I had to leave her. 'No way will I ever get bored of you.'

I never did.

7

THURSDAY

'I'D LIKE TO REPORT MYSELF AS ALIVE AND WELL,' I SAID. HUMOUR, I FAN-cied, was the best bet.

'Right,' said the lady at the front desk of the surgery, drawing the word out to three syllables.

'I was at casualty on Tuesday evening. I have reason to believe there may have been something of a mix-up.'

She glanced behind her, looking for the focus of my stare. 'I do appointments and test results, my love. Did you need to book an appointment?' Her tone was somewhat familiar: that of someone who suspects they are dealing with a crank, with someone whose staircase does not reach the top floor.

'I think you may have reason to believe that I am . . . deceased.' I found myself lowering my voice as I said it.

My first idea had been to revisit casualty this morning, but I remembered what the kind nurse told me the other night, about contacting someone's GP when they die; hence the change of plan and the long walk to my regular surgery. I'd queued ten minutes to reach this Perspex-covered hole in the wall of the waiting room. The place was full of warm, germ-laden air.

'Someone telephoned here yesterday, I think,' I explained.

'I don't work Wednesdays.'

Her tapping at her keyboard gave me an idea. 'Would that

database of yours tell you if a patient of yours was believed to have . . . ?'

The lady glanced at those waiting in line behind me and rolled her eyes. 'What's the name?' The tone of someone humouring me.

'Raymond William Thorns.'

A rattle of keys.

'Steady on, steady on! My word, your touch-typing is—'

'Date of birth, love?'

'VE Day, would you believe it?'

She looked at me, unmoved.

'8th May 1945,' I clarified. We waited for her computer to do its thinking. A baby was howling from across the room; someone else was having a coughing fit. 'Gosh, one could come in here in perfect health and leave with all manner of—'

'Well, Mr Thorns,' she said. 'You appear to me to be very much still with us. According to our records, anyway.'

'Right. Well, that does surprise me.' I made brief eye contact to emphasise my surprise.

She drew her cardigan closed across her chest. 'So did you want to make an appointment. Because if not, I really must ask . . .'

'Look here, I was in casualty on Tuesday night. I was with my neighbour, my *friend*, Barry. I think he may have had my wallet on him, you see. Well, not actually *on* him, as it were. But I think perhaps the ambulance people might have picked it up. He was in my house. And I *wasn't*. It's all a bit of a mess. And I didn't realise there'd been any confusion, not until last night.'

The lady gave a shake of her head toward a colleague at another desk.

'I'm not a crackpot,' I told her. It's a sad truth that it becomes a phrase uttered with increasing frequency past a certain age. Woe betide any person beyond seventy-five who finds themselves having to explain something abnormal.

'It seems everything is in order, Mr Thorns,' she said.

I began to feel agitated, could tell the chance to put this right was slipping from my grasp. I'd missed my usual charity shop visit yesterday; I wished for nothing other than getting this matter sorted so everything could get back to normal.

'I received a card,' I said. 'A sort of *With Sympathy* card, addressed to my family. Someone had been told that I'd . . . passed.'

'Please now. I will have to *call* someone if you're not able to move along.'

I raised a palm. 'Steady on,' I mumbled.

'Sir,' said a father with a buggy behind me. 'You really are holding a lot of people up.'

Muttering an apology I turned to leave. 'That computer!' I said, turning back as the thought occurred to me. 'At what point is it reprogrammed or . . . *updated* or whatever you might call it, when one of your patients . . . passes?' I wagged an unnecessary finger at the back of the screen in time with my words.

The lady huffed. 'Back office deal with that sort of thing.'

'So not *immediately*?'

'Well . . . perhaps.'

'I really do need someone to make a note of the fact that I am very much not dead.'

'It has been noted, Mr Thorns. Rest assured.'

'And that, in fact, the person thought to be me is a gentleman by the name of Barry Detmer. Have you got that? Please make a note of that. Barry. *Detmer.*'

'Yes, all noted. Now, please step aside.'

'This is very important. I mean, I suspect my brother has been informed, and I suppose this whole confusion will be righted when he's called upon to identify a body but all the same . . .' I was becoming upset and was unable to stop myself rambling. 'I'm not mad!' I told the queue behind me, with an involuntary stamp of the foot.

'Appointments?' the lady at the desk said, looking clean past me to the rest of the line.

'Yes please,' I replied instead, insisting that she take the time, that I not be pushed away. 'I'd like to see my doctor, please. Doctor Oduyami. Today—it's urgent.' This seemed my last hope of being absolutely certain that the matter was put to bed.

'Regarding?'

'I'd prefer it to remain confidential.' I felt myself flushing. I'm poor at confrontation but I was finding my stride.

'Doctor Oduyami is not able to deal with administration matters.'

'Perhaps we could let Doctor Oduyami be the judge of that.'

'She has a very full schedule.'

'I'm free all day.'

The firmest rattle of computer keys yet. 'Five-fifty this evening?'

'Thank you kindly,' I replied.

I shuffled past a queue that stretched as far as the doors, my eyes to the floor.

8

IT IS PERHAPS NOT OBVIOUS JUST HOW MUCH SANCTUARY ONE IS AFFORDED
by *routine*. A good routine is a bit like Little Boy Blue's cage (which
he had chosen to return to by my lunchtime visit today). A solid
routine creates parameters, life is framed for you; so it becomes
safer and easy to understand. Forced to compromise my routine
for a couple of days, I had become exposed. It's a feeling I've experienced before: the passing of my mother and the unexpected
ending of my career being good examples. Just as now, those occasions left me without a schedule to keep, and therefore vulnerable. And perhaps, with a faint and frightening sense that beyond
sight there might be something new, and unwelcome. Lying in
wait—the unknown.

I say this only in the hope it offers some excuse as to my
behaviour that afternoon. Having seen a man dying in my own
hallway, and still dealing with the fallout, I needed more than
ever to do something ordinary. In fact, I was *desperate* to do so.
Kept for just such a rainy day (closer to sleet, in reality), I had a
die-cast model of the Mallard locomotive. Midsixties, the paint
had become a rash of a thousand fireside rug collisions, axles and
wheels buckled by generations of children growing too fast to
know their own weight. With the blues of Robert Johnson on
the record player and the joyful initial strip-down completed, I
went to the understairs cupboard in search of an emery cloth.

There was a scratching sound from the outside of the front
door. The noise of someone fumbling with the lock. I froze,

gripping a low shelf attached to the underside of the staircase. In the front room my record had reached its end, the needle *bump-bumping* as it skidded round.

A key scritched into place. The lock tumbled and the door opened a crack. I'd not given anybody a house key.

Had I been less out of sorts, perhaps I'd have confronted the intruder. Instead, and I'm somewhat ashamed to admit it, I withdrew into the darkness of the cupboard, unprepared to react, let alone fight. I pulled its oblique-shaped door towards me till it was within an inch from the frame.

Footsteps in the hallway. The sound of clutter being pushed aside to clear a path.

'Fucking hell,' a gruff voice said.

My pulse hammered fit to give me a heart attack.

'What *are* we going to do with you, Ray?' the man muttered to himself, standing not three feet from the cupboard. 'God rest your bloody soul.' He kicked at the stacks of local papers lined up against the wall. 'My Christ, look at this. Look. At. This.'

I'd not spoken to Denny in nearly four decades, though his voice was unmistakeable. He hadn't set foot in this house since Mum and I lived here together—even then he'd done so rarely. I'd liquidated my pension and taken a mortgage to buy Denny out of his half of the inheritance; twelve thousand pounds, which had seemed a fortune. But it would appear that I never requested he return his key. I would've had no reason to ask.

'Ray, Ray, Ray. What a *fucking* mess, old chap.'

This was unquestionably my chance to make myself known. And I very nearly did so, my shaking hands reaching for the door. It was a wonder Denny couldn't hear my erratic breathing anyway. Had I been sure he was alone I would have revealed myself.

But as I went to grip the handle, a trot of boot heels on the front path. Divine perfume permeating every nook and cranny of the hallway, breezing through the crack around the cupboard door as if on a mission to find me. A million memories stirred. Competing desires to smile and to cry. And I rooted even more firmly to the spot.

'Who the hell lives like this?' Denny said, tut-tutting.

'Oh no,' she said softly. 'Oh dear, dear.'

I was sick to my stomach with nerves. Just an inch of timber separated me from my sister-in-law.

How many decades had passed since I had been this close to Junie?

9

'WHAT SAY WE TURN AROUND, GO HOME, AND LET SOMEONE FROM THE COUN-cil worry about all . . . this?' Denny said.

'Yeah, thank you, Den,' Junie said crossly.

'Would fall to *me*, wouldn't it?' He was poking around in the hallway near the cupboard, his movements amplified by the walls around me.

I had turned my back on the door, in the irrational hope it might reduce the danger of being discovered.

'Terribly, terribly sad,' she said. 'I was expecting—I don't know—a bit of a mess, maybe. But not *this*.'

I throbbed with embarrassment. Was it really *that* bad?

'He was always a slovenly git, wasn't he, Ju?'

'Was he, Den?' she said, sounding exasperated. 'Bit of a *magpie*, I suppose.'

'This is some bona fide hoarding, this is.'

'Bloody hell,' Junie said. 'Where on God's earth would we even begin?'

'I think I'll be worrying about that another day. It'll involve a skip, or ten, I imagine.'

Junie's heels tapped across the kitchen lino. 'Let's have a cuppa.'

'Really? You sure you want to risk it?' Denny said. 'Not sure I'm in the mood for a dose of botulism.'

'Yes, all right, Den,' she replied. 'I'll give the cups a damned good clean first. Don't you fear, darling.' Was that sarcasm I detected?

I heard a kitchen cupboard opening followed by a squark of surprise. I was fairly sure it was the second one from the end, judging from the noise its contents made as they avalanched to the floor.

With the growing promise of cramp in my calves, I ever-so-slowly turned and lowered my backside onto the Hoover. I glimpsed a slice of Denny in profile through the crack between the door and jamb. At eighty-one, still the very upright *big* man he'd always been. His grey slacks, hands resting in pockets, and his leather bomber jacket gave him the appearance of a retired villain; a quite deliberate affectation, in spite of a career spent in insurance brokering. Denny had always been the more image-conscious of the two of us. He once hired an Aston Martin for a school reunion.

He mooched about the place whilst Junie made tea, prodding around in boxes and cases and muttering expletives to himself. The stairs squawked and showered dust onto me as Denny ascended them.

I was still shaking. How ridiculous that, still, a woman could make me so nervous. Contrary to the accepted wisdom on such matters, it had got *worse* with age, not better. As a teenager, the anxiety would last only as long as it took to break into conversation, but as years began to pass without sight of her, yet with little let-up in the business of *thinking about* her, she became increasingly mythical. On the rare occasions we encountered each other during proper adulthood, I was never at ease. Her physical presence had become no longer exciting, but terrifying.

I took deep, quiet breaths and willed myself to relax—here I was, a seventy-nine-year-old man, sitting in a dark cupboard hiding from a girl.

'You're not going to believe this one, Ju,' Denny said, his descent from upstairs like rolling thunder.

'Go on then,' Junie said. 'Tea's up. Just had to bin half a Chinese takeaway from the fridge.'

A loud slurp. 'The man had to eat.'

'It's really sad, Den.'

'I know, I know.' That warm voice of his that could be switched on in an instant and was guaranteed to get him anything; a still familiar sound from another age.

'Do I *want* to know what's upstairs?' Junie asked.

'Mum's old room.'

'What about it?'

'Like a museum piece, Ju. I doubt a single damn thing's been moved since she died.'

'Sometimes people don't feel like . . . changing things.'

'Go and have a look. Bed made up, her old purple dressing gown hanging on the door, make-up still all laid out on her dresser, rings in that little saucer on her bedside table. She's been gone *forty years*.'

'Oh shit.'

'But it's *spotless*, Ju. Old Ray might not have been too keen on housekeeping, but he's bang on top of his game in there. Not a speck of dust!'

'Jesus, this is awful. For forty years . . .'

'He was a card, our Ray! Wasn't he just?'

This riled me. There was nothing strange about keeping things that way in Mum's room; I didn't desperately need the use of it for anything else, and repurposing would've meant finding new places for all of Mum's things, and who was going to help me with that—not Denny certainly. Logical then to leave it as was. And I was certainly not minded to apologise for keeping it *clean*.

'Funeral directors have come back to me,' Denny said, responding to a bleep from his mobile phone.

'How's their availability?' Junie asked.

'Pretty good. They can do something early next week, if needs be.'

'We should go and see them.'

'Yes, that *has* occurred to me,' Denny said, the sarcasm clear in his voice. 'Where would I be without you, dear?'

I rose from my seat on the Hoover. Electrified, I was seized in a half standing, half squatting stance.

How had this happened? How did I get here? Cowering in my own cupboard, as my brother and his wife inspect my home, my belongings, my life. All because I invited a neighbour in to warm up, have a spot of tea? And now there's talk of a funeral. A funeral, for crying out loud!

What of the . . . body? Why had Denny, my *next of kin*, not been yet called upon to make an identification?

I offered my watch up to the light seeping between the hinges: just gone half past three. This evening, I would be seeing my GP and putting this to bed once and for all. Should I leave it that long, even?

I buried my face in the many old coats hanging on the back of the door, closed my eyes, and gave myself a talking to. Any second now, I would reveal myself. No more mucking about!

'I suppose that's what we do?' Denny said. The kitchen stool squawked at the taking of his weight. 'A funeral?'

'There are other options?'

'Who's it going to be, Ju? You and me? Would there be any-body else?'

'What about Steven? He'll want to come. Ray is—*was*—his uncle.'

'Maybe. Three of us, then,' Denny said.

'I'll speak to his neighbours. Didn't anyone from the school sound like they might do the decent thing and show their face?'

'I don't reckon the person I spoke to had the foggiest idea who old Ray was.'

This, at least, explained the card.

'That place remembers him,' Junie said. 'That *is* the reason I was so keen for you to call.'

I was ready to go. I really was. Any second now.

'So you were, dear,' he said dismissively.

'There'll be people, Den. Who'll want to come. We'll . . . find some.'

'I'll be very blinking surprised,' Denny said with the know-it-all's conviction. 'Is it worth the . . . you know . . .'

'The bother?'

'Yeah.'

'Den, come on.'

'What we going to do? Go to all the trouble, to stand there like lemons—you, me, and Steven—and then what, go down the pub, have a pint and a sandwich and call it a *wake*?'

'If it is just the three of us, and I mean *if*, we'll pay our respects all the same. Do you not think we at least owe him that?'

'Be outnumbered by the pallbearers,' Denny said, with a snort. 'You ever heard such a thing?'

Noiselessly, I sank back into my place. Who *would* come? I hated to admit I was in agreement with my brother: Why go to the trouble?

In my rather glum self-reflection, I managed briefly to ignore the fact that I was not actually *in need* of a funeral. But the wind had gone from my sails. Imagine the position I'd be putting them in if I were to have burst forth at this moment! They were guilty only of speaking the truth freely.

'I'll have a decent check round, I suppose,' Denny said, on the move again. 'Make sure everything's secure. Then I reckon we'll call it a day. Hand it over to house clearance.'

'Don't do anything rash,' Junie said.

'You want to be going through all this?'

'Steven will be wanting to have a look through Ray's stuff. He'll want to keep some bits, I expect.'

'You reckon there's anything of enough value to get Steven off his backside and round here?'

Junie huffed. 'He looked up to Ray.'

'That's a new one on me.'

The shadow of Junie swept past like the ghost of another life. I could hear her picking up my restored models from their various places. There was a scratch as she lifted the needle from my record and clicked the turntable off, doubtless in the belief it had been spinning for days after my demise.

Eventually I allowed myself to move closer to the gap between the understairs cupboard door and its frame, affording myself a view through the lounge doorway directly opposite me. Feeling invasive but unable to look away, I watched as Junie wound the mantel clock and tapped it a handful of times, though it wouldn't be ticking again anytime soon; it had stopped working some thirty years ago and I'd opted not to repair it in the belief that the seven minutes past nine on the dial might prove some sort of omen.

A soft clacking sound. I knew exactly what she was handling. They'd been on the mantelpiece since Mum went, and before that they had lived on display above my bed. It makes an unmistakeable sound when knocked, carved ivory.

'What you found?' Denny asked, barely interested.

'Oh, nothing,' Junie said. 'Chess pieces, that's all.' Her voice was quiet and lacked the assurance it'd had earlier.

All thirty-two pieces were there, lined up behind a hundred less significant trinkets and projects. It's a wonder Junie spotted them at all. But then, they were familiar to her. They had once been hers, and before that, her father's. I was only looking after them as I'd been instructed: a down payment on a chess game never played.

10

IT WAS THE SPRING OF 1963, AND JUNIE AND I HAD BEEN EXCHANGING LETters and the occasional photo for nearly three years. It was a long, restless, visceral time. Her father had eventually come up for relocation, no longer a curate but a fully-fledged vicar now. Much as Junie and I had prayed for a London placement, he was deployed to a church near Macclesfield. Two hundred miles from me, give or take. It might just as well have been another planet. This was to be his permanent parish. Our misadventures in the churchyard by the coast began to feel like they'd been a vivid dream; deeply ingrained yet as fantastical as something that happened to somebody in a book or a movie. No girl ever compared.

A couple of train trips were eventually made, where we met halfway in Coventry for a few hours and made it no further than the back row of the Saturday matinee at the Empire. It was when I passed my driving test that I finally made the full distance.

'You must have been driving all bloody night,' Junie said. She wrapped her dressing gown tight around her. It was a little after eight and the April morning was bright but cool; it'd been especially chilly at around 4:00 a.m., just before the sky had begun to lighten on my right.

'Pretty much,' I said, a touch embarrassed, scuffing a foot through the dewy grass. 'Sorry if I woke you.'

'Anytime.' She grinned, prodding my arm. 'Where did you get the car?'

'You like it?'

As gently as if it were a pussy cat, she stroked the front wing where rust pricked through the green paint. 'I'm in love with it.'

'I bought it from a fellow I've done a bit of work for. It's called an MG TD.'

'Can't believe you've got yourself an open-top sports car.'

'Well, it's hardly a *new* one.' I'd paid six pounds (exactly a week's money as it happened) for it. It was twelve years old. There were great rust holes in the chassis, and most of the bodywork was frilly at its edges. The canvas of the roof was so slack and shredded that it was impossible to top fifty without fear of it being ripped free.

'I bet you feel like bloody James Bond driving around in this,' Junie said.

I chuckled, but had no idea who she was on about.

'When did you get it?' she asked.

'I picked it up yesterday evening,' I told her. 'About seven-ish.'

She grinned. 'And this driving test of yours. You passed that when?'

I didn't meet her eye. 'Friday,' I confessed. 'Afternoon.'

She laughed shyly.

'It's okay me coming over?'

She hugged me and kissed me on the lips. 'Yes, darling man. It is very much okay.'

I didn't mention that I had insufficient money to pay for insurance. It was part of the reason why I'd stuck to the back-doubles for the nine-hour drive up. When I think of it now I shudder. There is no condition in this world that makes one careless like that of being in love.

'Well come on then,' Junie said, climbing in. 'God, doesn't it smell amazing?'

'Warm oil. Think it might be leaking a bit.' I lifted the roof clear and let the morning sun pour over us. We'd endured a relentless winter, the worst of all time; long enough to forget that sense of nothing being beyond reach that blooms along with the spring. 'You don't want to get dressed first or anything?' I asked her.

'I can't think why I would,' she said, sitting with her slippered feet tucked beneath her.

With Junie giving directions, we went on a tour of the locality, voices raised over the eternally whining gearbox.

'I *told* you I live in the middle of bloody nowhere,' she said as we gathered speed along a deserted road in the foothills of the Pennines. She snuggled against my side as a green breeze whipped around the cabin. 'Tell me about your work,' she said.

'I don't mind it, mostly. Did a porch roof by myself the other week. Timberwork and the tiles. I enjoyed that.'

'And it's still standing?'

'Don't know. I daren't go back and look.'

'I'm sure it's just perfect,' Junie laughed. 'And that boss of yours, he's treating you okay?'

'Like a dream. He's a nice chap.'

Stan Mockford was a friend of Mum's. They'd met when he'd done some repairs at the solicitors where she worked. He was soon visiting our house one or two evenings a week. Doors that hadn't been right for years were soon a precision fit, leaky taps watertight once more, electrical sockets relocated to where most needed; there is work of Stan's that survives in the house to this day. When I'd left school a year earlier, he'd offered to take me on. As a general builder, I learned a bit of most trades from him.

'I like carpentry best,' I told her. 'Maybe that's what I'd like to do, eventually.'

'So grown up,' Junie said. 'Job, nice car, money.'

'Hardly *grown-up*. And I don't have much money, believe me.'

'Beats being at school.'

I looked across at her, hair flailing everywhere, wind peeling moisture from her eyes. Seventeen, and very much a *woman*.

'What you got, six weeks left?'

She nodded. 'Nearly free.'

'And you're still going to pursue the music, yes?' I said. 'Because you really, really must.'

She was quiet next to me for some minutes.

'You can't let it go to waste,' I said. 'Too much talent.' Since that first time she played for me on the beach, I'd only heard her play down the telephone. But her voice had matured, like it had known a century of joy and sorrow; and her harp playing was gentle and melancholy. She could play a guitar now too. I knew from her letters that she'd had nothing but compliments when she'd auditioned for radio shows and clubs, but the reasons they gave for passing on her followed a familiar theme: this wasn't the music people wanted to listen to nowadays.

'Maybe let's park up,' Junie eventually said. 'There's something I want to tell you.'

We stopped in a lay-by. The early chill had been burnt away. It was warm.

'I've come to a bit of a decision,' Junie said.

'Okay,' I said, sounding calm despite how I felt.

''Round here. It's hopeless.'

'Pretty though,' I said, gazing across the rugged countryside that we were overlooking.

'I told you about the festival, didn't I?'

'Sure. It sounded amazing.'

'It *was* amazing, Ray! I wish you'd been able to come.'

She'd mentioned it in many of her letters. The American Folk Blues Festival had taken place in Manchester six months earlier in October '62. I'd had neither the funds nor the ability to get away from work, but I'd thought about nothing other than her and the time she must be having for that whole weekend.

'You ever been somewhere, Ray, and thought you . . . *belong* for the first time?'

I shrugged my shoulders.

'All those people I met, people who see the music like I do. Like *we* do.'

'I'm just a listener,' I said, feeling an imposter. Sure, I loved those blues albums, but I'd been introduced to them by Junie and was therefore not approaching them with impartiality.

'I was jamming with these guys I met there. It was like magic. And it felt like this could really be . . . the start of something.'

'You're incredible. You'll make it—I know you will.'

She flashed a touched smile at me, as if to thank me for my faith, before returning her gaze to the horizon. This was a conversation yet to reach its crux.

'It's no good *here*, Ray.'

'Macclesfield? The . . . North?'

'It's all Acker Bilk and Cliff *sodding* Richard. People wouldn't know a decent record if it punched them where it hurts most.'

'You're thinking of leaving here?'

'I've got it figured out, Ray. It's only the thought of you that's held me back. I've been dreading telling you.'

'Don't you dare let *me* hold you back.' I said it because it was the right thing to say, but surprisingly enough I did mean it.

'My exams will be over and done by the start of June. I come into a little bit of money on my eighteenth—not a fortune, but *enough*. I'm going to Chicago.'

'I think that's a great idea.' A shortness of breath broke the sentence in two. The mere thought of the distance was a shock.

'It's where it's at. If I want to make a record, if I *really* want that, that's what I've got to do.'

'You must do it then.' I held the hand she'd put on my left thigh. One of us was shaking, perhaps both.

Neither of us could have predicted it, but inside a couple of years, the British rhythm and blues scene was set to explode. Some of those guys she'd jammed with in Manchester were destined to become household names. Chicago was about to export its best to London. But we couldn't have known that then.

'I'm so sorry, Ray,' Junie said. 'I've thought this through, over and over and . . .'

'Don't say sorry. You'll be a star. I just know it.'

'You don't have to be this good about it.'

'It's great news. I'm really happy to hear it.' I was exaggerating a touch, but not lying. I was genuinely excited for her.

She hugged me tight and whispered in my ear that she loved me. I told her I loved her too. We'd written it in letters before, even said it down the phone, but it was the first declaration in person. A sense of the world adjusting around us, an indelible addition being made to the record of all things.

IT WAS LUNCHTIME WHEN WE MADE IT BACK TO THE VICARAGE. JUNIE'S FAther was home after the Sunday morning services. Still in his dog collar, he greeted me like an old friend, with a robust handshake and a penetrating smile. Whilst Junie finally washed and dressed, he and I chatted easily in his study. He poured us a tankard each of bitter from a barrel—like all good home brew it was fruity and foamy and potentially lethal.

I asked him about his decision to become a clergyman, and he explained how it wasn't really a *decision*.

'It's a *calling*,' he said. 'And I can't really tell you what it feels like to be called, only that it is unmistakeable when it happens.'

I found him fascinating. 'When did you hear this calling?' I asked him.

He told me he'd served in the navy. He'd gone down with the battleship HMS *Barham* in '41. Two-thirds of the crew perished, and he had spent ten hours in the sea at the dead of night, injured and waiting for rescue, or for God.

'When you come face-to-face with your own impermanence,' he said, swigging his beer and leaving a foamy moustache, 'the world starts to give up its mysteries. *That* was when I felt myself being called.'

He bitched a little about his flock and the excess of administration, and then said something I've never forgotten: he told me how I'd make a good vicar. Though I've no idea what he saw in me.

Over lunch (roast lamb, fluffy roasties, a gravy I've yet to taste better), Junie's mother asked my advice on maintenance issues around the vicarage, and on their idea of building a sun lounge. She was grateful for my thoughts and made notes on my suggestions.

A strange, alien feeling was growing in me; I couldn't place it straightaway. I was being treated like an adult—that was it. I'd spent much of my life till then stuck in a worst-of-all-worlds limbo: at school I'd been like an awkward grown-up around children my own age, bookish and introspective and thought dull due to my lack of frivolity; at home it had always been necessary to be solid and reasonable. I'd become used to the weight of maturity, but without the accompanying clear run at the buffet of life's options. Here, with the woman I loved and a sense of something akin to respect, I was finally seeing what it was to have the spoils that come with the responsibility.

'You've heard about our Junie's plans, I gather?' her mother said. There was a coded exchange of glances about the table; an issue on which opinions varied, clearly.

I smiled at Junie and circled a fork in front of my mouth. This mouthful of meat—tender though it was—was proving difficult to dispatch.

'I'm really pleased for her,' I eventually said. 'She's going out and getting what she dreams about.' I could sense the mood soften in the room, and it buoyed me. 'I'm proud of her.'

'Amen!' her father said. He winked at me when no one else was looking and mouthed *good lad*.

'What are your plans for this visit, Ray?' her mother asked. 'You must've been awake all night driving up here. Tell me you're not planning on returning down South today.'

I shrugged. 'I'll be fine. I'm expected at work tomorrow morning.'

'You *could* stay the night,' Junie said.

Her father made a display of poking his fingers in his ears. Loudly, he sang some emergency lines from the Eucharist: 'Christ has died! Christ is risen! Christ will come again!'

Junie and her mother gave identical shakes of the head. 'I'll make you up a bed,' her mother said. 'I'd rather you stayed.'

There was no sense in arguing.

By the time Junie's father returned to work for evensong, Junie and I were ensconced in her bedroom. It was the first time we'd slept together. The first time I'd slept with anyone. As for Junie, it was not my business to ask.

It was not the world-changing event I expected it to be: neither explosive, nor something to embarrass my future self over. It just *was*. It was brief, but not excessively so; intimate, yet reserved; pleasurable, but not euphoric. Foundations on which, together, to build. And twenty minutes later, the building began.

In the eventual darkness of that room, between dozes and sticky snuggling, we began to fancy we could be rather good at this.

'I really can't stay the night,' I said, lying an inch apart from her. At the foot of the stairs their longcase clock was striking eleven.

'Stay with me a little longer,' Junie whispered. With the bed sheet wrapped around her, she fetched a chessboard and rested it on the mattress.

'One game won't kill me, I suppose.'

She set out the same ivory pieces of her father's that we'd played with at the beach.

'You could come with me,' she said, attempting a very obvious *scholar's mate* on me. 'To the States.'

'How would that work?'

'Maybe we'd make it work, Ray. I don't know.'

The idea was a pipedream, almost unimaginable. 'You need money for something like that.'

'And airfare, maybe,' Junie said casually. 'Worry about everything else later.'

'It's a nice thought.'

'Think about it, though.'

'Yeah.'

'Another game?' Junie said minutes later, as she sent my queen flying across the bed, leaving my king nowhere to hide.

'Stan will be expecting me in for eight o'clock,' I said miserably. 'I've got to hit the road if I'm going to stand a chance.'

'You need *sleep*, Ray.'

'I need to keep my job.' Despite having driven clean through the previous night, the several naps I'd had between bouts that evening had left me refreshed. 'We'll have another game before you know it.'

Junie scooped the pieces into their timber box. 'You take care of them. Until next time. I've no wish to play anyone else.'

'Likewise,' I said. Taking them from her, it was as if a part of that evening was leaving with me. If I could keep hold of them, perhaps this day would never truly be over.

I didn't take the same care on the drive home as I had on the way up; if I got caught without insurance, so be it. For a time, I picked up the newly opened M6. As I motored across that billiard-smooth surface, the silhouettes in the moonlight of chimneys and mining towers receded in my mirror. It felt, that night in the spring of '63, like I was on the very ridge separating two eras, that one was giving way to another. I wasn't sure that I liked it.

Thoughts of Chicago were inevitable. Could I do it? Could I see myself there? By the time an amber dawn was bleeding through the London smog up ahead, it had become a possibility.

'YOU'D BETTER HAVE A DAMNED FINE EXPLANATION FOR WHERE THE FLIPPIN' heck you've been,' Stan Mockford snapped down at me from the top of the stairs at home.

I was speechless. It was 7:00 a.m. I'd planned to sneak inside, take a wash, and be ready to meet him on time for today's job.

'Sorry,' I mumbled. 'I didn't realise . . . how come you're . . . *here*?'

'I am well and truly up the creek,' he said. 'Mark my words, boy. You have no idea.'

I'd worked with him nigh on a year, and I'd never seen him in such a state. He was an easy-going man, generally speaking.

'I thought we were in Crystal Palace today,' I said. 'Fitting a lav in that barbers. I thought you said to meet you there at eight.'

Stan was next to me in my own hallway now, throwing on his jacket and lurching for the front door. 'Fitting that bog is the least of my worries, boy. The bloody *least* of them.'

'You still want me at work today? I'll be ready in ten minutes.'

'You just sort your mother out, yes?'

'Mum?'

He leaned close to me. 'I've been here all bloody night, Ray.'

'Is she . . . okay?'

'I've been up the hospital with her,' Stan said, halfway out the door. 'She's all right. Wish I could say the same about me. Where the hell have you been?'

'What's wrong with Mum?'

He held up a palm and backed away. 'What am I supposed to tell the wife? Christ sake.'

I bounded up the stairs three at a time. Outside, a roar of engine and a howl of wheel spin.

'What's up, Mum?' I asked, dropping to my knees beside her bed.

She was sitting up in her dressing gown holding a cup of tea. 'Oh, don't you worry yourself about me.' She huffed as she spoke, trying to catch her breath.

'Tell me what's happened. Stan said you've been to the hospital.'

She closed her eyes. Perhaps she was gathering herself, but she drew out her response, stoking my impatience as I asked the same question a number of times.

'I had these ghastly chest pains yesterday,' she whispered.

'Your heart?'

'Well, they don't know. Quite possibly.'

'Where was Denny?'

'Raymond, where is that brother of yours *ever*? I for one have given up trying to keep tabs on him.'

It was a sound point: Denny was nineteen, an office junior up in town, and enjoying a throughput of women that was rapid even by his own standards. We saw him sporadically.

'I'm sorry, Mum, that I wasn't here.'

'I would have telephoned if I'd had any idea where you were,' she said.

'I'm sorry. I was . . . there was somewhere . . .' I was longing for her to interrupt me, but instead she hung on my next words with wide eyes. 'I needed to go somewhere. It's done now.'

'Gosh, don't *you* apologise.' She squeezed my hand. 'You're a young man. Out enjoying yourself, no doubt. The last thing you need is to be worrying about *me*.'

'What did they say, at the hospital?'

Another long pause, a few sips of tea. 'All a bit—what's that word they like?—*inconclusive*.'

'Not a . . . heart attack?' The term felt horrid as it left my mouth.

'Nothing's been ruled out. They were terribly good there, Raymond. I had *three* doctors come and see me. I was quite the source of fascination!'

'Have they given you any medication?'

'No. no. They did some tests which I suppose we'll hear more on in due course.' Her voice became breathy again. 'I didn't want to hang about there, being a nuisance.'

'You must rest up, Mum.'

'We'll see.' She smiled at me. 'Poor old Stan. I think he'll have some explaining to do.'

Stan tended to be over at ours for a couple of evenings during the week seeing Mum. It was an unspoken fact that the weekends were out of the question. 'He was here all night?'

'And yesterday afternoon, to boot. Who else could I have called on, Raymond?'

'I'm sorry.'

'Stop it! You've nothing to be sorry for. Out gallivanting and enjoying your time—good for you!'

'How are you feeling now?' I asked, stroking her arm.

'Oh, I'm fighting fit,' she said, taking a deep breath. 'I'll be running marathons before you know it.'

I stayed home and kept an eye on her that day.

Stan didn't visit again. Mum always referred to it flippantly as his *diplomatic incident*. Inevitably, I was in need of a new employer.

Mum was back to full health almost immediately, though the worry hung over me for months. I'd ask periodically about the results of her tests, but there was no news. There was no recurrence of the chest pains. Not for quite some time, anyway.

Chicago, as perhaps it always had been, was out of the question.

11

IT WAS GETTING ON FOR SIX; I WOULD BE MISSING MY DOCTOR'S APPOINT-
ment. Trapped still in the understairs cupboard. I could hardly
go freeing myself now. It was all I could do to sit tight and pray
that neither of them decided to take a nose in here.

By electric light, the house was calm. Denny had been
busying himself for an hour or more, floorboards occasionally
creaking upstairs. Junie was picking through cases in the living
room, methodically, respectfully. She had listened at low volume
to that Robert Johnson LP I'd played earlier, following it with
some Muddy Waters from my collection, and now Slim Harpo.

'Anything of interest?' Denny asked when he returned to
the room.

'You sound like a police officer,' Junie said. I permitted myself to watch through the gap between the door and the frame
once again. She was thumbing through textbooks from my
teaching days.

'What on God's earth are you listening to?' Denny asked.

'The blues,' she said absently.

'And you're enjoying it, are you?'

'Not all musicians wear tuxedos and croon over a big band,
dear.'

'You'd take this over a bit of Vic Damone or Sinatra, would
you?'

'I think I might,' Junie said, not looking up from her browsing.

'Righto,' Denny said.

'Make yourself useful and put some more tea on,' she said.

'*You* put the tea on if you want one,' Denny replied. I leant against the wall to my left, adjusting my field of view. He was picking up the card that Allonby House sent yesterday from the mantelpiece.

'Quick off the mark, this lot,' he said.

'Ray gave his life to that school.'

'Still, fiver says they won't be sending no one to pay their respects. Card sent—matter closed.'

I heard the door from the front room to the garage open, and the plinking of fluorescent tubes firing. 'My Christ,' Denny said. 'It's still here, Ju!'

'The MG?'

'Looks like bloody brand new!'

'Of course it's still here. It was his pride and joy.'

'Have a look.'

Junie leaned forwards as if she was about to stand before freezing halfway. She dropped back onto the chair, looking somehow . . . defeated. 'Please be careful with it, Den,' she said.

'When do you think this last saw the road?'

It was my regular drive till the late sixties, by which point she was so tired as to be worthless. The restoration began in the early seventies, and took something over a decade to complete. It had performed a lap or two of the block since returning home.

'Got to be worth a few bob,' Denny said.

'No doubt,' Junie mumbled.

'What a case you were, old Ray.'

'Please stop calling him a *case*.'

Denny busied himself in the garage: I could hear the familiar sounds of the doors and bonnet opening, switches being pulled. Whistles of appreciation. As unfamiliar as it felt to have people touching my possessions, I was strangely pleased to have impressed him. I silently willed Junie to look around it too.

Instead, she opened another old suitcase. I knew exactly what lay at the top of it. 'Oh my!' she whispered, grinning. 'My godfathers!' She withdrew the record sleeve from the protective plastic I keep it in. Holding it almost as gently as I do, she studied both sides with a look of wonder.

Junie had cut just one record in Chicago, a six-track EP of electric blues numbers of her own composition. I've no idea how many copies ever existed, but I know mine would be irreplaceable were anything to happen to it. It's been among my most treasured possessions since it arrived by airmail in '64. I play it only occasionally to avoid wear and never leave it at the mercy of dust or sunlight.

For a minute or more, she held the naked disc between her palms. She cast a glance in the direction of the record player, smiling but choosing instead to return it to its sleeve. When Denny emerged from the garage, she cast it away onto the hearth like a dirty secret.

'What a bloody mess,' Denny said, yet again, rifling the drawers of the bureau.

'What you looking for?' Junie asked.

'Oh, just, you know . . .'

'You're after something.'

'I'm not,' Denny snapped.

'You're looking for a will, aren't you?'

'No, I'm . . .'

'You—'

'Who cares what I'm looking for?' There was something threatening in his voice. 'Why don't you mind your own business?'

'You are! You conniving old bugger!'

Junie laughed. Almost a giggle. It was the first time that day that I'd really *recognised* her. Both her amusement, and the source of it, were a part of her character that the decades hadn't eroded.

'So what if I am?'

'You're the *card* round here, dear, if anyone is.' She did a poor impression of his gruff-Londoner voice: '"We should go round, Ju. Make sure the house is safe, Ju. Check nothing needs doing, Ju."'

'All right, all right,' he said, raising his voice.

'Patience, dear man,' Junie said calmly. 'I dare say you'll discover in due course what you've been left.'

He'd be disappointed, no doubt. It had, in fact, not occurred to me to make a will. Or rather, it *had*, but the thought always led to such unease that I would abort the idea immediately. Of course, there *was* still time for me to produce a will, although it took a good moment for me to remember that fact, such was the gathering pace of the deception I'd got myself snarled up in.

'Oh, have a look!' Denny said, spotting the record and picking it up. 'How's that for a blast from the past? You look very . . . serious, dear.' He was studying that stunning black and white cover image of her singing into a bullet mike.

'I *was* serious. Be careful with it please.'

'And a sort.'

'Thanks,' Junie said sarcastically.

'*June and The Electros Have Got the Blues Alright!*' Denny read aloud. 'How did you think that one up?'

'It was a long time ago,' Junie mumbled, embarrassed.

'Let's put it on.' I recognised Denny's mood: a behaviour that dated back to childhood. Having been shamed for searching for my will, he was compelled to level the score. 'Can't be any worse than this crap,' he said, cringing at the sound of Slim Harpo's 'Baby, Scratch My Back', an absolute classic.

'Leave it please, Den.'

'Come on! Be a sport, Ju. I'm fascinated.'

'You've heard it before.'

'Years ago. I'm curious.'

'Don't put that record on, Den.' She said it almost pleadingly.

'"Them Churchyard Blues",' he said, reading aloud the track listing. 'Racy stuff!'

It was a racy song, racier than he would dare imagine; the lyrics were coded, but of clear enough intent.

'"The Love We Leave Behind". Who, dear, were you thinking of when you penned that one?'

Junie returned to searching through the suitcase.

'Was that one about old Ray?'

'Please, Den. I didn't even *know* you back then.'

'You think I'm being jealous? Ju, give me some credit. Come on . . .'

'Put the record away.'

He considered it in his hand for a moment, before carelessly dispensing it from its sleeve. His fingertips were on the vinyl itself; it'd never been handled so roughly in sixty years. The Slim Harpo slurred to a stop.

'I want to hear it,' Denny said.

Junie spun around. 'Den, stop being a cunt.'

Silence. 'I'm sorry?' he eventually said, very *properly*, the London swagger gone from his voice.

'I called you a cunt, Den,' Junie said. 'There a problem?'

He raised a finger to make a point. 'I beg your—'

'Might there be a better term to describe the way you're acting? I can't think of one, you see.'

My heart was thumping, yet I caught myself smiling. She was still the woman I'd once known.

'You ought to wash your mouth out with soap,' Denny said. He had the confused tone of a bully receiving some overdue retaliation—a scene I encountered more than a few times in my professional life.

'I was a girl with a dream. At least I was once. I'm fascinated that you find that so worthy of your derision.'

'I'm having a joke with you, Ju. Remember *jokes*?'

She brushed past him and recovered the record. 'Perhaps I *would* like to listen to it again. But alone, without your mean-spirited commentary, if that's okay?'

'I'm not trying to piss on your chips.'

'Oh, you've pissed on my chips all right. And since you chose to ask—yes, some of those songs were written with your brother in mind. How's that for you, Den?'

Denny snorted. 'Whatever floats your boat.'

'Ray didn't spend his time laughing at the idea that someone might want to *do* something with themselves.'

'Yes, what an absolute *rock* the man was. Terrible shame he was also such a mummy's boy, you two could've really had something.'

There was a lengthy silence.

'Don't you *feel* anything, Den?' she asked. 'Being *here*. Your only brother, gone. Don't you feel . . . something?'

'Evidently not as much as you.'

'Jesus Christ.'

'All right, yes, I'm sad about it. Yes, perhaps it would've been nice if we'd had some sort of relationship. But I didn't choose that, did I?'

'Well I don't mind admitting that I'm . . . *very* sad about it. And I really couldn't give a toss if you take issue with that.'

'What's got into you, woman?'

She turned her back and mumbled something to herself.

'I'm calling it a day,' Denny said. 'Everything's secure.'

Junie began reassembling the stack of cases. 'There's a lot here I want to sort through. There's a whole life here. I'm going to carry on tomorrow.'

'You've stumbled on a blast from your past, and now you can't keep yourself away?'

'Shut up, Den.'

'You'll be on your own—I'll tell you that much. I'm at golf. And even if I wasn't . . .'

'Suits me. I might see if Steven fancies it.'

'I'll be in the car,' Denny said, spinning a key ring round his finger.

She checked over her shoulder after the front door closed. Certain she was alone, she took a last look at her record, gazing at it for a minute or more. I listened as she washed up the teacups and turned out the kitchen light. With her coat on, she returned to the mantelpiece. I would later discover that it was the black rook she'd chosen; at that moment I wasn't aware of the possibility that she might have slipped something into her handbag.

I willed my breathing to be silent as she paused not three feet from the door hiding me. She was staring at my favourite Allonby House school photograph: 1982, year of the Green Hair Incident. There was a small, private laugh.

'Night, night, dear old Ray,' she whispered. She couldn't have been more than six inches from the picture glass.

Her perfume hung in the hallway after her departure. I stretched myself out in the darkened house, my lower half roiling with pins and needles.

For a man, if official reports were to be trusted, whose heart gave out two days hence, I was feeling overwhelmingly alive. I was unable to keep still for some hours once outside the cupboard.

She was—possibly—planning to return tomorrow. Could I allow it to happen? My doctor's appointment already missed, surely in the morning I really *must* set things right. Get back to normal. I could not allow myself to be complicit in the continuation of this charade. Tomorrow. Then I forced it from my mind for the night.

Instead, I thought about Junie. I had, for the first time in decades, enjoyed a little time in her company. And, just possibly, it seemed I still meant something to her. Even if I was worth more dead than alive.

12

IT WAS NOT WHAT I WAS EXPECTING OF A JOB INTERVIEW. THE HEADMASTER of Allonby House was a fellow by the name of Rhind-Jones. He was the most devout Christian I'd encountered so far in life; within moments of my arrival he'd told me he'd read the Bible cover to cover five times. He went on to say he was a lay reader at his church, and I explained that my beloved's father was a man of the cloth, but this didn't impress him the way I'd hoped.

Feeling guilty over the business with Stan Mockford, Mum had found the job ad and nagged me to apply: *Trainee caretaker's assistant at boys preparatory boarding school, 5d 6s per week and some benefits.*

In the headmaster's study, I was introduced by Rhind-Jones to the current caretaker, a Paul Sheehan. The man was ancient and stooped, and considered me with a poker face. He had breath that could ruin a room and, like most people so inflicted, held conversations mere inches from his victims' faces.

'Let's see what you're about, lad,' he said to me.

I nodded, breathing cautiously through pursed lips.

Rhind-Jones left Sheehan alone with me to do his worst. The old man led me no further than the door the headmaster had just exited by.

'He keeps complaining,' he told me. 'Says it don't lock properly.'

'I see,' I said, testing it myself. The key turned as one might expect, but with a shove the door could be opened. 'The deadbolt doesn't align with the keep,' I offered. 'The door's dropped in the frame, I think.'

'Off you go then.' He slung his tool bag at my feet.

It was a simple enough fix: a little packing to the lower hinge, a run of a plane over the top corner, reset the keep plate's position, a drop of oil on everything.

'He was a good help to me,' Sheehan said when Rhind-Jones returned and test-drove his newly secure study door. Then he gave me the job.

The tone of my early days at Allonby House was very much set by that job interview with Sheehan: he'd tell me what needed doing, I'd do it, he'd take the credit. He died of a stroke a year later and his role was never advertised; it was simply accepted that his job was now mine, albeit without a conversation about wages.

I inherited Sheehan's former office, which was essentially no more than a storeroom. However, it said *Caretaker* in (oft-polished) brass on the door and it shared a corridor with the prefects' lounge and the headmaster's study.

BEFORE I BECAME *SPIKE*, I WAS BRIEFLY *JEEVES*. IT WAS A NICKNAME GIVEN to me by the older boys. One of my tasks in those early days was to set a fire in the grate of the prefects' lounge every winter's evening. Though it was hard to credit it, there were barely five years between myself at eighteen, and these boys who were soon to leave for pastures new. To them, this age difference was half a lifetime again. To me, the gap wider still. These were broadsheet-reading young men. In that first term on the staff, I was discreet in their presence; when necessary to speak with one of their number, I would address them each as *young master*; it was my own fault that they named me after fiction's most memorable butler. But I didn't mind it a bit.

'What are the principal themes, Jeeves, in your opinion, of *The Great Gatsby*?' a young man named Edmund asked my turned back as I fanned the kindling to life during the frozen February of '64.

The prefects regularly discussed their prep of an evening and, though this was the first time my opinion had been sought, I often had a thought or two I could bring to the debate.

As I faced the room and the many boys seated on their mismatched old settees, I noted a collective embarrassment aimed at Edmund.

He considered me through metal-rimmed specs. 'Any thoughts, Jeeves? I'd be enthralled to know.'

All other eyes found the floor or hands in laps. It was not so long since I'd left school myself to not understand this situation; lord knows I'd been pilloried widely enough in my own day. This Edmund fellow was in no way characteristic of most of the young men I came to know in my long career at Allonby House, but there were a few of his type. Privately, I thought of all such boys from then on as *Edmunds*. And when, much later, I had cause to meet the fathers of some notable Edmunds, I realised that these boys had invariably endured a poor education on matters of manhood from an early age.

'Don't people say it's about the American dream?' I replied, looking down into my hands.

'So they do,' Edmund replied.

'Or perhaps I should say—that the American dream is something of a fraud.'

I looked up to find a couple of faces nodding at me.

'You're writings essays about it?' I asked.

A murmur of agreement.

'But I'm not sure that's what I took from it,' I said. 'I think it's a story about love.' This felt like a dim point to make, but I *was* dim in this company. Surprisingly enough, I was met with a handful of interested-looking faces.

I'd been a casual reader for most of my days but had become a devourer of novels since Junie left. Pasternak, Salinger, Graham Greene. And of course, *The Great Gatsby*. Forty years since its publication, but only now was it making waves on this side of the Atlantic. There was wisdom in those pages that likely would have meant little to me a few years earlier. With Junie and me corresponding at least fortnightly, my next letter was eternally being composed and edited in my mind, its prose all the more eloquent for the great literature I was enjoying.

'I'm not sure there are many things other than love that drive someone to produce something so artful as a novel,' I said to the prefects, mumbling a touch.

'That's a tad . . . sentimental,' the Edmund said.

A couple of red-faced scowls were fired his way.

'What do you fine gentlemen think of it?' I said, nervous now all eyes were on me. I was expecting an education here but was met mostly with comments like 'It's all right' and 'Not my favourite'. I laughed when one fellow remarked: 'It's too short, and it's too long, all at the same time.'

'That's an incredible observation!' I said. 'How perfectly put.' He looked somewhat surprised at my reaction. 'A small amount of plot, written in—how can we put it?—such *flowery* language.'

'But maybe,' said a bright spark named Bellinger, 'that's a deliberate way of the writer telling us how these characters are all about style and—'

'Not substance,' offered another.

Forgetting myself, I swung a fist through the air—a nail had been struck on its head.

A few pencils twitched, a note scrawled here and there.

'It's a jazz age novel,' a more assured voice said. Plenty of nods.

'I've heard that said,' I replied. 'What does that really mean, though?' I became aware that some of the boys were leaning in their seats towards me. I stepped away from the fireplace, which had begun to crackle and snap behind me, taking up a place in a gap in their circle of furniture.

'I don't care too much for jazz,' I told them. 'I'm a blues man.' Silly as it sounds, I was wary discussing matters of personal taste, so fresh was the memory of my failure to conform during my own school days. I was, however, met with nothing other than mostly blank faces. 'The blues is quite something!' I reassured them, catching myself smiling. 'But what does *jazz* mean to you gentlemen?'

'A bloody racket,' offered Edmund.

'Well perhaps.' I remembered myself and my eyes found the floor at my feet.

'The characters behave like jazz!' snapped a wisp of a lad by the name Lloyd. This earned him some sniggers.

'That's exactly what I was thinking,' I said. The mirth was extinguished and once again I was the focus of attention. I had a curious sense of not finding it uncomfortable. I lowered my backside onto the arm of a settee, although I wasn't entirely at ease in such a stance.

'No rules,' Bellinger offered.

'Free from the constraints of rules,' I added. 'Like jazz itself.'

'And that's why they act so badly?' another asked.

'Perhaps there's nothing quite like taking away the rule book to see who people really are,' I mused. 'In the case of Gatsby's friends, they use the freedom to have affairs and to party nonstop and even to commit murder.'

There was a moment of quiet as some notes were made. 'And, you were saying,' began a boy called Ogilvy, before reddening, 'about . . . love?'

This got some baying from the lads. 'Who could you possibly be thinking of?' cried out one, hooking an arm roughly round poor Ogilvy's shoulder, who was beetroot-coloured by now.

'Steady on, steady on.' I turned and addressed Ogilvy directly. 'It happens to the best of us, I'm afraid to say. Look at our friend Gatsby. What else could possibly drive a man to spend years and years and every breathing moment becoming filthy rich, just so he can hold wild parties in the sole hope that the person he's crazy about might one day show up?'

This statement split the room. Some thought the idea impossibly far-fetched.

'I found it all somewhat relatable,' I said, and Ogilvy, still glowing, nodded along.

A voice called out to me: 'Maybe you could put a word in for him with Miss Hornery, sir.'

Ignoring that this was the first time I'd ever been addressed such, I implored the room to calm down. I pretended to not hear Ogilvy's expletives. I was not about to berate a thirteen-year-old chap who was mired in the horror of an unrequited crush.

'Ah, Miss Hornery,' I said. 'Yes, young master, I see your predicament. She is quite . . . striking. That I'll grant you.'

The lady in question was no more than twenty-five and taught mathematics. Though I'd never had cause to speak directly with her, it was impossible not to have one's eye caught. In any boy's school, there is always a member of staff whose image the pupils will remember for life, and Marina Hornery was Allonby House's.

'Hasn't she got a fiancé?' someone asked me.

'I believe there is a ring,' I mumbled.

'He was checking for a ring!' This observation led to much joshing at my expense.

'I'm a one-woman man . . .' I declared through a grin. 'I merely noticed it in passing . . . Oh, steady on, please!'

Bellinger said loudly: 'Even Rhind-Jones thinks he's in with a ghost of a chance.' This was rather dangerous ground and had the effect of hushing the room. I was looked at warily.

I chuckled. 'I don't think our esteemed headmaster has such things on his mind. He has a wife of his own, and five children to boot.' Not to mention that it was hard to imagine such an austere, God-fearing man, attempting to woo anyone. Though I had nothing other than respect for him, he was somewhat charmless. I saw him most days and was largely invisible to him, eliciting at best a stiff 'morning' but no more.

'He seems to drop in to her form room rather a lot,' Lloyd said. Ogilvy appeared ever increasing degrees of heartbroken. I gave him a wink.

'Now, now, boys. This is how rumours begin,' I said, smirking.

'Ogilvy's going to get himself caned. For looking at Rhind-Jones's sweetheart the wrong way!'

I put my fingers in my ears in response to Ogilvy's 'Fuck off'.

'Gosh, that's a fate that doesn't bear thinking about,' I said. The man was an evangelist for discipline and the proximity of the caretaker's room to his study meant that I'd witnessed a clutch of his poor victims making their pained exits.

'I trust none of you gentlemen have had the misfortune?'

This prompted a show of hands. At least a third had received a caning from him, and these were boys who had made the grade as *prefects*. Many of them in line for scholarships.

'He makes you say *thank you*,' one told me.

'Thank you, sir,' another simpered. 'Thank you so much for beating my arse raw. Thank you for being such a sadist. So jolly kind good of you.'

'Rhind-Jones gets a stiffy,' young Lloyd giggled. 'When he's doing it.'

Everyone laughed riotously.

'He does *what*?' I asked.

'If you will insist on looking *there*!' Edmund said.

'I swear it,' said Lloyd. 'I could've hung my blazer on it.'

There was a roar of distaste, some thrown cushions. 'My word,' I said, mopping my brow. Not that I believed a word of it, of course. To even think such a thing.

'His trouser legs were up round his calves,' he added.

Enjoying the horseplay though I was, it was at this point that I felt—for professionalism's sake—that I should return to busying myself with my caretaking duties. In any case, the fire I had come here to set was blazing a treat.

I was never *Jeeves* again. It was the first of many fine evening debates with the prefects, company in which I quickly found myself more comfortable than I ever had in my own schooldays. I forget exactly when *Spike* was first coined, but it was not long after that evening. It rather stuck.

IT TOOK LESS THAN A YEAR FOR ME TO FALL FOUL OF MR RHIND-JONES myself.

Nowhere on earth does one feel the changing seasons quite so vividly as at an English boarding school. Those misty spring dawns on wooden corridors, the stifling midsummer afternoons, the autumn chill that finds your toes first. But nothing came for you in that draughty old building quite like winter.

I was sent for one evening to attend to a leaky pipe in the youngest boys' dorm. It was gone ten and their housemaster took advantage of my presence by escaping for an assignation off-site. These boarders were no more than eight years old. It was a wonder that any of them were able to sleep—it was Baltic in there! Icy wind whipped through the uncurtained window, which was open by three inches. As I leaned over the bed nearest to lower the sash closed, the occupant looked up at me. 'No, sir,' he whispered sharply. 'It has to be kept open.'

'Why on earth . . . ?'

'Rules,' a voice from across the room muttered. I could hear the shiver in his voice; hardly surprising given that all that these boys had to keep them warm was their pyjamas and a blanket each that likely dated to before the war, given how thin they'd worn.

There was not a teddy bear in sight, nor a family photograph, or loving note from Mum pinned to the wall. Gosh, it made me appreciate how fortunate I was to have had my upbringing.

I closed the window to within half an inch—still open, technically. I did the obvious. In a jiffy I'd fetched some small logs from the wood store. The dorm's fireplace was a cobwebby black hole with a rusted basket. The chimney still pulled a treat though despite the lack of use and I had it roaring like a Bunsen burner within minutes. I made good the pipework I'd been called out to and left the lads sometime after midnight, every one of them fast asleep and a soft orange glow in the grate.

'We do things a certain way for good reason,' Rhind-Jones told me. I was seated in an awkwardly low chair; he towered over me on the other side of his desk as if sitting on a throne. It was not yet nine the next morning and already the boys' housemaster had carried out an interrogation.

'I would never doubt it, sir,' I told him.

'We are not in the business of leaving the boys' care at the behest of *manual staff*.' He chortled as he said this and I smiled along.

It had been some time years since I'd found myself in trouble with a teacher, but the sensation of being crestfallen and tearful was still familiar. 'I *am* sorry, sir,' I said. 'I just thought, with fires being my domain, and the room so cold, and . . .'

'You imagine you know better?' he said.

I shook my head.

'Imagine you know better how to prepare young men for the world? The Empire was not won by mollycoddled men, *Raymond*.' He was finding my name strangely light-hearted.

'No I can see . . .'

'We care very deeply here at Allonby House, about setting our boys up for life.'

'Certainly. I wouldn't—'

'British values,' he said. 'That is what we instil here. Along with the teachings of the Christian church, of course.'

'Amen,' I said, nodding. This was more comfortable ground and I relaxed a little. I felt I'd been acceptably briefed on such matters by Junie's father. I smiled, remembering an embroidered Bible verse sampler from his study that I'd been rather taken with, that day we'd drunk homebrew together. 'Fathers,' I began, 'do not provoke your children to anger by the way you treat them. Rather, bring them up with the discipline and instruction that comes from the Lord.'

Rhind-Jones leaned towards me. I couldn't quite read his expression: he looked surprised by me, but not in the way I'd hoped. 'And from where did you glean that?'

'Oh, I'm not sure. Ephesians, perhaps.' It was chapter six, verse four, but no one likes a smart alec.

'I was not aware I was in the presence of a religious scholar.'

'Steady on,' I replied shyly. 'I'm no *scholar.*'

His silence encouraged me to continue.

'The thing about Christianity,' I said, 'is that we should all be *real.*' This was of no relevance to the discussion; I was merely regurgitating some of Reverend Burnham's wisdom, which had rung very true to me. I was hoping it might make me appear educated, I suppose. 'God wouldn't have made us the way he did, if he wished us to be something different.'

'It's a theory,' he eventually replied. 'I was at school with the now *Bishop of Coventry,*' He enunciated each word of this title. 'We remain *close* personal friends. I generally conduct my discussions of theology in *his* company.'

He offered some thoughts of his own on God's plan—he was

quite staunchly in the fire and brimstone camp. I nodded along, but had become distracted by the dark elm cabinet in the corner of his study, which hung open. There was a pair of trousers hanging on the rear of the door, a match to the suit he was wearing. Was that a precaution all well-attired men took, I wondered?

You see, following the prefects' salacious claims, I had noted some odd behaviour from our headmaster. Given the proximity of the caretaker's room across the corridor from his study, I had witnessed his trot to the lavatory after meting out one of his infamous canings. A man of such perfect posture, yet he had made that walk with a distinct fold about his middle, hands in pockets.

'Do I disinterest you?' Rhind-Jones said, snapping his fingers. I returned my full attention to him. 'Fortunately for you, I have morning prayers to lead.' He reached for his gown and sent me away with a flea in my ear about leaving the boys' dormitory arrangements to their housemasters.

As the school year wore on, I began to observe something else too. I kept it to myself of course, but Miss Hornery had become a regular visitor to Rhind-Jones's study. There had been much speculation amongst the older boys about her now absent engagement ring (her beloved succumbing to typhoid, leaving her for a Miss England frontrunner, gruesome speedboat incident). I chatted with her once in the refectory about the business with Zambia. She was intimidatingly intelligent but with something of the lost soul about her. Those light-footed trips to the head were made always afterhours. Rhind-Jones was a family man. It came naturally for me to assume the best of him, to not jump to conclusions. But I was under twenty-one and—on reflection—encountering one of life's truths for the first time: that people with the most conservative views are simply those who wish to stop others indulging in the misbehaviour they permit themselves.

IN EARLY '66 I SPENT A WEEK ON THE ROOF OF THE MAIN BUILDING, REPLACing storm-damaged slates and pointing the chimney stacks. Four storeys up with just a transistor radio for company, it was a fine job. The new Post Office Tower rose out of the London smoke, Wilson was in Number Ten at last, Chicago rhythm and blues had made it onto the radio here and there, courtesy of some local lads called The Rolling Stones. In my breast pocket was a junk shop fob watch I'd bought for pennies, set six hours behind the trusty Ingersol on my wrist. Chicago time. Ticking away close to heart.

It was the fourth morning of the job when I saw the boy up there. Not yet eight o'clock; the day pupils were yet to arrive and the boarders were at breakfast. I'd been busying myself on the north-facing flank and only spotted him when I crawled up to the ridge for more nails. He was at the gable end where my ladder had been affixed all week. Clinging to the edge of the roof and crouched as if he'd expected this to be a laugh and had now discovered otherwise.

'Higher than you think, isn't it?' I said, having scurried across a third of the building along the ridge in record time.

The boy nodded once. His face was pale and blank, so very blank. I moved to within six feet of him and he shakily sidled away from me. He was a couple of feet from a sheer drop.

'Steady on, steady on,' I said. 'Do your friends know you're up here?'

'No.' He shot a look towards the top of the ladder.

'I can help you back on,' I told him. 'It's lashed to the wall. Nice and tight. But it can be a little scary, getting on, I know.'

The sun had been on the rise for half an hour, but it was still chilly. Grafting as I had been, I was still glad of the two jumpers beneath my old wool jacket. The boy had nothing over his shirt and tie.

'You'll catch your death up here. Nothing to stop the breeze, see. Might only be five miles per hour this wind, but it's a northerly. Barely nothing between us up here and the Thames ten miles away.'

'Listen,' I said, as a gentle gust licked the roof. 'Can you hear the whistling. It's the gaps between the slates. Like the reeds in a harmonica.'

I steadied myself with a heel against a batten and eased out of my coat, offering it to him at arm's length.

'I'm all right,' he said. His expression didn't change, eyes stuck to the middle distance.

Shuffling over to the gable, I looked down to the concrete below. No mates daring him on. No one at all.

'What's your name?'

'Timothy,' he eventually said. 'Tim.'

'I'm Ray,' I told him, keeping to a distance that didn't spook him. 'Pleased to meet you, Timothy Tim.'

'Hi,' he whispered. This, it seemed, was just him being unable to forget his manners; nothing about him suggested he wanted a conversation.

'You didn't fancy any brekka?'

Tim shook his head.

'I've got some ginger nuts, if you might like one?'

'No, thank you.' His voice was unbroken and immaculately spoken. I'd later discover he was eleven, but he looked younger.

'I wasn't much of a fan of school,' I told him. 'I quite liked history. And reading, I like that still. You like books, Tim?'

'Sometimes,' he said after a while. 'Used to.'

'You will again. Have to read the right stuff, that's the key.'

Tim shifted just slightly, let his backside settle more firmly on the ridge tile.

'Of course, you see, I didn't *board*,' I said. 'I don't know if I'd have liked that a great deal. I suppose if you've got good friends it might be fun. I didn't have too many friends really. You've got friends, Tim?'

'Sort of. One or two.'

'Ah, well that's good. You'll make hundreds more as the years go on. I know I did, eventually. I was never lonely for long.' This isn't true, but seemed a decent line to take. I dared to take my eyes off Tim, scanning the area for anything that could be of use. There was a length of rope attached to one of my roof ladders thirty feet away: it was hard to imagine retrieving and making good use of it without unsettling the boy.

I shuffled a little closer to Tim. 'Sleeping at school, though. I don't know about that.'

'I don't sleep.'

'I hate that. When there's stuff on my mind. I do feel for you.'

'Never,' he said, choking on the word. 'I can't sleep. I just . . . can't.'

'I'm sorry. God, no wonder you feel shitty. That'd make anyone feel shitty.'

'I can't even think,' he whispered. Tears ran from those hollow eyes, for which he apologised several times.

Shuffling on my backside I moved in, resting my old jacket over his tiny shoulders.

'There's some fruit gums in the pocket. And some slate nails. Don't eat those.'

Below, I could hear the pupils leaving breakfast and the shouts of a master. But they were too close to the building; at this height the two of us would only be visible at a fair distance away. We sat silently awhile. High above us, a jet plane arced slowly across the clear sky. Heading west, America bound. My heart beat out of rhythm.

'Nice to be away from people,' I said after a time. 'Would you listen to that!' I nodded towards the fir trees at the school's perimeter and the frantic chorus emanating from its branches. 'Chaffinches. They do love to make a racket about this time. Funny thing, birdsong. There so often that we can forget to listen to it. Foolish of us, really.'

'Did you get in trouble at school?' Tim asked me.

'Not much. Sometimes, I suppose. My brother on the other hand, well he was another matter. Never seemed to do him any harm, though.'

'I do *try* not to.'

'What is it they get angry over?'

Tim shrugged. 'Not listening. Not . . . concentrating. Forgetting stuff. It's not deliberate or anything. I just can't . . . do stuff. I used to be able to.' He withdrew his hand into his shirt cuff and wiped his tears with it.

'Clean hanky in the top pocket,' I said pointing.

'They think I do it on purpose. That I don't care. That isn't why. I don't know why.'

'We must have a chat with your masters. This started when you stopped being able to sleep?'

'Don't know. Maybe. Can't really remember what happened when. Nothing's in order anymore. Sorry, that sounds really stupid.'

I shook my head. 'Tell me about your mum and dad. Only if you don't mind. What are they like?'

Tim's gaze edged toward the gable, and the sheer drop, to the other side of me. He said nothing.

'You ever worked on a roof before?' I asked.

'Helped my grandad once. Just a shed roof, though.' A flicker of a smile.

'Felt. Yes. No felting to do up here. Perhaps you could help me on one of the stacks, though. Many hands, and all that.'

He nodded slightly.

'I'd have to tie you on, though. Safety first.'

I watched his every move as we sidled along the ridge to the scaffold stage I'd erected around a chimney. With a rope around his waist I showed him how to rake out poor pointing with a chisel. We slowly worked a flank each with the radio playing between us.

He told me how his grandad had died back at Christmas. How his mum and dad weren't getting along. It was hard to know what had come first: the worry, the sadness, the sleeplessness, the getting into trouble. But each in turn had made the others worse.

'I'm going to take you see the nurse,' I told him. 'Today, if you don't mind.'

'There's nothing wrong with me,' he said, confused.

'Even so. I think she'll help.'

'I'm not *ill*, or anything. What would I tell her?'

'Just the things you've told me. Nothing you've said is at all silly. You can do that, yes?'

'I don't know. Maybe.'

'I'll come too, help if you need me to.'

'Okay.'

'What do you reckon of this song?' I asked. I was brushing sand off the scaffold as The Beatles' 'Nowhere Man' played on the radio.

He listened for a minute. 'It's good, I suppose.'

'There's lots of great music being made.' I was of course biased: a young man in love does not evaluate the soundtrack of the day impartially. 'Imagine how much more there is to come. All those great things to be heard for the first time, things to be seen for the first time, things that we'll *feel* that we can't even imagine feeling right now.'

'Maybe.'

'Are you ready for us to make that visit to the nurse?'

Everyone was in lessons as we scaled the ladder to the ground, me two rungs below Tim and imploring him to *steady on* the whole way.

I kept an eye on Tim after that day. He joined me every now and then during his free time in the early evenings. He'd lend a hand with lining out the football pitch or cutting the perimeter hedge, or whatever was on my schedule. Sometimes, he came with a couple of friends too. It was an education for me: to see how these boys from such well-heeled beginnings took the same joy as I did from the free mind that comes with busy hands.

Our little club was disbanded when Tim and another lad were seen behind the pavilion and reported to the head. They'd been helping plane timbers. I made representations on their behalf, but they were out of bounds and that was that. A caning inevitably followed.

It was mere days later that Rhind-Jones was caught in a compromising position in his study with Miss Hornery. It had taken no more than a firm knock from a prefect to send his door opening. There had been a continuous recurrence of the door lock issue that was thought previously repaired.

He stood firm for a while. But the scandal, far from going quiet, grew daily. By the time it came to the attention of the governors, he'd run out of choices.

His replacement was Charles Sethi, a five-foot-three giant in a Savile Row three-piece and a turquoise turban. He'd climbed the ranks the hardest way and the altar he worshipped at was that of common decency. There began a bright new era at Allonby House.

13

FRIDAY

I SAT ON THE ARMCHAIR IN BARRY DETMER'S CHILLY FLAT. THE POWER WAS still out. I ate a beef pasty washed down with a takeaway coffee (*freshly ground*, and boy did it taste so). Junie and Denny had disposed of my few perishables yesterday, but even a presumed-dead man has to eat. I'd taken a walk to the petrol station at the crossroads and treated myself to their hot hold. It had occurred to me that perhaps I shouldn't risk being seen out and about, but trusted to the camouflage of anonymity that one wears after retirement.

The absurdity of my situation had hit me anew in the morning light. I'd slept well, surprisingly enough. But I had become torn: a desire to do the right thing, yes, but since Denny and Junie's visit yesterday I'd rather lost my desperation to return things to *normal*. Normality had lost something of its . . . attraction. Was I complicit in a deception by allowing this to continue? For just one more day? Any moment, wouldn't Denny be called upon to identify a body, putting the matter to bed once and for all? And hadn't I *tried* yesterday, at the doctors? Done my best?

In exasperation, I slapped my hands onto the arms of the chair. On my lap was the local paper, delivered sometime yesterday. I sprinkled the flakes of pastry it had collected onto the coffee table and clicked my fingers to gain Little Boy Blue's attention.

He had now—forty-eight hours on—colonised the entire flat, no longer fascinated by, or fearful of, his new freedom. Perched between the net curtain and the window glass, he looked out at a golden new day that more than hinted at spring. He was vocal as ever, but there was something wistful in his song. It put me in mind of a finely played harmonica.

'Here, boy!' I kept repeating, but nothing would draw his gaze from the big wide world.

I was keeping an eye out too. If indeed Junie were to make good on her plan to return today, she surely wouldn't be over till later, but still my heart fluttered every time a car slowly passed my own front door across the road.

The knowledge of who's chair I was sitting in struck me afresh. 'Oh, Barry,' I said out loud, 'I'm sorry.'

I took a walk around the flat, guiltily shedding pastry as I went. In his bedroom I looked again at those few photos of his family in Spain. Barry's mobile phone was where I left it in the living room the other day. A nice solid Nokia. No evidence of a single person attempting to call him since the phone was last in his possession on Tuesday evening. I inexpertly navigated the menu. His most recent text messages dated to Christmas: brief festive wishes from a couple of grandchildren.

A day more, would it *really* matter?

An opportunity to spend an hour or two close to Junie, before getting everything in its rightful place.

Flicking through the local paper, I separated out the business flyers to take home and put with the others. To the back pages: births, marriages, and deaths. I read each one slowly as I always do. My wariness was foolish: of course I wasn't there—too soon, and who would think to place the notice? I made light work of the crossword; so many clues they'd used before.

Absently, I began sketching notes for a will. The time *would* come eventually, it seemed I could face that idea now. Denny should have something, I fancied, but not *everything* as Junie suggested he would in the absence of instructions. Half the house maybe, and the other half to charity? That sounded decent. But who else? I wrote the name *Steven*. What for my nephew? We'd not seen each other in decades. The MG perhaps? Did he drive? Would he take care of it?

Yesterday had taught me something: It wasn't just the avoidance of contemplating death that had kept me from making a will. It was the matter of all the stuff around me, all that I've *accrued*. What plan does one make for the reappropriation of such? Oddly, watching Junie, and even Denny, pick through it made both the house, and me, a little lighter. I gazed out across the street at the place, my home for over seventy years. Bizarrely, I found myself fantasising about it being broken into and stripped of everything by some undiscerning burglar. A fire even. No option but to start afresh. Something about the thought *appealed*.

With Little Boy Blue's toileting cleaned away and his food replenished I was performing my final checks about the flat when I heard it. An alien bleating sound.

I crept back into the living room. Glowing green and doing its vibrating dance on Barry's coffee table. Moving slow, as if his phone might attack, I peered at the screen. *Unknown Number.*

Frozen with my hand inches from it. Would answering it condemn me? Would failing to answer it cause more questions?

Someone wished to speak to Barry. The decision had been taken out of my hands. It was, unavoidably, time to do the right thing.

With a shaking finger, I answered.

It was Lauren. Arranging a time for an engineer to look at the power outage.

I hung up.

14

I WAS GIVING UP ON THEM EVER SHOWING WHEN I HEARD MY FRONT DOOR go. I slipped into my bedroom office. The day had disappeared in a melee of guilty dithering. Eventually doing a deal with myself that I'd sort matters once and for all tomorrow, I'd made arrangements for lying low about the house. The ludicrous risk of the understairs cupboard had haunted me since yesterday—how easily they could have stumbled upon me! Far better this former fitted wardrobe in which my small desk and personal computer reside, offering a stool and a (somewhat blinkered) view out through the louvred slats of the door when up close. To the interior face of each of the two doors were a pair of coat hooks. I had established that the placing of a wooden coat hanger across these hooks served to secure the doors from the inside. I drew a blanket over my knees.

An hour or more passed after Junie's arrival, hearing only muffled voices from downstairs. She was not alone. There was the friendly peep-peep of the old MG's horn, followed by the sound of the engine being briefly run. Pleasant petrol fumes wafted up in time. Twilight closed in before a soul set foot upstairs.

I'm not sure I'd have recognised Steven were I to have passed him in the street. He remained an adolescent in my mind, yet here was my nephew, in his late forties. He had been one of those children who are forever regarded as being at imminent risk of *going off the rails*, a promise he delivered on at least once. He and I had been close for a time during his teenage years; he'd even worked with me for a few fine weeks. But we drifted I'm saddened to say, for which I myself am partly to blame.

Holding my breath, I studied him as best I could through the narrow slats. He flicked on the light and navigated the narrow path around my bed. There was a certain jogging motion to his arms even when standing still, as if he was so brimful of energy he might start jumping on the spot any moment. Taller and wirier than in my memory, intricate tattoos wove down his forearms onto the backs of his hands.

'In a little minute, Mummy dear,' he said in reply to Junie calling him down for a cup of tea.

He picked up the manila folder I'd left on top of everything else on my bedside table. The inscription of PRIVATE CORRESPONDENCE in block capitals upon it obviously proved too inviting. It was a file that lived eternally close to my bed and was regularly browsed by me, although it was at the top of the pile now only because I'd shuffled it there a couple of hours earlier. Why did I wish it to be in plain view? I felt dreadfully silly now, seeing it in Steven's hands. Be it discretion on his part, or embarrassment, he glanced only at the topmost leaf, before replacing the file where he'd found it.

He was more interested in my flat caps, picking one from its hanging spot on a wall light. He put it on. Making faces at himself in the mirror, he tried it at various angles, eventually settling on a position with the peak diagonally rearward.

Out on the landing, he lowered the ladder from the loft hatch. 'Oh my word!' he said, poking his head into the attic. He gave a long whistle and began to laugh.

'I dread to think,' Junie said, arriving upstairs.

I recoiled into the cupboard. My foolishness assaulted me. What on God's earth was I playing at?

'If you think it's bad down here,' Steven said. 'You ain't seen nothing yet.'

'What are we talking?' Junie asked.

'Don't you worry about it. More crap, that's all. Literally to the rafters.'

Tea in hands, they both wandered into my bedroom. Backed away from the wardrobe door, I was viewing them in narrow stripes as if watching the world through a partly closed Venetian blind. Steven lay on my bed, resting his trainered feet on the bedstead. Junie slapped his legs and he duly returned them to the floor.

'Take that off,' she said, laughter in her voice. She pulled at the flat cap but Steven pinned it to his head and she soon let go. 'I can't take you anywhere.'

'Bloody loving those Doc Martens,' Steven said.

I caught sight of one glossy pink boot being raised.

'I don't go treating myself often,' Junie said.

'Damn right. Enjoy them.'

'I felt a bit silly, this morning, buying them. I wondered if the girl at the checkout was going to laugh at me—this dappy seventy-nine-year-old tart buying a youngster's shoes. I don't know, they just seemed to be *speaking* to me.' She giggled.

'Telling you to live in the moment?'

'Something like that. Though right now, they're telling me I should've packed some blister plasters.'

'Yeah, DMs are a bastard for that. Trick is to smash the backs in with a hammer before you wear them. Reckon Ray's got a hammer or twenty stashed somewhere?'

'I'll be doing no such thing to them,' Junie said.

'Pack them with newspaper then. That'll save your ankles. Now, have you seen any newspapers anywhere round here?'

Junie slapped the back of his hand. 'Stop it!' she said, sniggering.

'I expect Dad will have something to say about them.'

'Oh, I've given up worrying about what he thinks.'

I'd done no more than glance fleetingly at her face yesterday.

To stare had felt invasive. But I allowed myself now, her position low on the bed aligning with my shuttered view. It may seem a nonsensical claim, but not only was she still recognisably that girl from a lifetime ago; to my biased eyes, she was almost entirely unchanged. Perhaps there was a wrinkle here or there, I forget now. Her eyes were as electric as ever they'd been, her smile as infectious. She's never to my knowledge had long hair, and it now sat in a blond bob. *Chic*—I fancy that's the word.

'There's months of work here, Mum,' Steven said.

'And the rest.'

'It's not your problem, you know that?'

'Yeah, I know.'

'Take a keepsake or two if you must, and then leave it,' Steven said.

'There's nothing you want?'

'Maybe, I'll see. Look, I really like Uncle Ray. Really *liked* Uncle Ray. He was one of the good guys. It's been a while, I know, but he was very bloody good to me, back in the day. I kept meaning to get back in touch with him, you know that? But sorting all this out? There'll be some cash in his estate. You can throw money at the problem to make it go away. I know a couple of people who'd take the job.'

'Dad found six hundred quid in a Yellow Pages yesterday,' Junie said. 'And another eighty in the airing cupboard.'

Steven had a good laugh at this. 'I'll find you someone honest, Mum. Any cash and they'll be handing it straight over.' He mimed punching his own palm.

As far as I'd seen or heard yesterday, Denny had kept quiet about finding that money. Presumably he'd had an attack of conscience afterwards. In any case, he'd only found two of the seven hiding places I used. Or were there eight? Nine, now I thought about it. A job tomorrow for me.

'I want to do something to . . . help,' Junie said.

'Help who?'

'Does it sound strange to say that I like being here?' Junie asked after a long moment. 'I feel like I *should* be here.'

'Guilt's a useless emotion,' Steven said with a smile. 'Never trust it.'

'I want to do something for him. Treat his stuff with a bit of respect. It feels—I don't know—*right*.'

'I get it. It's like being close to him.' He spoke whilst looking at his mobile phone in his lap. He huffed and typed out messages at lightning speed.

'You've seen his mother's room?' Junie asked.

Steven sniggered without looking up. 'Afraid so. Still smells of old dear, doesn't it?'

'That woman,' Junie said. 'That . . . fucking *witch*.'

'Now, now, Mummy dearest. Is that any way to talk about my grandmother?'

'I'll speak about her any way I damn well please. I've earned *that* right.'

'I'm kidding about. What was I—six, seven when she died?'

'1985. Be grateful for small mercies. No chance to get her nasty little claws into her only grandchild. Mind, she'd have to have trampled over my dead body first.'

'Christ, since '85!' Steven said. 'That's how long that room's been perfectly preserved.' He emitted a whistle. 'A bit . . . creepy, would we say?'

'Nothing surprises me with that woman.'

'I'm not sure we can pin this one on her. You know, what with her being . . .'

'Oh, she knew how to manipulate.'

'From beyond the grave?'

Junie ignored his point. 'What that woman did to poor old Ray.'

'But not to Dad, though,' Steven said. 'Riddle me that.'

'Denny and Ray are very, very different people. *Were.* Christ, past tense. Bloody hell.'

Steven cast his phone away onto my duvet. 'Come here, Mum.' He hooked a long arm over her shoulder and squeezed her.

'The irony's not lost on me,' she said. 'That I married the only man in the world who shared the same mother. But Lil was totally different with each of them. Denny was a wild one. Ray was kind and dutiful. He was her puppet on a string. Someone to fill the hole left when her husband buggered off back when the boys were tiny.'

I felt dreadfully bad for Mum, listening to this. But nothing Junie said offended me as such. She hadn't known my mother well enough; that was the thing. Mum had her moments, sure. Can't we all be demanding every now and then?

'You would tell me, wouldn't you?' Junie said. 'If I ever interfered in your life. Ever forced my own wishes on you?'

'Well, now you mention it . . .'

'I'm serious, Steven. If I ever made you feel like you can't be your own person . . .'

'Do I look like a man without his own identity?' Steven asked, doffing my flat cap and resetting in an even sillier position.

'If ever I'm interfering, you tell me, yes?'

'Yeah, whatever.'

Steven tapped his foot against the box at the bottom of the stack next to my wardrobe. 'Want a new microwave?'

'Jesus Christ,' Junie said. She knelt and inspected it. 'Still sealed. Actually it looks like quite a good one. Better than mine, I think. Maybe I *do*.'

It was a decent one. An irresistible bargain in the Curry's sale some years ago.

'There's unopened new stuff everywhere,' Junie said.

'Another microwave in the back room,' Steven said.

'You're kidding me.'

'Nope. Looks eighties. Early nineties tops. All taped up, still.'

In my defence, I had forgotten about the presence of that when I purchased the one presently in my bedroom. And the microwave in the kitchen is still going strong so I've had no call to press either into service.

'I'll pop it in the car,' Steven said, shimmying it free from the stack above it.

'Can I really just *take* it? It feels wrong.'

'He'd be glad someone's making use of it.'

Steven was dead right on that.

'What's it all about?' Junie asked, cuddling her mug of tea up to her chin in both hands.

He laughed. 'This, Mummy dear, is how men behave when they don't have women keeping them sane.'

'I think this may be an extreme case. Bloody hell, what makes someone . . . behave like this? Surround themselves with . . .'

'A load of old shit?'

'Quite.'

'Some people just can't throw anything away.'

'It's more than that,' Junie mumbled.

Was it really so bad? Were Junie and Denny and Steven's reactions warranted? I must confess, I was beginning to see this collection that I'd amassed as something a bit, well, eccentric.

How had it begun? When Mum was alive, the house was kept well. She had no tolerance for clutter. Whatever I chose to hang on to was squirrelled within my own domain: the garage, the potting shed, my bedroom. A little discipline was lost with her departure, I suppose. It was after retirement, though, that was when things really took off, if I'm being honest. A tumour-ing of the massed contents of my home.

I had *time*, that was the thing. Charity shops were such a haven: so many things to which one can bring new life! And the litter picking. You wouldn't believe what people simply *drop*. Newspapers, Tupperware, once even a skateboard! And skips too. Consider this: on the average build, one fifth of the materials ordered are wasted. Timber, screws and nails by the kilo, good straight pipe. Why not make use of such so-called waste? It was all just simply *there*.

But—there were things I began doing, post-retirement, that I knew were a bit odd, even at the time. I experienced a kind of difficulty in simply putting a bag of rubbish out. It became necessary to empty the bag on the kitchen floor, to ensure there was nothing within that could be salvaged. Such has also been a long-standing habit with the Hoover bag: when full, it is dissected. And still, checks made, the rubbish became painful to part with. On occasion, I've written *sorry*, or *goodbye*, on a used piece of kitchen paper or a soiled container, before discarding them.

'The only constant in life is change.' Charles Sethi told me that. I'm sure he was right. But it's not always easy to *welcome* change, is it? Things over which we have no control. People, jobs, our rank, our *standing*. But the objects that surround us, those are something we *do* have control over. Those things *can* be constant. We get to choose if they've served their last purpose, get to choose when is the last time we ever see them. Even a dirtied tissue, when discarded, is condemned for eternity.

'I'm gonna make a start on those newspapers in the hallway,' Steven said, draining his mug. 'Get them out for recycling. It's a start, innit?'

'A fine idea.'

'What's Dad had to say about all this? I mean, I can imagine . . .'

'Wouldn't you expect him to be at least a little . . . *upset* at the loss of his brother?'

'They say people grieve in funny ways,' Steven said.

'Does he feel anything, do you think?'

'Ask him.'

'Oh, we've pretty much given up talking,' Junie said. 'That's hardly anything new. Sorry, I'm not going to burden you with all that crap.'

'Don't worry yourself. The half-the-house-each arrangement you've got going is a bit of a giveaway.'

'How bloody pathetic!'

'He's not the easiest of blokes, my old man.'

'He was bloody intolerable last night. Constant digs about Ray, about *me* and Ray.'

'He's not let that one go yet? Christ!'

'I damn near called you to cancel today,' Junie said. 'Didn't seem worth all the earache.'

'Insecure over his dead brother. Daddy, Daddy dear! What *are* we gonna do with him?' Steven's phone trilled once again and he snatched it up from the bed, muttering expletives to himself.

'You're jolly popular,' Junie said.

'Yeah, I'm gonna have to make a couple of calls.'

'Don't let me get in the way of your . . . *dealings*.'

'You make me sound like a two-bit spiv, Mummy.'

'Perish the thought. Are you sure we're all right for time?'

I'd paid it no attention earlier, but I spotted now the gold bracelet watch on Steven's wrist, with what were perhaps gemstones circling the dial. It looked to be of enormous value.

'I said I'd come with you, and I'm not going to rush you out the door again. I can spare an hour or two more, no sweat.'

He shimmied around the bed and grabbed the file he'd peeked inside earlier. My rather too-obvious plant. 'Might be of interest,' he said, passing it to Junie.

I felt nauseated. Glancing upwards at the coat hanger holding the door, I panicked that maybe I'd misjudged its security.

'What have we here?' Junie said.

'I've not read them. Don't worry.'

She opened the file. 'Gosh. Wow!' She put it to one side. 'Very long time ago, Steven.'

'It's not my business, Mum.'

'People did write a lot of letters back then. It's no indicator of . . .'

Steven raised a palm. 'Mum, it's fine. I know there's a bit of . . . history. Ray kept your letters because—'

'Because he kept everything?'

'Well, there is *that*.'

'There are years' worth,' Junie said, flicking absently through them.

'Honestly, I've not looked.'

'What's to see?'

Steven gave her a suspicious smirk. 'It's all right. Enjoy a trip down memory lane.' He sidled out onto the landing and descended the stairs.

She began to read them, as I have a million times. Blood rushed to my face and I turned away. Would she laugh at them, at how foolish we'd once been? Cast them out for recycling with the newspapers?

I eventually allowed myself to watch her. She wore a look of solemn concentration as she studied her own words. From those earliest missives from Sussex, through her time in Macclesfield and Chicago. Until it inevitably all began falling to pieces, as perfect things often do.

That's the trouble with people and things—they *change*. They are not like the items and possessions we surround ourselves with. They cannot be held close and safe, kept constant.

15

FEW THINGS IN LIFE REQUIRE QUITE SO MUCH THOUGHT AND PLANNING AS the act of *being spontaneous*. Well, I was hardly just popping over the street to make a surprise visit on Junie. I had to cross the Atlantic!

I expected I'd be nervous, and I suppose I was during those small hours mooching about Heathrow Airport, but it was more a sense of not belonging, of feeling perfectly unreal, that was the order of the day once aboard that Boeing 707, a little like beginning a strange book and feeling oneself being immersed in the otherworldly. I gripped my armrests and let take-off exhilarate me. Even the hour of lolloping turbulence was thrilling despite the air hostess's many wobbly-heeled apologies; I only took the precaution of placing the paper bag on my knee due to the relentlessness of ten straight hours of cigarette smoke.

The guilt had gone nowhere, even by the time we were beginning our descent. Mum believed me to be in Normandy. In my defence, she herself had embarked upon a romance with a gentleman who worked at the lido, which was keeping her busy. He was younger than her, which she mentioned often. I fancied that his presence on the scene might mean she'd feel my absence less keenly. I'd told her I was away with the school for four days. I felt sick doing so. However, it offered perfect cover for the trip up to town to obtain a passport, and for the 4:00 a.m. start.

Silly, really. There was so little Mum and I couldn't talk about, yet I'd kept Junie a secret too long to come clean now. My paranoia had consumed me in the days leading up to my departure; every time she remarked upon how impressed she was that they'd asked me as caretaker along to a field trip, I panicked that she knew the truth (as it would be quite some years before I'd genuinely be accompanying the boys on such jaunts). She'd also taken to cooing and shaking her head here and there, muttering the word *France* in an impressed fashion.

My living dangerously was, in part, the fault of Charles Sethi. When he took to the lectern at his inaugural assembly, he gave the most rousing speech about daring to be great, about the fleetingness of our time on this planet. 'It is easy to forget,' he told us all, 'that life is supposed to be an adventure.' We were all inspired for days! Never mind that my return ticket had cost me the entirety of my savings, a sum that amounted to nine months' earnings. I couldn't conceive of a better way of spending it. Three whole days in Junie's city.

Chicago O'Hare sweltered in the August heat. A sign on the terminal building declared it 'The World's Busiest Airport' and they weren't kidding. I queued for three hours to have my passport checked in a clamour of bumped shoulders and mumbled apologies with the perfume of kerosene in the air. The acres of glass focussed the sun upon us. My suit was soaked through in no time. It was the only one I owned: navy blue and wool and not ideal.

I rode the bus through the early afternoon as far as the Loop. I swear I could see the steam rising off the river. Mosquitos nipped at my neck. The air smelt so different to anything I knew. I wasn't quite sure if I was loving or hating being here. Even my underpants were soaked by now. I bought a Coca-Cola in a small store and drank it with my suit jacket slung over my shoulder and my case between my legs; when I caught my reflection in the grubby window glass I found it jolly pleasing, I was a real *traveller* now. I scanned the hordes of people and wondered if I might happen upon Junie, though this was something I had a habit of doing even at home, ridiculously.

From my case I pulled the map that the library back home had ordered in for me. I'd been writing to her for nearly three years and knew her address by heart. Kenwood was a few miles south, it appeared. I set off and the vertigo-inducing skyscrapers and important men in suits and hats soon gave way to a street market where vast cars burbled past, inches from the kerb and my own backside.

'You want leather sandals, yes sir?' called a man. I looked him briefly in the eye and smiled. He blocked my path. 'Perfect for the beach,' he told me, offering up a pair close to my nose.

'Yes, indeed. Aren't they beautifully made.'

'You're a man with style,' he told me, arm around my shoulder.

'It's very kind of you to—'

'Try them on. Come on.'

'Look, I'm a little short on—'

'These ones?' he said, offering a pair in darker tan. 'Five bucks. Come on now, sir.'

'They're quite remarkable, I'll give you that.'

'Four. Best I can do.'

I was waylaid for some time. Having declined every sandal, we moved onto purses. I eventually parted with one dollar fifty for a trinket pot, and expense I could hardly bear with just thirty-six dollars to see me through my trip. I thanked the gentleman profusely and went on my way.

'Afternoon, good sir,' called another voice. I smiled and returned the greeting. Another arm was soon at my hip, this time a fine display of rainbow trout for my perusal. It took five minutes or more to leave both politely and empty-handed. Stalls stretched as far as I could see. I found a taxi.

'You're new to Chicago,' the driver said as we roared through back streets, 'and this is the first place you want to go?' He shook his head, checking again the address I'd scrawled for him. We were heading south and the lake was visible here and there between dishevelled buildings. A hot wind blew through the open windows.

'My friend lives there. Junie Burnham. Are you a fan of the blues?'

'Sure.'

'Ah, well you may have heard of her.'

'She one of Len Chess's?'

'One day. Any day now, in fact.' Leonard Chess ran the record company that had launched the career of all Chicago's fine bluesmen. 'She plays all over. You're likely to have seen her. Not someone easy to forget, I can tell you.'

'Uh-huh?' He eyed me suspiciously in the mirror.

I wracked my brain for the names of the clubs she played at which she'd told me about in her letters. 'Now, let me see. There's the Green Room. The Kaipa Lounge. The Kasbah.'

His expression shifted. Amusement, *pity* even? 'I'd have remembered if I'd seen her at the *Kasbah*.' He didn't elaborate and I was soon outside my destination being lightened by another dollar (including a tip, of course).

My heart raced. The house was three stories high and weatherboarded in what may once have been white-painted timber. A Pontiac Coupe slumped at the kerb, rusted and windowless and punctured. An equally tired old man occupied the back seat. Barely a block away rose scores of tall buildings, not metal and glass like those back at the Loop but concrete instead. The sound of children playing floated down on the breeze and it was as happy and familiar a sound as ever it was, grounding in this new and strange place.

'Pal, keep your tits on,' said a long-haired man, after I'd knocked several times. He was English and already his accent sounded out of place, as they do in Hollywood movies. He looked exhausted. The house was dark behind him and it oozed the smell of sleep and incense.

'Junie?' I said in a tone that struck even *me* as prim.

'Right.'

'I have the correct address, I believe.'

'And you'd be?'

'Raymond Thorns.' I looked for a flash of recognition that didn't come. He was joined at the door by a young lady. I found myself able to breathe again. 'Gosh, how many of you are there here?'

'A few,' he said exasperatedly. 'Junie's at work, pal.'

I checked my watch (set to central time since the very instant the landing gear left British soil). It struck me as early for a gig, but I was in the home of the blues—what did *I* know?

'The Roosevelt Hotel,' he told me.

'Ah. The Cabaret.'

'The chambermaids,' he replied. 'And that ain't the name of her band.'

'Yes. Very good.'

'You walking?'

'I fear so.'

'Follow the lake up. You'll find it eventually.'

'That's jolly helpful.' I raised my suitcase up by my side and mimed pinching a hat brim.

'And try not to talk to anyone. Or look at anyone.'

'Noted.'

'And if it gets dark, run like buggery.'

IT WAS HER LAUGH I HEARD FIRST. I STOOD AND WATCHED AWHILE, TO THE right of the hotel's façade. There was a group of four of them, chatting and smoking outside in their mint green uniforms as they sorted linen from a trolley into various trunks. Junie had her back to me. Legs and arms tanned. Blonder and more slender than before. Think about her all the time though I did, the sight still knocked the wind out of me.

'Are you lost, sir?' one of the ladies asked as I sheepishly approached.

'Fancy seeing you here,' I said as Junie turned. A line—preprepared of course—that would've been smoother were I not obviously shaking. My God, she was beautiful.

It took her a long moment to compute. 'Ray? *Ray?* What the f— What are you doing here?'

I shrugged. 'Surprise.' I mumbled, phrased it as a question.

She stepped towards me but stopped a few feet away. 'How did you *get* here?'

'I . . . flew. My arms are jolly tired.'

She rolled her eyes. 'Come here, you old fool.' We hugged, but much too briefly.

'How's about an introduction,' called one of her friends.

'This is Ray,' she told them.

'Your English gentleman?'

Junie grinned. 'The very same.'

I felt a hundred feet tall. She told me it was a half hour till she got off shift, but her friends insisted they'd cover for her and we were soon meandering alongside the lake. The sun had sunk into the land on our right and everything glowed reddish.

'I wish you'd said you were coming,' she said. An open space strolled between us.

'A bit spur-of-the-moment. And, you know, the post—it takes a while.'

'It's just a part-time thing, the hotel.'

'You mentioned about maybe getting a job.'

'I just help out here and there, that's all.'

'The musician's lifestyle. Working all hours of the night! I'm impressed you have the energy for a day job too. All credit to you.'

She cringed briefly at this. The gap widened a touch.

'Are you playing tonight?' I asked. It took me a moment to orientate myself in time. 'Gosh. Friday night. Of course you're playing.'

'Maybe. You got here today, right?'

'Six a.m. out of Heathrow.'

She reached for my hand. 'You need some rest. You must be jet-lagged halfway to hell. Get your head down tonight, Ray.' She jiggled my arm by way of insistence. There was little tenderness in her handhold.

'Yes I suppose, but . . . well . . .'

'Where are you staying? Here I am dragging you off to the arsehole end of nowhere.'

'Oh, it's not so bad. Your housemate was . . . friendly enough.'

She slowed and released my hand. 'You've been to my . . . place?'

My cheeks flushed, and not due to the heat. 'It's the address I have for you.'

She shook her head and lit a cigarette from her bag, looking over the water in silence for a moment. I rested my hand on her back.

'Sorry, Ray. Shit, sorry,' she said. 'It is really good to see you.'

'And you!' I scoffed. 'Bloody hell . . .'

'I can't believe you went to the house.' She said this more to herself than me.

We walked by a couple of gentlemen who looked down on their luck. 'Good evening, fine people,' one said.

'And a very good evening to you.' I doffed an imaginary hat.

He was at once in our path. 'What could you spare?'

'Ah, now . . .' I dug around in my pocket.

'We're unable to help,' Junie said firmly, weaving around them both tugging me away.

'Gosh, sorry,' I mumbled back as we sped away.

'Stop being so bloody polite, Ray,' she said.

'Oh, yes, sorry.'

'And stop apologising.'

'I'm sor . . . Yes, noted.'

'Tell me about back home,' she said, slowing.

'Let me think. Denny—my brother, you'll meet him one of these days, you'll like him—he's moved out. I mean, he's hardly spent a night at home in three years, what with him keeping half the beds in South London warm. But he's left *officially*. He gave me some of his shirts though—swings and roundabouts. In fact, this is one of his, as it happens.'

Junie accepted my invitation to examine the striped fabric. 'Looks expensive,' she agreed.

'And Mr Sethi—my new boss—has given me a raise. Perhaps that was in my last letter.'

Junie shrugged. 'It's nice to listen to you anyway. What else is new?'

'Mum has a . . . a *man*.'

She smirked. 'In addition to you?'

'Yes, in a manner of speaking. His name's Douglas. He's a lifeguard at the lido.'

'And they're . . .' Junie smirked, '*stepping out* together?'

'I fear they may be doing rather more than that.'

'Oh God!' Have you been hearing things through the wall?'

'If only it were just that.'

Junie grinned properly for the first time. A dazzling sight which alone made the trip worthwhile. 'Do tell, darling.'

'Just Mum, you know.' The guilt returned with all its weight. 'She doesn't have people to talk to about . . . things. No real *friends*, that's the trouble. I'm pleased, I suppose, that she turns to me. Not that I'm exactly an expert, am I? On affairs of the heart. Not to mention . . . other matters.'

Junie looked wildly intrigued.

'Well, he's somewhat younger than her,' I explained. 'And in excellent fettle. It all leaves her a little *doubting* of herself.'

'How on earth are you helping with that?'

'I'm afraid I'm no use. Rather too quick to change the subject.' Really, I was betraying Mum in what I mentioned next. '*His way*,' I mumbled.

'Sorry, what?'

'Mum tells me he keeps asking if they can . . . do it *his way*.'

'Fucking hell, Ray! What are you supposed to say to that?'

'I was initially not sure I understood what was being got at.'

'Nor wanted to, I imagine.' Even Junie looked a little flustered.

'Quite. The subject has arisen more than once, though. Over morning coffee at weekends, bizarrely. Should she . . . permit things *his way*? she asks. Is that a normal thing to do? Is it something *I* do, she's curious to know.'

Junie glared wide-eyed at me.

'Oh, she's just got no one else she trusts enough,' I said.

'You *do* know what she's talking about, Ray?'

I grimaced. 'I fear I may.'

Junie shook her head and began to laugh. I sniggered along for a moment before the guilt struck me anew.

It was not long after that Frank Sinatra would record his best-known hit, and I would for years find myself cringing whenever I heard him sing *I did it my way*.

'So, tonight's big gig,' I said. 'Where are we off to?'

'I'm not sure if I'm . . . I *might*, I guess.' She drifted away from me once again.

'There'll be people expecting to see you, I'm sure. Not least *me*!'

'Maybe tonight's not the best time. It's not the greatest

line-up. Sorry, I'm not trying to put you off. Just not really your scene, maybe.'

'If you're playing, it's my scene all right.'

She looked frustratedly at me. 'Where are you staying? I could come over later maybe. Or tomorrow?'

'Yes, well, I must make some arrangements, I suppose.'

'You've not booked anything?'

I shrugged and held my small suitcase aloft. 'I thought I'd get by on my wits.' This sounded highly improbable coming from me. I was feeling crestfallen and therefore acting overly jolly. I was not about to admit that I'd imagined I would stay at Junie's. Her letters had talked of the big house she'd been lucky enough to find, where a handful of British musicians and other such bohemians cohabited in harmony.

'It must have cost you a fortune, getting out here,' Junie said.

'No real bother,' I replied casually.

She looked perplexed. 'A *bloody* fortune,' she said, the full extent of the expense occurring to her. 'I mean, I could only afford to get out here thanks to dear old granny popping her clogs. I'd be dashing home to see you all the time if the cost wasn't so absurd. How the hell *did* you afford it?'

'A little that I've saved here and there. I'm a working man, after all. And I hardly live lavishly!'

She looked at me, stunned, for a long moment. Behind her, the lake was fading to indigo. Her face, washed with the last of the sun, softened. Tears came fast to her eyes. 'I *am* happy you're here,' she said. 'I really am. It's just . . . I'm not a *liar*, okay?'

Taken aback, I assured her the thought had never entered my mind.

'I can't bear to be boring,' she said. 'To be . . . disappointing.'

'I'm not sure I follow.'

She took my hand and squeezed it. 'No one wants to hear

about running out of money, and jobs that pay peanuts, and gigging for free because—well, if I want to gig . . .'

'You imagine I'd think ill of you?' I was grinning with incredulity.

'When I write you, I want to be that girl that's living her dream. Always with a story to tell. I want to be the person you *think* I am. The person I *am* when you're about, let's be honest. Just not when I'm on my lonesome a long way from home, it seems.'

'There's nobody I've ever known who's bold enough to do this!' I told her.

'It's been three years. And what have I done, really?'

'This *is* success. Just being here makes you a success.' I meant it, of course. And anyway, I'd detected from her letters that life here wasn't always rosy, but I tended not to dwell on such in my replies. That was the trouble with us: we'd seen each other's best sides since the beginning and these were the identities we'd stuck with—her bold and daring, me relentlessly upbeat.

'I don't care if you're hanging in rags and sleeping in a bin,' I said. 'This is really living.'

'Ray, stop it.' She hugged me, properly this time, her cheek soaked against mine. 'Thank you,' she whispered. 'This is the best surprise ever.'

We kissed, at first a little clunkily, but we remembered our way soon enough. How our bodies fit together just perfectly, how our senses closed off to everything that wasn't each other. For a while I simply held her in my arms as we gazed out over Lake Michigan, calm and infinite. I had a curious sense of being completely untroubled, having that impossibly rare sense of there being no other place nor time in the world that mattered.

'So I guess you're watching me blow some harp tonight,' she said after a time.

It was a night of firsts for me. My first trip to an after-hours club, the first time I'd seen bands playing live, the first time I'd set eyes on a firearm. The latter was no pistol either, but a full-size shotgun leaned against the wall in the club owner's booth which we shuffled past on our way in. The place was called The Tone. It was nothing like the striped-awninged bars I'd seen downtown earlier. Next door was a tyre shop and the façade of this building was almost indistinguishable from its neighbour, including the boarded upstairs windows and soot-stained bricks. The only hint to the establishment's nature was a ten-foot-high mural of Muddy Waters.

Everyone there knew Junie.

The bartender was a giant by the name of Claude. 'Take good care of my man,' Junie called to him over the racket. She planted a kiss on my lips and patted a stool for me to sit on before whisking into the crowd with her little case of harmonicas in hand.

A beer appeared in front of me uninvited. 'Any friend of June's,' he said, looking terribly serious, before returning to his business.

I'd been feeling a little overdressed ever since leaving the airport, but no longer. I was sorry I'd left my tie at Junie's with my suitcase when we'd stopped off before heading here (she'd permitted me no further than the dark hallway, so ashamed was she of the place). Boy, did the people here know how to dress! Sharp-fitting suits and trilbies, tiepins and collar bars, dresses in vibrant fabrics pinched tight at the waist.

'You gotta tell me your secret, man,' Claude said as he passed me by.

A band was taking to the shallow stage across the room. The crowd and thick smoke obscured my view. It had a distinctive smell, which I would later learn was marijuana; to this day the scent of the best of times.

'She ain't interested in any other man, whole time I've known her.'

'Ah, yes, I'm not sure there's a . . .' He was walking away as I spoke. Our *conversation* would continue in this way for most of the night: him breezing past and musing (never unkindly) about how rich I must be, or what might be residing in my underpants et cetera, then going about himself before I answered. I liked him. After the beer, he poured us both a generous bourbon.

The blues, played live, reached my very soul. It was enough to make a buttoned-down Englishman punch the air and shout *yeah!* Gruff men sang words that I couldn't always discern, yet their angst and longing was like a language I understood completely. Electric guitars screamed, in pain and with euphoria. I cried, at how beautiful and divine sadness could be.

And then there was the way that harp was played. A pocket-sized horn section all by itself.

'What an incredible talent!' I said to her after the band had finished. 'I knew you could play, but *that*, that was . . .' I waved my hard around looking for the words.

'You're bloody cooked!' she said grinning. 'I never thought I'd see the day.'

It was something close to 3:00 a.m. and I'd had more than my share of spirits. And then there was the heat, the haze of drugs, the fact I'd been awake for thirty hours. 'I'm proud to know you,' I said, my lips feeling a touch rubbery. There was a relentless screeching in my ears.

'It was a. . . nice gig,' she said, as if this was a surprise to her. She sat down close to me and rested her hand on my thigh.

'You were on fire!' Claude said, serving her a beer. The crowd was fast slipping away into the night.

'I enjoyed it,' Junie said looking half-surprised at the fact. 'That's what it's all about, I guess. They asked me if I'd play the After Midnight with them.'

The bartender whistled. 'The After Midnight! You just remember your old friend Claude when you make it big.'

'It's where the scene's at,' Junie told me. 'Kind of a feather in the cap to be asked.'

'This isn't your regular band?' I asked.

'There's not really regular bands. We all just drift in and out with each other.'

'They aren't the gentlemen playing on that fantastic record of yours?' It had been nearly two years since my treasured copy had arrived back home.

Junie shuddered faintly and took a deep swig of beer. 'The guy on bass, he played on it I think.'

'And how's it selling?'

'Oh, Ray, don't bring things down.'

'Come on! How many people have cut their own EP?'

'Every person in this goddam town who's silly enough to waste their cash.' She put a ciggie to her lips and Claude lent over the bar, flicking open a golden lighter.

'It's a masterpiece,' I said glumly.

She ran her fingers through my hair. 'You want to sell records, you got to be played on the radio.'

'Kim Mack's R&B on Midwestern,' Claude interjected. 'He's the man who makes the kings.'

'And what's old Kim's problem with you?' I asked, in strident tone.

Junie smirked. 'There's a lot of records, Ray. I guess he hasn't found mine in the pile. Or he took one listen and tossed it out with the trash.'

'And you've asked him to play it?'

She chuckled at my naivety. 'You send a copy and you hope. People don't *ask*.'

'Why on earth's that? Do people not know where to find him?'

'On South Archer. It's just not what you do. You'd be—I don't know—*laughed at*. Probably.'

'Is that all?' I said, hardly a stranger to such a fate, forgetting that being laughed at is the greatest fear of the *cool*. 'Maybe we should pop over and—'

'No,' she said. 'I couldn't possibly. Just . . . no.'

'KIM MACK,' JUNIE SAID TO THE GLAMOROUS LADY AT THE RECEPTION. THE walls were coated with gold discs and nicotine.

'He expecting you, honey?'

'He said to swing by sometime,' she said without missing a beat. 'I mean, if he's not free or—' I cleared my throat noisily behind her. 'I need two minutes of his time.'

It was another blazing morning. I was hungover halfway to hell after the club. I'd shared Junie's single bed in a room of four others, where I'd fallen unconscious the moment the weight was off my feet. A sweat broke on my back and I reversed onto a chair in the waiting area.

On our way back last night, I'd been passing off Sethi's wisdom as my own. 'It's easy to forget that life is supposed to be an adventure,' I said to her. 'Every so often one must stand back, look at what they've done, and remember to be proud.' This, particularly, seemed to cut the mustard. She was raring to go this morning.

'I'm feeling *cocky*,' she said, as we marched the three miles to the home of Midwestern Radio.

A man in a maroon suit three sizes too big emerged from the studio door. 'I got five minutes for you, young lady.' He talked through teeth that clenched a cigar. Someone crueller than I might describe his as a *good* face for radio, but there was a kindly sparkle in his eyes. Junie looked starstruck. It was a voice known the length of the electric blues world.

As nervous as I could remember being, I waited, listening to the thrum of two songs of hers which I knew so well playing beyond the closed door.

'All sorted out,' Junie said, emerging moments later looking a little bewildered. She thanked the receptionist and we left.

And that was that. They'd play it. It seemed she only needed to ask, not that she could quite believe it.

'Thank you,' she said, as I hurried to keep up with her frenetic walking pace.

'I've done nothing,' I replied.

She mulled this point over awhile. 'That's love, isn't it?' she said. 'The person who brings you closer to yourself.'

The more I considered it, the harder I nodded.

We tuned in that evening, and sure enough, Kim Mack played one of hers: a flat tyre shuffle called 'Tell Me in the Morning'.

For my remaining two and a half days we lived like honeymooners. We took a boat trip, we swam in the lake at dusk. Junie got us some cut-price tickets to Riverview Park—the first (and only) amusement park I'd been to—where we rode rollercoasters and the log flume. We fed baby elephants at the children's zoo. We bought the last of the day's trout catch and cooked it in Junie's front yard using an abandoned shopping cart as a grill. She found out from her fellow chambermaids that a room at the Roosevelt Hotel had been taken as an *afternoon special*—a term in the trade for a room that was paid for in full but vacated by evening in order that the residents could return to their respective spouses. Junie remade the bed and we took it for ourselves. And made full use of it. At one point, she—with cheeky grin—asked if I'd like to try things *his way*. I politely declined, though grateful for the kind offer. At the break of dawn, we left via the fire escape.

When we parted at O'Hare I was down to my final few cents. Enough for one last Coca-Cola each. We both cried, her first but me for longest. Most of the way home, in fact.

It was the time when we were closest to each other. It was the time when we were the closest to ourselves.

16

COULD IT REALLY BE THAT FIFTY-SEVEN YEARS HAD PASSED SINCE I'D LAST been this near to Junie for such a length of time? Logic would say it should've felt like reliving a ghostly memory from a past life, but instead it seemed more a return to something familiar; as though our proximity *then* and *now* was separated not by a string of decades but by a gossamer-thin screen. A strange sensation indeed.

By the light of my bedside lamp, she'd studied each letter. Her mug was rested beneath her chin but never sipped. I've long considered that a sign of a decent read: cold tea. Behind the jammed doors of my computer cupboard, I listened to her breathing and the occasional turn of a page. Every now and then she'd looked up and cast her eyes about the room, letting them settle once or twice in my vague direction. Could she sense my presence? Humans do, don't they? They get a feeling of being watched. I'd hung my head each time her glance came my way.

'Made you a fresh one,' Steven said, returning to my bedroom, steaming cup in hand. 'It is now possible to swing a cat in the hallway, believe it or not. Well, a kitten at least.'

For an hour or more I'd heard the occasional phut of newspaper bales being dumped at the kerbside. So many articles I may have wished to reread at some point. I wondered if I might check the piles later on and salvage anything of interest. It didn't seem a pressing concern; certainly I felt no desperation at the thought of their disappearing forever, which surprised me.

'How's memory lane?' he asked.

Junie cast the folder aside. 'Oh, vaguely interesting I suppose.'

'Funny. Seems Uncle Ray found them *vaguely interesting* enough to keep them right to hand at his bedside.'

'Maybe he'd been having a bit of a sort out or . . . Don't raise your eyebrow at me like that!'

'A sort out?' Steven said. They both laughed.

'They're just silly letters between two people briefly . . . entwined.'

'I'll put them out with the papers, yeah?'

'Fine, yes.'

Steven straightened the contents of the file and put it on Junie's lap. 'Keep them, Mum.'

'Maybe I'll hang on to them for—'

'There's no need for Dad to know about anything.'

'Bollocks to Dad.'

'We're all allowed a bit of history, Mum. Speaking of which, I saw that record of yours downstairs.'

'Come on then, let's get it over with.'

'Get what over with?'

'I've already had your father's ten cents' worth on that one.'

'*I'm* not taking the piss.'

'We were all young and foolish once.'

'I thought it was cool, actually.'

'Give over.'

'You made a record! And you went to bloody Chicago to do it.'

Junie nodded. 'It was a tougher thing than people imagined.' She patted the file of letters.

'You know what I thought seeing that record? I'm thinking— why am I seeing this for the first time? There should've been a copy of this framed at home forever. You have *got* a copy?'

'Somewhere, sure. In the loft.'

'In the loft. Fuck's sake, Mum.'

'You promise you're not taking the piss? It really makes you proud of me?'

'Damn straight.'

'Well, that's nice of you to say.'

'I'll be showing it to my grandkids. And they'll be showing it to theirs.'

'You may need to have some *children* first.'

'All in good time, Mummy dear.' Steven, who appeared unable to keep still for any length of time, had begun poking around my bedroom again. Silently, I gripped the doors hiding me, augmenting the improvised coat hanger bolt between them. My heart rate accelerated once again. Thankfully, he was more interested in my wardrobe.

'It seems that clothes are the one thing he didn't own millions of,' Junie said. 'I had a nose in there yesterday.'

'Very . . . beige, aren't they?'

'He was never much fussed about things like that. I mean, he was always smart and everything, but . . .'

'What is that *old man* smell?'

'It's a nice smell,' Junie said. Was that a sad smile I detected in her voice? 'I read somewhere that you should get rid of all of someone's clothes as a matter of urgency.'

'Not sure they're the most pressing problem round here.'

'Before the funeral, they reckoned.'

That bloody word again!

'Helps with the grieving process, they said,' Junie went on.

'Any more of a clue on the funeral arrangements?' Steven asked.

'Dad's on the case. Or rather, when he decides it's more important than his bloody golf, he will be.'

I talked myself down from my panic. The matter would resolve before going *too* far: to arrange a funeral Denny would be needing a death certificate; to obtain such he'd need to formally identify the body. Things would be righting themselves imminently, even independently of me.

'I can really . . . *feel* him,' Junie said thoughtfully. 'Around here. Is that a weird thing to say?' Again, the sweep of eyes around the room.

'Of course you can,' Steven said. He was standing close to my louvred door, darkening my cupboard with his shadow.

'You too?'

For a long moment, it was as if he knew full well of my presence and was braced for a *big reveal*. About to tear the doors open.

'You're in the house of a man who died three days ago,' he eventually said. 'Of course you can feel him.'

'Sure, sure,' Junie said. She sat rapping her fingers against her letters. 'Would it be silly—to listen to my record?'

'Bloody hell, Mum, if I'd ever had the talent and the drive to record an album, I'd be listening to it every day of my life. Tell me, when did you *last* listen to it?'

'A while ago, I suppose. Twenty years . . .'

'Those'll be twenty old person's years, yes? So, sometime in the nineteen seventies then.'

'What's an old person's year?'

'Anything that you describe as happening more than five years ago usually predates the fall of the Berlin Wall.'

I smiled. What a lovely thing it was—the sound of voices and mirth in this house!

'Cheek! I guess it's a while since I last had a listen. Why would I, I mean—'

'Go downstairs and listen to your record, Mum.'

'We should be getting back and . . .'

'Mum. We'll make a move in a bit, but you have time for at least the A-side, okay?'

'I'm being a silly old tart.'

'Take your tea downstairs. Put it on quiet if my opinion terrifies you so much. I'll entertain myself up here.'

'Two tracks,' Junie said, on her feet. 'Then we'll make a move.'

'Live dangerously, have three!' Steven called after her.

It was not long till the familiar sound drifted through the house. First up, a groovy shuffle called 'Minding My Business' in which her voice sounded almost indistinguishable from Etta James's, and a harp solo that could've been played by one of the greats; it certainly stopped Steven in his tracks as he mooched about the bedroom.

My enjoyment was shattered by Steven trying the doors to my tiny office. The fingers of his right hand, calloused and cracked, poked through the gap between the louvres. I reversed silently against the desk and held my breath. He rattled the doors back and forth. The coat hanger wedged across the metal hooks on each door jiggled in its place but held firm. I was damp with sweat by the time he let them be.

The contents of my wardrobe instead drew his attention. He picked out a couple of jackets and cardigans. Surely he wasn't acting on Junie's suggestion? What was I to do if they disposed of my clothes? It would leave me with just the jersey and rather tired house trousers I had on now.

Smirking at his own reflection in the mirror attached to the wardrobe, he offered up each of my ties to his neck. Settling on the wool paisley (my favourite), he raised the collar on his polo shirt and tied it in a rather vulgar full Windsor. Judging by the increased pace of his eternal bodily fidgeting, he found this look agreeable.

He slipped on my sage green cardigan next. It rather suited him. The elbows had long since worn through and the cuffs were frilly but there was life in it yet. Steven posed with the neck slung rakishly down his back, before setting it correctly and looking at himself very seriously.

The ensemble was completed with my tweed sports coat. He emitted a sheepish laugh. I'd never considered myself dapper, but I was quite taken with how he looked. He walked repeatedly to the landing and back again. It seemed he was refining the walk. Shoulders hunched, head down, short but fast steps. An exaggeration perhaps, but I had to accept it was *my* walk.

Steven certainly enjoyed the performance as he approached the mirror once more. 'Steady on. Steady on,' he said, in a whispery voice, holding two palms up. He repeated it a number of times, experimenting with different intonations. He retrieved his oft-bleating phone and took some *selfies*.

I sensed there was no ill meant by his behaviour. Merely amusing himself, in the way people must when faced with human mortality. Is it egotistical to admit that I was touched to be remembered, to be worthy of caricature? Especially given that it had been twenty-five years or more since the pair of us had been close.

It was pleasing to see the man Steven had grown into. He'd not had the right start in life. In the distant past when I was in sporadic contact with Denny and Junie, when Steven was a young child, there'd been some minor misdemeanours: a football through a window at his school, the discharging of a fire extinguisher. Enough for an invitation to Denny from the headmaster. And that was that. At seven years of age, Steven's identity had been settled upon. He was, his father would report wherever possible, a delinquent.

If my time spent teaching taught me anything, it is that there are no inherently naughty children. There are children easily bored, children who work at a different pace to most, children with an irrepressible sense of fun.

Denny enjoyed remarking that his son would by adulthood be either a millionaire, in prison, or dead. I had done what I could for the young Steven, as any uncle surely would.

'Steady on. Steady on,' he said again, scurrying along the narrow track round my bed. He swapped the cap he was wearing for various others in my collection. He began checking in my bedside table. What was he looking for? A pair of my glasses perhaps? My watch? A skim of every drawer in my dressing table didn't turn up whatever he sought.

Without fair warning, his hands were on the doors to my office again. He pulled firmly on the left handle. The doors parted by an inch. The coat hanger held fast, straining against the hooks. It was a wonder it didn't snap in half. Steven's fingers slipped into the gap between the doors. He ran them up and down, feeling for the securing bolt. Twice he searched the woodwork but found no obstruction.

Mercifully, he let go. I hardly dared look, but on the other side of the louvres I saw him step back. Any hope that he'd busy himself elsewhere was short-lived. Another yank on the left door, all his strength. There was a great crack of tortured timber as the door opened nearly a foot at the bottom, but remained in the frame at the top. He let go and it slammed back into place.

There came a shout from the foot of the stairs: Junie enquiring what the hell was going on.

'Just having a fight with a locked door, Mummy dear,' Steven called back. 'Don't worry yourself.'

This time he grabbed the edge of the door and held it out well clear of the frame.

I knew I should pull the door closed from inside. Instead I reversed as far into my desk as I could. I glanced up at the coat hanger charged with keeping me safe. It was holding, but to my horror one of the hooks it was threaded through was pulling its screws out of the timberwork. A childhood reflex, I closed my eyes and covered my ears.

A second later, the coat hanger leapt free, ricocheting off the walls of my tiny office. The door flew open.

Through squinting eyes, I watched Steven stagger backwards and stumble against my bed.

'Sorry,' I whimpered. 'Please, Steven. I'm sorry.'

He swept my cap from his head. 'What?' he said, stunned. 'What are you . . .'

'I never meant this,' I said in a hurried whisper. 'Please. Don't be mad.'

He shook his head, eyes wild. 'What the . . .'

'Stead . . . calm down, Steven.'

'Jesus fucking Christ.' He was stuck halfway between standing and sitting. Huffing, he put a hand to his chest. 'You've gotta tell me what the hell is going on.'

'Yes. Yes, of course.'

It was the very least I could do.

17

ALLONBY HOUSE HAD BROKEN FOR SUMMER ONCE AGAIN. AFTER FOUR YEARS in Chicago, Junie was back. Amongst the massed hordes of holiday-makers, we slowly drove towards the West Country. Tucked safely in my breast pocket—tight to my heart—a little surprise for some-time over the next few days.

I had no longer felt compelled to keep anything from Mum; she knew Junie and I were serious. It had taken several sleepless nights and days of limited appetite, but I had built myself up to tell all. Why I'd been so fearful, I don't know. She was delighted for us! So delighted in fact, that she'd insisted on paying for this holiday. Mum had recently given up her job, but a legacy be-queathed to her by a little-known cousin meant she was flush for the first time in a very long while. And she was generous with it. Without the use of her former employer Fletcher's place in Sussex, she'd instead found a perfect cottage in Ilfracombe advertised in *The Lady*. Not trusting my old MG to make the journey, she'd even hired the Ford Cortina I was at the wheel of.

'How long is it since you've had a break away?' Mum asked as we ground along past Stonehenge.

I didn't dare make eye contact with Junie in the rearview mir-ror. One thing Mum still did not know about was my sojourn to the States a year earlier. 'Oh, some time,' I mumbled vaguely.

'Having a nice little doze, dear?' Mum asked, reaching be-hind and patting Junie's leg where she was lying across the rear bench. 'You're probably jet-lagged, my darling?'

'I'm just dandy,' she replied.

'You sound so *American*,' Mum said.

'Some words she does, some she doesn't so much,' I said.

Mum lit a cigarette and sat in the way she tended to in a car, half turned towards whoever was driving.

'Still comfortable?' I asked her.

She massaged her thigh. 'Oh, I'll live.' Her sciatica had been playing her up, which had meant riding up front was the only option.

'How's the search for work been going, June dear?' Mum asked.

'Give her a chance, Mum!' I said. 'She's only been back five days.' Since landing she'd been home with her folks up North. I'd picked her up from Euston just this morning; we'd had no more than half an hour alone together and I'd largely wasted that getting over my nervousness.

'When we're back from Devon I'll have an ask around,' Junie said. 'So many pubs and clubs in London putting on blues acts now. It's a crazy scene.'

'I heard on the grapevine of something going at the dry cleaners up the way from us,' Mum said. 'If you were planning on hanging about, down South?'

'I appreciate you keeping an eye out, Mrs Thorns.' Junie and I smiled at each other in the mirror.

'*Lil*,' Mum said. 'I don't know how many times I have to say.'

'Sorry . . . Lil,' Junie said. It sounded odd.

'They pay their girls all right, I'm told.'

'I'm not quite ready to hang up the old harmonica just yet,' Junie said.

'Of course you're not,' Mum said. 'And why the hell should you?'

Although we'd yet to discuss it in depth, Junie's return was in part due to a running out of money. Getting radio play for her record had brought with it kudos, but little hard cash.

'Strange as it might sound,' Junie said, 'the Chicago blues coming out of London town is getting more of a following than what's coming from Chicago itself. All over America, people are listening to blues played by London musicians. They're literally buying their own music back.'

'What a cockeyed arrangement!' Mum said. 'It doesn't make any sense.'

I did my best to explain: 'To a lot of America, their own bluesmen don't . . . look quite right.'

'Well what *do* they . . .' She stopped herself short. 'Oh, right. Gosh, how dreadfully depressing.'

Warm wind blasted through the car as I made an opportune overtake on a camper-van. Even at seventy this brand new sedan was steady as an express train.

Mum tapped my knee. 'Isn't he a fine driver?' she said to Junie.

'So, talking of Junie getting a job . . .' I said to Mum. I kept my eyes on the horizon.

'Oh yes?' She could, I'm sure, detect my nerves.

'If she was to find something in London, she'd need to have some sort of . . . digs down here.'

'I expect you would,' Mum said, turning around. 'I could have a word about. Would you like that, June?'

'Mum, haven't you been saying about a lodger?' I said.

'Oh, I don't *mean* all that. That's just me talking . . .'

'She'd have her own room, of course. No funny business. A proper, professional arrangement.'

'*That's* not a concern. But—'

'And we could use a bit of help making ends meet.'

'I'm quite capable of keeping home, thank you very much. Besides, your housekeeping money keeps our heads above water. No, I won't have it said that we can't stand on our own two.'

I tried to find Junie in the mirror, but she wouldn't meet my gaze. Much as I knew I'd have to pick my moment for this con-

REPORTS OF HIS DEATH HAVE BEEN GREATLY EXAGGERATED 143

versation, I had been quietly confident of success. Now I wish I'd kept my mouth shut.

'Have a mull on it, maybe,' I said, breaking the silence.

'It's not you, June love,' Mum said with unexpected jollity. 'Of course it's not *you*! I'd like nothing better—another lady in the house, stop me being ganged-up upon. But it's Denny's room, see?'

'He's moved out, Mum,' I said. 'What's it been now—fourteen months?'

Denny was living with a Portuguese dancer who was earning well in the West End. They'd rented a flat in Camden Town.

'Who knows when he'll be back, tail between legs,' Mum said. 'You know what he's like.'

'I don't think wild horses would drag him back to living with his mother and little brother,' I said.

'Nonsense,' Mum said, looking hurt. I thought better of mentioning that I was actually *quoting* Denny; I'd met him for a beer in town a few weeks ago in order that I could take him a couple of pairs of his cufflinks and a shaving mirror, saving him the trip south of the river.

'I couldn't just give his room away. He'd never forgive me.'

'It's okay,' Junie said. 'Honestly Mrs . . . *Lil*.'

'He's a bit of a boy, that one. Hard to keep up with who he's with one week to the next. Have you met him, June?'

'I've not had the pleasure. His reputation rather goes before him, though.' She and I smirked at each other in the mirror.

'He'd like *you*,' Mum said. 'My, would he!'

'Terrence and I,' she went on, 'that's Raymond and Denny's father. We never spent a single night under the same roof till we were good and married.'

'The times they are a-changin',' said Junie, in her best Bob Dylan.

'As well they may be, but what was good for us is good for anyone else.'

'It's okay, Mum,' I said. 'I'll help Junie find something.'

'I'd love to meet Terrence one day,' Junie said.

'I don't imagine that'll be happening anytime soon,' Mum said.

'Is he not still in the area?'

'Lord alone knows where that man's got to.'

'Blimey, I didn't realise,' Junie said. 'You don't see him at all? Aren't you still married, though?'

'In name alone,' Mum said sharply.

Junie's eyes met mine and I looked at her, confused. We'd talked about Dad many times; she knew we'd not heard a whisper of him in fifteen years.

'I didn't realise things had gone to pot quite so dramatically,' Junie said. 'I'm dreadfully sorry, Lil. I shouldn't have brought it up.'

'Don't be silly, dear,' Mum mumbled.

We crossed a fair portion of Dorset in silence.

'SHE BLOODY HATES ME,' JUNIE SAID.

'She does not.' I sat at the end of her bed and massaged her socked feet. 'How could anyone possibly hate *you*?' The small room was cold and musty smelling. Rain slapped the window; the third day of our holiday and the weather had barely lifted for more than ten minutes at a time.

'Everything I do is wrong.'

'I don't know what you're talking about. Mum keeps telling me what a sweetie you are.'

'She's lying.'

'Oh right. Okay. That makes perfect sense.'

'All the time, Ray. I can't even make a cup of fucking tea

without her telling me there's not enough leaves in the pot, or more milk than you like, or . . .'

'You're being overly sensitive.'

'Piss off.'

'Please, keep it down a bit. She's only next door.'

'God forbid she might overhear anything.' She pulled her foot from my grip. 'What an unbearable risk that would be.'

I looked at the floor. 'It's not ideal. Perhaps when the weather clears we might have the place to ourselves and we can . . .'

I looked up at her hoping for any sign of understanding.

'It just doesn't feel right here,' I whispered. 'Not with Mum . . .'

'Can we at least sneak out tonight?' Junie asked. 'There's a nice-looking pub we passed on the way in.'

'I don't see why we shouldn't.'

'Just the two of us, though.'

'Look, I'm not sure it's fair to—'

'Yes, forget it. Let's all play bridge again.'

'You like bridge.'

'Too much of a good thing, as they say.' She turned away from me and hugged her blanket.

'Sorry if you're not enjoying yourself. I was really looking forward to coming away with you.'

'Same,' Junie said. 'But I wanted to come away with *you*.'

'Mum's been very kind, paying for all this. She's not exactly flush. But this is her treat.'

'So she keeps saying.'

'That's not fair. I think we should be . . . grateful.'

Junie sat up suddenly. 'Has she said something?'

'I'm just saying—'

'She has!'

'Look—'

'She thinks I'm an ungrateful little bitch?'

'Please,' I urged her, palms raised. 'She's only next door.'

'You and her have been having *quiet words* about me. Marvellous.'

'Maybe just . . . say *thanks*, or something. Sometime. Oh, I don't know.'

'I'm tempted to say *something*.'

I gazed out the window. 'I think the sky's lightening a touch. In the west. Might be a pleasant evening.'

Junie snatched her copy of *The Prime of Miss Jean Brodie* from the floor, wrenching it open and reading immediately. 'I'll be sitting the cards out tonight, if that's okay with you?' she said.

THINGS CAME TO A HEAD. THE TRICKY CLIMATE—METEOROLOGICAL AND interpersonal—was playing havoc with my intention to propose. As is the way of the inclement British holiday, we were taking a lot of drives. A different beauty spot each day where we'd usually buy ice creams and take a siesta in the Cortina.

On one such jaunt, I offered to give Junie a driving lesson. She'd had a few goes behind the wheel in the States she'd told me, though she had no experience of 'driving stick' (an expression that was endearing at first but began to grate, much like her downshifts). This aside, she was proficient with an enjoyable tendency to get a move on.

Mum had to ride in the back. I was pretending not to hear the muttered complaints as she was thrown this way and that, forced to dust cigarette ash off her skirt. Junie took it in good humour at first. The road that wound steeply up to the cliffs at Baggy Point rather challenged her composure, though. Mum grumped as we took a hairpin too fast. She clutched her lower back.

'Been doing it *his way* too often?' Junie asked through gritted teeth.

'I'm sorry, June?' she said.

'It's nothing, Mum,' I said, glaring at Junie. Quite apart from anything else, she knew perfectly well that Mum and Douglas from the lido were long finished.

We slid to a stop in the gravelled car park. Wind shimmied the car on its springs. This was the summit.

'Thank God for that,' Mum said.

Junie stared out through the windscreen. Quite the view: furious clouds, steel sea, shafts of sun like searchlights cutting through here and there.

'I am sorry if I'm not good enough for your son,' Junie said. Coolly, matter of fact.

'Gosh, June, I . . .'

'I've no doubt you have an idea in your mind of exactly who he should be with.'

'Now, come—'

'But I love him.' She was red in the face, teeth bared, and still staring dead ahead. 'Is that not enough?'

'June, dear, I never . . .'

'You've got two options, Mrs Thorns. Like me, or damned well put up with me. Because I'm back now, and I'm back for good.'

'*Lil*,' she whispered.

I waved a calming hand, but the look Junie shot me made me put it away.

She spun around so that her head was between the front seats. In raised voice: 'There's enough of him to go round, *Lil*.'

Facing the front once again, Junie rolled the driver's window down and lit a cigarette, drawing heavily on it.

I glanced around at Mum and forced a quick smile. Her face was contorted, stunned and incensed. She said not a thing, instead silently opening the back door and slipping out onto the clifftop. With one hand pinning down her hair, and the other taming the skirt snapping at her legs, she walked slowly away from the car.

'Don't you sodding dare,' Junie said, glaring at my hand which was creeping reflexively toward my own door handle.

'I wonder if I should—'

'She's fine.'

'Yes, yes. I'm sure.'

'Sorry, Ray, but sometimes . . .'

I nodded as it was safest. Fifty feet away from the car, Mum stood looking out to sea, swaying gently from foot to foot.

'Give her a few minutes, yes?' Junie said, softening. 'Sit with me awhile.'

Somewhat petulantly I remarked, 'I just wish things could be like they were in Chicago.' This was something I'd been opining to myself hourly, but I'd not voiced it aloud till now.

'God, yeah.'

We were soon reminiscing about those glorious few days, though I must confess I kept half an eye out of the windscreen.

'Mum *is* very close to the edge,' I said, after once again catching her shuffling forwards a few inches. She turned side-on to us, the wind rippling at her cheeks and jetting her hair back. Her expression was hard to read, misery perhaps but also the stuff of good photographs.

Junie flung open the driver's door and stood leaning against it. 'Not going to jump are you, Lil?' she yelled. 'Come on, I didn't mean you any ill.' I could detect amusement in her tone.

Mum turned her back on the angry Atlantic. Her expression melted into a broad smile. She sauntered back toward the car.

'I think I can see Lundy Island,' she said. 'Would you credit it on a day like this?'

'Probably just another storm coming in,' I offered.

She clutched Junie's upper arm. 'Are you familiar with Lundy, dear?'

Junie shook her head. 'I'm a northern lass, me.'

Mum eased herself without complaint into the back seat. 'Well now, let me bore you then with a tale that takes us back to the nineteen thirties!'

'Go on, Lil,' Junie said, gesturing for me to slide over to the driving seat.

'No, no,' Mum said, reaching out for Junie's hand. 'You're really getting the hang of things. Do drive us back.'

TO OUR LAST FULL DAY AWAY. A LITTLE BEFORE TEN AND THE MIST HAD burned away to reveal, finally, an utterly glorious morning. My mouth was dry, heart racing. The sea was flat and a deep green, seagulls having a party with last night's dinner leftovers. Junie and I were sitting at the table in the garden, sharing a pot of tea in our dressing gowns.

This wasn't as I'd planned it. Imagining that this reunion holiday would involve a rerun of our best memories, I'd intended to do this after some sunset assignation on a deserted beach. Still, no time like the present.

'Junie,' I said, terribly seriously. With a hand in my dressing gown pocket, I clasped the small velvet box. I knew I should drop to one knee—certainly that's what I'd done whenever I imagined this moment—but self-consciousness prevented me from so doing. It seemed the sort of thing an American might do. Instead, I opted for a sort of halfway-there position, leaning forwards uncomfortably with my backside contacting the very edge of my seat.

So abashedly that it came out sounding almost like an apology, I *popped the question*.

She was suddenly bolt upright. Both hands covering her mouth. 'Are you being serious?'

The correct answer: I've never been more serious about anything in my life. What I actually said (warbly voice, eyes to ground): 'Erm. I suppose so.'

'Oh my God! I didn't think you were going to ask. I mean, I wanted you to. I've been praying you would, but . . .' She performed a little sitting-down dance.

I remembered the ring at last, flipping the lid open.

Junie's face crumpled in on itself, tears falling.

'What do you reckon?' I asked.

'I reckon *yes!*' She clasped my face between her hands and kissed my lips. 'Yes, you beautiful man. A million times yes!' She was shaking more than me by now.

I grinned like a maniac. The setting may have been compromised, but the outcome was everything I dreamed it would be.

'It even fits,' Junie said, holding her finger aloft with the gemstones glinting in the sun. 'It's beautiful, Ray.'

'You really like it?'

'It's perfect. Bloody perfect.' She hugged me tight and gave me a wet-faced kiss.

'Let's hear her answer then!' Mum said, standing a few paces clear of the table and grinning. She cupped a hand behind her ear. 'Is that wedding bells I can hear in the distance?'

Junie sprang to her feet. 'You know what, I think it is.' She and Mum hugged.

'I'm over the moon for you both,' Mum said. 'Ray won't tell you this, but he's been so worried. And I've been telling him there's no need. I knew exactly what your answer would be. You two are *besotted* with each other.'

'We are,' Junie said.

'So pleased to have you in the family, dear,' Mum said, squeezing both her hands.

'You and me both,' she replied, beaming at me.

I could've cried. Everything—my fear she'd say *no*, the tension between Junie and Mum, even the weather—had all come perfect in this moment.

'A real diamond, and a sapphire,' Mum said, holding Junie's finger. 'Stunning.'

'Wowee!' Junie said.

It looked a million dollars, somehow even more striking than it appeared when Mum had tried it on when we were shopping for it. 'Must have been to eight jewellers,' I said.

'And the rest!' Mum said.

'Mum helped me choose,' I told Junie.

'Oh, I didn't do anything,' Mum said. Then in a stage whisper to Junie: 'I made sure he didn't skimp on the price!'

This wasn't quite accurate: left to my own devices I'd have parted with the entirety of my savings, but Mum reined me in a little.

'You'll think I'm silly,' Junie said, 'but I've been practicing my signature. I've been doing it for years. June Thorns—wow! That's actually going to be *me*.'

'I can't wait.' I said.

'One thing at a time,' Mum said. 'Take some time to enjoy being *engaged*. You're both still so wonderfully young.'

'Twenty-two, Mum,' I said. I hadn't felt anything close to young for some years. And I was earning okay at last. I saw no reason for a lengthy engagement. The idea of next spring rather appealed when I'd thought about it privately; one of many exciting things to mull over with Junie.

'And here's a proposal of my own,' Mum said. 'Let's go out for lunch. Preferably somewhere where they do wine. And it is—no arguments—my treat.'

'I think that sounds like a fabulous idea, Mrs Thorns,' Junie said, somewhat theatrically.

'Well that's sorted . . . Mrs Thorns.' Mum stumbled on the words, like she'd decided halfway through that they weren't as funny as she'd imagined.

That evening, Junie and I finally did find a beach that was ours alone. And in the quiet of a midsummer's evening, we took advantage.

It may have been the best day of my life.

18

'I'M AFRAID I'VE RATHER DUG MYSELF INTO A HOLE,' I WHISPERED TO STEVEN.

'Jesus Christ, Uncle Ray.' He began to snigger. It built to a fit of barely muted laughter. The colour had returned to his cheeks during the five minutes I had spent—hurriedly and hushedly—telling him of the events since Tuesday night: Barry, the case of mistaken identity, my scotched attempts to correct the record.

He was clutching my duvet with one hand, slapping the bed with the other. A tear rolled from one eye. 'Fucking hell!' he said.

'Steady on, steady on,' I said. Junie could've come up the stairs any second.

'Come here, you stupid bastard.' He put his long arms around me.

I held firm for a moment, but then wilted, involuntarily. My face fell into my own cardigan, which he was still wearing. Steven patted my back. It really was the most wonderful feeling.

'It's good to see you, Uncle Ray,' he whispered. 'Really bloody good to see you.'

'You too,' I said rather stiffly.

He passed me a piece of toilet paper from the roll beside the bed and pointed at my face. I wiped my eyes and the paper came away translucent. I'm not sure what had come over me.

'Shit!' Steven said, shrugging off my clothes and dumping them on the bed. 'Sorry, I didn't mean any . . . I was just having a bit of a . . .'

'No apologies necessary. You looked rather good. If you did want to hang on to anything I dare say I'd manage.'

He grinned. 'You'll be needing these.'

'Yes, I suppose so.'

'The whole lot damned near got sent to the charity shop. What would you have done then?' Steven began to chuckle again at the absurdity of my predicament. I found myself joining in.

'I hadn't thought too much about it.'

'Sorry, I've dumped your papers. You want them back?' Steven asked.

'Gosh no. If I feel there's any I can't live without, I'll fetch them in myself.'

'Oh Christ, and Dad's pocketed six-hundred quid of yours.'

'That's the least of my concerns.' It really was.

We stood facing each other in silence. Downstairs, Junie's record was still playing, side two now.

'She's on a proper nostalgia trip, bless her,' Steven said.

'I don't think I can face her,' I told him. 'Are you going to tell her?'

'You want me to?'

'I don't . . . gosh, I just don't really . . .'

'I won't go telling on you. I may be many things, Uncle Ray, but I ain't no grass.' He said it with steel in his eyes. I looked at his solidly tattooed arms.

'She'll be furious,' I said.

'She'll be bloody delighted,' Steven said. 'Mark my words.'

'What the hell am I to do?'

'Everything all right up there?' Junie called up.

Steven put a calming hand on my shoulder. 'Fine and dandy,' he shouted back. 'Sleep on it,' he whispered to me. 'I'll help you sort this.'

'It's not your problem.'

He smiled again. 'Bloody hell, I've never met anyone who's faked their own death. I'm impressed.'

'No life insurance to live it up on, I'm afraid.'

'Shame. Look, I do need to go.' He checked his mobile phone again with a look of frustration. 'Lot of people wanting a piece of me. I'm gonna take Mum home. I'll pop in on you tomorrow, okay? We'll fix this up together, yeah?'

'I really wouldn't want to put you out. You've already been very good and—'

'I'll be round tomorrow, Uncle Ray. Now, do you need anything before I go?'

I shook my head. 'I already feel like a very fortunate man.'

Steven winked at me before flicking off both the bedroom and landing lights, leaving the upper floor in darkness. 'You old legend,' he whispered, sniggering as he descended the stairs.

19

SATURDAY

A DIFFICULT MORNING. I WAS PERFECTLY MISERABLE. A TRIP MADE AT THE crack of dawn to feed Little Boy Blue. It would likely be our last meeting. Maybe Barry's relatives, once informed, would allow me to continue with the job; or perhaps they'd think me far too much of a deranged crackpot to shoulder such responsibility. I kissed the budgerigar goodbye on the warm, wispy crown of his head, which smelt of Fairy Liquid—God knows what he'd been up to. He returned to his cage with minimal coaxing and I locked him in—defeat was accepted with grace.

Guilty that I'd been away for nearly a week, I visited Mum. Usually the first perfect blue sky of spring and the flurry of blossoms over the cemetery would cheer me. The grass had grown at the edges so I gave her plot a swift back-and-sides with my scissors. A spritz of Pledge on the headstone. I never spoke aloud to Mum (do people do that?) but I did so in my head. Ordinarily, I'd reach the wrought iron gates separating this ethereal ground from the South Circular with the answers to my questions complete. Not that I necessarily attributed the wisdom to the spirit of Mum. No, I fancy it was more like the explanation of prayer that Junie's father once gave me: the solutions are within us, we must peacefully listen for them.

But there were no answers today.

At home, the thought of pressing on with restoring one of my models, or grabbing my litter prodder and sacks, didn't interest me. Worse: they *appalled* me. I'd spent the previous days in a panic, trying to put matters right, in order to return to the life with which I have long been content, but which now horrified me.

In dying, I'd gained the ability to envisage a *future*, stretching out before me for years, potentially. Unfathomably, it looked so . . . pointless.

That card from Allonby House caught my eye once again. I reread its empty sentiment: *He is remembered fondly* . . . Fondly, my foot!

I was drawn to the hallway (easier to navigate courtesy of Steven's efforts). I took the famed 1982 school photograph from the wall; where Mr Thorns—*Spike*—wore green hair. In my armchair, I gazed at it on my lap. I've heard it said that the high water mark can only be seen from a distance. How true.

I had no appetite, for lunch nor anything else. Feeling like a condemned man in the cell nearest the gallows, I waited for Steven.

20

IT'S EASY TO IMAGINE, ESPECIALLY FOR TWO YOUNG PEOPLE, BEING IN LOVE is enough. That this greatest of conditions will carry you both through whatever obstacles may be encountered. I thought this, and I was wrong.

It was seven weeks before our wedding, a beautiful April day in '68, when Junie told me she was pregnant. We were sitting in my MG outside the Viscount Café a mile from home. Inside, Junie's parents were awaiting the arrival of us, and Mum. It was to be the official *meet the in-laws*, an event that had already been put back twice for health reasons (Mum both times: attack of vertigo on occasion one, a cancer scare the other). Junie was living in digs in Putney, working in a pub and depping in a couple of rhythm and blues bands. She was only permitted in our house till 8:00 p.m. though this seldom got in our way, as evidenced by Junie's current *predicament*.

'We've never really discussed . . . a family,' Junie said. Her legs and arms were pinched so tightly that she barely occupied half the passenger seat.

'No, but I mean, that would always be the . . . you know, I can't imagine us *not* . . . it's a bit of a surprise, but that doesn't mean, well, you know . . .' It was a touch chilly for April and I was infuriatingly shaky. 'How long do you think you've . . .'

'Doctor says I'm about eight weeks. They say not to tell everyone till twelve weeks, but I'm not about to keep it from *you*, am I? I don't think I'll be showing for the wedding.'

REPORTS OF HIS DEATH HAVE BEEN GREATLY EXAGGERATED   159

'November,' I mumbled. 'When it'll be . . . due. That's right, isn't it?'

'There or there abouts.'

'This year. Wow.'

'You are okay with this, Ray?' She put her hand on mine where it gripped the handbrake lever. 'I know it's a . . . surprise. At least *I've* had twenty-four hours to get used to the idea.'

'Sure. It's good news. Really . . . lovely news.'

'For what it's worth, I think you'll be a bloody amazing dad.'

I grinned, though I didn't share her confidence.

'Look, I know it's not quite like we might've planned,' Junie said.

'No, it's great,' I told her. But just then, I didn't *feel* it was great. I was in shock. Does anyone greet the expectation of a child with carefree celebration, I wonder, like in the movies? But I would come around quickly. Even by the time we'd crossed the road and were being escorted to our table by Mum's long-time admirer Italian Tony, I was getting high on the idea.

Mum was running late and I made hopelessly distracted small talk with Junie's parents who'd come down from Macclesfield for the day. We sank two coffees apiece during the wait.

'Mrs Thorns!' Tony said eventually, dashing to the door.

Evidently not in the mood for his usual niceties, Mum swatted him away like a wasp when he held a chair out for her.

'So wonderful to meet you both at last, Mrs Burnham and . . .'

I'd told Mum there was no need to call him *father* or any suchlike. Without a dog collar as he was now, he looked like an ordinary man anyway.

'Rudolph. Rudy to friends, as I know we'll very soon be,' he said, reciprocating Mum's very square handshake.

'So sorry to keep you all,' Mum said, flustered. 'Today's been chaos.'

'It's all fine,' Junie's mum said softly. 'We've only just arrived ourselves.' Though I knew they'd left home at 5:00 a.m. and I felt bad that they could have had a little extra time in bed.

Junie's father took charge of the conversation, enthusing about the cake selection and asking Mum about the area, dissolving all awkwardness. Had this meeting happened—as was intended—the previous autumn, there would've been much to discuss: venue, guest list, the delicate matter of the tab. But, with only a month and a half till our big day remaining, these had been addressed already at a distance.

'Important diplomatic mission to attend to this afternoon,' Junie's father said, having ordered the mixed grill from Tony. 'I shall be needing a full stomach. An audience with Reverend Bull of this parish.'

'You won't have any trouble there,' Mum said. 'You'll charm his socks off.'

'We're very territorial, us clergymen. Can't have any old Tom, Dick, or Willy taking over our beloved temples.'

'I think it's a lovely idea,' Junie's mother said. 'All in the spirit of union and compromise.'

Naturally Junie's preference had been to marry in her father's church, but Mum rather liked Saint Bede's near us, and there was the long drive to think of, and what with Junie wanting to make her life down here in London, and there were perhaps other good reasons too. There'd been correspondence between Junie's father and the incumbent of Saint Bede's, a deal struck such that he could officiate.

'I'll tell you this,' Junie's father said, 'I'm looking forward to this. You've done me a turn really. A new place to familiarise myself with! I only hope I'm up to it.'

Our lunch was on the table by the time the last of our party arrived. Denny was the only logical choice for best man. Customary as it may be to have a good mate in the role, the best and only friend I ever wanted was the person I was due to marry.

Denny was someone who could make a noisy entrance in complete silence. Everyone in the café looked at him. He had a wink for the two young mothers up at the front. His suit may well have been a Tommy Nutter; he had a fountain pen peeping from his breast pocket and an Omega Constellation on his wrist. I smiled at Junie. She and he had yet to meet and I felt proud that this man was my brother. It reflected well on me, I thought.

He had a handshake and a smile for my soon-to-be in-laws. 'And this must be the princess?' he said, having a good look at Junie and evidently approving. Junie blushed.

Denny and Junie's father instantly hit it off, holding forth whilst we ate on matters of the Vietnam protests and Enoch Powell. Only Mum was yet to finish her food when she seized an opening in conversation.

'There is something I've been wanting to bring up,' she said. She sounded nervous and I gave her knee a squeeze under the table. 'There is something, June dear, that I'd like you to have.'

'Sounds exciting,' Junie said. Our table fell quiet. Junie's mother wore a smile but seemed transfixed by Mum's plate and the remaining precise squares that she'd cut her open cheese sandwich into.

'I don't suppose you've seen the photographs of mine and Terrence's wedding?' Mum asked.

Junie grinned at me. 'Actually I have. Ray and I have been so overcome with wedding fever that we dug it out the other evening. You were very glamorous, Mrs . . . *Lil*.'

'You *are* very glamorous,' Junie's father boomed, shooting his daughter a where-were-you-brought-up glance.

Mum looked flattered. 'That's sweet of you all to say. And the thing is, June, I'd like you to have my dress.'

'Isn't that an incredibly kind thing?' Junie's father said, after an overlong silence.

'It was very expensive,' I said. Mum had told me—that morning—of her plan to gift it to Junie.

'Never mind *expense*,' Mum said. '*Exclusive*—that's more the word.' Adding in hushed tone, as though imparting something not to be spread around: 'Terrence was doing very well for himself at the time.'

Junie looked less elated than I'd expected. She squirmed on her chair. 'That's very kind of you, Lil. Really kind and—'

'It might need letting out a little,' Mum said. 'But I've already found a seamstress worthy of the job. I was *tiny* back then, you see. A nineteen-inch waist, would you credit it?'

Junie's mother sank back in her seat and gazed out of the café window. I gave Junie a knowing smile—the dress more than likely *would* need letting out, what with recent developments. She dodged my gaze.

'There's actually a dress I've got my eye on,' Junie said. This was news to me.

'And I did promise that it would be my treat,' her mother said.

'And just maybe,' Denny chipped in, 'she don't want to wear her mother-in-law's dress. It's all right, princess, you *can* say that. We're all friends here.'

'It's not that,' Junie said, blushing. 'But I've really got my heart set on this other—'

'The photographs don't do it justice,' Mum said. 'It could easily pass for Dior.'

'I completely agree, Lil. It's gorgeous. But maybe not quite . . .'

'The sensible thing here,' her father said, 'would be to try it for size. Who knows, it might just be perfect. And if not—well—it's an incredibly kind offer. Thank you, Mrs Thorns.'

'If someone had offered to gift me such a thing,' Mum said, 'I'd have bitten their arm off.'

REPORTS OF HIS DEATH HAVE BEEN GREATLY EXAGGERATED   163

Denny lent back in his chair, Dunhill smoke jetting from the corner of his mouth. 'Not exactly a good omen though, is it, Mum?'

I shook my head at him. Denny still hadn't learned when to shut up.

'Terrence loved the dress,' Mum hissed at him.

'You get married in whatever you want, princess. Sorry about this old family of ours. You'll get used to us, don't worry.'

Junie grinned at Denny. 'Thank you, Lil. I'm really touched by the offer. And of course you looked beautiful in it . . .' Both her parents nodded and made agreeing noises.

'You'd be making your mother-in-law very happy,' Mum cut in. 'As your father suggests, give it a try at least.'

'Just a try,' I added. 'Where's the harm?' I couldn't understand Junie's resistance. It was awkward; she looked ungrateful, which was not *her* at all.

The stare she fired my way was unsettling. 'Lil, I'm very appreciative. But I have a dress in mind, and that is what I'd like to wear. We have conceded to you the choice of church, the catering, two-thirds of the hymns, sixty per cent of the invitations, and precisely zero per cent of the bill.'

'Junie!' her father said without moving his lips. He smiled softly at Mum. 'There is no question of anyone other than my wife and me bearing the costs in full,' he told her.

'Thank you,' Junie said. 'I'm bowled over by your kindness, but I must politely decline.'

I was about to say something, but Mum shushed me. 'I fully understand,' Mum said, like she really meant it. I thought it very big of her.

'Please, I'd hate you to be upset,' Junie said.

Mum laughed. 'I'm not upset. Gosh, no. It was just an idea. But I can see your point entirely. I'm very . . . delighted you've found a dress. Such an exciting time!'

Despite the best efforts of Junie's father and Denny, things were stilted for the remainder of our lunchtime. My face and neck felt hot, vapour rising from the cologne I'd doused all over when smartening myself for this engagement. It'd been less smooth than I'd hoped. I might have been a touch depressed at the fact, were I not so thoroughly distracted by dreams of fatherhood.

WE ARE ALL FAMILIAR WITH NEWTON'S THIRD LAW: THAT EVERY ACTION IS met with an equal and opposite reaction. When looking back over things, one realises that this rule applies equally to life as to physics. It is not an obvious truth because, unlike science, reactions often do not immediately follow their causing action; the two can happen such a period apart as to make their connection unclear. But I've come to see that it is one of nature's irrefutable rules.

'June rang for you,' Mum told me. 'I should have said as soon as you came in. Sorry.'

'Isn't she working this evening?' I replied. 'I'm sure she is.'

'She only said to call her back when you're free.'

'Did she say if there was a problem?'

'Have your tea,' Mum said, barring my path to the telephone. 'You've been working hard.'

It was ten days since the café. I'd had a late finish at Allonby House having hosted chess club *and* sat in on prep.

'Are *you* okay, Mum?' I noticed as we sat across the kitchen table from each other that she was huffing as she breathed.

'A little green around the gills. Nothing to concern yourself with.'

'You do look pale now you mention it.'

'I'm all right. Coming down with something, I dare say.'

She jerked as she lowered her teacup, causing it to crash against the saucer.

'Mum? How long have you been feeling rough?'

'It's no bother. Most of the day, I suppose. On and off.'

'Should I be calling the doctor?'

She waved the idea away.

Somewhat distractedly, I returned Junie's call. Her landlady answered. It was some minutes before Junie came to the telephone. I should've known immediately that something wasn't right. She spoke quietly; I'd never heard her so flat. No explanation was given for her not being at her pub job. A three-minute conversation was hard work. She asked only that I go around there after suppertime. I promised I'd be there.

'How did she sound to you?' I called to Mum. 'Not her usual—'

I stopped dead in the kitchen doorway. 'Mum! What's wrong, Mum?' She had slunk off her chair and was sitting on the floor, leaning against the wall.

'Just a little . . .' She huffed and closed her eyes. 'A little faint. That's all.'

I knelt next to her and helped her up. Supporting half her weight I led her to the armchair in the sitting room. She brought a hand to her chest and grimaced.

'Tell me exactly what your symptoms are, Mum.' It was mere weeks since I'd attended a St. John Ambulance first-aid demonstration at the school. I'd shared what I'd learned with Mum. We both knew the signs of a heart attack.

'Just a funny turn,' she said. 'I'll be fine in a minute.'

'Mum, now is not the time to worry about putting anyone out. Now, tell me—do you have pains in your chest?'

She braced against an invisible force. 'Perhaps a little,' she whispered.

'Can you manage the walk to the car?'

She stared into her lap as she thought about it.

'Or else I'll have to call an ambulance.'

'No,' she snapped. 'I'm not having all the neighbours seeing me, well . . . Be a dear and get my shoes, Ray love.'

I'd never thrashed the poor MG like it as we battled through late rush-hour traffic. At casualty they had Mum to a bed in minutes. We drank sweet tea and waited on the doctor's verdict. Mercifully, Mum's breathing had improved markedly in our many hours there.

At just gone ten, it occurred to me to find a public telephone and call Junie. I got her landlady again, irate due to the hour. She told me Junie had retired for the night. I left a message with her: that Mum had been taken ill and I was with her.

The doctor was satisfied with Mum's heart rate and blood pressure. His diagnosis: inconclusive; minor angina perhaps, possibly nerves, indigestion even. There was the offer of a night of bedrest on a ward, but she insisted she'd be more relaxed at home. Dawn was bleeding into the sky by the time I got Mum comfortable and turned in myself, in the hope of an hour of shut-eye before another day at the school.

'SWITCH OFF THE ENGINE,' JUNIE SAID.

Friday evening now, outside her digs in the MG, picking her up as was customary. I did as I was told.

'I'm not hanging about.' She lit a cigarette in the passenger seat and faced the half-open window on her side as she smoked.

'And there you were telling me how easy it was to give up,' I said jokily. She'd been off the fags for months due to some rather questionable studies she'd read about how smoking could somehow be damaging to an unborn child.

'I changed my mind,' she said, dragging deeply. 'People do. Is that okay with you?'

'Sorry about the other night,' I said. It'd been three days of failed attempts to get hold of her. And now I had, she seemed hardly recognisable.

'Why apologise? You were doing the right thing.'

'I could hardly go leaving Mum. Not the way she was. But, even so . . .'

'I'm no longer pregnant. *We* are no longer pregnant.' She said it so matter-of-factly. It's a statement that I would hear in my mind for days, weeks to come. An auditory flashback that would bring with it each time the same shattering sensation that assaulted me when I first heard the news.

'What?' I asked. 'What?'

'I miscarried.' Again, so coolly put. She repeatedly ashed her ciggie against the top of the glass, the naked tip blazing red in the breeze.

I held my vibrating hand within an inch of hers, but she didn't take it. 'How did that . . . Did something happen to . . .'

'It just *happened*, Ray,'

'On . . .'

'Tuesday. Knew something wasn't right in the afternoon. Doctor came out. And that's that, as they say.'

'And it's definitely . . .'

'Trust me here, Ray.' There was something dark in her brief laugh. 'It's definitely, definitely.'

'But you've been fine. Did everything right and . . .'

'Not cut out for it, by the looks. Anyway, not worth dwelling on.'

'Why are you saying that? We've lost a . . .' My voice cracked and I took a deep breath. 'We can't just go forgetting about it. That's . . . absurd.'

Junie tapped a cigarette hard on the packet and lit it up, having only just ejected the last from the car. 'You do as you wish.'

'I'm so sorry I didn't come and see you. I was going to. I promise I was going to.'

'I was all right on my own. I can manage by myself.'

'Of course you can. But this is our . . . this was both of our . . .'

'It doesn't matter, Ray. I dealt with it.'

'This isn't fucking fair,' I said. I would cry every waking morning and every bedtime for weeks to come, but at this moment the overriding sense was one of being cheated.

We sat in silence for ten minutes or more.

'I've been thinking,' Junie eventually said. 'I'm not sure we should get married.'

'Why would you even . . .'

'I don't think there's really any need now.'

I turned and stared at her, incredulous. 'But that's not *why* we were getting married. We weren't doing it because we were expecting a . . .'

'Even so.'

'Junie, please. Just steady on, for God's sake. You're upset. I understand. I'm upset. But don't do this. I can't bear it.'

She took a deep breath and stared dead ahead through the windscreen. 'I don't want to marry you, Ray.'

'No,' I told her. 'I won't have it.' I was burning with upset and anger, but I couldn't find the words I needed. 'People have made arrangements. It's five and a half weeks away. We can't do that to people.'

'That's very considerate of you, to worry about that.'

'One of us must.' I was furious and, as I realised soon after, focussing my ire on the wrong thing entirely. 'What about our families? They've all made plans, and . . .'

'Has your mum already bought herself a hat?'

'I don't know if she's wearing a hat.'

'I dare say she'll get over her disappointment. You should probably get back home, Make sure she's still bearing up.'

'She's okay today.' I batted the subject away.

'Good,' she said bitterly.

'All the things that have been booked,' I snapped, returning us to the matter in hand.

'I'm going to speak to Dad. This weekend.'

It was more than five years later, when reliving this argument in my mind as I periodically do, that it dawned on me that the fact she hadn't *already* spoken to her father meant that, at this stage, things were still salvageable. It was possibly my very last chance. And I hadn't seen it.

'I don't know how you can do this to him,' I snapped, ignoring the true source of my agony—my own heart was being ripped to shreds. Why could I not understand that she was being driven awry by her own insufferable hurt?

'I'm going to go back inside now,' Junie said. 'I've said what I need to say.'

'Have you met someone else?' It was a stupid, ruinous question; I knew it when I said it.

That look she gave me. I've never forgotten it. Not sadness. Not fury. It was, I think, confusion. She seemed to wrestle for words, settling eventually on simply this: 'Goodbye, Ray.' She closed the door softly behind her. A curling haze of smoke lingered long after she'd disappeared into the house.

For a weekend I was madly aggrieved and kept my distance. Come Sunday night I sat still long enough to pen her a letter which I delivered by hand. I received no reply and her landlady wouldn't call Junie to the phone. Eventually, I heard from her father (who was kind and sympathetic and not even slightly angry) that she'd returned to Chicago. She'd saved a little money for the wedding and spent it instead on another shot at her music. I wrote a letter every week.

She replied only once. It was the last letter she ever sent. Three months had passed and she sounded her old self, insofar as one can tell from words consigned to paper four thousand miles away. She'd hooked up with some of her old pals and they were getting gigs, which I was ecstatic to hear. She said she was sorry. That it hadn't been fair to blame me. She missed me, she said. There was no declaration of love which had always been a staple of our missives, but not even this could detract from the wonder of hearing from her.

She even implied I could pay another visit out there, though I was certain it was a hollow offer, an excess of politeness and no more. In any case, they were keeping me busy at Allonby House, and it was increasingly necessary to keep a close eye on Mum's health. And a curious feeling had settled upon me by then: that I had lived through my summer and I was now holing up for winter.

It would be a full two years before I'd hear any more of Junie.

21

'FANCY THE PUB?' THESE WERE STEVEN'S FIRST WORDS TO ME WHEN HE AR-rived at my house.

'What an incredible car,' I remarked as he held the door for me at the kerbside.

'This old thing?' he started it up and revved the engine twice. The growl tore through the neighbourhood. 'You like it?'

It was a flashy Mercedes coupe of considerable size, with an interior of soft white leather. A skinny robotic arm offered me my seatbelt. I foolishly muttered a *thank you*.

'Ask it nicely and it'll wank you off too,' Steven said.

'It would need to be a bloody magician these days,' I replied with accidental bawdiness. 'Powers that have long-since waned, I'm sorry to say. I'm doing well to raise a *smile*.' We both laughed before remembering ourselves.

Steven drove in much the same way as he did everything: at speed and with an enthralling erraticism. Unnecessarily, he apologised for not being over earlier, explaining that he'd had a heavy session in the gym. I was a little surprised; he seemed too wise a man to give his time to furiously peddling a bicycle that doesn't go anywhere.

'This is your car?' I asked.

'Sure it is. Had this one a couple of months. Were you won-dering if I'd hired it just to show off?'

'Oh, nothing of the . . .'

'I'm not my father, you know?' He grinned. 'You heard about

the time back in the seventies when he rented an Aston for a class reunion at Longrove Grammar?'

'Yes, that escapade of Denny's did rather pass into folklore.'

'What an arse that man is!' Steven laughed.

'You must have a jolly good job,' I said, worrying it might sound like prying.

'A bit of this and that,' he replied, looking at me from the corner of his eye.

I replied with a knowing nod. It seemed safest.

'Somewhere comfortably off your patch,' Steven said as we pulled into a pub car park. We'd been driving over half an hour and were well into the wilds of Kent. 'Can't risk anyone identifying a dead man.'

'You may have overestimated my notoriety.'

How long since I'd been in a pub? A teacher's leaving do at Allonby, over twenty-five years ago. And this was a fine example of a hostelry: ancient, low-ceilinged, dark and woody, huddled Saturday drinkers conspiring or getting intimate.

'We should've been doing this years ago,' Steven said, as we took a seat at a bench in a garden to the rear. He chinked his pint of beer against the cider I'd ordered in a fluster. The view was quite remarkable—stretching for miles a patchwork of hilly fields in shrub, the breeze swaying the fresh growth this way and that, painting it ever-changing shades of green. 'I've really bloody missed you, Uncle Ray,' he said, offering me a cigarette which I declined, before lighting one himself and jetting blue smoke into the sun.

'Mum's taken it hard,' he said. 'Harder than I'd expect?' he asked himself aloud, pondering an answer. 'Dunno. Maybe not.'

'She knows that I'm . . .'

'I've kept my mouth shut. That's the least I can do for you.'

'I'm not sure I follow you.' I took a cautious sip of my drink; it was cloudy and divine tasting, a balm on my agitated innards.

'You didn't cause this,' Steven said. 'Enjoy it. You don't exist! You've got the perfect alibi. The invisible man! I'm jealous.'

'I can't see there's anything to *enjoy* about the sorry situation.'

He smirked at me. 'A man who hides in a cupboard rather than coming clean. It's all right—I reckon I'd do the same.'

'I doubt that.'

'So you're telling me you've not had a bit of a kick out of it, the ducking and diving?'

I swigged my drink instead of replying.

'Since the other day,' Steven went on, 'when I got that call from Dad, saying he'd been told you'd . . . passed. I've been thinking about you pretty much non-stop, Uncle Ray.'

'I'm very sorry for—'

He held up a palm. 'You've no idea what a relief last night was. I can't get over it. How often do we *really* get another chance.' Steven looked at me intently. 'I've been shit to you.'

'Steady on now.'

'It's unforgiveable, Uncle Ray. After everything.'

I had helped Steven out a little in his younger years. But I had no sense of being owed. After all, had I done *my* best to keep up with *him*? Not a bit of it.

'I'm here now, and I'll make up for whatever I can,' he said.

'This is more than enough,' I replied, raising my glass. It was the truth.

'We're gonna do exactly what you want to.'

'Well, I suppose we should go and see them at the hospital. And set my brother—your dad, rather—right.'

'Yeah, we'll get around to it. No sweat.'

'Denny hasn't started arranging a . . . *funeral* has he?' I winced with the word.

Steven waved the question away. 'Don't worry about that.'

'Seriously, Steven. The very thought gives me the willies.'

'Don't sweat it, Uncle Ray,' he said, far too dismissively for comfort. 'When has my dad ever got on with anything? Too wrapped up in his golf and his own life.'

'Well . . . okay,' I said, letting the matter lie. 'It sounds like you and your father don't get along too famously.'

'We're just about civil, Uncle Ray. That's the size of it. He's not exactly my favourite person.'

'He's always been someone rather . . . sure of himself. Little seems to have changed on that front, not from the view afforded from my understairs cupboard, anyway.'

Steven had a good chuckle at this. 'He's a bully, that's what he is. How Mum still sticks with him I've no idea.'

'They don't seem very happy.' I enjoyed the flutter in my chest brought on by thinking again about Junie.

'Enough about *them*,' he said, sinking a third of his pint in one draft. 'Tell me, what's been happening with you these last . . . twenty-five years?' He puffed out his cheeks at the absurd length of time for which we'd been strangers.

'Well, I retired in 2002, from the school. And since then, I've been, well . . .'

'Retired?'

I nodded, but looked only at the table. Could there really be nothing else to tell? How *had* I filled those two-and-a-bit decades?

'I bet they miss you up at that school,' Steven said. 'You were a legend, I don't doubt it.'

'I wouldn't be so sure about . . .'

'Didn't get the sack, did you?' Steven asked with a wicked grin.

I huffed. 'Not the . . . sack. Not as such.'

'Fucking hell, Uncle Ray. I was only having a joke. What happened?'

'They called it *early retirement*,' I said after a while. 'Things weren't really . . . working.'

'Oh, early retirement doesn't mean anything,' Steven said, waving his arms about. 'Probably showing everyone else up, weren't you?' There was something unnatural is his bonhomie.

'It's okay,' I told him. 'You've not upset me. Long time ago.'

He nodded. 'You miss it, right?'

'I do, I suppose. Still, change is life's one constant.'

Steven rolled his eyes at the tea-towel philosophy; I obviously couldn't deliver the line with the gravitas Charles Sethi always leant it.

'They sent a card,' I told him. 'Denny told them, I believe. About my . . .'

'Death?' Steven said grinning.

'To the family. Sending their condolences.'

'Good for them. You obviously weren't *sacked* then.'

'How do you mean?'

'I imagine they're only in the business of sending out cards to the people they think well of.'

'Or people they don't remember at all.'

'Oh, give over, Uncle Ray!' he said, necking the rest of his pint. 'You have a way about you with young people. It's almost . . . magical. Something I'll never forget, that's for sure. Mark my words, that school thought highly of you.'

'Steady on. It's kind of you to say, but . . .'

Steven again offered me a cigarette. I held up a palm.

'My smoking habits were limited to the occasional panatela with the school headmaster,' I explained. 'Usually coupled with a brandy.'

'Another?' he said, pointing at my glass.

'It's rather my round, I fancy.'

'No chance,' he replied, heading for the bar inside at his usual pace.

I thought about that card at home. Would they send such

a thing to someone who'd left in disgrace? Could there still be someone at the school who thought well of me? It was a pleasant thought that I almost let myself believe.

'Remy Martin,' Steven said, setting a brandy glass in front of me. 'Drink up!'

'Gosh, that's very—'

'And look what else I procured at the jump.' He pulled a cellophane-wrapped slim panatela from his pocket and performed an exaggerated mime of smoking it like an oil tycoon.

For some reason, the idea of lighting the thing frightened me, but I did so all the same. Accompanied by nips of the brandy, I felt conspicuous and silly for two minutes, and rather thrilled for the following ten.

'You ever been back there,' Steven asked.

'To Allonby House? I pass by on occasion.' Every couple of weeks, in truth.

'When did you last go inside?'

'Gosh, not since the day I left.'

'You must've wanted to? You gave that place your life.'

'I suppose part of me wonders how the old place might have changed.'

Steven's phone was back in his hands. For half a minute, his lips quivered as he speed-read to himself from the screen. He looked at that gold Rolex on his wrist. 'Ten past three on a Saturday,' he mumbled. 'Who knows?' He tapped the phone again. 'It's ringing,' he told me.

'Steven, what are you doing?'

His eyes were alive with that same spontaneous sparkle I'd seen when he was trying on my clothes yesterday. 'Seeing if we can pay them a visit. Take a look round the old gaff.'

'You have to go on an open day!' I hissed. 'Even then you have to book in advance.'

'Maybe.'

'Please, Steven. They'll think us fools.'

'That's possible.'

I flapped furiously. 'They think I'm deceased!'

'Ah, yes, hello,' Steven said, silencing me with his eyes, 'I wonder if you *can* help me. Tell me, is there likely to be a member of staff at the premises for the next hour or so?'

I stared at him, dumbstruck.

'Perfect, perfect. Sports fixtures till five, you say, Philip? That'll suit us just fine. There's a couple of items we missed when we did our site survey last month. *T*'s to cross and *I*'s to dot!' Steven emitted a professional-sounding chortle.

I'd found myself liking Steven immensely, although I was beginning to worry he cut his living as a confidence trickster.

'It's Leigh Delamere speaking, needless to say.' He winked at me. 'I'll be with a colleague.'

I caught myself smirking.

'Lovely. I'll put a call in to your head Doctor Plumpton,' he went on, expertly regurgitating the information he'd digested before calling. 'As a courtesy.'

He closed the call and drained his remaining half pint. 'We have a date to keep,' he told me, getting to his feet.

'Steven, I'm really not sure this is a great idea.'

'Sure it is.'

Had the brandy not gone to my head, I'm sure I wouldn't have followed him to the car.

'How did you know they'd had a *site survey* recently?' I asked.

'The key is, be *vague*,' he told me, starting the engine and revving it. 'And always say you're going to contact their superior, in order that *they* don't.'

'That's very insightful.' We were on the move again, as rapidly as ever.

Steven grinned. 'I'm not a wrong un, Uncle Ray. I'm just good at getting things done.'

'That name you gave,' I said. 'Leigh Delamere. Isn't that the . . .'

'Service station on the M4? Why yes! Yes it is. They do a mean lasagne and chips.'

'Why on earth did you choose that name?'

'Dunno. Because I thought you'd find it funny, I guess.'

I sniggered. 'Leigh Delamere,' I repeated. 'Yes. Very good.' The more I thought about it, the funnier it got. A touch tipsy, with the taste of a golden era on my tongue, and still presumed dead, I was soon laughing harder than I had in years.

22

'YOU APPEAR TO HAVE ACCRUED A BAND OF MERRY FOLLOWERS,' HEADMAS-
ter Charles Sethi said to me. It was a Friday evening and I'd
crossed the corridor from my caretaker's store to his study, where
we were each enjoying a brandy and a panatela.

'A few of the boys rather enjoy working with their hands,' I
explained.

'And seeing the fruits of their labours,' he added, wisely. 'Not
to mention the company of their good friend *Spike*!'

'Well . . . steady on.'

'Let's make it official,' he said, with his trademark decisiveness
that was akin to God saying *Let there be light!* 'The boarders have
little to do, of an evening, once they've completed their prep.
Have the sports store near the west gate. Do as you wish with it.'

And so, as the nineteen seventies dawned, the operation began. To clear the building, I quietly rehomed the shooting and
fencing equipment; it had been in enthusiastic use during Rhind-
Jones's reign but mothballed under the new administration. The
place was furnished with scrounged workbenches, a tea urn, a
good loud record player. In use, it soon gained posters of T. Rex
and Clint Eastwood and Neil Armstrong, a Scalextric track, and a
train set that would eventually circumnavigate the whole building. There was only one rule: never be mean, though even this
was rarely a problem. People have funny ideas about workshops;
those who haven't spent time in one tend not to appreciate what
a sanctuary they can be. It quickly became a haven for the boys,

and indeed myself: we were each learning to live independently of who we loved most.

It was illogical—I knew I was still made of the same flesh and blood, but I was utterly different to the man who'd been betrothed to Junie. Only in losing her could I appreciate love's greatest thrill: that slow acceptance that *yes*, *yes*, you *are* worthy of this near-mythical person's attentions, however improbable that fact. And so with the loss of love, the cruel realisation you weren't deserving of it after all. My cells, my DNA, unaltered maybe, but in the wake of her loss the very fabric of me had changed so drastically as to make me someone new. Somebody so, so much poorer.

Still, the positives—I had Mum, a fine job, and this new boys' club of mine, which kept me especially busy.

THE CHANGING CULTURE AT ALLONBY HAD BECOME EVIDENT THE MOMENT Sethi replaced Rhind-Jones. The cane vanished and was never seen again. The couple of moustachioed masters who had seen service in the Great War were finally pensioned off. But I wonder if nothing reveals the attitude of a school to its pupils better than how it conducts an assembly. In the eyes of Rhind-Jones, each boy before him was a sinner, in need of lengthy, daily prayers of penitence. His favoured hymns were like dirges, begging the Almighty for forgiveness, or vowing to be good, muscular Christians through song. Sethi however would make room only for a swift Lord's Prayer, before delivering a sunny anecdote sure to inspire. And the new repertoire of hymns! 'Amazing Grace' and 'Morning Has Broken' were greeted by the boys like they were Beatles hits. They could even be heard being sung in the corridors and dorms whilst the novelty lasted, if not by the boys then by Mr Sethi himself in his distinctive singing voice; what he lacked in tone he made up for in volume.

REPORTS OF HIS DEATH HAVE BEEN GREATLY EXAGGERATED   181

His approach to morning worship summed up his approach to the boys: they weren't here to serve, but to shine. No longer 'Onward Christian Soldiers', but 'All Things Bright and Beautiful'.

An incident in the early days of my new club would become the stuff of legend. We'd built skateboards that were ready for finishing. I'd negated to check the lid on a tin of matt black paint before shaking it up. In what seemed like slow motion, the liquid contents rose into the air in the exact shape of the tin, as twenty or more schoolboys looked on from the other side of the bench. As it descended it landed precisely on the crown of my head, forming—I was later told—a perfect umbrella of paint. I scooped a handful out of each eye socket and standing perfectly still, I scanned the stunned faces before me.

I'm unsure which of them uttered the famous line that followed: 'Steady on, Spike!'

I sniggered, which had the effect of igniting a firework of laughter. Some of them were crying. Our new youth club had now been christened: Steady On Spike's. In the fine oral tradition of school nicknames, it would pass down, leading each new generation of pupils to imagine it was they who made it up.

My MG, now so decrepit as to be unusable, was towed from the garage at home to the school. It was just one of our many projects. The rebuild took some fifteen years; there must have been several hundred keen young men who had a hand in the car's resurrection. Charles Sethi himself sprayed the bonnet, although I rubbed it down and did it again myself later that same evening. It became something of a tradition that after their last summer exam, the thirteen-year-old leavers would be allowed a drive in the old girl around the lower field, in whatever stage of reassembly it happened to be. I'd supervise from the passenger seat and we'd venture no further than first gear, though those with the knack of car control would be encouraged to pull some handbrake turns. Those were, I suppose, rather different times.

IT WAS A SATURDAY IN THE SUMMER OF 1975. EARLY EVENING AND ALL THE boys long gone after morning school and cricket fixtures. We had a forthcoming production of *Fiddler on the Roof* for which I was putting in some extra hours to finish the set. There was, I thought, nobody else remaining on site when I heard distant shouts and whoops from the opposite end of the grounds. I set out to investigate. As I drew closer to the melee, I could hear splashing noises too. There were people in the swimming pool.

Filled only during summer term, it was a small outdoor pool within a wire-fenced court. I found the gate to the court still padlocked shut, yet ten or more boys, and perhaps half as many girls, having themselves a party. They had evidently broken onto the grounds and then scaled the fence around the pool.

As is usually the way, these misbehaving youngsters looked intimidating at a distance, and harmless up close. In charge of chlorinating the water, I had the padlock key on my bunch and I let myself in.

I raised two palms in front of me: the sign language equivalent of *steady on*. The pool's cover had been pulled back and two of their number were in the water, both slight young things of twelve at most, in nothing but lurid Y-fronts. A makeshift barbecue had been assembled where Walls sausages were hissing and blackening. Music blared from a battery radio.

'You're having quite the party, I see,' I said. I had found myself facing a girl and boy, whilst everyone else huddled in small groups some distance from me.

The young lady turned the music down. 'We're not here to

REPORTS OF HIS DEATH HAVE BEEN GREATLY EXAGGERATED   183

cause trouble,' she told me. She looked no more than eleven, but had the demeanour of someone years older.

'I don't think any of you are pupils here, are you?' I asked, knowing it to be the case.

'Have you called the police?' the boy asked.

I shook my head. 'I hardly think this is a matter for *them*.' He seemed surprised by this answer.

'Put the cover back on,' the girl ordered the boys in the pool. They dragged themselves dripping onto the concrete and began doing as they were told.

Instinctively, I removed their sausages from the heat. They were about to spoil.

'Didn't think anyone was here,' the boy told me.

'Where are you all from?' I asked.

There was an exchange of glances, as though this might be a trick question.

'Watermead,' the girl eventually told me. It was a notorious estate, the butt of many jokes made by Allonby House boys.

'What brings you all the way out here?' I asked.

There were some shrugged shoulders. 'Bored,' someone mumbled.

'Used to go up the Ethel Burge,' the girl said.

I nodded. It was a community centre with a reputation for trouble. 'Didn't it burn down?'

'It wasn't nothing to do with us,' she said, very seriously.

I laughed. 'Gosh, I wasn't accusing anyone!' It was the last thing I would have thought; they were a bunch of harmless children making fun for themselves.

'We'll get our stuff together, and we'll be out of here,' the boy told me. Everyone appeared to deflate a little.

It was a glorious evening. The youngest of them were only nine or ten years old.

'Stay and have your sausages,' I said. Privately, I was a little impressed by their resourcefulness. 'Leave the place as you found it, that's all I ask. I'll be back to lock the gate in an hour.'

Again, I was looked at as if laying a trap, but thanked eventually.

'You really have nowhere to go?' I said as I turned to leave.

Shrugs all round.

'You could probably pop in,' I said. 'Weekday evenings. If you like? We have a little club of our own. You'd be welcome, I'm sure. Best to use the official entrance, though. If you're looking for something to do? At least till that Ethel Burge centre is . . . fixed.'

Worried I'd made a misjudgement, I ran it past Sethi first thing Monday. He was entirely relaxed on the matter.

'The generation before *us*,' he said whilst he read his post, 'they had no choice but to stand shoulder to shoulder with each other, regardless of their estate. And all were better for it.'

And so, for a few years as it turned out, Steady On Spike's even enjoyed a modest membership from beyond our own boundary.

CARL BRIGHT WAS AN ESPECIALLY MEMORABLE PUPIL. HE WAS CERTAINLY appropriately named. Not only for his academic acuity, but also his sunny demeanour and dazzling yellow hair; each of these attributes could light up a room. Everybody knew who he was. He was in my form group in 1982. I was, by now, spending far more time in the classroom than on the tools; not an official change of role, rather a habit of answering *yes* to Sethi's suggestions.

It was a little before the Easter holidays when Carl went absent. I'll never forget the visit from his parents. They told me he had leukaemia. I was stoic in the face of his desperate parents, but I did weep after they left. A child of eleven! As it happened, he would go on to make a full recovery, but, as one does, I feared the worst at the time.

Treatment would begin over the Easter holiday. I went to see him at home during that time. We watched *Knight Rider* together. He didn't look well at all. But his spirit was undulled; he wanted to return for summer term regardless.

'Will you look out for him?' his mother asked me in their kitchen, shakily pouring tea. 'Will you make sure no one makes him upset about how he looks?'

I promised I'd do my best. The boys at Allonby House were not cruel; I could hardly imagine anyone poking fun. But they may well have—innocently enough—stared and talked, that was the worry.

On that first morning back, I was dreadfully nervous. I had done what I fancied was the best solution, though by the golden light of that late April dawn, I worried my plan may have been ill-judged. I didn't mind the risk of looking a fool, but I couldn't bear to let Carl down.

He was a non-boarder so we arranged to meet in the form room early. The moment he set foot in there, a little colour returned to his complexion. That beaming smile that could only belong to a chap named Bright shone out.

'What have you done, sir?' he asked through giggles.

'I'm afraid I've no idea what you're talking about,' I replied. My straight-faced reply only served to amuse him more.

'You think you'll manage okay?' I asked him once he'd composed himself.

He nodded at me, a little teary now. He was an astute boy; I fancy he understood my thinking.

As always, the school day began with morning prayers, all three hundred boys filing into the hall through the front doors. I made my own entrance deliberately late, in front of most of the assembled staff and pupils. Initially, silence. Maintaining a look of nonchalance (easy enough given that I was petrified) I walked slowly past the lectern in the direction of the masters' seating along the side of the room.

I didn't respond to the giggles. Nor did I allow my eyes to meet those of my colleagues, who stared at me with varying degrees of incredulity. No—I remained unmoved, as if it were in fact all of they who were insane.

The whispers gave way, eventually, to laughter. My own form group, Carl Bright among their number, slipped in entirely unnoticed, as I shot exaggeratedly confused looks towards the many amused faces pointed my way.

It had required a trip some days earlier to Camden Town. Lime-green hair, set in Johnny Rotten spikes, was perhaps not a natural look on me.

But so far as I know, not one person remarked on the boy in the Boston Red Sox cap that barely disguised the bald head beneath; the boy who'd once had such remarkable yellow curls. I'm not so sure anyone really noticed. In any case, he quickly became part of the furniture again.

As for me, the wretched hair dye lasted damned near the whole term, not for the want of washing. I offered to sit out the school photograph that summer, but Sethi wouldn't have it. 'It'll be quite the memento for us all,' he said, reserving me a seat next to his deputy. He was, as ever, absolutely correct.

23

HOW ON EARTH HAD I MANAGED TO FORGET THE SMELL? FLOOR POLISH, powdered pencil lead, cleaning products unique to schools. Smell can take you back somewhere like nothing else, can't it?

'Has it changed much?' Steven asked, hands slung in jeans pockets, peeking around classroom doors as we walked the downstairs corridor.

'I must confess to feeling a little uneasy,' I said.

'It's occasionally necessary for me, during the normal course of my business, to *blend in* somewhere. And do you know what I do, in order to make my presence discreet?'

'Go on.'

'I wear a high-vis vest.'

'Yes, I think I understand what you're saying.' I did my best to loosen up.

'You're a *visitor*,' Steven said, pointing to where that word was printed on the lanyard around my neck. 'Totally legit.'

We'd been checked in at reception by a harassed games master who would barely have been born when I was last here. Steven had signed the visitor log—needless to say—as Leigh Delamere, and on my behalf as Mr Deadman. The car park was solid with Range Rovers and Teslas and the occasional old wreck with gaffer-taped mirrors. The grounds rang with that old Saturday sound: distant boots thwacking against distant balls, the shouted camaraderie of team sports, shrill blasts of whistles, the protestations of wax-jacketed fathers.

'This was my form room,' I said, stopping outside a door with panes of frosted glass. 'Till the mideighties. It got so hot in the summer of '76 that the Formica started melting free of the desks. Lots of windows, see. Boy did we have a laugh about it. "Mine's melting now, sir!" another boy would shout.'

'Go in,' Steven said. 'What they gonna do? Arrest a dead bloke for trespass?'

The room, though essentially the same as it always had been, revealed the limitations of my memory. It was smaller than I'd thought, the wood darker, everything smoother and shinier.

'What have they done to your blackboard?' Steven said.

'Isn't that quite something,' I replied, marvelling at the huge dark rectangle behind the teacher's desk. 'Is that some sort of television set?'

'Sure,' Steven said with a giggle. 'It's a big old flat-screen. No board rubbers to throw at the little shits anymore.'

'There were a few on the staff who went in for that sort of behaviour, I can tell you.'

I perched on the edge of the desk awhile. Had this really been my world? This polished, proper, prestigious place of learning?

'You all right, Uncle Ray?'

It took me a moment to get my breath. 'Yes, yes. Off with the fairies. Sorry.'

We strolled the remainder of the corridor, past rooms where I'd taught history, and science, and provided cover for every other subject.

'This fella looks familiar,' Steven said, stopping at a three-foot-high signed portrait on the wall outside the gymnasium.

'Ah, yes. Wes Lithgo,' I said, standing before that grinning man in his Union Jack sports vest. He was the former pupil of which Allonby House was most proud; an Olympian decathlete.

There'd been posters of him all over the school during his heyday in the eighties.

'Sure I saw him on something on the telly a few weeks back,' Steven said.

'He's still very much doing the rounds. Raises a lot for charity I believe. There's a big part of the school's internet site given over to him.'

'I've no doubt,' he said, face-to-face with Mr Lithgo's likeness. 'Nothing like a great British success story to justify the fees.'

'Indeed.'

'Did you teach him?'

'Not so I recall,' I said. 'It would have been back in the seventies when he was here. I do remember him making waves on the sports field. Hardly my domain, though!'

We continued our tour. 'These were once the dorms, many moons ago,' I explained as we peeked upstairs at state-of-the-art science labs.

When we set foot outside into the grounds, we came face-to-face with a group of boys and girls. This took me aback initially, though I knew they'd been admitting girls for some years now. Their teacher was hauling a netting bag of footballs behind her.

'Good game?' Steven asked.

There were mumbles of discontent.

'You win, or you learn,' Steven said. 'So either way you win.' He winked at their teacher. 'You have yourself a smashing weekend,' he said. I could've sworn I saw her blush.

'You are quite something,' I mumbled to Steven once we'd passed.

He put his hand to his heart. 'Thank you, Uncle Ray. Means a lot.'

There are essentially two types of people: those of us who forever exist a step behind the unfolding of time, always being taken by surprise, at its mercy, reacting; and those who are perpetually a beat of the heart ahead of the present, ready with a line to deliver and the right move to make. Steven, just like his father, was in that latter category.

'So, where to?' he asked.

I squinted as I walked. The sun was low, and what had been easily the warmest day of the year so far was giving way to the damp chill of evening. 'It's still there,' I said. 'The old stores by the west gate.' Up ahead, largely disguised by a fir hedge, were the familiar blockwork walls and corrugated flat roof. The home of the after-school boys' club—of Steady On Spike's. 'There was talk of demolition,' I mused.

Learning fast from my nephew, I operated the door handle without so much as a glance over my shoulder. Steven hit the light switch and the fluorescent tubes plink-plonked to a dull pinkish glow. It smelled damp. The place had been a storeroom before my time, and to that it had returned. Stacks of mouldy gym mats, superseded textbooks, music stands speckled with rust, an arsenal of 1990s Casio keyboards, which had required a fund-raising concert to buy. A last hurrah on the school premises before the final journey to the landfill.

'I wonder what they do for fun now,' I said, rather glumly inspecting the place. Is there any sadder place in the world, I wondered, than somewhere where there used to be laughter?

I gave Steven a rundown of the operation that had once been here.

I stumbled on a pair of craters in the blockwork. 'This is where we had our train set,' I said. Sure enough, there were similar large holes at the same height on all the walls. 'It lapped the full perimeter of the place. Three stations, signal boxes, remote control points, you name it.'

'They were lucky to have you.'

I flicked powdered masonry from one of the hollows. The brackets I'd made had been *hacked* from the wall. Levered off with a crowbar. Why? 'Could they not have at least unscrewed them?' I asked.

'Don't go sweating it,' Steven replied.

'I think maybe we'd best go now.'

Steven looked troubled. 'Look, this is supposed to be about happy memories. I mean, you loved this place. Maybe we could look somewhere . . . else? I reckon we can get away with another twenty minutes before they lock us in.'

My gaze flitted upwards as I turned to leave. There it was, on the ceiling. Ingrained in the building. A legacy of my time. A circle of about four feet in diameter, made up of a fine splatter of black paint. That accident I'd had shaking a paint tin in the summer of '71 that had brought so much merriment; I'd never thought to clean up the ceiling.

'What's wrong, Uncle Ray?' Steven said.

'Nothing.'

'I've fucked up here, haven't I?'

'Oh, not a bit of it. No, I . . . I . . .'

The weight of time past squeezed all the air from my chest. A sudden realisation that all those thousands of long, hard-to-fill days had stacked up to form decades. Decades that had whipped by in a flash.

'Come here, please,' Steven said, arms outstretched.

I found myself without the strength even to cover that small distance. Instead, I buckled at the knees and clung to an old balance beam to stop myself dropping completely.

It seemed unreal. Like I'd fallen asleep all those years ago and was seized by a nightmare, soon to awake, and carry on, and not be this shadow of a man on the eve of eighty.

It was akin to that feeling one gets when opening an old

book, and stumbling upon your own name inside the cover, written there when you were a child, in a prototype of your current handwriting. And it is as though simultaneously a lifetime has passed by, and no time at all. Steven kept asking what was up. I couldn't possibly explain—not without sounding utterly mad.

You see, the great winding sorrow that had overtaken me was that I *couldn't* go back. And yet I was so illogically desperate. Why did all those years have to have *actually* be real?

As Steven led me to back to the car, he kept telling me he was sorry for bringing me here. Dodging the glances of pupils and parents as they themselves left, I reassured him it had been a kind thought, and that I was a stupid old fool. We spoke little on the way home. I dabbed the few tears that eventually came.

'Would you like to come over to me tomorrow?' Steven asked, parked outside my house beneath a lit streetlamp. He was unusually serious.

'Oh, don't you worry about—'

'Uncle Ray, it'll be Sunday roast. That's what families do, I believe. I'd love to have you as my guest.'

'Well, yes I . . .'

'I'll be over for you at three. And I really *am* sorry.'

'You mustn't be,' I said, alighting the car. 'I should be thanking you. I've had a fine day.' Surprisingly perhaps, this was true.

In fact, as I let myself into the dark house, I had that rare feeling of wishing there was someone there still, to tell about the time I'd had.

24

THERE HAD BEEN NO GREAT FALLING-OUT BETWEEN MYSELF AND DENNY AND Junie. As much as it surprised people, I bore no hard feelings about their union.

In early '70, the two of them were at the Eight Bells in the City one night after Junie returned from Chicago the second time. They recognised each other from that ill-fated pre-wedding meet in the Viscount Café. It was just a drink and an exchange of pleasantries. Denny had split from his Portuguese dancer and was enjoying life's pleasures. Junie had taken a sensible job at an estate agent. I learned all this some months later, after Denny offered to take me for a beer. This alone should've made me suspicious; he made little time to see either Mum or me. He told me he wouldn't go with Junie if it would upset me. I said my permission was hardly necessary. But he insisted, and I gave it. Imagine what Junie would've thought of me if I'd said no! And who would I be to deny my own brother happiness? Denny was good-looking and charming and urbane; of course, Junie would go for someone like him. And as Denny kept saying with genuine surprise: 'She's a sort, *and* she's got a brain on her!' They would make a fine couple, no question. Yes, ugly jealousy gnawed away at me. But I was excited too, at the knowledge she was back around, her existence if only at the periphery of my own.

It wasn't till a year later that I encountered them as a couple. Hackney Town Hall in the summer of '72, where they were married. At twenty-seven and twenty-eight, they were, I suppose, at risk of being left on the shelf.

Denny asked me to be a witness. He rented me a nice suit from Moss Bros. Though he was adamant that I should simply enjoy myself, I took the job very seriously: I ensured that the day ran to an itinerary, of which I'd produced several drafts. The guests were seated a full fifteen minutes before Junie's arrival, split depending on family allegiance and each person's position deliberated over at length. Everyone was briefed on how to reach the Duke's Head half a mile away, the room above which was host to the wedding breakfast. Taxis were booked for those of a certain age and, list in hand, I directed each cab to a stop and escorted the passengers. What with the necessity of seeing to Mum as well, who was struggling with fatigue and requiring an arm to lean on, I was extremely busy throughout.

With memories of planning my own wedding four years earlier, it was somewhat surprising that Mum hadn't involved herself in the arrangements at all. She had little to say on the matter of it taking place outside church (let alone *her* church, which she'd been so keen on for Junie and me). Nor did she offer her wedding dress this second time around; Mum in fact said how chic Junie looked in the little maroon number she wore.

A handful of family on Junie's side fussed about my well-being and watched me from corners of eyes. There was no need. Reverend Rudolph Burnham, Junie's father, sought me out for a chat, though I had no choice but to be brief what with all my duties.

The wedding breakfast ended at five. Denny left soon after for another pub to celebrate with his pals (I was kindly invited but declined—much still to do). Junie and her mother cleared away the cake and presents from the function room. It was only then that I found myself face-to-face with Junie. How strange that two people once so close can both find themselves at a loss for what to say.

'Wishing you well,' I told her, with utmost sincerity.

'Thank you for coming,' she replied.

'My brother's wedding!' I remarked. 'I hardly need thanking like I'm some common or garden . . .'

'Thank you,' she told me again. 'You didn't need to come alone.'

I chortled and pointed a thumb across the room towards Mum.

'Who are you with now?' she asked.

I found myself a little stumped—that she'd assumed there was somebody. It took some time to make things clear. She kept insisting that I must be with *someone*. Her incredulity at my singledom became a touch awkward. Hadn't Denny mentioned there was no one *special* in my life?

'I'm jolly happy for you both,' I said. I was at something of a loss for what to do with my wretched hands as we spoke.

'You've enjoyed yourself? It hasn't been . . . I'd never forgive myself if I thought you'd—'

'I've had a ball. Not sure I'll know what to do with myself tomorrow, without this to organise.'

Junie grinned. 'Every time I've clapped eyes on you today, you've had your clipboard with you.'

'It's gone off a treat, I'd say.'

Junie nodded. 'You look like you're really enjoying life. You look . . . good. It's a lovely thing to see.'

'Yes, well, steady . . .' It was only later that I realised—crass fool that I am—that I didn't compliment *her* appearance.

'It's great to see you again, Ray.'

Isn't it funny how the sound of your own name from one person's mouth can be the most intimate thing in the world?

'Indeed,' I replied. 'Likewise.'

I turned on my heel. I was expecting to find Mum sitting by

the exit where she'd been since shortly after the cake was served. She was instead in an animated conversation with a cousin of Junie's. But I'd turned my back on Junie already, and we each returned to our business.

They set up home in Harrow. Mum and I saw them infrequently, though from what I did see life was treating them well during those early years. Childless and often promoted, they took foreign holidays, owned a brace of new cars, and ate at good restaurants.

They'd been married six years when Steven arrived. Mum and I were invited over to meet the new addition. The visit was one of those events that doesn't necessarily feel like a disaster at the time, but that comes to be regarded as such on reflection. It was the last time Mum set foot in their house.

The baby was asleep when we arrived. Denny and Junie had a shell-shocked look about them.

'Let me just take a peek,' Mum said, placing her foot on the lowest stair and passing the bulging bag of presents to me.

Junie glared at Denny, but snapped away when she noticed me looking.

'Yeah, Mum, let him have a bit of kip,' he said.

'He shan't even know I'm there,' Mum said. The stair groaned as her high heel pressed onto it.

Junie turned her back.

'Later, Mum,' Denny said, barring her way with an arm extended beneath the balustrade. 'It's quite a job to get him off. We should probably ask the doctor about it.'

'Oh nonsense,' Mum said, aborting her climb. 'I can tell you exactly how it's all done.'

Junie smiled. 'I'm sure you had two boys who slept fine. But I don't know if that makes you an expert on *all* children.' The barbs on the words seemed accidental.

As he led us into the living room, Denny confided to Mum

REPORTS OF HIS DEATH HAVE BEEN GREATLY EXAGGERATED

and me that he was rather in the doghouse: 'I've been going out to wet the baby's head a tad too often,' he explained.

Mum cast a look in my direction once we were seated by way of instruction.

'Fucking hell, Ray,' Denny mumbled as I knelt before her and gently removed her shoes.

'Back pain,' I explained to him. 'It's a struggle for her to . . .'

'Chronic,' Mum added. 'Thank you, my darling,' she whispered to me as I set them neatly aside.

They were good hosts. Denny was especially doting, fetching us tea and snacks, and brandy for him and Mum to toast the baby.

'The house looks marvellous,' I told Junie and Denny. 'So modern!'

'A labour of love,' Denny said, springing into action and showing off the alterations made. 'Knock through lounge,' he said, standing where once a wall did. 'Wall-to-wall carpets.' He ran a foot along the neat meeting of skirting board and brown nylon.

'I quite liked the parquet floor,' Junie said.

'Nah, this is luxury underfoot. And *warm*. Ripped out the old fireplaces. You know they dated back to the Victorians? Ancient!'

'They were pretty,' Junie said. 'But we didn't let that get in the way.'

'They were draughty,' Denny explained. 'Place was old-fashioned.'

'You've made a remarkable job,' I said.

'That's nice of you to say,' Junie said.

'It must've cost a fortune,' I added.

'Not 'alf,' Denny said proudly.

'More than the neighbours have spent on theirs, eh, Den?' Junie said.

'There are cracks showing,' Mum said, having raised her eyes to the ceiling around the knock-through.

'Shrinkage and expansion,' I said lightly, fancying I was the buildings expert here. It was a shame that Mum had to find that one glaring error in an otherwise smart renovation. 'I may have a little filler in the van I could leave you,' I offered. With the old MG still up at the school, I was getting about in an ageing Ford van. The load space had become brim-full with things I'd found in skips and junk shops. It was a habit that had spread to the shed at home, though not yet the house. I certainly *did* have some filler on board, assuming I could find it.

'Don't worry yourself,' Junie said, smiling properly for the first time.

Denny fussed over a spread of cold cuts and sandwiches. It seemed he'd been involved in its preparation and he was proud of it. He picked out a selection for Mum, though she was less than profuse in her thanks.

I felt sorry for my brother. It'd not struck me before how keen he was to please. To impress. Had it been me providing Mum a plate of food at home, she'd have been overly thankful if anything.

I'd always thought of him as a show-off, but I could see now that was unkind. He'd been closer than me to our father, and after he left Denny didn't have Mum's constant attention as I did. Was that why he so needed the respect of men in pubs, why he'd always courted the attention of women, why he'd famously hired that Aston Martin for his school reunion, even?

My own praise for his buffet was fulsome, even if he had been heavy-handed with the butter.

Steven finally awoke and Junie brought him down to join us. Mum set her food aside and took him in her arms. He immediately began to scream the house down. Junie took him back and calmed him. So began a dance: the month-old baby switching every few minutes between contentedness in his mother's arms and making a racket in his grandmother's. It was funny to begin with; Denny and I exchanged smirks.

After a time, Mum scooped Steven from Junie and began to sing a Billie Holiday number, carrying him off with her to the kitchen.

'Just give it a moment,' Denny said to Junie as she attempted to follow, looking distressed. 'Sit down and relax.'

The crying continued from the other room. We sat in tense silence. Eventually, Junie shot to her feet looking red-faced and furious. She shouted at Mum to return.

'I don't think he even knows who I am,' Mum said crossly as Junie soothed Steven. 'Does he know who I am?'

Once peace had returned, I was offered to hold him. I declined.

'It's okay,' Junie said to me more than once. 'I do understand, Ray.'

Yes, there were thoughts of our own child. How could there not be? But this was not why I didn't hold him. It's simply that I've never been a natural with babies, and I most certainly didn't wish to take away time that Mum could've had with her grandson.

When it came to leaving, Junie whispered 'thank you' into my ear. She hugged me. I had a sense of ten years of my life being undone.

IT TOOK LONGER THAN THE DRIVE BACK HOME FOR MUM'S OPINION OF JUNIE to crystallise. She made the comment several times that Junie was not content with taking one of her boys (me), she had to have her other son, as well. This became a refrain in the years that followed. 'You had a lucky escape there, my dear,' she would sometimes comment.

There were invitations to Mum and me for a Christmas or two. 'I'm not going north of the river,' was Mum's standard reply. Leaving her by herself was out of the question, though she always told me I should go.

I didn't have a policy as such to avoid them myself. But, as time wore on after that first meeting with young Steven, the idea of seeing them in their family home did bring with it an unexplained panic. I tended to drop Christmas presents round for them all, though I always ensured no car was on the drive before depositing them at the doorstep, with a promise to myself that I'd knock and say *hi* next time. It would be some years before the cruellest of fates would bring us together once again.

IT WAS THE DAY AFTER WE RETURNED FROM HOLIDAY WHEN IT HAPPENED. The summer of '85. When I think about it all, I always go back to that last evening Mum and I were away. She was so happy. I don't understand it. I never have.

We were at the Hydro in Hove. We'd been staying there annually for some time. Historically it had been an indulgence afforded us by Mum's cousin's estate, though that had eventually run dry. I was now earning close to a full teacher's salary; it was the absolute least I could do.

'Another bottle of the sparkling Chardonnay?' a stiff young waiter in a bowtie asked.

'Shall we, hubby?' Mum said. We smiled at each other.

'As the lady wishes,' I said, rather without conviction.

'Please. He spoils me rotten,' she said, her hand on the waiter's set-square forearm. 'That's why I snapped him up!'

This had been a running joke between us since we'd arrived three days ago. Regulars to the hotel though we were, we'd not previously met Shona, the crinkly-haired young lady on reception. She had assumed on sight that we—Mr and Mrs Thorns—were a married couple. We had played along with the charade as long as it had taken to escort us to our conjoined rooms. Shona was dreadfully embarrassed! She needn't have been: Mum at sixty-five was immaculately made-up and dressed in Jaeger; at forty I was already greying, balding, and worn from summer term. It was a simple mistake that had brought joy to Mum; who was I to not play along?

'Isn't this just bliss?' Mum remarked, gazing out of the dining room window to the twilit beach below. A jet ski tore to and fro and I enjoyed a second-hand exhilaration at the sight; in a different life perhaps it might have been my kind of fun.

Nodding, I washed down the last of my steak with a gulp of wine. Mum as ever ate slowly, two-thirds of her chicken main still on her plate, diced by her into perfect cubes. We were at our usual table, reserved for both breakfast and dinner for the duration of every stay.

A booming laugh came from the bar. Mum and I smirked. It was a gentleman we'd been chatting to earlier. He'd generously bought us both a Gin and It 'on the tab'. He was a big, tan man with the arms of a jersey draped over his shoulders and signet rings on cigar fingers. Named Gordon, he'd told us all about his holiday home *portfolio*. 'There goes our gawdy Gordon,' Mum said with a wicked sparkle in her eyes.

'You're terrible,' I said, quietly.

'You were loving the nonsense he was talking too.'

'I'm not sure you needed to encourage him quite so much. You needn't have looked so . . . impressed.'

'What a great buffoon!'

I stifled my laughter and shushed her. My mother had reached a point in life, by her own admission, where she no longer cared what people overheard her saying.

We'd had a fine holiday. The perpetual sunshine and warm

coastal breezes had quelled Mum's health worries: there had been no instances of the chest pains that so often landed us in casualty of an evening back at home, nor any of the unexplained breathlessness that left her immobile some days. She'd managed just fine dressing herself and had needed no assistance with the bath. We'd shopped in Brighton's Lanes, *promenaded* arm-in-arm along Hove's lawns with ice creams in hand, even made a trip to a blustery Beachy Head.

'The twentieth of July,' I said to Mum. 'I wonder if Steven's having a good birthday.'

Mum slid her half-filled plate over to me and lit a Silk Cut. 'Oh, I'm sure. Seven is a lovely age.' She looked out of the window as she said it with a quick smile.

'I hope he got our card on time.'

'We sent it with days to spare. If he hasn't got it, there'll be only one reason.' She exhaled her smoke noisily. 'There was five pounds in there.'

I nodded, terribly guilty that in fact I'd removed the fiver before posting, and replaced it with a twenty. It was devious behaviour and felt now like a slight on Mum's generosity. A few weeks earlier I'd seen in a shop window a Peugeot mountain bicycle with five gears; I had so wished that I could've nipped in and bought it for my nephew. The truth was I had no idea whether or not he already *had* a nice bike.

'Motor racing–themed party,' I said. 'I bet he's in his element.'

'They saw their way to inviting *you*?'

'I'm sure I told you,' I lied.

'Don't let me get in your way.'

'We'd already booked this! I mean, not that I suppose I'd have gone even so, but . . .' I'd only have found myself another excuse anyway.

Mum shook her head, dismissing the subject.

'Cheers, my darling,' Mum said, raising her glass of port

and brandy. She smiled and jetted smoke up to the ceiling. She looked so relaxed. So *content*.

Coffees were brought to the table, together with a slice of gateau for me and another port and brandy for Mum.

'Isn't this the life?' she said.

I swear to it: those were her exact words.

I've scrutinized the memory so many times. Did she really *mean* it? Could I have missed something?

The two of us had spent so much joyful time together in eateries, going back as far as our *dates* in the Viscount when I was eight years old. I hadn't the first clue this would be the last time.

'I should speak to the hotel,' I said. 'Get a date in the diary for next year. You know how early they get booked up.'

Mum, without hesitation, thought this a fine idea. On our way back to our rooms, we stopped at reception and spoke to Shona. We all joked once again about us being a married couple. A reservation for Mr and Mrs Thorns was made for the same week the next year.

TWO DAYS LATER. THE WORST DAY OF MY LIFE. I'D SPENT A MORNING UP AT the school, catching up on things whilst the boys were off on their summer holiday. That Mum was yet to rise when I returned didn't alarm me. There were days (and they were *very* occasional) when she wouldn't emerge till the early evening. 'A touch short on vim!'—that's how she'd previously explained such late risings.

So I didn't check on her till mid-afternoon. The tea I'd taken her at seven in the morning was where I'd left it, a milky swirl resting on the top.

I whispered in her ear a few times. Squeezed her hand. Her cold, cold hand.

For a time, I lapped the house in something of a trance, periodically returning to her bedside. Eventually I called the doctor.

'What can I do for you, Ray?' he asked, sounding like a man tiring of me. We had cause to speak most weeks.

'It's Mum,' I said.

'I've no doubt,' he replied.

'I think it might be her heart,' I told him.

'Are you all right, Ray? You don't sound quite your usual . . .'

'I'm okay, thank you. It's Mum.'

'Ray, might I speak to her?'

'No, I don't think she's able . . . . She's . . . asleep just now.'

'I need to call you an ambulance, don't I, Ray?'

The telephone receiver was shaking violently against my head; I just couldn't keep the wretched thing still.

'It might be nothing,' I tried to tell the doctor. 'Perhaps I'm being . . . silly.'

'Sit down, Ray. Deep breaths, there's a good lad. I'll be right with you.'

An ambulance was sent. The doctor followed along too.

It had happened many hours earlier, he told me after they'd taken Mum away. It wasn't her heart, he explained. Not this time.

'You weren't to know,' he said. 'There's nothing you could've done.'

Could I have done something? She must've been so desperate. Should I have noticed? Treated her with more care?

Was her happiness an act? It never, ever seemed so. I'm certain of it. Was she simply too kind, too adamant not to put upon anyone?

What was she thinking?

I don't know.

I don't know.

I *still* don't know.

We buried her a week later. They played 'Blue Moon' by Billie Holiday. I took to the lectern and read that poem by Henry Scott Holland, about just slipping away to the next room.

'I'M TERRIBLY SORRY FOR YOUR LOSS, RAY,' JUNIE SAID TO ME IN THE KITCHEN.

'I'm sure we've some decaffeinated coffee somewhere,' I said. It's a sentiment I've never been sure how to respond to. In a fluster, I knocked over half the contents of the cupboard, and this was when everything about the house was still ship-shape.

'They'll live without it,' Junie said, her hand on my back making me stop dead still.

There was a gentle hubbub of chatter from the living room and the rattling lid of boiling tea urn. The house smelt pleasantly of buffet; Italian Tony from the Viscount had happily taken the catering gig (now a distinguished silver man of sixty), though it was clear I'd ordered for far too many mourners.

'Everyone seems to be enjoying themselves,' I said. 'Not *enjoying* themselves per se, but . . . satisfied, I think.'

'You've laid on a lovely spread. And the house all looks just so. You've done your mum proud, Ray.'

I smiled at this. Mum did like a good wake. She could never bear to go to funerals, found them too sad, but always would be along for the wake. 'People have travelled,' I said. 'A light lunch is the least I can do.'

'And would you say that you're doing okay?'

'Oh, yes. As much as, as much as. A little busy. Administrative business.' I found it very tricky to look at Junie whilst speaking to her. Now forty years of age there was something so mature and efficient about her. It was hard to imagine we'd once been something close to equals.

'Have you eaten, Ray? You should. You're shaking.'

'A good hearty breakfast, yes. Just the ticket.'

'Perhaps you should take it a little easy. Everything's going just fine.'

'That's good to hear.'

Junie leant around the door and requested someone pour me a sweet tea.

'I hear you spoke to my father,' she said.

'It was incredibly kind of him to telephone.' It had been a stilted conversation, despite him sounding very much like his old self. We'd not properly spoken in some eighteen years; I suppose that was the problem. He said nice things about Mum. And he kept telling me that it was okay to be angry. He said that was important. Not to forget that, he said.

'Denny, Steven, and I,' Junie said, 'we're your family. And we want to support you. We never see you, Ray!'

'Thank you, but everything's all under control.'

'Let us help. You're clearly coping admirably, but—'

I found myself chuckling. 'Yes, well. As much as. Getting on with things.'

'I could come over and help with your mum's things? Sort out her room, that sort of thing. If you don't think it an imposition? It really might take a little weight off.'

'Oh, you've better things to do! No, I'll have it done in a jiffy. Two jiffies, perhaps!'

I had already broken a wish of Mum's. She had periodically said to me in recent years that after she'd popped her clogs I wasn't to let Junie ('That bloody wife of Denny's' as she had become known) in the house. It was said always with a laugh, but never in jest.

'It makes me sad that we hardly ever see you, Ray,' Junie said. 'This could be a fresh start. A chance to forget about . . . the past.'

'Forget about what?' I quipped, a moment too late for it to be funny.

'Our door is always open,' she said.

Again, a moment too late for comic timing, I retorted: 'Gosh, your heating bill must be horrendous!' It was clear humour wasn't the thing. 'That's awfully kind,' I said. 'It really is, and . . .'

We were mercifully interrupted by the appearance of the seven-year-old Steven.

'Mummy, you seen Uncle Ray's old car?'

'Not for many moons,' Junie said with a grin.

'It's well cool!' He skipped a lap of the kitchen.

The MG was by now fully restored, better than new, and back home once more.

'I've been meaning to carry out a check of all the lights and the horn,' I told him. 'Perhaps you could help me with that.'

'Already tried all the switches,' he said.

'And all seemed well?'

'I think so.'

'That's a load off my mind. Thank you. We should probably start her up too, make sure the oil pressure's good.'

Steven jumped on the spot. 'Yeah!' he said. 'Let me do it.'

'Who else?' I said, following him to the garage.

Junie tapped my arm as I walked away. 'Think about it,' she said.

'Of course,' I replied, nodding profusely.

That was the last time the two of us spoke.

25

SUNDAY

I FOUND MYSELF THINKING A GREAT DEAL ABOUT STEVEN.

I'm ashamed to confess that, after Mum's wake, I didn't see him for a long while. There was a generous enclosure in every birthday and Christmas card I sent, but I knew even at the time that it was a poor substitute for being present in his life. And so, when the doorbell went one wet summer's afternoon in the midnineties, I almost didn't recognise the seventeen-year-old standing there, lanky and baggily dressed.

'All right, Uncle Ray,' he said, as though we'd seen each other only last week.

I rather played along with the spirit of familiarity, inviting him in to disguise my awkwardness.

'Was just in the area,' he told me. 'Trip to the deep south, innit! Thought I'd say hi.' He spoke in that energetic, rasping way so common to boys not long out of puberty.

'How's . . . school?' I asked, putting on tea.

'Ah, don't bust my balls, but I'm calling it a day. Gave sixth form a year, but I'm done with it.'

'I suppose it's not for everybody. So what's the plan from here on in? College, an apprenticeship perhaps?'

'All in good time, Unc. Don't you fret.'

'You'll work it out, I'm sure.'

I turned, looking for biscuits in something of a fluster. His gaze was flitting all around the kitchen and the hallway. He froze when he realised I was looking at him. I turned away, sparing his blushes, though I had noticed something wasn't right about his appearance. The sheen about his hair and complexion was something more than just hormonal excesses. His clothes had that crumpled, slept-in look about them.

'So how are Mum and Dad?' It was just small talk, though I felt a flutter of nerves.

'Same old, same old. You know what they're like.'

I mumbled in agreement, though I had no idea. It'd been ten years since I'd seen them.

'Mum's still a bit sad, I guess. Pretends she isn't. Since Grandad . . .' He did a somewhat distasteful mime of a man dying.

It took me a moment to assemble the family tree, to realise to whom Steven referred. 'Junie's father?' I said. 'Rudolph? The vicar?'

'Been ill for yonks. Cancer. Think they said cancer.'

'Gosh, that's awful news,' I said, passing him a tea in the largest mug I owned. 'That's quite taken the wind out of my sails.' I shook my head at this tragedy. Not to mention the silliness of my distance from his parents that meant such a thing could happen without my being informed.

'He was a tremendous man,' I said.

'He reckoned he was ready to—you know—*go*.'

I fetched myself a chair from the front room as Steven had the stool. 'Your parents must be devastated.'

'Dad not so much. Says Grandad's bothering God in person now.'

'Reverend Burnham was a jolly decent fellow,' I said, hollow at the thought of just how much I'd looked up to him.

Steven had necked two-thirds of his tea and was fiddling with a cigarette paper.

'You've come quite a distance,' I said. 'Perhaps you'd like something to eat?'

'I could go a bit of nosebag, sure. That's kind of you, Uncle Ray.'

'Bacon, eggs, and sausages?'

'You're a diamond, you know that? Sorry to ask, but don't suppose you've got a bit of baccy lying around?'

'I'm afraid you're out of luck. My smoking habit was limited to a weekly cigar with my old headteacher. But since he retired last year, I've been—'

'I'll live,' Steven said, crumpling the paper into a ball and jiggling where he sat.

'You're welcome to use the phone,' I said, firing the stove. 'Let your parents know where you are. I could even drive you back there after we've eaten if you like. Not in the old MG I'm afraid, but I've a van for running—'

'It's fine, Uncle Ray,' he said, jollity back in his voice. 'A bit of grub would be magic. Then I'll be out of your hair.'

'You might like to take the opportunity to freshen up?' I hoped the offer didn't sound loaded. 'A quick shower? Perhaps a bath if you like? Whilst I'm cooking.'

'Yes, Uncle Ray! I think I'll do exactly that.'

Whilst he was upstairs, I began preparing something of a feast; it was a pleasure to have another hungry mouth to feed. Baked beans, fried bread, some chipped potatoes, a five-egg scrambled, mushrooms with a dash of cream, you name it! He'd been gone a few minutes when it occurred to me to dig him out a fresh towel.

The bathtub was filled but unoccupied. The door to Mum's room was ajar. I stepped gingerly inside. Cool air, still with a note of her perfume a decade on.

'Steven, I said. 'Now, I can't imagine what reason—'

'Just having a wander round.' He thrust his right hand into his pocket. 'Sorry, I'm a bit nosey. Curious, you know . . .'

From the far side of her bed, I glanced at the little dish of rings on her dressing table. It was there that his hand had been hovering till a moment ago. There were six rings that she wore regularly, and that is where they lived by night. And now there were five. No surprise that it was the two-thirds carat diamond engagement ring—the one legacy of my father—missing.

'I'm going to return to the kitchen, Steven. In my absence, I shall trust you to return anything that you might have accidentally picked up whilst looking around.'

'I wasn't trying . . . I was just sort of . . . Look—'

'Dinner will be ready in twenty minutes. You get in that bath before it gets cold. You're a decent lad. I know you'll leave things as you found them.'

We ate, kept from silence only by the rhythmic splash of his tracksuit and T-shirt in the washing machine.

'You've got yourself into a little trouble, haven't you?' I eventually said.

He shrugged but didn't look up from his shovelling of food.

'Maybe you'd feel better telling me about it?'

Another shrug, something mumbled.

'You're always welcome here. Please know that.'

'Cheers,' he said. He appeared to struggle swallowing his beans. It was the most serious I'd seen him.

'So, you're short of money?'

'A bit.'

'Do your folks know?'

He shook his head and snorted incredulously.

'Well, they have a lot on the plate. A bereavement can leave people at sixes and sevens.'

'Yeah,' he replied. A whiff of sarcasm.

'You owe somebody?'

He nodded.

'What are we talking?'

'Dunno. Two hundred quid. Two-fifty maybe.'

This was a relief. He'd nearly made off with something of my mother's insured for ten-times that. He probably had no clue of its value.

'And would you be offended if I offered to settle this debt for you?'

'Why would I be *offended*?'

'I suppose not everyone's comfortable with charity.'

'I'll pay you back as soon as I can. I promise.'

'There won't be any need. I'm pleased you've felt able to come to me.'

'I didn't come for money. I just . . . I'm sorry, I don't know why—'

I held up a palm. 'Desperate times. I understand. I think I've enough cash at home. Are you able to tell me to whom it is owed?'

'Been getting a bit too much on tick, that's all.'

'We're talking . . . drugs?'

Steven stiffened at the word.

'There's no need to fear being honest with me,' I said.

'A bit of smoke. Weed, nothing else.'

I nodded, unsurprised. There had been a rather pleasant whiff of marijuana about his clothes when I'd bundled them into the machine. 'I would suggest these are not people you want to be owing money to.'

'We're not talking actual *drug dealers*,' he said, doing quotation marks in the air. 'Just mates who sell a bit.'

'Right. Let me run you back home after dinner, and you can clear your account first thing.'

He glanced down at the jersey of mine I'd loaned him.

'As soon as your clothes are done in the dryer, then,' I conceded.

'I'm not really . . . *living* at home at the moment.'

'They've not thrown you out?'

'Not *officially*.'

'Where have you been staying?'

He stared into his plate, which he'd mopped to a shine with a slice of buttered bread. 'A mate,' he mumbled.

'I'll take you back there then. He's in your neck of the woods?'

'It's all a bit of a fuck-up,' he said, arms flopping to his side. 'I kinda got myself thrown out of theirs too. I know, I know, what a fucking loser.'

'What is wrong with people?'

'What's wrong with *me*—I think that's the question. Everyone's had a skinful of me.'

I considered logistics for a moment: Mum's bedroom was definitely out, the other small bedroom was filled to the ceiling. 'Would you like to stay here? It would have to be the sofa. And I'd insist upon you telling your parents you're safe. But you are most welcome.'

Evidently something was troubling him as he mulled over the offer. 'Nah,' he eventually said. 'Cheers anyway, Uncle Ray. I want to try going back to my mate's. Make up, you know?'

It was to a rather smart detached house that I drove Steven later that evening. He'd tried to hide it, but he was nervy all the way there: large gulping swallows, a pale greyness around the eyes. He was out of the van in a flash when I stopped at the mouth of that generous driveway; striding with mock confidence to the front door.

I'm not sure why I chose to do so, but I lapped the block and returned, parking a few car lengths from their house. I had a *vibe*, as a youngster might say. Steven had not yet made it inside the house. A discussion was going on with whoever was in the hallway. The body language on display suggested it was less than friendly. Then came the shouting. Steven at first: demanding to be let in so he could 'just explain'. A terrible torrent of expletives from the woman of the house. And then a man stepped outside, grabbed Steven firmly by the shoulder and marched him off the premises.

'I just want to talk,' Steven kept saying. He had begun to cry.

I started the engine and drove to level with them. 'Let's take you home, Steven,' I said through the opened passenger window.

'Are you his father?' the man asked.

'No, no,' I said. 'Just a concerned uncle.'

'You want to keep him away from my . . . *child*,' the woman said.

'Steady on, steady on. I'm sure this can all be resolved amicably.'

'Just let me inside,' Steven said, fully sobbing now. 'For a few minutes? *Please!*'

'I suggest you take him away,' the father said.

'What can possibly have happened?' I asked.

Steven stared towards an upstairs window. 'Please!' he yelled. 'I need to see you.'

'God help me,' the mother said, 'if you don't get this grubby little . . . bastard away from our house.'

'I fancy that's the best thing for everyone,' I said, making firm eye contact with her. She snatched her top across her chest.

He kept telling me he was sorry as we drove into the blue evening.

'First love,' I mumbled.

Steven shrugged, but it was clear now: he was a man obsessed, his entire sense of self at the mercy of another's whims.

'What on earth's got into her parents?' I asked.

'It's complicated,' was all he said.

'You need to be back with your mother, don't you?' I said. Steven nodded and gave me directions once we were close.

'Be sure to settle those debts,' I said, parked several houses down from Junie and Denny's.

'Sure. I'm really grateful, you know,' he said, noisily sniffing. 'Sorry, I know I'm a stupid arsehole and I—'

I held up a hand. 'What are your plans for the rest of the week?'

He shook his head. 'Jack shit.'

'I've a job on, over the summer holidays. It's for my former headmaster, Charles Sethi. I'm converting his double garage into a snooker room. I've bitten off more than I can chew if I'm honest. I could really use another pair of hands. It's a paying job of course.'

'Yeah, why not,' Steven said, in the rueful manner of someone with nothing left to lose.

'Say, fifty quid a day?'

This perked him up a little. 'Where do I need to get to?'

'I'll pick you up from home. Well, let's say the end of the road. 6:30 a.m. to miss the traffic. You can bear that?'

'No sweat.'

'Could I ask a favour?' I said as he was stepping out of the van. 'Would you mind dreadfully not telling your mum and dad that you've seen me?'

To my immense relief he gave me a thumbs-up and made no scene about this rather odd request.

Rather to my surprise, he was waiting for me the next morning. The pair of us made light work of the job over the next fortnight. He was the best labourer I ever had. As I gained an education (whether I liked it or not) in The Prodigy and Cypress Hill to name but two, Steven became proficient in first-fix wiring, laying blocks, and basic woodwork. It was as a plasterer that he really excelled; a notoriously tricky skill to master yet he was putting my efforts to shame as a mere beginner.

'I'M ACTUALLY REALLY SAD THIS IS FINISHED,' STEVEN SAID, AS HE, CHARLES Sethi, and I enjoyed a topping-out beer and cigar. I was due back at school in a week, with no other building jobs on the horizon.

'Perhaps you should be thinking about a career in this,' I said.

'It seems your calling,' Sethi seconded. 'There's no shame in working with one's hands. Quite the opposite, in fact.'

'It's crossed my mind,' Steven said with a smile. He was almost unrecognisable from the lad he'd been two weeks earlier: relaxed, focussed, tanned, and healthy-looking.

I took him to Davy's Hardware, an Aladdin's cave of a shop over whose counter much of my hard-earned had migrated over the years. It was my great pleasure to treat him to a tool bag packed with all the basics, and much besides. 'Life is easiest when one has a tool for every job,' I told him.

He called me a few weeks into term. He'd got a late enrolment into a technical college on a construction course. I was ecstatic. He said he was all right for money but, rather crassly, I insisted on having his bank account number in order that I could provide him a small monthly *sub*, enough to keep that arsenal of tools growing if nothing else. We spoke every few weeks on the phone for a while. Steven was getting on very well indeed.

It was the following summer when I let him down. His eighteenth was a month away, he said when he called. A party was planned. Junie and Denny had booked a sports club. Food, free bar, disc jockey, all his college pals. He was insistent I come, that I 'throw some shapes' on the dance floor. I said I'd go and I didn't. I couldn't.

It wasn't his nature to hold it against me, though our phone calls became sporadic. On the occasions we did speak, I had a strong inkling his enthusiasm for college had waned. Eventually, our conversations were no more.

I had only myself to blame.

26

'I HOPE YOU'RE HUNGRY?' STEVEN ASKED.

'Famished,' I said, riding once again in his flash Mercedes.

'Fore-rib of beef. Stilton and port gravy.'

'Stop it!' Nerves had kept me from food all day, but it was gone four now and my mouth was watering at the thought. 'No longer a North London boy?' I asked. Having been on the road an hour, we were free of the city limits, weaving through the lanes of Hertfordshire.

'I appreciate the quiet life these days,' he said. 'All the old gits together.' It was easy to forget he was a man of forty-six.

We turned onto a narrow track with high banks to either side. At the end was a grand farmhouse with flint walls and a vast glass extension wrapped around the sides and rear.

'This is . . . yours?' I asked as we crunched to a stop in front of a canary-yellow front door. 'It's stunning. And . . . enormous.'

'I've been kind of lucky,' he said, with unusual modesty. 'I'm glad you like it.'

We stepped into a hallway big enough for its own three-piece suite (in fuchsia pink, no less!). The house smelt of charred logs, and clean linen, and roasting Yorkshire pudding. A Siamese cat studied me from the mezzanine above. Steven took my coat and flung it over the banister.

'Bloody thing,' he said, elbowing a grandfather clock whose dial was jammed at twelve o'clock.

'Early Georgian,' I said. 'Jolly nice indeed.'

'Look, I promise this isn't why I invited you over, but you wouldn't mind taking a look as some point?'

'The least I can do,' I replied. I was instantly more relaxed. It had been a long time since I'd been a dinner guest of anyone's, but I had always been most comfortable when able to find something about the host's home that I could fix during my visit.

'Also, there's a body in the barn. If you wouldn't mind helping me . . .'

'Yes, very good,' I said, following him into a kitchen worthy of a TV chef.

'Hello, hello!' said a gentleman, tending a tray of roast potatoes. He tossed his oven glove to one side and dashed over to me. 'Stevo insisted I call you *Spike*, but I'm going to settle for Ray until I'm told otherwise.' He shook my hand in both of his. 'I'm Kwan. What a pleasure to meet you.'

'Indeed, yes,' I replied, keen not to look at all confused.

'Stevo speaks very highly of you. I was relieved myself when I heard you were actually *un*dead.' He roared with laughter at this.

Steven winked at me and grinned.

'Sorry, I'm a bad man,' Kwan said. 'Let us fix you a drink. When are we thinking of eating?'

'I'm in your hands,' I replied. 'It smells marvellous.'

'Where's the hurry,' Steven said. There was a pop of champagne cork and he made a grab for a flute. 'I think bubbles are called for. Now, I bet you didn't think I'd have my own private chef did you, Uncle Ray?' He jabbed Kwan in the ribs.

'Gosh, right. Really?'

'Yup. I mean, he's a bit of a wanker, but at least he's cheap.'

I smirked awkwardly. 'You're . . . friends, I take it.'

'I wouldn't go that far,' Kwan said, taking Steven's champagne glass and returning to his stove.

'Kwan's my fiancé, Uncle Ray,' Steven said.

'Oh, right. Gosh. Great! I didn't realise . . . well. Wonderful! I—'

Steven watched me with a smirk. 'It's fine, Uncle Ray.'

'I'm very pleased for you. Really pleased.'

'I know you are. I can see. And thank you.'

'So, how long have you chaps been . . .'

'Three years in April,' Kwan said. 'And we're getting married later this year.'

I instinctively raised my glass and they both clinked theirs to mine.

'September,' Steven said. 'In Nice. Just a few close friends and family. There'll be an invitation landing on your doormat very soon.'

'Right. Wow. That's . . . incredible. Of course, I don't have a passport. I only ever had one and that expired back in, gosh . . . But I suppose I could *apply*.'

'Probably best we sort out the whole *deceased* business first.'

'Yes,' I said, returning to earth. 'We must talk about that.'

'We'll get round to it, no sweat,' Steven said, glugging more champagne into our glasses.

'We really would like you to come, though,' Kwan said. 'It would mean a lot.'

'In that case, well . . . I suppose I'll have to give it . . . I'm very touched to be asked.' A flashback to all those refused invitations to family dos, to Steven's eighteenth. 'But of course, yes! Whyever not?'

Steven laid a hand on my shoulder. 'Lots to take in, I know. I've put you on the spot. No need to RSVP right now. Come on, I'll show you round the place.'

The house was magnificent. Four bedrooms upstairs, each of which could put a good hotel to shame. And then, up another staircase to a knockout of a loft conversion: one huge bedroom with exposed beams covered with twinkling lights, and a bathroom separated by sheets of green glass. The stuff of glossy magazines!

'And just when you thought it couldn't get any better,' Steven said as we returned to the ground floor. He flicked a light on in a small room. 'My office.' It was chaos. There were box files and papers everywhere including several piles on the floor. There was no more than a square foot of usable space on his desk.

'One thing's for sure,' I quipped, 'we're definitely related.'

'Don't,' Steven said. 'This is the one place that's my domain. Kwan won't set foot in here. Gives him a panic attack.' He cleared a tub chair for me and he sat at his desk.

I studied the wall above me, on which was pinned an artist's impression of a row of houses. 'You're a . . . builder?' I asked.

Steven smirked. 'Yeah, I build. I've got a redevelopment on the go out Stanmore way. A derelict warehouse—proper old characterful one. It's made for some stunning little flats. And there's this lovely old dairy near here—that's going to be a piece of work.' He couldn't sit still, so enthused was he about these projects. 'It's not just building, though. A bit of demolition too. I get very excited about recycling, see. I see a dilapidated building the same way a chef sees a pig: nothing can go to waste. And there's an affordable housing project I'm getting stuck into. It's madness, Uncle Ray. People can't afford to live these days. It's a proper little eco-village we're planning, carbon negative.'

'And this place?'

'God, this was a breeze. This place was like a bit of fun on the side.'

'Incredible.'

'A wise man once told me I was a natural. He bought me some tools too.'

'I thought you were—I don't know—doing something *dodgy*.'

Steven nodded and grinned.

'Maybe a con man,' I said. 'Some sort of criminal mastermind.'

'Yeah, I know you did.'

'Why didn't you set me straight?'

'I was enjoying it, I must admit.'

'All those phone calls you get. They're just . . .'

'Work. That's right. I'm pretty busy, you see.'

'I'm so terribly sorry. Denny—your father—he always used to say you'd end up in prison, and, well I suppose . . .'

'Or be a millionaire, I believe was the quote. So, without wishing to brag, the bitter old wankpot wasn't totally wide of the mark. Not that I'd recommend anyone take notice of him.'

'Gosh, Steven. I'm incredibly proud of you. You really have . . .' I dabbed my eyes with my handkerchief.

'I owe a great deal to you, Uncle Ray. I promise I've never forgotten that, even if . . .'

'Please, Steven. You don't owe anything to me at all. An uncle who can't even be bothered turn up for your birthday parties.'

He looked intently at me. 'I do know there's a lot more to it than that.'

'I've been a fool. And it's cost me my family.'

'Stop it. I'm the one doing the apologising, thanks very much.' Our champagne glasses had long run dry. Steven grabbed a bottle of scotch which was on the floor in the corner and poured a decent tot for us both. 'You must believe me,' he went on, 'I've never forgotten what you did for me. And it's unforgiveable that I've not made more effort to get in touch.'

'There's nothing to apologise for,' I said.

'There bloody well is, Uncle Ray.' He thumped his desk, causing an avalanche of A4. He was reddening around the eyes and I felt a compulsion to change the subject.

'I'm not going to insult you with excuses,' he said. 'But I can attempt an explanation. The thing is, this life I live now, it's pretty new. Having things in order, that's a recent development.

Only since I've been with Kwan. Life's a fuck-sight easier when you've got the right person holding your hand, you know that?'

'Yes, I think I perhaps do.'

'I've kind of made sense of a lot of things in these last few years. Trouble is, Uncle Ray, I was so *ashamed* of myself. I'll tell you, it wasn't too much fun being at school in the early nineties and being gay. That was a dirty little secret, all right. The biggest lesson I learnt in that place was to fucking hate myself.'

'I'm so sorry, Steven. I wish you'd told me.'

'*I* wish I'd told you. I think I could've told you.'

I smiled sadly at him. 'That house I took you back to, when you were seventeen, it wasn't a girl's like I thought?'

Steven shook his head. 'My once best mate, Terry Scott. I was crazy for him. And I let on to him. What the hell was I thinking? His parents treated me like a serial killer.'

'Appalling.'

'Wasn't about to make that mistake again. Spent my twenties and thirties living a lie. A chaotic, miserable lie. You know I only came out to my folks in my forties? Nuts, innit?'

'I dare say it made no difference at all to the esteem they hold you in.'

'Mum was totally cool. Of course she was. I'm not so sure about Dad. We weren't exactly best of buddies before anyway. Trouble is, the bloke's spent his whole life making jokes about poofters. Not about to have a complete change of heart, is he? He's kind of okay, as long as there's nothing distressing for him to see, like—I don't know—hand-holding.'

'I can only apologise for my brother.'

Steven rolled his eyes at me. 'Up till these last few years, everything was a mess. My work was all I had.'

'You've made a staggering success of it.'

'Maybe. But at a cost, Uncle Ray. I was always flat-out, at it seven days a week, sixteen hours a day. I was like a junkie, but my substance of choice was *work*. And you know what, it was probably killing me just as quick as any shit I could've been putting up my nose. People say *workaholic* like it's a good thing. It ain't, Uncle Ray. Sure, things are cool now. I'm enjoying the spoils of my labour. But was it worth it? I dunno . . .'

'I only wish I'd been around for you.'

'You weren't because I didn't let you. I was a self-absorbed dick. Didn't let anyone in. Not until . . .' He gestured towards a black and white portrait of Kwan among the mess on his desk.

'He must be quite something.'

'Sure he is. Things are good now, Uncle Ray. I've finally got my house in order. I've put myself through a bit of counselling. I'm not ashamed to admit that—it's done me a power of good. Oh, and I've been diagnosed with ADHD—that's made sense of a lot of stuff, I can tell you!'

'You were always somewhat . . . energetic.'

'Usually confused with being a naughty little shit. Not by you, though, Uncle Ray. Never got any judgement or grief from you, did I?'

'It's kind of you to . . .'

'There's twenty years of my life that could've been so much better spent, Uncle Ray.'

'Yes, well I'm rather coming to know that feeling.'

'But please believe me when I tell you that I never stopped thinking about you.'

'Nor I of you, Steven,' I said.

'And lately, I swear to you, I've been saying all the time that I must get in touch with you. Go ask Kwan. Seriously, ask Kwan.'

I raised a hand. 'I believe you.'

'And then when I got that call from Dad the other night. It killed me, Uncle Ray. I'd left it too late.'

'Stop this, please.'

'Fucking hell, when I *do* actually see you again, I'm prancing round your bedroom wearing your clothes. What an absolute fucking prick!'

'It was a rather pleasant distraction, actually.'

'Believe me when I say I was always planning on inviting you to the wedding. I'm not bullshitting you, I swear. We haven't sent out the invites, but you've been on the list right from the start. I promise.' He began tearing through a filing cabinet. 'I've got the draft guest list somewhere. I can show you.'

'There really isn't the need.'

'I need you to believe that I never forgot about you.'

I put a hand on his shoulder to still him. 'I'm very touched. And the silly thing is, had this recent . . . *debacle* not happened, I'd most probably have declined to come. Isn't that just pathetic?'

'You *will* come though, right?'

'You have my word.' Our glasses met and we both necked the contents.

Steven's mobile phone, which had been mercifully absent thus far during my visit, was in his hand again. He grinned as his thumb danced over the screen.

'A lot of people have looked up to you over the years, Uncle Ray,' Steven said. 'Not just me. All those boys you taught . . .'

'It's kind of you to say so but—'

'You are a legend in your own lifetime!'

'Hardly.'

Steven raised his eyebrows at me. 'You do yourself down.'

'I was lucky enough to take some classes, and I had some good students. They were the best of times. But I was no teacher. It was deemed by someone far more intelligent than I that the classroom was not my natural habitat. I joined that school as a caretaker, and I left as a caretaker. That was my station in life, and I'm not ashamed of it.'

He wore a smirk as his gaze flitted between his telephone and me.

'What exactly are you up to over there?' I asked.

'Not a thing!' he replied.

We were interrupted by the doorbell. Steven leapt to his feet, sending some of his in-tray floor-wards.

'I'm on it,' came a shout from Kwan.

'Our last dinner guest,' Steven said. 'About time too. I'm bloody famished.'

'I wasn't aware we were expecting any . . .'

'Ah, yes. Now look, Uncle Ray, don't be mad. But you know, who better to set the record straight with? Who better to break the delightful news of your cheating of death?'

'Steven, who—'

'It's really no biggie. I often have Mum over on Sundays.'

'Your mother?'

'Don't look so worried, Uncle Ray.'

'Junie's here?'

'She'll understand. You'll be fine.'

'Steven, I really don't think . . .'

'Nonsense! What's the worst that could happen?'

27

IT WAS PROBABLY MY OWN FAULT. I DON'T RECALL HOW MUCH EFFORT I MADE to get along with Charles Sethi's replacement—a gentlemen by the name of Ceawlin Brown—but there was something of the oil and water about us.

'Mr Thorns!' he said, shaking my hand over his desk. 'Take the weight off!' He'd been in post for a term and a half, and this meeting between us was to follow an established format: greeting me like an old friend, aloof from there on.

'Firstly, I'm not minded to be making any changes to the maintenance staffing arrangements just now,' he said. He looked up at me briefly, flashed what may have been a magnanimous smile. 'We'll soldier on as we are.'

'It's an arrangement that works,' I replied, though it was hard to tell if he heard. For the past twenty years or more, whilst I'd been officially in the caretaker role, I'd had a full-time assistant in order that I could tend to my tutor group and many classes. There'd been mutterings since Sethi's retirement that this was somewhat inefficient, with the inevitable possibility that I might have to return fully to my original job.

'But woodwork,' Brown went on. 'I wonder if it's run its course.'

'It was always so popular when we had pupils boarding.'

'Yes. In the *seventies*.'

'We had boarders till '88,' I pointed out. My craft classes had continued nonetheless, in the old Steady On Spike shed, and forty or so boys still gave up an evening once a week. The train set was going strong too, and the Scalextric had grown to Nurburgring proportions.

'I'm not sure that learning to work with wood has quite the . . . relevance it once did,' he said.

'It's not just wood. We do a bit of metalwork. Electronics. We even work with plastics!' I hoped this last point might appeal to his enthusiasm for modernity. 'And a good few boys pop in of a lunchtime too, for their own amusement.'

'Our world is changing,' he said. It was a sentiment that was everywhere at the time, what with Tony Blair's oft-repeated promise of *New Britain*. It put me in mind of three decades earlier, when *The times they are a-changin'* was the mantra of the day, although the prospect had mostly excited me then. At what age, I wonder, does newness become the enemy?

'Our obligation,' Brown went on, 'is to prepare our young men for the world they will step into. This is a new era, Mr Thorns!' For a second, the two of us were engaged, his eyes aglow. 'This is the age of *media*. And that is where our focus must be.'

I nodded firmly, as if to prove my commitment to our students. I kept it to myself that I wasn't entirely sure what *media* meant. 'Perhaps there's a little room for everything.'

He shook his head; I hadn't been asked in for a debate. 'Our brilliant boys are destined to be the trailblazers. We have some bound for Eton! A few even for Harrow—my own old stomping ground!'

'I understand, sir.'

'You see, theirs is a generation who are unlikely to need to ever . . . build a shelf. We needn't be . . . troubling them with skills they shan't put to use. This is fast becoming a service-based economy.'

This was another vague claim that was becoming ubiquitous. That old notions of class were dying, and noble trades with them. Someone in power had decided that those of us who work with our hands needed to be rescued. Tempting as it may have been, I didn't ask Brown who he imagined *would* likely be building shelves for these men of the future. I instead took my leave, feeling thoroughly depressed. A room of computers, together with a green-screen video facility was assembled. Branded the *Media Suite*, it kept the young men busy when my own operation came to an end.

IT WAS WHEN THE HEADMASTER GOT SHOT THAT THINGS WENT DOWNHILL. Our summer production was to be *Bugsy Malone* and, as had fallen to me for many a year, I took charge of the set and prop making. In view of Ceawlin Brown's attitudes, I didn't seek out a team of helpers, but regardless a good number came to me as they always had. We had a fine time: mock smoky speakeasies with crystal soda-siphons and demijohns of lurid liquids, seedy New York back alleys, a moonshine runner's hot rod that rolled across the stage. But nothing gave us quite the kick that making fifteen splurge guns did.

There was a good amount of prototyping involved. With a can of inexpensive shaving foam as ammunition, we discovered that the key was to connect the aerosol to a very narrow tube of twenty-eight inches in length. The result was a quite startling range and power. This established, we spent a week of lunchtimes and early starts building lifelike rifle bodies in which the can of jollop could be hidden in the stock.

Brown paid our little factory a visit one Friday. The boys and I got to our feet.

'How are you fine young gentlemen progressing?' he boomed from the doorway. He brimmed with bonhomie and was liked by the students, if not *adored* in the way Sethi had been. I think he sensed as much, and this was probably one of the reasons he and I didn't click; few things are as unpopular with new management as a protégé of their predecessor.

'Well aren't these quite something?' Brown said, glancing at the boys' fine work and emitting an impressed whistle.

'I think the boys have very much enjoyed making them,' I said. I meant it only as chatter, not as a dig.

He picked one off a nearby desk and studied it in his hands. 'Put 'em up!' he shouted, jerking into a *firing from the hip* stance.

There was a peal of polite laughter from the boys, a few pairs of hands held aloft. The boys were still standing, as was protocol.

Laughing richly, he lowered the gun. 'Perhaps I should hang on to this,' he joked. 'Keep you boys in line!'

I hold none of them responsible for what followed. Not even highly trained police officers are immune to the itchy trigger finger that comes from spending a great deal of time holding a potent weapon; even such professionals can become so excitable as to loose off a few rounds at the wrong moment. Our splurge guns were in the paint and polish phase. They were armed and dangerous.

Standing at the front, I saw the great arc of jet-propelled white foam shoot across the back of the room. Brown however, had no warning. Had it been machine gun fire, he'd have been perfectly bisected down his midline, such was the stripe drawn upwards from his groin to his chin. He stood perfectly still. The only sound in that room was the foam fizzing as it expanded, the line blooming to a girth of six inches.

Calmly, beginning at his chin, he scooped the stuff away in handfuls, chucking it to the floor. 'Very funny,' he eventually said. 'Yes. Very good.' He was wearing a pair of orange slacks, and it was hard to ignore the darkened patch around his crotch where the mess had soaked in.

'Gosh, I'm so terribly sorry,' I said, hopefully loud enough to cover the sound of desperately repressed sniggering from around the room.

REPORTS OF HIS DEATH HAVE BEEN GREATLY EXAGGERATED   231

Brown's own laughter was forced. 'Well it wasn't *you* was it? Now, perhaps someone would care to own up?'

'I don't imagine it was deliberate,' I said.

He strode to the front of the room. 'I enjoy a laugh as much as the next man, but I would appreciate it if the person responsible would reveal themselves.'

Silence.

'It's not a serious matter.' Oddly, his words dripped with warmth and charm, as if to reinforce how reasonable a man he was. 'But if everybody could sit, accept the person who just . . . gunned me down, that would be appreciated.'

Slowly, everybody sat.

'Just a bit of general horseplay,' I said. 'No malice intended, I fancy.'

'What I'm requesting is very simple,' Brown said. 'Would you not all agree?'

Murmurs of agreement.

'Mr Thorns, are you able to tell me who fired the shot.'

'I'm afraid I. . . can't be sure.' This was partly true. I knew from which direction it had come; I could've narrowed it to three or four suspects.

'I'm not angry,' Brown said, though his eyes suggested otherwise. 'Not about the . . . foam. But I'm not happy about the unwillingness to step forward.'

In my years at Allonby House, I'd encountered a handful of men who'd been educated at England's very finest public schools. Just as Ceawlin Brown, they were dramatically confident, and pathetically thin-skinned.

The silly standoff ran for some minutes. 'It's a matter of principle,' Brown repeated several times, whilst appearing to laugh off the crime itself. I was watching the embodiment of that philosophical conundrum: what happens when an unstoppable force (him) meets an immovable object (the class).

'Mr Thorns,' he eventually said in calm yet grave tone. 'I'll leave this in your capable hands. If you could establish the perpetrator, and present them to my study at end of school today, please?' He didn't wait for my answer before taking his leave.

'That wasn't terribly clever was it?' I said to the boys.

'Sorry, sir,' a young man named Nathan Baird said.

'Is this a confession?'

He shrugged, but before he could speak the boy next to him piped up: 'It was me, sir.'

'I'll thank you to spare me the *I'm Spartacus* routine,' I said. Blank faces all round. 'Look it up,' I added.

I took the decision to present all seventeen of them to Brown's study that afternoon. 'We are all equally responsible,' their appointed spokesman explained.

'And each in turn would like to apologise for today's misbehaviour,' I said to the headmaster. 'Whatever punishment you deem fit will be accepted graciously, and shared.'

It was clear this did not meet with his approval. There was something in the look he gave me that said: I set you a test, and you failed. The boys were dismissed with a jovial 'Don't do it again'. At the time it seemed such a minor incident, but on reflection it was the moment he wrote me off completely. In life as in physics, every action leads to an opposite reaction, at some point or another.

With each timetable issued, I had fewer classes of my own. When my assistant caretaker left for pastures new, he was not replaced. My last tutor group graduated in the summer of '98—I was not given another. By the time the burgeoning IT department was bracing for the arrival of the *Millennium Bug*, my role at Allonby House had reverted to one of maintenance alone.

REPORTS OF HIS DEATH HAVE BEEN GREATLY EXAGGERATED 233

I IMAGINED THAT I, LIKE SHEEHAN BEFORE ME, WOULD WORK TILL I DROPPED.
But three years after my final demotion, I found myself in the
headmaster's study for the last time.

'You've rather made an error here, haven't you, Ray?' he
said, looking gravely up at me from behind his desk. I'd not been
offered a seat.

I fizzed with panic over the trouble I'd got myself in. My
bottom lip quivered. A man of fifty-seven! I stared down at my
boots where the silver toecaps had worn through the leather.

'Would you care to attempt an explanation of your behaviour yesterday?' he said.

It was first period Monday morning. I'd not slept a wink.
'I'm sorry, sir,' was all I could say.

I'd made a mistake. Jamie Gale—there's a name I'll not forget—a rather delicate-looking, long-limbed, long-haired young
man. He was so clearly being picked on. We'd been short of staff
the previous week and I'd been helping supervise the refectory.
What a joy it was to spend a little time chatting to the lads whilst
I worked once again. Poor Jamie though, this wisp of a thing,
who day after day I noticed discarding every item off his plate in
turn; into pockets, onto the floor, even his shoes. It was a well-honed act, a fine sleight of hand. I spoke with him a couple of
times as he left for afternoon school; he was sweet and chatty and
said it was *delicious* when I asked how lunch had been.

In *my* day at Allonby, no one would've thought twice about
paying the parents a visit, about asking the school office for the
address. Theirs was a road closed to the public; I drove as far
as the barrier blocking the way and set off on foot that Sunday
morning. The estate consisted of a pristine green, around which
the private road ran. It was on this central green that I ran into
Jamie and a younger companion. He was as charming as ever.
I asked if he might show me to his house—a quite enormous

residence as it turned out. He led me around the back and introduced me to his three golden retrievers.

After a time, the boy's mother made an appearance. The marching walk with mobile telephone pinned to her ear were warnings I should've heeded. We did not get off on the right foot, to say the least. My explanation that I was school caretaker seemed to worsen the situation, not mitigate it. My assertion that I was worried about her son, stoked rather than damped her fury. I was ordered to leave. I did so.

'I imagine you can appreciate the situation you've put me in?' Ceawlin Brown asked.

'I was worried for the boy,' I eventually mumbled. 'He's unhappy, I think. Boys are picking on—'

'Of which I am well aware, thank you,' Brown said in a patronising tone. 'You may not realise this, but we do *have* policies and procedures for dealing with bullying. And they have been actioned in the case of this pupil. Needless to say, as *caretaker*, we haven't felt it necessary to run that past *you*.'

I reddened. 'I'm not sure he's eating quite as—'

'This is grossly inappropriate behaviour, Ray. A child's home, at the weekend? Snooping to obtain an address.'

I nodded. Put like that, it was indefensible.

'It's not as if this is even the first cause for alarm, Ray. A member of staff has already come to me recently about your conduct.'

For a moment I was utterly confused.

Brown briefly met my eyes and read my expression. '*Kitchen* staff,' he added.

'Ah, yes,' I replied. This had been nothing more than a misunderstanding—over a large tin of baked beans of all things. The tin was opened, and therefore the contents bound for the bin. As I had pointed out at the time, my taking it home was an act of recycling not one of theft. With so much more time on my hands since being relieved of my teaching duties, I had come across much wastage around the place; my van and shed at home were packed with materials and fixtures that the school had carelessly tossed away.

'Can't quite sweep that under the rug, now can we. And to say nothing of that you seem quite,' mused the head, 'keen to be . . . *friends* with the boys. I must say, I find it all increasingly . . . uncomfortable. In this day and age.'

'No, I suppose . . .'

'I take my obligation to students' safety very seriously.'

'Yes, now that is something I—'

'I've spoken with the governors, Ray. A rather generous decision has been made to offer you an early retirement package. I'm sure you'd rather that than for matters to go beyond these walls?'

'No, I suppose—'

'We'll report it in the weekly newsletter *email*,' Brown said, raising his eyebrows with the word. 'That *you* have made the decision to take a well-earned retirement.'

I was put on *gardening leave*, advised to leave the premises before the morning was out. It had taken less than three minutes in his study to bring my thirty-nine years of service to an end.

In this day and age. That phrase of Brown's rolled around my head as I removed my bits and pieces to the van on that cool, milky-skied Monday. Morning break began as I carried the last load. Three boys stopped by to chat. I'd not been taking classes for three years, but all the same they asked some advice on a maths puzzle they'd been set which I did my best to help with as I walked. They of course had no idea I was leaving; it was scarcely unusual for me to be taking boxes home (though had they been more familiar with my self-imposed schedule, they'd have known that at precisely this time on a Monday I'd be checking the water tanks in the attic).

The bell rang and I was alone. I stood awhile beside the loaded van and took a long look at that beautiful old building.

At those tall arched windows, beyond which the school hall: venue of so many fine productions for which I'd made props and the set, site of the green hair incident, home to Sethi's rousing, noisy daily assemblies (now a thing of the past; the whole school gathered only weekly, with Ceawlin Brown delegating the job to his deputy). I looked up too at the roof I'd repaired, at the chimney where I'd sat with that troubled young man. How did the London skyline look from there now, I wondered.

I had found myself in a world I didn't recognise, no understanding of my place within it and its new rules. The *You Are Here* arrow had been erased from my own map of all things.

28

'PLEASE, STEVEN,' I SAID. 'DON'T LET HER JUST WALK IN AND FIND ME.'

'I could see if we could find you a nice comfy wardrobe?'

I could hear that old familiar voice in the hallway, exchanging pleasantries with Kwan.

'She'll have a heart attack, Steven. I know you probably think it'll be funny but—'

'Uncle Ray, I'm not a complete moron, all right?'

'Sorry. I'm just incredibly . . . Perhaps if I could pop out for a little air. You could explain and . . . oh, I don't know.' I glanced down at my hands. Bloody hell, stop shaking, man!

'Take a seat. I'll deal with my mother. You chill for a minute.' Steven slipped out into the corridor, pulling the door to behind him.

I listened as they greeted each other. Junie's perfume crept around the door and made its usual beeline for my nostrils. My own pulse squelching in my ears.

'I'm going to fix you a drink, Mum,' I heard him say. 'And then there's something I need to tell you about.'

'Steven?' she said warily.

'You'll love this, I promise,' he replied, their voices trailing away.

They were not gone nearly long enough. I had scarcely composed myself.

Junie from outside the room: 'I want you to remember just how many times I've said that I don't believe you. Okay? So you can't go round saying "I got Mum a corker on that one."' Her tone wasn't quite jovial. She sounded scared, tearful perhaps.

'Mum, I'm not going to joke about something like this. Frankly, you couldn't make it up.'

He tapped the door. 'I hope you're decent in there, Uncle Ray,' he said, gently swinging it open.

Junie hands flew to her mouth. Her eyes were wide and puffy. 'Ray!' she whispered.

My gaze fell to my lap. The trouble I'd caused these people. The upheaval! 'Sorry,' I mumbled. My knees jiggled.

'Ray!' she said again. She had every right to be furious but there was no hint of anger. She moved her hands from her face, folding them outwards like a butterfly's wings. 'My darling Ray.' She approached in half steps, eventually reaching out and cupping my cheeks in her hands, which were wet now with her tears.

'Up you get, Uncle Ray,' Steven said, jabbing my arm and laughing. 'No one ever tell you to stand when a woman enters a room?'

I shot to my feet. 'Yes, gosh, of course. I'm so sorry, I'm a bit . . .' Junie and I were barely two feet apart. Too close for a comfortable handshake, but I offered awkwardly all the same.

She took my limp hand between hers and stroked the back of it. 'I really thought we'd lost you, Ray.'

Hadn't I been lost for quite some years?

'I really am dreadfully sorry for all the trouble I've caused,' I said, nodding firmly. 'I've put you all out.'

Junie looked up into my eyes. 'My God, Ray. You really are still the same old berk you always were, aren't you?'

Steven roared with laughter. 'Didn't I tell you, Mum? The guy just can't help himself!'

'All this effort you've had to go to on my account,' I mumbled, too close to her to conduct a conversation in a comfortable manner.

'What are we going to do with you?' Junie said, grinning at me. Her tears were coming fast now. She put her arms around me and I hugged her back. At first stiffly. But then, a curious thing happened, I felt something somewhat akin to melting. That distantly familiar form of her frame, the shape of the ear resting in the crook of my neck, the warm, perfumed heat rising from her uncovered shoulder, the vibrato of her breath as she cried gently close to my ear. We stayed this way for some moments. Leaving her embrace was like being snapped awake from a wonderful dream.

She'd not been in my arms since the April of '68. Yet those intervening years seemed now to have passed in a flash. Could it be that there are only really two modes of existence: being with the person you love, and waiting?

'YOU BOYS DO LIKE TO CUT THINGS FINE, DON'T YOU?' JUNIE SAID, HER GAZE switching between Steven and me, once we were all seated at the dining table and tucking in. Despite Kwan's muttered complaints that his meat had overcooked, it was proving to be among the finest meals I'd ever eaten.

'How long, exactly, have you known?' she asked Steven. She was trying to sound stern but kept breaking into a grin. Her cheeks were flushed since we'd opened the second bottle of wine.

'Friday night,' he replied.

'Just the forty-eight hours, then? No wonder you seemed so distracted when you ran me home.'

'I *had* just encountered the fucking ghost of my dead uncle.'

Junie shook her head. 'I swear I could *feel* something in that bedroom. Like I wasn't alone. I thought I was going quite mad.' She pointed her fork at Steven. 'I am pleased you've at least had the conscience to set the record straight before the funeral.'

'The thought of anyone planning such a thing was horrifying me,' I said.

'Oh, so Steven's not told you?' Junie said. 'My word. This is priceless.'

'Come on now, Mum,' Steven said, palms raised. 'It's been one step at a time. I think Uncle Ray feels bad enough about everything.'

'Absolutely terrible,' I added.

'I think we've established that, love,' Junie said, patting my hand where it rested on the table. I expected her to pull her hand away, but she left it on mine. 'But what my darling son had neglected to mention is that a funeral has already been very much arranged.'

'Surely not?'

'*Arranged* is a bit strong,' Steven said. 'The crematorium's been booked. A hearse. What—a few phone calls made, that can perfectly easily be unmade.'

'And a few . . . people have been notified.' Junie said. There was something panicked in the exchange of glances between the two of them.

'There's hardly a need to protect me from the fact my funeral would not be a grand affair.' I opted to keep my counsel about overhearing her and Denny's discussions, about how the idea of no funeral at all had been floated. 'I'm hardly bloody Churchill, am I?'

'I'll get on it first thing tomorrow, Mum,' Steven said. 'It's the weekend, innit? Couldn't have sorted it anyway.'

'Not that you thought to try,' Junie said.

Steven fumbled over a reply but Junie held up a palm to quiet him. 'Tuesday,' she said, looking me in the eye.

'*This* Tuesday?' I asked. 'As in, the day after tomorrow?'

'Yup, that's the one!' Junie said.

'Hell's bells!'

REPORTS OF HIS DEATH HAVE BEEN GREATLY EXAGGERATED 241

'North Lambeth Crematorium. 11:00 a.m.'

'It'll be dealt with first thing,' Steven said.

'Dad's supposed to be collecting a death certificate tomorrow,' Junie said. She rested her forehead in her hand and stuck a forkful into her mouth. She was stuck somewhere between despair and laughter.

'Did he not need to identify the body?' I asked. 'I'd been rather counting on that settling the matter.'

Junie huffed and gave me what was surely a pitying stare. 'The people at the hospital, they did ask Denny if he wanted to . . . see you. He didn't feel that was . . . needed. Oh, Ray, I am sorry. I'm not sure that an official identification is necessarily required. Not if there's no doubt about who the person is.'

'One old geezer looks much like the next,' Steven added.

I nodded, though Junie shot him a glare.

'We'll all be laughing about this by next week,' Kwan said, topping up everyone's glasses.

'Mum, it'll all be fine,' Steven said. 'I'll talk to Dad tonight. We'll deal with the undertaker's and the crem. I don't think he's even got around to booking the pub for afterwards.'

'Barry Detmer!' I said, a little too loud. I was struck by guilt that he'd not been weighing so heavily on my mind these past couple of days. 'He's who would've been cremated.'

'The neighbour who expired on your doorstep?' Junie said. 'Steven did explain.'

'More at the foot of my stairs actually. Or possibly in the bathroom. Of course, he didn't actually *die* till sometime later.'

'All will be taken care of,' Steven said. 'Fear not. Family will be made aware.'

'I've been keeping an eye on his flat, see. And feeding his bird. It's a rather beautiful little budgerigar. Bright blue, would you believe? But regardless . . .' I was aware of Junie grinning to my side.

'Bloody hell, I've missed you, Ray,' she said, holding my hand tighter than ever.

'I do wish you'd told me, Steven,' I told him. 'I wouldn't have dared meander through these past couple of days had I known such . . . things were so imminent.'

'Exactly,' he said, tipping his glass my way.

'I don't quite follow.'

'Uncle Ray, I was well aware that the minute you knew of an upcoming funeral, you'd have outed yourself. And something that's become very apparent is that you are not living a life that you're *loving*. I didn't want you simply returning to that. I couldn't let you do it.'

'I'm not sure it's *unhappy*, as such.'

'So why didn't you put this right immediately? Save yourself all that hiding in cupboards?' This got a good laugh from all except me.

'Well, I . . . tried to,' I said. 'Of course I did.'

'Oh okay,' Steven said, smirking at me through his wine glass.

'It's just a pleasure to spend a little time in your company, Ray,' Junie said.

'Amen to that,' Steven said, and yet another toast was made. Glasses topped up again; we were tearing through the booze.

'I can hardly believe I'm here,' I said.

'You two must have a bugger-ton of catching up to do,' Steven said.

'We've not said two words to each other in—what—forty years?' Junie said.

I shook my head: the pointless sadness of it all was almost too much. 'Thirty-nine years, seven months, and perhaps sixteen days.'

A cheeky smile bloomed on Junie's face.

'Mum's funeral, see,' I added. Her expression shifted: a single serious nod.

'Let's get a date in the diary, then,' Steven said. 'Come on, just the two of you. A chance to put the world to rights.'

'Yes, I suppose that would be . . .'

'A game of chess, perhaps,' Steven said with a grin. 'That was the thing, wasn't it? In all those letters you wrote each other?'

Junie rolled her eyes at me. My cheeks were aglow. 'What else did you read?' she asked.

'Relax, Mum. I do have *some* discretion. I'm not sure I have the stomach for all the gory details. So come on, how are you both fixed? Mum? Uncle Ray?'

I shrugged. I hardly needed to embarrass myself with a run-down of my diary.

'I think if we are to learn anything from recent events,' Steven said, 'it's that there's no sense in putting anything off. How's . . . tomorrow?'

'Look, let's not get carried away with our—'

Junie interrupted me. 'As it happens, I was planning tomorrow to draw up the order-of-service sheets for your . . . well, you know, Ray. And if I got those all printed with time to spare, I thought I might take a trip round to the house, to make a start on your clothes. Sorry, I hope you don't mind me . . .'

'I appreciate the effort,' I said frankly.

'So I do find myself at something of a loose end. Shall we seize the day? I hope you don't consider that too *forward* of me, Ray, darling.'

'I've known you to be rather more forward.' My confidence ran dry and I delivered the last of the sentence down to the dining table.

'Oh, enough already!' Steven shouted. He mimed vomiting onto his plate.

'Looks like you have a date tomorrow,' Kwan said.

'If you're not busy, Ray?' Junie said.

'I suppose that might be . . .' I stammered.

What useless instincts! After everything, I was reaching for an excuse such that I could spend tomorrow in the same way as damned near every other day in the past twenty years. Litter picking on the heath. Scouring the charity shops. Getting the bread.

To hell with it!

'Yes,' I said.

Steven wrung his hands together. 'Excellent! And meanwhile, Dad and I will see to all the dull administrative matters, starting with the undertakers. Mum, what time can Uncle Ray expect you?'

She turned her palms upwards. 'What shall we say? Ten o'clock?'

I nodded. A whole day. Might that be a bit . . . *much*? 'Perfect,' I said.

We ate plum crumble made with fruit from Steven and Kwan's own orchard. There was a cheese board and dessert wine, port and brandies to finish. The two of them talked about their wedding, and Junie and I were asked our advice on all manner of details.

All four of us retired to the fireside, where I played my first game of Scrabble in close to half a century. Kwan was in a league of his own, going *all out* twice. Steven took much joy in spelling out *STAIRS*, and asking if perhaps I'd like to go underneath.

'I know how much you enjoy being under stairs,' he repeatedly quipped.

Soon after, Junie played the word *CLOSE*, to which I added a *T* to the end.

'I may have spent a day or two in there myself,' I remarked, 'but that's nothing on Steven.' There was a moment's silence in which I feared I'd made a misjudgement. The collective intake of breath was followed by an eruption of laughter from Junie and Kwan.

'Yes. Touché,' Steven said.

'I don't think I appreciated just how much I was missing you all,' I said to him when eventually the evening drew to a close and he walked me out to the minicab he'd ordered.

He hugged me. 'Nor just how much people have been missing *you*.'

'Oh, nonsense,' I said, climbing aboard.

His mobile phone, which had been unusually absent for some hours, was back in his hands, eliciting excited noises from its owner. 'You just wait, Unc,' he said.

He winked and walloped a hand twice on the roof.

29

MONDAY

WHILST I APPRECIATE THE MAGNITUDE OF OUR ENVIRONMENTAL CRISIS, I must confess to still finding something stirring about the rich smell of an ancient petrol engine running on choke in the cool of morning. I blipped the throttle and listened to that familiar stumble before the old girl cleared her throat. Ticking over a treat and oil pressure perfect, I switched off. It was early and I'd no wish to rudely wake anyone.

Now for a jolly good sweep-up to clear the way out to the road. I took the initiative and swept the hardstandings fronting my closest neighbours' houses too; there'd been a time when I knew every one of them by name, been at their beck and call for a leaking radiator or an unruly lawn. At what point had those acquaintances been lost to residents oblivious to my passing away? Time to set that right. The fine day promised by the weatherman was materialising; by the time I turned in for breakfast my shirt back was drenched.

I'd slept poorly; one of those nights where every hour is glimpsed. By half five I'd surrendered and made tea. In the living room, disorderly since Junie began the sort-out, I'd found myself resting my feet on a box marked *Good China*. Last opened when, I wonder? How much life do we lose, withholding the best of everything for some notional special occasion? We surround ourselves with the things we love, that we worked for, only to save them for *best*. A dazzling spring dawn on the rise, and being alive. Maybe there are no bigger days.

The old MG hadn't left the garage in thirty years. It'd been no further than round the block since its return from Allonby House in the 1980s. What a waste.

'NOW YOU'RE TALKING!' THESE WERE JUNIE'S FIRST WORDS WHEN I OPENED the door to her. 'God, it's even more gorgeous than I remember.'

I'd watched from the upstairs window as she'd admired it on the driveway for a minute before knocking.

'It's due a little run,' I said. 'Keep things moving. I could do it later of course. I've popped the top down, because, well, why not? There's no need necessarily for you to accompany . . .' I was waffling, eyes at her feet which were shod in those pink Doc Marten boots.

She stepped closer and reached for my hand. 'A little fresh air is just what I need this morning. That's why I'm so bloody late. I'm hungover to buggery. It's been a while since I've put it away like we did last night. I look an absolute wreck.'

The confidence I'd had in her company yesterday had seemingly left my system along with the alcohol. It was an effort to meet her gaze. Her eyes were as piercing blue as they'd ever been. She looked, and smelt, as gloriously fresh as the breeze. Hair blond and bobbed just as it was in '63, big hoop earrings in delicate silver. How had she not grown *old*? 'No, you're . . . fine,' I told her.

'I made a picnic,' she said, swinging a basketwork bag by her side. 'I wasn't sure if you had an idea in mind. It's just sandwiches and a few bits. We can feed them to the ducks if you like.'

'No, a picnic is a marvellous idea. I've not been for such a thing since . . .' Royal wedding day, 1981, with Mum. 'Oh, I don't recall.'

'Marvellous.' She heaved the bag over the closed car door and stowed it inside. 'So where's it to be?'

'I suppose we could venture over to Richmond Park?' I said it casually, though it was further afield than good sense would permit in the car. Something local was a better bet. 'Or Streatham Common perhaps? The blossoms will likely be out.'

'When did you last see the sea, Ray?'

'I drove a minibus of fifth formers to Great Yarmouth. Let me think, that would've been—'

'For your own enjoyment?'

'Ah, now, some time ago. You fancy a trip to the coast?'

'I'd really like that.' There was uncertainty in her expression; if I didn't know better, I might've thought her nervous. 'Of course, we *could* go in mine.' She pointed to a small Volvo parked across the road. 'It is terribly unexciting, though.'

'The thing is, I've not got breakdown cover. Can you even *get* cover on a car from the fifties? Who knows! I suppose I could pop a toolbox in the boot. But even Brighton, we'd be talking *sixty* miles. And, in modern traffic—'

'I'm being a silly old tart, Ray.'

I shook my head. 'No one uses the best bloody china, do they?'

'I don't follow.'

'Let's see how far we get. I don't suppose you brought a headscarf?'

'Erm, no, I . . .'

'It's going to be exceptionally blowie.'

'Blowie, indeed,' she said, sniggering.

'I could lend you one of Mum's?'

'All right, go on then.'

I was back in a flash. 'It's Chanel,' I explained, handing her the square of turquoise and gold silk. Even Mum had saved this one for special occasions. For *best*.

Junie tied it under her chin and lowered herself into the passenger seat. She glanced at her reflection in the chrome of the windscreen surround and broke into a chuckle. 'Come on then, sweetheart. And don't, whatever you do, spare the horses.'

30

WIND-BURNT AND EXHILARATED, AND WITH A RINGING IN THE EARS, WE stopped at a somewhat *olde worlde* tearoom. We'd been on the road for two and a half hours and were the far side of the South Downs now, the sea a strip of grey in the distance.

'I can smell the salt,' Junie said as we set foot beneath a doorway that forced me to crouch, into a large, low room with various cosy nooks. It had an oddly insulated feel about it, a little like a soundproofed booth. The place burbled softly with chatter and the clinking of teaspoons.

'Yes it's rather wonderful,' I said, pulling out a chair for her from the only unoccupied table. 'A very popular establishment, it would seem.' To my surprise, this observation caused a number of the patrons to look over and smile. I tipped an invisible hat to them.

'Well driven, darling,' Junie said.

'There was a hint of a misfire out of Horsham, but otherwise she was faultless.'

'Testament to the restorer.'

'Very many hands were involved. Hundreds. Boys who'd be, gosh, middle-aged men now.'

'Beautiful car,' the lady at the table nearest the window said to us, breaking from gazing out to the car park.

'A latte would be magic,' Junie said to the young waiter who appeared at our side. 'A big one if possible.'

'And for you, sir?'

'Oh, now, I wonder . . .'

'Another large latte?' he suggested.

'No, I think I'll have a coffee please.'

He gave me an odd look.

'A milky one?' Junie asked me.

'Yes, why not.'

'Two lattes,' she told the waiter.

Once again, I was aware of people looking over. I tapped my fingers to the muted jazz that was being piped in.

'How do you think the boys are getting on with the funeral directors?' Junie asked. She checked her mobile phone. 'Not a word.'

'I do hope it's not caused too much trouble. If there are any fees due, I shall be settling them.'

'Do funeral directors have a cancellation policy?'

'What a jolly good question! I can't imagine it's enacted very often.'

'Perhaps you could leave it on account with them,' Junie said. 'Become their first ever repeat customer.'

I supressed a laugh. 'Poor old Barry,' I said, refusing to ignore the gravity of the situation. 'In their mortuary. Known by name that's not his own. How . . . undignified for him.'

'Do you think he'll make a complaint?' she asked, looking at me with wild eyes that couldn't fail to put me in mind of those days back in her father's churchyard.

'Now, look—'

She put on a gruff cockney voice: 'Who the 'ell's this Barry Dermot? Never 'eard of 'im. Reckons it's too cold in our bleedin' fridge.'

'Detmer,' I corrected her. 'He has a family in Spain. Not seen them for a while. But all the same . . .'

'It's all in hand, sweetheart,' Junie said. I felt the leap in my chest that I did every time she uttered an endearment. 'I know

Steven's a bit of a loose cannon, but he's got his head screwed on. And Denny's with him too, for what it's worth.'

Our drinks were delivered in tall glasses. I watched a sugar lump as it drowned into the froth of mine. 'What did my brother make of your plans for today?'

'Do you know what, Ray? I think I may have neglected to tell him.'

'Would it have caused ructions?'

'I'm hardly having an affair, I suppose.' She flashed a grin at me. I detected a faint shift in the tearoom at large, a stilting of conversations around us. 'More exciting having a few secrets, isn't it?'

'He knows I'm . . . alive?'

'Yeah, yeah,' she said dismissively. 'Steven filled him in last night. He was happy about it, in fairness to him.'

'He was.'

'Even our Denny still has something of a heart left about him.'

I nodded, relieved I suppose that my aliveness was welcome news to my next of kin. Buoyed by the thought, I ventured a little further.

'Things are not . . .' I waved a hand about in the hope it might communicate something. '. . . between you two.'

'Oh God. Poor. Very. Yes.'

'This is a recent thing?'

'Oh, only the last . . . how long is it we've been married?'

'Fifty-three years.'

'The last fifty-two, say.'

'I don't believe that,' I said.

'Okay, so I'm embellishing a little. Not much, mind. You've not been married, Ray. It may not be quite the voyage into the sunset you imagine.'

'You're still together, though. That counts for something?'

'If you like.' She sipped her coffee.

REPORTS OF HIS DEATH HAVE BEEN GREATLY EXAGGERATED 253

I sensed I'd said the wrong thing. 'Of course, I don't understand these sort of . . .'

'People can get lazy, Ray. Settle for things they shouldn't.'

'He wasn't always the simplest chap to live with,' I said, remembering the feral independence he'd had as a child that drove Mum potty.

'We are two people who coexist. Denny has his golf, and his pals. I'd like to think he's no longer indulging any of his other . . . little hobbies. Not *these* days.'

'And you?'

'Me?'

'What is it *you* have?'

'Right, yes. I keep myself out of trouble, I suppose. A bit of admin for Steven's business. Two afternoons a week at the theatre in town.'

'You're playing music? Marvellous!'

'Wouldn't that be nice?' she said, smiling at me. 'It's a tea dance. For people even more ancient than I am. I help with the catering, bake a cake here and there. A bit of volunteering.'

'That's jolly noble of you.'

'Cheers.'

I blushed. 'You're still blowing those harps, though?'

'Would it disappoint you terribly if I said I'd not clapped eyes on them since I got married?'

'Most dreadfully.'

'In which case—I play them morning, noon, and night, Ray.'

I laughed along with her. 'That's fine then.' A silence followed, during which I took too big a gulp of my coffee. It scalded my throat and it was all I could do not to eject it all over the table.

'These other hobbies of Denny's you mentioned?' I eventually said. 'That he's given up?'

'I should really know when to shut up, shouldn't I?'

'Gosh, I've no wish to pry.'

'It's all right, darling.' She snapped in half the little biscuit on her saucer and spent an undue amount of time sweeping the crumbs into a pile on the tablecloth. 'I think it was the risk of finding irrefutable proof, that's the thing that terrified me for years.'

'Proof of . . .'

'In the early days anyway. You see, *suspicion* counts for nothing. You can talk yourself out of it, tell yourself you're being silly. It's not the thought of one's husband *playing away* that cripples you, because that fear's there anyway. No, it's the worry that one day you'll unwittingly stumble on *proof*. Because that's when the denial dies. Denial's like a nice, warm blanket, Ray.'

'Yes, I can perhaps see that. A blanket one wears over the head as well as the body.'

'Quite.'

'You found . . . proof?'

'Eventually. Accidentally. Yes.'

'There was someone else?'

'Some*one*?' She gave a dark laugh. 'What a quaint thought. Back when Steven was young, it was always the young girls he worked with that I wondered about. More recently, it was the *golfing* holidays. Him and the same three of his miscreant *mates*. Were they really spending ten days at a time in Spain, just to hit a ball about?'

'Sounds a lot like our own father.'

'Viagra,' Junie said, letting the word hang in the air.

It felt as though the entire tearoom stiffened, ironically enough.

'You remember that old joke?' Junie went on. 'What's worse than finding a worm in your apple?'

'Finding half a worm?'

'Precisely. And the only thing worse than finding a full packet of impotence meds in your husband's luggage, is happening upon a blister pack half consumed.'

'Oh, that really is most—'

'And I can tell you hand-on-heart that not a single one of those little blue wonders had been sunk for *my* benefit. That ship has *very much* sailed. Turns out my instincts were correct: he *was* paying for more than just green fees on these jolly-ups.'

'I'm so sorry, Junie.'

'Oh, don't pity me, Ray, for fucksake.'

Four tables away, a back straightened and a knife slammed against a side plate.

'Was this long ago?' I asked.

'Ten years back, maybe.'

'What on earth did you say to him?'

She leaned back in her chair and gazed around the room. 'That's the question, isn't it?'

'Denied everything, I imagine,' I said sharply. 'Charmed his way from trouble. Believe me, I saw it. Back in the day.'

'Perhaps he would have.'

I was slow to catch her drift. 'Junie, you can't just let—'

There was a flash of anger in her eyes. 'Don't lecture me. There comes an age where one can do as they damn well please.'

'He *still* doesn't know that you . . . know?'

Her features softened into a resigned smile. 'What difference would it possibly make?'

'He's got away with it. He's a . . . goddamned . . .'

'It's me who's got away with it, Ray. Don't you see? Had I confronted him, and then stayed, what would that make me? Every time he clapped eyes on me he'd have less and less respect for me.'

'You could've left him.'

Junie offered her bank card to the passing waiter and waved away my resistance to her paying. 'If I were going to leave him, I'd have done it years ago. Back when I first suspected. When I first *knew*, let's be honest.'

'I'm horrified.'

'Sure. Isn't it pathetic?'

'I don't mean you!' I snapped.

'I know I'm a fool,' she said, shaking her head at me as I went to argue the toss.

She retrieved Mum's headscarf from her bag and folded it ready. 'So where to now, darling man?'

I let the matter lie. 'By my geography,' I said, 'we're a mile and a half from Worthing. Just the place for such a glorious day?'

'My God, Worthing! I've not set foot there since we upped and left for Macclesfield. Bloody hell, 1961!'

'I suspect it's changed a little,' I said.

'I used to walk there from Dad's church in Ferring. Along the sand sometimes. Took an hour each way. The place was impossibly glamorous!'

'Perhaps we should drop in on Ferring too.'

'Visit that *private* beach you and I were so fond of? You dark horse, Ray!'

'Gosh, no I just thought . . . maybe see the old church and—'

Junie's eyes were alive again. 'Another skinny dip?'

'Oh, do you mind?' came a man's voice from the table home to the noisy cutlery. He and his female companion were a good fifteen feet from us. 'The foul language is off-putting enough.'

'Excuse me,' Junie said, glaring at him like he was dirt. There was a table of four between us and him who all self-consciously busied themselves. The entire tearoom was silent. 'May I make a suggestion?' Junie went on, in prim, *incensed of North London* voice. 'If you are liable to being offended by the private conversations of others, perhaps don't earwig on them.'

'Nobody is *choosing* to earwig,' the gentleman said.

'Hardly a *private* conversation,' his companion muttered, not looking at us.

'The pair of you would be well advised to mind your own bloody business,' Junie said, getting to her feet.

'It would be nice to have that option,' he replied, turning his back.

Junie looked around the room for moral support, shaking her head with incredulity.

The lady at the window who'd previously complimented us on the car gave a gentle smile. 'You have been talking at quite a volume,' she said. 'It's been no bother to me, of course.'

I was minded to apologise as I turned for the door, but not a bit of it from Junie. 'I didn't realise we were in a library,' she said.

'At first I wondered if you were both a trifle deaf,' the lady said. There appeared to me a sense of agreement from all corners. 'But then it occurred to me. The car! You've been on the road some time, have you not?'

I nodded. 'All morning.'

'All that wind noise. It must dull the senses terribly.'

'Indeed.' I said. It was true: even my own voice sounded odd to me. It explained the muffled feel about the tearoom (which had now abated a little). Not only had the wind been terrifically noisy at a steady sixty, but the exhaust had roared and the canvas of the folded roof had flailed and cracked in our wake. Our ears had beaten a retreat!

It seemed Junie was readying a counterattack, until instead she simply said: 'Yes, I see.'

'Just my tuppence worth,' the kind lady said, 'I think your husband doesn't deserve you. Fancy finding . . .' She made an excessive show of mouthing the word *Viagra*.

Outside, Junie walked a pace ahead of me toward the car. Her face was thunder.

'Thought we were a trifle deaf, indeed,' she mumbled.

'Thought what about death?' I asked.

'Not *death*, Ray! Deaf!' She began to smirk.

'Yes. Right.' I held the passenger door open for her. A snort of laugh escaped her. 'A trifle *death*,' I remarked. 'Perhaps that's rather a good description of my week.'

She shook her head. 'The things I've just told everyone in there!' Her voice swooped upwards as she spoke.

I started to snigger.

Junie clutched the front wing of the MG. She did an impression of the old lady mouthing *Viagra*.

'Gosh, how embarrassing,' I said, unable to deliver all the words in a serious tone.

Junie had begun to sound like she was having an asthma attack, long shaking exhalations punctuated by great honks as she drew breath. 'Fucking hell, Ray,' she said, sagging at the knees such that she needed the car to hold her upright.

I caught sight of the old lady, sitting inside. She looked at me with confusion through the glass. 'We're all right, thank you,' I attempted to say. But it was no good: I was completely and inappropriately overcome by a fit of laughter. My chest ached in places numb for fifty years.

It was some minutes before I found the composure to pass Junie a handkerchief for her tears, and to wipe away my own.

'Let's get the fucking hell out of here!' Junie said as I fired the engine.

31

'I CAN'T GET OVER HOW BUSY IT IS,' I SAID AS WE SAUNTERED ALONG THE front, squinting in the face of the sun.

'Rather wonderful,' Junie said. 'Everyone making the most. It is all a little more . . . concrete than I recall, though.'

I unbuttoned my cuffs and rolled my shirtsleeves to the elbow. To our left the sea glittered with gold. A busker played violin on the hardstanding. Junie gave her a pound as we passed.

'The smell!' I said. 'Do you find you forget how things smelt?'

She closed her eyes and took a long sniff, waving her hand like a wine connoisseur. 'I'm getting fish and chips, and donuts, and candy floss, and seaweed, and fags.'

'Yes, magnificent.'

'Bumper cars!' Junie said, turning me around by my shoulder. 'What do you say?'

'Would I be a dreadful party pooper in saying that I'm rather enjoying a break from being behind the wheel?' This was an understatement; I had forgotten how taxing it was to drive any distance in a sports car designed before the war. 'I could certainly handle an amusement or two, though,' I said, catching sight of the lurid signage of an arcade up ahead.

We were soon in amongst the sensory assault of ascending electronic bleats and flashing neon and blaring music. With a pocketful of change, I took on the coin pushers. Junie wasn't messing around though: she was straight to ones marked *Over 18s Only*. I enjoyed an initial win of over seven pounds, but I soon fed those twenty-pence pieces back into the machine from which they'd come with no further luck; a concise demonstration of the ills of gambling.

My pockets were empty but Junie was in no hurry to leave, having commandeered the help of a young man with a sparse beard. I waited outside. A girl of about seven was sitting against the wall, transfixed by the multicoloured toy in her hands. I used to often chat with children when out and about, before I became gripped by the surety that one shouldn't. A great shame—no one makes better conversation than a youngster.

'What's that fascinating thingamajig you've got there?' I asked, noting her obvious frustration.

'Called a ruby cube,' she told me. 'I won it on the grabby machine.'

'Aha!' I crouched level with her. 'It's been some years since I've seen one of these. Mr Rubik sent the whole world potty when he came up with this.'

'Mummy says it's from the olden days.'

This gave me a good laugh. 'The olden days indeed! Your mummy is, of course, quite correct.'

'What does it do?'

I took it from her and held it in my palm like a revered artefact. 'It's the most incredible puzzle in the known universe. Only a few people know the secret of it. And they keep it to themselves.'

She giggled. 'Do *you* know the secret?'

I made a show of looking about myself. 'I do,' I said quietly, hoping memory wasn't about to let me down. 'And I'm a very old man. It's time I passed it on.'

The young lady moved closer.

'White first,' I said. 'Remember that. Make a cross of white squares.' I passed it back to her. 'You do this one.'

Inside five minutes, we had two-thirds complete. 'And now,

the famous yellow cross,' I said, muscle memory coming back to my fingers, the blocks flicking this way and that.

Three more children were now watching. There were some adults a pace behind too.

'Now, listen up,' I told the girl whose cube it was. 'There will come a time when you too will be old. And it will fall to you to pass on these secrets. Eighty years from now, you'll run into a small boy, at this very spot. And you will show him as I've shown you.'

'Okay.'

'Promise?'

She nodded.

'I myself, learned from a very old lady. Right here. She looked very much like you, just much *much* older. Tell me, what's your name?'

'Elsie,' she said, giggling.

I stopped dead still. 'Elsie? No! That was *her* name!' This got a titter from our few onlookers. With one swift movement, I tapped the cube onto the ground and spun the last squares into place. I passed it to her and bade her farewell, striding towards Junie who was watching from a safe distance.

'If ever there was a man who I just *know* could solve a Rubik's Cube . . .' she said.

'I'm not sure I had a single boy beat me at Allonby in that great craze of '81. Whole lessons were wasted.'

'I can well imagine.' She raised the flap on her handbag to reveal a stash of loose pound coins. 'I must say, that was a rather lucrative detour. Sixty quid! And that's after splitting the winnings with young Callum. He said you have to know which machine's not paid out in a while, they're programmed to get sympathetic.'

'A fine tactic. You always do that—find yourself an expert?'

'Just an idea that came to me. I was feeling, I don't know . . . *cocky*. Do *you* find yourself feeling a bit cocky today?'

'Cocky . . . Yes, I think so.'

We wandered onto the pebbled beach. The tide was low. We set out the picnic blanket at the foot of the stones, a little way from the crowds. Almost windless, tiny rolling waves flopped onto the sand as if too tired to go any further. In the distance to our left, that old haunt of ours, Ferring Beach, was hazily visible. Far out over the sea, a kite hovered, its body just a speck, a squiggle of red tail giving it away. I thought of those that I flew there, on a full mile of catgut line. Again, hit by that sense of decades slipping from my grasp, leaving barely a trace. A bizarre cosmic sleight of hand, it was as though I could have traced that invisible kite string to where it made landfall along the coast, and find it in the taut-skinned hand of a young man with a lifetime ahead of him.

'It's nothing other than I deserve,' Junie said, out of the blue. She was opening Tupperware pots of sandwiches and small savoury pastries.

'I'm sorry?'

Junie shrugged. 'Come on, get stuck in.' I did as I was told. She snapped the ring pull on a can of lemonade and passed it to me. 'When one makes bad decisions, it's only right and fair they live with them.'

'And the bad decision you're living with would be . . . ?'

She smiled. 'You know who I mean.'

I nodded sympathetically, chewing on a rather delicious smoked salmon sandwich.

'I didn't do it to get at you,' she said. The humour was gone from her voice. She was gazing out to the horizon. 'Marry him, that is.'

My mouthful became hard work. 'I never thought that was—'

'Of course you didn't, Ray. Because it's not in your nature. You're too damned nice. Too innocent.'

These assessments of my character had been made by a few people in my past. And then, just as now, they hurt. They were words given only half as a compliment, and received half as an insult.

'Or rather,' Junie went on, 'I didn't *think* I went with Denny to punish you. He was fun and uncomplicated and charming, and *unencumbered*.'

'There's no sense in raking over it,' I said, more through discomfort than anything else.

'And I liked knowing you were close. If I was with him. I think that was part of the attraction. Does that make sense?'

'Yes, I rather think I too—'

'But you know, maybe part of it *was* to get at you. I didn't realise it at the time. But, looking back . . .'

'Gosh, we'd been . . . over for some time when you and Denny started out. Two years?'

'So you'd forgotten all about me, yes? After those couple of years apart?'

'I suppose . . . no. Not entirely.'

She looked at me in a school-teacherly fashion. 'Nor I of you, sweetheart.'

'Would you look at those gulls,' I said, watching as six or more set about a washed-up crab.

'When you and I lost a child,' Junie said. 'I've never been in such a—'

'A very long time ago. Tell me, what *is* this you've put with the egg and cress?'

'Crème fraiche,' she said irritably.

'Yummy.'

'*Was* it a long time ago, Ray?'

'April 1968.'

'I struggle to think of many more pivotal events since. Steven, certainly, but not much more than that.'

'No, well . . .' She had me here. There was not one, though I felt ashamed so didn't admit it.

'She'd be fifty-six,' Junie said. 'Or *he*, of course. I don't know why but I always thought it was a girl.'

'Yes. A girl. Me too. I was sure of it.'

Junie smiled at me. 'You think about her still, don't you?'

I was silent for a minute, which revealed it all. My eyes felt warm. 'Fireworks,' I said, watching the sea. 'Remember, remember, the fifth of November.'

'Not sure I quite—'

'Her birthday,' I said. 'I mean, we never had a precise due date, did we? But my maths said the first week of November.'

'Thereabouts.'

'It started that first year. I heard fireworks, and I thought of her. I think she'd have liked fireworks. Particularly the ones with every colour at once. We'd have gone to lots of displays, I think. A real birthday treat.'

'Sure you would.'

'Some kids don't like the loud ones,' I rambled on. 'But I think she'd have been okay. Brave. Certainly by the time she was three or four, big enough to stand on her own and hold hands.'

'I'm sorry, Ray.'

'I'm an old fool. Listen to me!'

'It's lovely to listen to you. You do still think about her then?'

'When I hear fireworks, mostly. Other times too, I suppose.' I omitted the detail that I have a running fantasy: that every approximate birthday I picture what she's doing, who she's with, the web of relationships she's woven over the decades with characters I've imagined and become intimate with by dint of how much time I've spent visualising them. I could hardly admit this without appearing a crackpot, though I fancied Junie had something of an inkling. The strange thing was, there was nothing wistful about these imaginings of our daughter. They were all happy thoughts.

'Erika,' she said. 'That's what I thought we might have . . .'

'Brenda,' I said.

'Brenda? Really? Come on, Ray. Seriously?'

I reddened. 'No, I suppose. But I sort of made my mind up at the start, and, well, it stuck.'

She sidled closer to me and rubbed my forearm. 'I'll never forgive myself for how I treated you. When I up and left, dropped you like a stone.'

'Steady on. Forget about it.' My tone was all wrong, like I was reassuring a stranger who'd bumped into me.

'You were grieving too. And look what I did to you.'

'Such is life.'

'Ray, stop it!'

'I'll concede it was a . . . difficult time.'

'And I was a . . . fucking bitch to you. I was just so full of anger. Not at *you*. At losing our child. I didn't even feel upset. Not really, not till later. It was just this all-consuming fury.'

'I understand.'

'And when I needed you most, you were running round after your bloody mother. I couldn't stand it. Knowing I was always going to come second. To *her*. That's why I walked, why I fucked off to Chicago again.'

'I missed you very much.'

'Bloody hell, Ray, we were about to get married! I missed you every second. I was a mess. But the fury . . .'

'It's okay.'

'It isn't. Why did it have to happen, Ray?'

I nodded along, no answer to give.

'Those first few weeks in Chicago, I was lost. Booze, bars, mandies, men. I'll spare you the details,' she added, in response to my obvious discomfort. 'And then I caught up with some blues players I knew out of the London scene. We played this festival one Saturday night, out at Grant Park, by the lake. Full-on eight-piece band. Otis Spann himself got up and did a number with us!'

'Blimey!'

'It was an incredible gig, Ray. We played till two in the morning, it was so sticky and humid! But you know what? Blowing the harp that night was the first time since. It was the first time I'd not thought about . . . *it*. I was completely free for a few hours.'

'The meditative power of the blues,' I said. 'I know it.'

'And I sat down. And the sun came up. And I wrote you.'

'I remember the letter well.'

'The last entry in that lovely file of yours.'

'I suppose you could send me another,' I said, another attack of feeling *cocky*.

'There's a thought,' Junie said, smiling. 'It was my white flag, that letter.'

'I don't remember it saying as much.'

'For God's sake, Ray, no one says what they actually *mean*. I think you're old enough to have worked that one out.'

'It was lovely to hear from you.' I could still clearly recall the buzz from spying that envelope on the mat with her handwriting on. 'I'd imagined there'd never be another.'

'If you'd dropped everything, and come out to Chicago, we'd have made it together. You know that?'

'Well you see, Mum wasn't in great health.'

A flash of malice in Junie's eyes and then it was gone.

'Your bloody mother.'

'Who else would've kept an eye on her?'

'I know, sweetheart,' Junie said. 'I know.'

I stuffed a cube of carrot cake into my mouth and gave an emphatic thumbs-up; it was quite delicious.

Junie had eaten her fill, and lay back on the blanket, hands behind head, sun on face. 'She shouldn't have done what she did to you,' she said.

'Oh, I don't think—'

REPORTS OF HIS DEATH HAVE BEEN GREATLY EXAGGERATED

'You are a man of pure kindness. But you were barely more than a child. No mother should take that all for herself.'

'I never begrudged doing my—'

'She liked being doted on far too much, Ray.' I could sense Junie was holding herself back, minding her words.

'Perhaps there's a little truth there,' I eventually said.

'Steven and I have talked about her. He reckoned she must have had—what did he call it?—*abandonment issues.*'

'All sounds a bit *New Age.*'

'There's something in it. Your father had walked out on her. Denny went his own way, as he does, bless him. *You* however, she clung to you. Knew that *you* wouldn't abandon her. She made sure of it.'

'Yes, I see. Steven's a bright boy, isn't he?'

'Not half.'

'Being abandoned. Yes, perhaps that was her greatest fear.'

'That's before we start on the many boundary issues.'

This struck me somewhat as psychobabble. 'She's long gone though,' I replied.

Junie patted the blanket next to her, inviting me to lie down. 'I'm not trying to get on at you here, sweetheart,' she said. 'No one should be ashamed of loving their Mum. Quite the opposite.'

Her leg rested against mine. It was a most pleasant feeling.

'Tell you what, though,' Junie said, jokiness in her tone as she gazed up at the sky. 'Whenever I see an old woman—let's be honest, a woman of *my* age—being followed around by a hen-pecked, unmarried son who's never been allowed to leave home, I have an overwhelming desire to have a word. Say to her . . .' She began to giggle. 'Oi, you cunting narcissist! Let him go!'

'Maybe *don't,*' I said, laughing along. We lay in silence awhile. I found myself almost overcome with a sense of well-being. So perfectly unwound and unworried, as if we didn't realise all the discomfort of *being* except in a moment like this when the discomfort was gone.

'I'm terribly sorry,' I said. 'Hearing about your marriage.'

'Don't be, darling.' She wove her fingers into mine. 'It was never like it was with us with Denny. It was never like that with *anyone* else. I think I just assumed that what we had was this *young love* thing, something you only get to have, to *feel*, once. So I ended up settling for something that came nowhere close.'

'Oh, I'm not sure that's entirely—'

'I paid the price for being selfish, didn't I? I *could* have shared. There was enough of you to go round. A bit for me, a bit for old Lil.'

'It was my fault. I let you down when you needed me most.'

Junie propped her head against her elbow and leaned over me. 'Do you think it's about time we said "bollocks to the past"?'

I turned on my side and locked eyes with her, our faces inches apart. 'A fine idea. Mine is somewhat less exciting than yours, anyway. All that talk of strange men, and what have you . . .'

She smirked. 'Less fun than you'd imagine.'

'There's only ever been you,' I said. It was thrilling to make such an admission.

'Poor you.'

'I've never felt I've missed out.'

'Darling man!' She laughed softly and stroked her hand on my hip. It was incomprehensible that it had been sixty-five years since we were first this close. Ludicrous that she was recognisably that same beautiful woman.

'Where did all those years go, I wonder?' I said.

'Are we too old, Raymond?' she asked.

'For what?'

'To not settle. To turn our backs on discontentment. Can a pair of geriatrics like us ditch our worst habits?'

'If someone had asked me a week ago, well then . . .'

'Absolutely!' Junie said, nodding emphatically. 'But things seem . . . different now, don't they?'

I assumed a learned tone: 'I have become reacquainted with the art of possibility.'

'Steady on, steady on,' she said.

32

IT OCCURS TO ME THAT WE LIVE ACCORDING TO A SET OF SELF-IMPOSED rules. Anything beyond these parameters risks committing a grave offence: that of acting *out of character*. It's a dangerous thing of course, because if we break one arbitrary rule, might the whole damned system be at risk of falling apart? Might *character* actually prove to be something malleable, after all?

So it most certainly seemed that afternoon, given what happened next.

We had fed the scraps of our picnic to the seagulls and were back on the promenade. A stone's throw from the pier, we waited in line at an ice cream van. The violinist from earlier had gone. Her position was taken by a tall, cadaverous gentleman with a gnarly grey beard. He slumped against the wall behind him with a mic around his neck and a Telecaster in his hands.

Long-nailed fingers picked out a groove; what's known in blues circles as a box shuffle. He began to sing. What a voice! His small amplifier crackled and fuzzed under the pressure. My foot tapped. Though it was familiar, I struggled to place the song at first.

'"Keep It to Yourself",' Junie said. 'Sonny Boy Williamson.'

'So it is.' The track had been on the first compilation record I'd bought on the recommendation of Junie.

'He's bloody good,' she said.

I stepped out of the queue; waiting for ice cream seemed suddenly so mundane. I'll admit that my boldness was assisted by a rather hippie-looking young lady. She wasn't so much *danc-*

ing in front of the busker as *embodying* the music, hands aloft and gyrating like her whole body were the flame of a candle. It would've been difficult for anyone else to look silly.

That said, it was *my* idea; a fact I still have difficulty believing.

'Shall we?' I said, stretching out an arm to her.

'Are you serious, Ray?' Junie said. Her eyes were wild. What a thrill it had always been to impress her!

I walked slowly backwards, grooving a little. Elbows raised, an open palm offered Junie's way.

'Yeah, man!' the busker said between phrases.

She gave me the sort of grin that was worth any amount of embarrassment. 'Fabulous!' she said, half strutting my way.

We held each other in a close hold and swayed at the hips. My Clarkes loafers behaved a little like anchors, but nonetheless I managed a bit of sidestep this way and that, in the East Coast swing style.

I'd not danced in years. Not since Mum passed anyway; she and I would sometimes take to the floor if there was entertainment laid-on at a hotel. It was she who taught me the little I did know: how to hold, how to lead. Though no expert, I was aware there was only one way to dance: unselfconsciously. No use boogieing like a self-aware teenybopper caught in the sweep of a *Top of the Pops* camera.

Our presence had imbued the busker's performance with a new energy. He played that guitar like it was bass, rhythm, and drum kit all in one, all the while howling like one of the greats. Junie's hips were lithe against mine. She drew away from me and held my hand aloft, twirling left then right.

'All right!' shouted the busker as we grooved up close to him. He had deep, timeless eyes, and smelt wonderfully of marijuana.

He finished the song and, with barely a moment for us to get our breath, broke into a familiar Muddy Waters riff. He winked at us.

'Cheek of it!' Junie said, wagging a finger at him.

'*I may be getting old,*' the man sang. '*But I got young fashioned ways.*'

A fine classic. We took each other in both hands, and let the music carry us. Were people looking on, laughing at us? I've no idea. No one paid us any undue attention when, four songs later, we took our leave. I was joyously breathless. I slipped a tenner into the gentleman's guitar case, and I made a note of his internet site.

'Have you thought of selling CDs?' I asked, but I don't think he heard.

Seldom have I enjoyed a Flake 99 as much as I did then, with one arm around Junie. The sun, cool and red, lay down into the sea.

'Perhaps time is a little tight to visit your father's old church,' I said. 'A long drive ahead. And the poor MG's headlamps aren't to modern standards.'

'Something for next time,' Junie said.

'There's an idea.'

She turned to face me. 'And let there be no doubt—there *will* be a next time.'

And as if it were nothing at all, she kissed me on the lips.

IN TOTAL I'D BEEN AT THE WHEEL NEARLY SIX HOURS. I'D BEEN UP SINCE FIVE. Yet, back home and alone that evening, sleep was far from my mind. I grabbed a bag of bags from the kitchen, one of the many Russian dolls of used carrier bags I have about the place.

Cup of tea in hand, I headed upstairs. I creaked open the first door on the left. The air was cool in there: a little musty, a little Elizabeth Arden. I tugged free a good-sized bag and splayed it on the pink bedspread. *Woolworths* it said in faded letters. I chuckled at my own ridiculousness.

I permitted myself a minute or two of internal debate, of double-checking. Briefly, there was that same illogical feeling that had come over me when I considered doing this job forty years ago: that somehow she might return and be mortified to find her stuff gone.

But no. No. It was time.

'I love you, Mum,' I said out loud. 'But you've lived here long enough.'

33

TUESDAY

AND SO, TO THIS MORNING. A DAY THAT BEGAN WITH A NAGGING MELAN-choly. It put me in mind of those heading-home days down at the coast in my teens when it seemed that life could never again deliver the wonders of what was already history. At the slack pace of the morose, I sorted the bags of Mum's things on the landing in order of which charity shop should receive what. I'd assembled a box of jewellery which would need the attentions of a professional valuer. The thought of the money they might yield excited me not at all.

It was not yet eight when the phone went. A breathy voice introduced itself as Leigh Delamere.

'Very good, Steven,' I said. 'To what do I owe the pleasure at this ungodly hour?'

He scoffed, boasting that he was up at four most mornings. 'I'll be round for you at ten thirty sharp.'

'Did we make a plan? Sorry, there's been so much going on, and—'

'Just being spontaneous, Uncle Ray. You're free, yes?' I detected a snigger from him as he asked this.

'I've a few bags of things that could use rehoming, but—'

'Blimey, just a few?'

'Yes, all right. Steady on, steady on . . . Nothing that can't wait one more day, I suppose.'

'That's the spirit.'

'So where are we off to?'

'A redevelopment across town.'

'One of yours?'

'None other.'

'Well that's worth clearing my diary for.'

Another hearty laugh. 'See you in a bit, then. Oh, and wear something smart. Might shout you lunch somewhere posh if you play your cards right.'

'Right, that sounds . . . ten thirty it is, then.'

And just like that, my return to normality was postponed by another day.

With a schedule to keep, I marched over the road to Barry's. His flat felt immediately different: no longer stale and cold and dominated by the smell of bird. The power had at last been reinstated, evidently without any need to enter the property after all. It had taken ten days; it was what had brought him to my door a week ago. Finished the poor fellow off, no doubt. I brought Monday's *Advertiser* in from the doorstep together with a number of circulars. Little Boy Blue chattered fit to bust.

'I know all about it,' I replied to him. 'Almost tropical, isn't it?' I turned the thermostat down a couple of degrees.

There was nothing to suggest anybody else had set foot inside since I was last here: everything where I left it, the note I wrote on my first visit still on the coffee table, my feathered friend's dishes empty. The reconnection of the electric supply was incidental, it seemed. Still, following on from Steven and Denny's record-straightening yesterday, it was safe to assume the undertakers now had a correct name to hang from a toe; his next of kin would be aware soon enough.

I discarded my previous note and wrote a new one. A few gentle words of condolence to the family, a little about what a fine man Barry was and how I valued his friendship and wit. An elongation of the truth, granted, but no use having them all worry that he'd been lonely. For them, no second chances.

Little Boy Blue faced outwards on the window sill, tail all of a quiver.

I added a footnote, to say that if no one else could house Barry's budgie, I'd be only too happy to do so. I was, after all, embarking on quite some spring clear-out; I'd find room for the cage. I had never in my life had a pet. What a thing to deprive oneself of! With his dishes replenished, I hung about awhile to keep him company.

I was absent-mindedly skimming through yesterday's *Advertiser* in Barry's one armchair. Two pages from the back and there it was. I felt a little sick. It was logical enough that it should appear, yet I was not prepared for the reading of my own brief obituary.

Some of the death notices were treated to double-size ads, framed in black. Mine the same small size as the listings on the opposite page for the many lawnmowers and bikes for sale. I was grateful for Denny's parsimony on the matter, at least.

'RAYMOND THORNS,' it said. '*Died peacefully on 25th March. Funeral 11:00 a.m. on Tuesday 1st April, North Lambeth Crematorium. No flowers. Donations to Albert Cresswell Funeral Directors.*'

Like passing a gruesome car accident, I kept looking away then returning to it.

Barry's phone was hung from a cradle in the entrance hall. Inelastic from age, the coiled cable reached to the armchair. Business cards for three betting shops were taped to the handset. I dialled the stop-press number in the paper.

'It's a matter of a retraction,' I explained to the young lady. 'I'm hoping I might make the cut-off for Thursday's edition. I'm happy to pay any fees incurred.' My death had been made a matter of public record, and that surely needed righting post-haste.

I was transferred to Classifieds, where I found myself speaking to Jed.

'So you're telling me this Ray isn't dead?' he said. There was suspicion in his tone.

'Absolutely. Alive and well.'

'Right.' He stretched this to several syllables. I could hear that he was eating—most impolite on the telephone.

'There's no need to bore you with the whole saga. Unless of course you'd like me—'

'Let's have it right. You're telling me that this fella ain't dead, because you're him?'

'Quite so.'

'Listen up, yeah? Do you wanna know how many wind-ups we get, handling obits?'

'Yes, I suppose I'd like to.' Only in the silence that followed, aside from chewing, did I realise Jed was being rhetorical.

'A lot,' he eventually said. 'Several. Every year.'

'I can imagine. But this is not a wind-up, you see.' I baulked at the phutting sound of the seal between fizzy-pop bottle and lips being broken and remade.

'Ray Thorns, yeah? It says the funeral's this morning. Hardly any sense stopping the press now, is it?'

'I don't honestly imagine any of your readership are likely to be dashing out to pay their respects to . . . me, this fine morning. But people will have been given misinformation, you see. I'm sure, as a *journalist*, you understand the problem.'

This appeared to curry some favour. A tapping of keys. 'You got access to the net there?'

'Not here. I could pop back over the road, I suppose. My old personal computer is connected to the—'

'Let me tell you this: I'm on the website for Albert Cresswell's as we speak.'

'The funeral directors?'

'Your death notice is very much up there, Ray.' He emphasized my name, as if it were an alias.

'This whole . . . *muddle* was only set right yesterday. They've obviously not had an opportunity to correct their internet.'

'Maybe so. Though I'm not sure I'll be retracting your obit. Given the circumstances . . .'

'You should be an investigative journalist,' I remarked, though I sounded less salty than I wished to. 'Your talents are wasted in Classifieds. Perhaps a detective, even.'

A few grunts. 'Crem too,' he said, a whiff of triumph in his voice.

'I'm sorry.'

'The crem are listing it. Eleven this morning. North Lambeth. The Elgar chapel. Perhaps they need to update their *internet* too?'

'It would appear they do,' I replied, ignoring the sarcasm. 'So you're flatly refusing to do as I ask?'

'That's about the size of it.'

'I'm not happy about this,' I told him. As ever when faced with confrontation, I couldn't find any better words. 'I'll be calling again, and I shall—'

'Bye, fella.' Line dead.

I paced the flat. Why were the crematorium still billing it? Administrative inefficiency was the most likely reason: a simple failure to update the listing. Such logic didn't calm me for long, though. Doubts gnawed my gut. What if someone had failed to relay the information from Steven and Denny yesterday, to all the necessary people? Could I live with myself if there was even the faintest chance of a body being misidentified?

Directory Enquiries put me through. The *At Rest Crematoria Group*. One of those wretched automated systems. When prompted, I said, 'Lambeth North.' The pre-recorded lady was sorry, they don't have a branch of that name. Saying it louder didn't help. I tried 'Elgar chapel' too, but got the same response.

'You *do* have a North Lambeth Crematorium!' I said firmly. 'You bloody well do!' I immediately apologised, in case an actual human was listening in.

I pressed *three*, for upcoming ceremonies. Then *one*, for today. My word, they had a number of crematoria (this plural was new to me). We eventually rolled around to the correct branch. Sure enough, 11:00 a.m.: 'Raymond Thorns,' a gentleman's voice precisely said.

Heart racing, I called again. *Eight* to speak to a team member. Too many minutes wasted listening to dead air punctuated by soft clicks. I smirked, remembering Junie's comment yesterday: the funeral business doesn't need to concern itself with repeat business. Boy, did they behave like it, I thought, slamming the phone into its cradle.

Steven. That's who I needed. He'd know exactly what was afoot, put my mind at rest. But now that I thought about it, I didn't have his number. An idea occurred. I bid Little Boy Blue goodbye and sped over the road to home. He'd been the last to call. I made three attempts at dialling the last caller; no answer each time.

It was approaching half past nine. He'd be over in an hour to collect me for our jaunt. I was probably panicking about nothing. But hadn't all of this week's confusion been caused by my failure to speak up, loud and clear? Granted, I was probably faced now with nothing greater than an administrative oversight. But the stakes were creeping alarmingly high.

I looked at my *London A-Z*. The crematorium was four miles away by my measure. In morning traffic it was likely a half hour drive or more. Wait for Steven, and the opportunity could be missed. The 352 bus might just be the quickest way. Or a 46, plus a brisk walk.

No, there was one way only.

34

WHY DO CREMATORIUM DRIVEWAYS NEED TO BE SO BLOODY LONG? IT WAS hardly appropriate to gun the engine. In any case, there'd been a recurrence of the misfire that struck briefly yesterday; power was well down. I'd done well to make the journey. Up ahead, a hearse was stopped in front of the building. The stroke of ten, by my watch. Too early to be for me; or Barry, rather. At a second-gear crawl, the car spluttering and surging as ignition was lost and found, I made my approach. I swung left before I reached the hearse and parked on a cobbled track among sombre Japanese hatchbacks. The old MG, mischievous and gleaming, felt distasteful here.

'Beautiful,' a black-suited gentleman remarked as he passed by.

Yesterday, the attention the car had attracted had been quite a thrill. Today, I didn't have the vim for it. I felt like that most ungainly of creatures: a shy man in bold clothes.

I mooched around the building. The sun had burnt through and it was warm again. An oasis of silence in London, just the soft chatter of spring high in the trees. No officials were in evidence, with whom I might speak. But I was calmer, being here. Funny places, crematoria: in some respects, like a plain-bricked municipal building, a library perhaps; but then those gothic flourishes, arched windows, grand wooden doors. Something of the theme park about the place.

The stillness was interrupted by a door to the rear of the building clicking open. Mourners filed out, to Monty Python's

'Always Look on the Bright Side of Life' leaking from the chapel. I kept my head bowed as they filed past flowers on the ground, studying each with the attention one might give a painting in a gallery. There must have been thirty people, mostly my age or thereabouts. It fascinated me wondering what life the deceased had led to pull such a crowd.

I moseyed inside once everyone had gone. Those powered curtains around the coffin had been opened and the undertakers were manipulating the box onto a trolley. I don't know why this fascinated me so. Had I *really* imagined that the closing of curtains was the last time the departed was ever seen? What—that they plummet through a trapdoor? An absurd idea, yet watching these two tail-coated gentlemen manhandling the coffin like removal men might tackle an armoire was a little like catching one's mother in the act of playing tooth fairy.

'Are you okay there?' a lady asked me. She stood before me, head slightly bowed, oozing kindness.

'I probably shouldn't be in here.'

'There are few rules round here.' Both the *in* and *out* doors were open and a floral breeze swirled through the chapel. 'I'm very sorry for your loss. A friend of yours?' she asked, gesturing to the coffin which had now begun its *actual* final journey, on a stout tea trolley.

'No, no. I'm here for . . . another . . . I'm a bit early.' I looked her briefly in the eye.

She tightened her cardigan. 'We've nothing on for a while now. Not in this chapel.'

'There's no eleven o'clock?'

'Next is not till half past one. Who are you here for?'

'Sorry, you're saying there are no other funerals this morning?'

'Delius—that's the chapel next door—they have one at twelve. If you can tell me who you're—'

REPORTS OF HIS DEATH HAVE BEEN GREATLY EXAGGERATED

'Oh my word. Oh, that really is the most almighty relief. Gosh, I can't thank you enough.'

She looked at me as if I was potty. 'Perhaps I can check for you what time it *is* scheduled?'

'Look, I've no wish to put you out. Everything's . . . in order, I think.'

'Whose funeral are you here for?' She looked very intently at me as she asked, as one might address some crackpot on a geriatric ward. It wouldn't have surprised me if she'd asked me to confirm what the year was.

'Raymond Thorns,' I said, shaking my head dismissively.

'Ah, now I *have* come across that name.'

'There was something of a mix-up.' I hoped she wouldn't probe me on this.

'I'm going to check in with the office,' she said. 'It's not one of mine. I'm one of two officiants here, see.' She backed towards the doors, holding a finger aloft: *one minute.*

'There's no need to go to any trouble,' I said, but she left regardless.

Alone in the chapel. How silly I felt! All this running about! Twenty past ten now. Steven would be calling for me at home shortly. The thought that I might miss him saddened me. I walked as far as the door but felt it rude to simply dash off.

'You're here for Raymond Thorns?' said a bald gentleman in a precise pinstripe suit, strutting into the chapel with the lady celebrant following.

'Honestly, it's no problem. I must be going.'

'Change of venue,' he said, tapping his finger on a clipboard. 'A bit last minute.'

'I'm sorry?'

'It was scheduled here, eleven today. But it's been moved, I'm afraid. All Saints Church. Wimbledon Park.'

'At eleven, still?' the lady asked.

Notes checked. 'I'd have to confirm. So it seems.'

'It's still . . . on?' I asked. 'Are you . . . certain about that? It said on your website that it was here, see?'

'I do apologise, sir,' the man said. 'That really should have been updated.'

'Would you like us to call you a cab,' the lady asked. 'You should still be able to make it, with a bit of luck.'

'There shouldn't be a funeral,' I said. 'This is all a terrible mistake.'

An exchange of glances between them.

'When exactly was this . . . *relocation* carried out?' I asked, scrabbling to order my thoughts.

'Perhaps only in the last day or two,' the gentleman said. 'I can only apologise for the confusion.'

'By whom?'

That perfectly trimmed fingernail shook as it probed the clipboard. 'We have as our contacts a Dennis Thorns and a Steven Thorns. Brother and nephew of the deceased.'

'And they were here yesterday? To change the venue?'

'I'm afraid I was off yesterday.' He turned to the lady celebrant, who shrugged her shoulders.

'I think we should get you over to All Saints, don't you think, love?' she said.

I turned my palms outwards. 'I don't appear to have any other choice.'

'How about that taxi, then?'

I dithered for a moment. I could scarcely afford the wait. 'That's kind but no,' I said, my back already turned as I exited the chapel and broke into a run across the forecourt.

35

'HAVE I NOT ALWAYS DONE THE RIGHT THING BY YOU?' I SAID. 'AND I'VE ASKED so little in return.'

The engine picked up a little. The car had started up well enough, but we were barely off the crematorium premises when it began misfiring again. I nursed the clutch out ever so gently and made it away from the traffic lights. A mother and child waved from the pavement. I waved back, doing my best impression of someone not harassed.

What in God's name was Steven playing at? The man likes a laugh, of that I had no doubt. But allowing this to go ahead, wrong body and all? In the house of the Lord? I struggled to believe that even *he* could be so flippant.

An acceptable downhill run towards Clapham. Traffic heavier now. 'No you bloody don't!' I cried. Engine petering in and out.

Quarter to eleven.

A sweet spot found in the accelerator's travel: anything over a third and power disappeared completely, together with a strong smell of petrol. 'Come on, you can do this!' I told the old girl.

Stationary in a jam. Shaking my head. No, I wouldn't have it. No one, loose cannon or otherwise, chooses to relocate an erroneous funeral instead of cancelling it, for what—comic value? And even if Steven *were* so deranged, he would've had to get the idea past Denny. Probably Junie too. Absurd! The car shunted and shook as I nursed it up to walking pace. Should I return home? Trust to my confidence the staff at the crematorium had the wrong end of the stick?

Either way, I had about three miles to travel. I limped as far as the top of Tooting Broadway. Straight on for the church. A left turn for home. It was increasingly unlikely the MG would survive distance to either. At the lights—no more dithering now. On autopilot, I took the middle lane. Struggling to believe it as I was, going anywhere other than the church would be the height of folly.

The car sounded like a lawnmower phut-phutting on a single cylinder. It was running at a steady rhythm though, and all the while I was on the flat I could maintain a steady fifteen miles per hour.

Five to eleven.

Bloody hell! People hooted and overtook where they could; when I didn't pull into an obvious layby to let the accumulated masses past, I was gestured at and called unrepeatable things. The goodwill this car usually attracted had been lost. Not least by its driver.

The air was cooler and sweeter when I reached the edges of Wimbledon Park.

Six minutes late already.

'Excuse me,' I called out to a young lady on the pavement. 'Would you have any idea where I might find All Saints Church?'

She popped an earpiece out and grinned at the car. Leaning on the opened passenger window, she asked the same question of her mobile telephone.

'All Saints Church is zero-point-six miles from here,' said a disembodied voice.

The young lady showed me a map on the screen, my route scribed in blue. I thanked her profusely.

A left turn made. So nearly there. Somewhere along this narrow tree-lined street. The uphill gradient was at most one

REPORTS OF HIS DEATH HAVE BEEN GREATLY EXAGGERATED

in twelve. But no amount of slipping the clutch would do it. I stalled and restarted countless times. Each time, just as I got rolling, the engine would die.

I rolled backwards, swinging into a parking bay marked *Residents Only*. To hell with it.

I jumped out, and began to run.

36

I WATCHED FROM THE OUTSKIRTS OF THE CHURCHYARD. THERE WAS—TO MY very great relief—no hearse outside. Something appeared to be going on, though. The tall, heavy main doors were open, leading into a dim foyer. Soft music spilled out; inexplicably it sounded like the blues at this distance, something of Elmore James's slide guitar about it. I kept well back.

A lone man approached the open church. He was ancient and stooped so extremely so as to take on the shape of an apostrophe. He walked slowly, propped by a cane of Regency appearance. Bald and barely four and a half feet tall, he was dressed in a fawn suit that was somehow cut perfectly for his unusual frame. It was hard not to stare. Navigating the wide arc of the churchyard boundary, I stood such that the trunk of a sycamore tree kept me obscured from the view of this frail, fascinating character as he made his way inside.

'Looking for somewhere to take a leak?' a voice called over to me from twenty feet away, making me jump. Evidently the church's gardener, he was edging the grass where it met a pathway.

'Oh, sorry, I . . .'

'I know,' he said. 'Same for everyone. Feels kinda blasphemous to drain the old snake on consecrated ground, doesn't it? But you're all right.'

'It's not that. I'm just . . .'

He looked bemusedly at me.

'I was told something was on,' I said, tripping on my words. 'But I think I've been given duff information.'

'Right. Not here for the funeral?'

'No, I don't think I am.' I laughed as I said this. 'I certainly hope not.'

He looked at me strangely and began working his edging knife into the ground again. 'From that posh school,' he said, signalling the church with his eyes.

'I don't follow.'

'The funeral. He used to work up at that posh boys' school, Wandsworth way.'

'Allonby House?'

'That's the kiddie. Snob school, innit? Are you all right, chap? Where you off to now?'

I didn't *know* where I was off to. I marched around the rear of the building. No clue what the hell was going on or what to do. But unable to stand still.

Beneath a towering stained glass window, I paced circles. Stared at my open palms.

As I emerged on the far side of the church, there was a man standing with his hands on his hips. I froze. He had his back to me. He was dressed in a busy floral shirt tucked in to smart grey slacks. Before I had a chance to make myself scarce, he turned.

For a moment he peered hard at me. The deep, worried creases in this unfamiliar sixty-something man's face began to unfold. A smile bloomed. 'Ray?' he said, walking slowly towards me, head bowed, arms outstretched in greeting.

I nodded, nailed to the spot.

'What a blessed relief it is to see you!' he said. It was only as I shook his warm hand that I noticed the dog collar attached to his loud shirt.

'This is . . . your church?' I asked him.

'For my sins,' he replied, not releasing my hand.

I tugged it away with childish petulance. 'There's been a terrible mistake.'

The vicar nodded. 'Now, don't you worry. I have a bit—'

'I've been such fool,' I snapped. A panicked tear ran free. 'I'm sorry. This is all my—'

'Ray. Please. Everything's all in order.'

'You're not listening to me. Why will no one ever . . .' My complaint was cut short by the sight of a familiar, grinning form lurching from the church's side door and coming our way.

'Now, didn't I say I'd be collecting you at half ten from yours?' Steven said, hugging my head when he reached me.

'We're all here now,' the vicar said. 'That's all that matters.'

'Panic over,' Steven added, with a theatrical sweep of hand across his forehead.

My gaze flitted between the two of them. 'I'm sorry, I really don't . . .'

The vicar silenced me with his smile. 'I think we rather owe you an explanation.'

37

'FIRST OFF, A LITTLE ABOUT ME,' THE VICAR SAID. HE, STEVEN AND I HAD taken to sitting at a bench in the churchyard with the lazy sun warm upon us. 'Tim Fry, parish priest here at All Saints for some thirty-two years, believe it or not.' He had a voice one could bathe in. Once again, he took my hand in his. 'And I must say, it's so wonderful to see you.'

'I'm pleased to . . .' I stopped myself saying *meet*. Was I supposed to recognise this man? '. . . *see* you too.' Rude as I felt, I couldn't place him.

Steven was repeatedly glancing at that gold watch of his.

'Just a few minutes late,' the reverend Tim said to him. 'Not a problem.'

'Late for . . . what?' I said. 'If I may ask?'

The vicar laughed warmly. 'Now, Ray, you must forgive the two of us. I wonder, have you ever heard of such a thing as a *living funeral*?'

'Well, I'm . . .'

'Steven and I, between us, wondered if it might not be a nice idea. I've not conducted one before, but they've been around for a few years now.'

'We weren't quite expecting the last-minute wild goose chase, though,' Steven added.

'A *living* funeral?' I said.

'Why not?' Tim said. 'A chance to give thanks for a life,

whilst that person is still around to appreciate the love that surrounds them. I think it's a lovely concept. Don't you?'

Instinctively, I thought of Mum. How much better for everyone to have gathered and said those nice things about her, when *she* could've been there too. Maybe then, she wouldn't have . . .

'I can see the logic, I suppose,' I said.

'You see,' Tim said, 'when I contacted your nephew here to communicate my condolences, and I was told the rather wonderful news that you were still with us, it struck us both as a rather marvellous idea.'

I glanced again at his face. I *was* supposed to know this man. And indeed, there was a whiff of something familiar about those eyes—watery blue and oddly vulnerable.

'Why do we wait to honour people in death?' he continued. 'When we can instead honour them in life?'

'Amen,' Steven said.

'And with arrangements already in place at the crematorium, it was a simple case of a change of venue. Those wishing to pay their respects are still able to do so.'

'A lovely thought,' I said, though I was red with embarrassment. This kind vicar had likely been expecting a generous congregation. Perhaps something like the twenty or more who turned out for Mum. 'Although there was no need to go to such trouble.'

'It's no trouble,' he said.

'I'm just not sure I can . . . see the point.' I squirmed where I sat, eager not to sound ungracious.

There was an exchange of glances between Reverend Tim and Steven.

'Ah, nonsense, Unc!' Steven said, slapping my thigh. 'Must be nice being back in a churchyard?' he asked, changing the subject. 'You and my old Mum . . .'

I smirked, thinking of the letters he'd browsed. 'Steven's grandfather was a man of the clergy,' I told the vicar. 'A great man. Feet very much on the ground.'

'Yes, your brother Dennis was telling me.'

'Denny's here?' I asked.

'Inside,' Tim said, shooting a look towards the open side door.

'And . . . Junie?'

'She was hardly going to miss this!' Steven said.

The flare of excitement at the knowledge of her being nearby was quickly extinguished; what a fool I would appear. Having my eulogy heard in a near-empty church, without having the good grace to be dead for it.

'I'm not terribly sure about all this,' I told the two of them. 'I mean, this is an awful lot of effort for, well . . .'

Another look between them. 'There are a few people who've turned out,' Tim said. 'Ray, humour us, if you would?'

'All this upheaval I've caused!'

'I understand,' Tim said, looking upon me kindly. 'All a little overwhelming, no doubt. Here's a plan—why don't we fix you a seat off to the side? A little privacy, till you make friends with the whole thing? At least while I do my welcome? See how you feel then?'

'There's a great idea,' Steven said. 'Now we are getting on for twenty minutes late.'

'I do appreciate all the kind thought,' I said, rising to my feet.

'So we'll find you a spot out of the way?' Tim asked. 'Let you find your feet.'

I nodded as we walked around the outside of the building.

'My absolute pleasure,' the vicar said, looking pleased with himself in an almost suspicious fashion. 'I think that might work rather well, actually.'

38

HOW APT THAT, ONCE MORE, I WAS WATCHING FROM THE SIDELINES. I'D FACE Denny and Junie and whoever else (*whoever else!*) in a short moment. I was seated in the hard chair Reverend Tim had given me in his vestry; a small room packed with hymn books and choir gowns. The door to the main nave was open, giving me a sidelong view across the very front of the church—to the altar and communion rail, to an unoccupied organ keyboard, to an ornate brass vicar's lectern. I could see nothing of the congregation area, and they nothing of me. Like an actor waiting in the wings, I'd be clapping eyes on my modest audience soon enough.

A familiar guitar riff was playing over the sound system. Howlin' Wolf's 'Smokestack Lightning.' I was rather touched by this. The sound of life at its very freshest.

The music faded. Reverend Tim emerged from the unseen main body of the church, striding behind his lectern. He turned side-on to it and gave me, thirty feet away, a calming smile.

'Well, isn't this quite something?' he said, after a long pause spent gazing outward and then heavenward. His glorious baritone sounded even creamier through loudspeakers. The decision to amplify his voice should have struck me as odd, but I gave it no thought.

'What a wonderful occasion,' he went on, tipping a quick nod my way. 'A chance for us to give thanks for the life of Raymond Thorns.

'Now, as you all know, we've gathered here today to have a

REPORTS OF HIS DEATH HAVE BEEN GREATLY EXAGGERATED 295

living funeral. For those of you not familiar with the practice, as it is still rather a new idea, you can expect some familiar touchstones throughout. The main difference being rather obvious,' he said with a slight grin.

He went on to explain how the service was to work: essentially as a regular funeral, with singing and a reading and an address.

'We are, all of us, surrounded by our legacy,' Reverend Tim said. 'For many, that legacy is in clear view; it's evident in the children we have, and in turn their children, and the family tree that grows and weaves forth from us. But others leave something that is not so immediately tangible. Possibly something far greater. Their legacy instead is in the lives they've touched, the good they've done for whom they owed nothing; it is in the stories of heroic decency that become folklore and long outlive their subject. Raymond didn't have children of his own, and yet here we are. So many young lives better for having known him.' He locked eyes with mine and smiled.

I returned the smile, though I felt absurd. So grand and overblown.

'If we have a purpose in this life,' the vicar continued, 'perhaps it is this: to leave this world a little better than we found it. Now, *that* is a legacy.'

He turned his head this way and that. 'Those of us who've yet to become acquainted, a little about me. Before I was Reverend Fry, I was plain old Timothy Fry. Allonby House, class of '67. And I had the great pleasure of encountering Mr Thorns in the early days of his illustrious career.'

I looked hard at him in profile. There again, the faintest shadow of a memory.

'Each of us, if pushed, might be able to assemble the names of those people we've met along life's path, who have come along, and made things better. Most of us might need a while to compile such a list.' He folded his arms on the lectern and rested his chin against them. 'It wouldn't take *me* a while to think of the first name on that list,' he said. 'This is a happy occasion, so I shan't bog it down with tales of misery. Suffice it to say, though, that I endured some dark times at Allonby House. I haven't forgotten my privilege,' he added quickly, 'I was *fortunate* to be educated at such a place. But I was *not* fortunate to endure what we'd correctly now call a mental health crisis, under the gaze of a school administration that would seek to beat such a thing out of a child with a length of birch.

'I don't dwell often on this.' His eyes were wide and damp as they swivelled once again to me. 'But when I do, it's always the ladder I remember most vividly. And the cool sun in those early mornings, which shone for everyone except me. This ladder, it was lashed to the school building's chimney stack. Up three storeys then further still to the peak of the roof. I thought about it for more than a week. All day, and all through those wide-awake dorm nights.' He looked straight at me. 'When you don't know how to cry anymore. That's when you know you're done.'

I nodded slowly. 'Timothy,' I muttered. 'Of course. Tim.'

After our first meeting on that roof, he'd leant me a hand with all manner of jobs: cutting hedges and tending the field and repairing the sports pavilion. Well into his sixties now perhaps, but he *did* still bear a resemblance to that eleven-year-old. I tingled with goose bumps, so touched to be remembered by this fine man.

'On ground that was flat and hopeless, that ladder was the only way out,' he said. 'A climb to freedom. Four days it took of walking past, looking at the first rung. Knowing if I could just do *that*, I might do the rest too.

'Easy way out!' he boomed, causing the sound system to distort. 'Isn't that what they say? What fools! I hope they never find themselves where I did.'

He turned, leaning an elbow on his lectern and addressing me. 'On day four, I began the climb. And I was right. After the first rung, my course was set.

'Most of us will be two minutes from death only the once. That's surely how close I was. But instead of meeting the oblivion that this desperate, *desperate* small boy craved, I instead met Raymond Thorns.' His face lightened. Smirking, he looked up into the rafters. 'It's enough to make anyone believe in a higher power.' There was a strange weight about the murmur of gentle laughter from the body of the building.

He began a slow stroll across the front of the church towards me. 'And so nearly, I never did say *thank you*. How unforgiveable of me! But today, we've been given a gift.'

Reverend Tim reached the open vestry door and stopped. 'Thank you,' he said quietly to me.

'Steady on,' I whispered, shrugging my shoulders. 'It was nothing at all. But you're most welcome.'

Standing ten feet from me, he at the door, me within the vestry, he stretched out both arms. 'Would you care to join us, Ray?' he said.

'I think I'd . . .Yes. I'd like that,' I replied, getting to my feet.

Still shielded by the door, he hugged me in his big arms. 'You deserve this,' he whispered into my ear. 'Enjoy it.'

Laying a hand on my shoulder, he led me into the church.

There was a muted cheer. The clatter of a few handclaps.

'Welcome, Ray,' the vicar said.

It became applause.

'I don't under . . . I just don't . . . What in the name of . . .'

We reached the lectern and he held me at his side.

It was absurd.

'This can't possibly be for . . .'

'There's no need to look so petrified, Ray,' Tim said.

The place was damned near full.

There were a few whoops and whistles, the applause was still going strong.

'Who are all of . . .'

'Oh, just a few of your former students, for the most part. You are a man held in very high regard.' He swept an arm from one side of the congregation to the other. 'By a good many.' He joined in the applause himself.

'I don't believe this,' I told him, shaking my head. 'How—'

'All in good time,' he said.

He led me to a space in the front row, next to where Steven, Junie and Denny, and Kwan sat. Not to appear rude, I managed a quick, nervy smile to this large crowd. A limp wave of the hand.

'Weren't expecting that, were you?' said a grinning, yet rather red-eyed, Steven as I took up my place next to him.

'I don't understand,' I said.

Junie leaned behind Steven. 'So glad you could make it,' she said with a smile I'd swap all I own for.

'You're . . . in on this?' I mumbled.

'Only since yesterday. Forgive me?'

From the row behind, palms belonging to people I didn't recognise patted my shoulders.

To the far side of Junie sat Denny. He was excessively re-clined with legs crossed. 'Good to have you back,' he said, tip-ping me a nod and a wink.

'Sorry to spring that on you,' Reverend Tim said, back at his lectern now, the congregation quieted. 'We owe you an explana-tion, I fear.'

He spoke softly, close up to his microphone, eyes locked on mine. 'What on earth is everyone playing at? That's rather the question, isn't it?'

I looked at him wide-eyed and shook my head. There was a further rumble of mirth from the assembly behind me.

'So, as you're perhaps aware, Allonby House last week announced the sad—and mercifully erroneous—news that you had passed on. On their website, and their *socials*. Are you familiar with the lingo, Ray?'

More laughter. I was keeping up thus far.

'Your brother Denny here subsequently informed the school of today's funeral, which they duly announced.'

'Now, something that may come as news to you,' Tim went on, 'you have long had something of a fan club amongst your former pupils. The famous Facebook *Spike Thorns Appreciation Society*. Inaugurated back in, gosh, 2008 I believe!'

Steven's mobile telephone was in his lap, screen tapped at a pace.

'Some six hundred and fifty members at last count,' said the vicar, beaming.

I shook my head again. How could there be so many?

'And as the desperately sad news of your passing broke, there began the rather touching plan to have something of a reunion at your funeral. Give thanks together for a man who touched so many of our lives.'

Steven nudged me and passed me his telephone. There it was on the screen: *The Spike Thorns Appreciation Society*. Beneath the main title it read: *Reminiscences about the greatest man ever to walk Allonby's corridors*.

My hands shook. 'I don't believe it,' I mumbled.

'Now, I myself,' Reverend Tim said, 'was as bereft as anyone on hearing the news about you, Ray. I did a little detective work, and got in touch with this nephew of yours.' He and Steven smirked at each other like a pair of old crooks.

'Mainly to offer my condolences. To share a few private memories of my own. But also, to offer the services of this rather lovely old church, should your family so wish. And I was met with the miraculous news that in fact, as Mark Twain might have said, reports of your death were *greatly* exaggerated!' he held his palms up to the heavens. 'What wondrous news: Spike's alive!' This elicited a cheer.

I glanced over my shoulder. *So* many people.

'Sunday evening,' Steven told me quietly, leaning close to my ear. 'When you were round for dinner. I was *literally* about to message the school and get them to run a retraction.'

'So the plan was hatched,' the vicar continued.

I looked down at Steven's phone in my hands. With a finger to the screen, I rolled at speed through the list of members of this group. I had the sense of a light coming on in a long-closed room in my brain; so many names that I'd forgotten, yet could recall instantly.

'They . . . they're all here for me?' I whispered to Steven.

He closed his eyes and nodded.

I looked behind me once more.

'And so, a chance for us all to give thanks,' Reverend Tim said, a crack in his voice. 'For the life—the *continuing* life—of Raymond Thorns. Good old Spike!'

A peal of warm laughter. Yet more applause.

I looked down at Steven's phone again, skimmed little vignettes, some written fifteen or more years back, regarding events of four, five, even six decades ago. It was hard to believe these things I'd been involved in were worthy of anecdote, of being reminisced about by men in their middle age. A Harvey Moore (quiet boy, mad on military aircraft) recalled the term they were tasked with writing blues songs and the multiple complaints about the noise. There was Mansoor Mahmood (talented artist, once suspended for using the C-word within earshot of the deputy head), telling of an assignment I set of writing a volume of our own fairy tales; he'd kept his copy of the book I had bound for each of the class; he's been reading it to his own young children lately. Andreas Villaverde (wonderful character, inappropriate posters removed from dorm at least twice) wrote of the Saturday morning detentions I supervised, and the games of sponge football in the school hall that they descended into. The list of stories went on and on, far too many to digest.

I had mattered.

I *had* mattered.

39

'AND NOW,' THE VICAR SAID, 'THOSE OF YOU WHO CAN, PLEASE STAND, FOR our first hymn: "Morning Has Broken".'

The shuffle of very many feet behind me. One line of the melody on the pipe organ before we began to sing. The words were projected onto a large screen.

I began mumbling along. The congregation droned in the customary way.

A lone voice amongst us began to cut through. '*Sweet the rains new fall*,' belted out a gentleman a few rows behind. He was gruff sounding with a strong vibrato. Somebody old. '*Sunlit from heaven*.'

Steven sniggered next to me, and upped the volume of his output. Likewise Junie, who'd lost none of her vocal abilities. But still, bolder and bolder, this elderly, somewhat tuneless voice trounced us all.

I'd no wish to stare, but I like everyone cast a glance towards the source of the sound. It was the same chap I'd seen making his way into the church when I first arrived: that tiny man, curved and ancient. Mouth agape, he looked up at the words. We caught each other's eye.

It couldn't be! He smiled with his eyes, though his singing continued unabated. It was unmistakably him. He was no longer wearing that trademark turquoise turban, the years had taken his hair and more height than he could afford to lose, but he was as alive as ever. Charles Sethi! I did the maths: he was something around ninety-five years old. I couldn't stop grinning.

A realisation began spreading through the church of exactly who the old man making all the noise was. He'd overseen the greatest thirty years in Allonby House's history. There was a murmur of excited chatter about the place.

And then something rather magical began to happen. This hymn had been a staple of morning prayers, ushered in during Sethi's reign. And buoyed by that loud voice, and no doubt the knowledge of to whom it belonged, everybody began to let themselves go—just as we did all those years ago when this hymn was fresh and optimistic. With such a wall of sound, I had no reservations myself in singing at the top of my voice. From all corners the sound grew and grew. We were all at school once again.

After the last line reverberated through the place, there was an instant of silence. And then, more laughter.

'Didn't that blow the old cobwebs away?' Reverend Tim said, red in the face.

In keeping with the funeral format, there followed a biography of me. Is it grandiose to admit that I caught myself rather enjoying it? From my arrival on VE Day morning, our time in the countryside with Dad, our move back to London after he disappeared.

'And now,' the vicar said, 'it gives me great pleasure to welcome a special guest.'

I gazed up at the very tall man on his way to the front. That familiar, somewhat famous face of Wes Lithgo winked at me. He reached out and shook my hand. 'Good to see you, Spike!' he said, before skipping up to the lectern.

He had long been Allonby's most notable former pupil. As Steven and I had discovered during our impromptu visit, his portrait took pride of place on their wall. He'd competed at the

'88 and '92 Olympics and been a national champion many times over. Still now, he turned up on television and in a newspaper articles, talking about some charitable endeavour or another.

By my calculation, he had to be around sixty, but a member of that burgeoning generation who still appear preposterously young even at such an age. Lean and wrinkle-free and dark-haired, he stood at the front in trousers so tight they revealed the absence of socks beneath his brogues.

''Ello all!' he said, leaning close to the mike. 'You'll be pleased to hear that for once I'm not gonna be banging on about the Olympics.' There was a comedic sigh from somewhere behind me. 'And I'm not here to pester you for your time and money for *Level the Field.*' The name rang a bell, and Wes correctly read my expression. 'It's a charity we founded fifteen years ago. We help talented children from underprivileged backgrounds find their way into professional athletics. And if anyone wants to know more, or to donate a year or two's salary, I will happily make myself available afterwards.

'I spend my life doing talks to kids,' he said. 'And the thing I'm always chatting about is *hard work*. Nothing comes without hard work, not in sport. Everyone knows that. But there's something I'm a bit slower to tell them. Thing is, hard work alone won't cut it. Because you need something else too. You need *luck*. Without luck, you're nowhere.

'I won't bore you about my upbringing. Plenty had it worse than me. It's all on Wikipedia anyway. But I'll summarise by saying that I had the sort of background that tends not to produce—forgive my arrogance—top-flight sportspeople. Not so *lucky*, you might think.'

The strength of his South London accent had never really struck me on television, but in here, in contrast with the impeccably spoken vicar, it was marked.

'I was about ten or eleven. And as was pretty standard, I was up to no good. Me and a group of lads were in the habit of *letting ourselves in* to places. Imagine our excitement when we found a private school with a fence that was no stress to clear for a future decathlete! A private school—with an outside swimming pool. Irresistible!'

I shook my head. It had never occurred to me that this fine man had been among that group of trespassers that I'd dealt with all those years ago. To this day, I could remember the faces of the ringleaders. The young Wes Lithgo must have been one of the many quieter ones who'd loitered in the shadows.

'First stroke of luck right there,' he said. 'We were met with none other than Spike Thorns! And instead of treating us like dirt—and trust me, that was how we were used to being treated— or calling the police, Spike says: "Come and join our club."'

Our discussion had been somewhat more convoluted than that, but I smiled all the same.

'I know he's not the only person I have to thank, mind.' He pointed a hand towards our frail old head. 'Mister Sethi played no small part, as well—something I've discussed with him many times over the years. But without Mr Thorns, and his generosity of spirit, and his utter decency that stops him from casting judgement on a single soul; I would've been booted off Allonby House's land there and then.

'Instead, I was *included*. That alone changes you. Being around that thing we call *potential*. Spending time around all these bright kids from well-to-do homes. Seeing that they're pretty much the same as you. Makes things less . . . *unobtainable*.'

'It wasn't just that you let us in,' Wes said, speaking directly to me. 'You trusted us enough to give us a bit of free rein. And it was out on that playing field, that you said we could help ourselves to, that I came to the attention of old Davy Charlton.'

I smirked at the memory of Allonby's games master of the nineteen-seventies. He smoked sixty a day and was so breathless on the football field he couldn't blow a whistle, instead resorting to hand signals.

'Charlton saw a bit of potential, helped me train. Got me hurdling at county level. Then came Mister Sethi's offer of a sports scholarship on old Chimney Charlton's recommendation. Two years at Allonby House, and another scholarship—this time to Angmering College. And the rest, as they say, is history.'

Sport has never been my thing; perhaps that's why I didn't remember Wes specifically from back then. But I *did* remember letting those who came by to Steady On Spike's from outside school use the sports and music equipment if they so wished. How wasteful to withhold such things that were only lying dormant anyway. I could hardly see that I'd been even faintly generous in so doing. They were not—let's be honest—mine to give.

'I've been blessed,' he continued. 'More than my share of *luck*. But there'd have been none of that without that first bit of good fortune, half a century ago. Without *you*, Mister Thorns.'

There were a number of *Hear hear*s about the church.

'I work with a lot of kids these days. Every one of them, every single girl and boy, bursting with talent. And you know what they want? They want to be *heroes*. I hear the word *hero* a lot.' He rolled his eyes. 'I blame the London Olympics.

'And you know what I say about being a hero? I tell these kids that they've got to put in the work. Being a hero ain't about one great triumph. It ain't about one chance alignment of the stars in front of a watching world. There's no quick route to greatness. It's about putting in little bits of effort every single day of your life, without reward or applause. It won't feel like heroism, I tell them, not for years. But they'll multiply up, all those little, quiet efforts. Until one day, you'll be victorious.'

He stepped off the low stage and addressed the church whilst standing a couple of feet in front of me.

'Small efforts, every day of his life. Driven only by a sense of fairness. Of a desire to do the right thing. And here he sits, a *hero*.'

I was blushing. I shook my head at him.

He swept an arc in front of himself. '*This*,' he said to me, 'this appreciation for you. This *love* for you. This is what it looks like when you put the work in for long enough. This is what being a true hero looks like.

'I think I speak for us all when I say I'm sorry that we nearly left it too late. For a nasty moment, we *had* left it too late. Looks like I've had another stroke of *luck*.

'Spike Thorns! I think it's about time you took a bow, don't you?'

He stood in the aisle and slammed his palms together.

Wes Lithgo crouched level with me. 'It's okay,' he said. 'You can *look*. Please look.'

'Come on, Uncle Ray,' Steven said, putting an arm around my shoulder.

I did as I was told. The applause became cacophonous. For the first time, I really *looked* at the assembled mass. Took it all in.

I began to allow myself to believe it. It was ridiculous, absurd; but it *was* real.

Shakily, I rose to my feet. I certainly wasn't going to honour Wes Lithgo's request for a bow; but I smiled. I held palms up. I'd have implored them to *steady on* if only it could have been audible. Instead, I looked at the ground and mouthed the words *thank you*. I retook my seat.

When eventually there was silence, Reverend Tim introduced our next hymn. 'Jerusalem,' another Allonby House staple. After a tentative opening few lines, propelled again by Charles Sethi, it enjoyed the same raucous rendition as the previous number.

I caught the vicar's eye as we sang. He came over to me.

I spoke up before the spell upon me wore off. 'I wonder,' I said to him, 'should I perhaps say a few words. Everyone's gone to so much effort, and . . .'

'I think that's a splendid idea,' he replied.

40

AT LEAST A HUNDRED PAIRS OF EYES WATCHED ME. I RECOGNISED A FEW OLD colleagues, some members of extended family. But the majority were unfamiliar. Predominantly male, most exuded that officer class self-assuredness that successful men over fifty tend to. There'd been a ripple of applause when I took to the lectern. Silence now.

Twice I went to speak, but stopped myself. I had thought that I'd thank everyone for coming, for giving up their Tuesday morning. To not express my gratitude would've been impolite. But in the thirty seconds I spent looking out at the congregation, a peculiar thing happened. I began to feel *not scared*. More than that. Not quite comfortable, perhaps. More . . . thrilled.

Wasn't this how standing in front of a class felt? How being invited to lead a morning assembly always excited? Wasn't *this* the very high that made my school maintenance work feel so mundane by comparison?

I had nothing prepared, of course. Had I ever, though?

'Newton's Third Law,' I said into the microphone, after a moment's more thought.

Inexplicably, this got a titter. Many a gleeful expression. I was buoyed.

'Come on, boys. Who's going to give us a definition?'

Both Steven's and Kwan's hands shot up. But I picked a red-faced gentleman who was evidently wrestling with his memory.

'If object A . . . and object B . . .' he said. 'Oh, now what is it? If A acts on B, then . . . oh, this is pathetic. Sorry, sir.'

'On the right lines, young man,' I said. 'In layman's terms: for every action there is an equal and opposite reaction. It's an irrefutable law of physics. We've covered it in many previous lessons. Despite the lapse in memory from . . .' I sent a mock-chiding glance his way.

'Burstow, sir. Edmund Burstow.'

'Indeed.' I grinned. 'Class of . . . '86. Ate raw pasta as a break time snack. Played Adrian Mole in the summer production. You look . . . a little different.'

He nodded and slapped his shaven head.

'Newton's Third,' I said again, only half an idea what I'd follow this point with. 'It's been on my mind of late. I've been wondering if it's not just a *scientific* principal, see? I've been wondering if *everything* we do elicits an equal and opposite reaction. But life's rather more complicated than science, isn't it? Somewhat messier. So one can't always *see* the equal and opposite reaction to our actions. And then there's the timescales involved: sometimes the reaction, though equal and opposite, may not occur till months, years, even decades after the action.

'But I have decided, recently, that this law *does* apply to the human realm. Although it seems I've made an error in my theorising.' I leaned forward on the lectern and studied the fascinated faces before me. How I missed this!

'I made the assumption that this only applies to our *errors*. To our misjudgements, our lapses in consideration towards those we love.' My eyes were drawn to Junie in the front row. She gave me a smile.

'I've recently become sure in the knowledge that our mistakes echo down the years, their counterpoints turning up to punish us when we've long forgotten our initial misbehaviours.

'But you good people—you generous, gracious people—you've made me see the full picture. That this law of Newton's is *truly* universal. It's not just the errors, is it? It's *everything*. All

REPORTS OF HIS DEATH HAVE BEEN GREATLY EXAGGERATED

that each of us does, reverberating throughout our histories, every action causing reactions in the most unexpected places, at the most unpredictable times. A great criss-crossing web of causes and effects running down the generations, tying us all together.'

I was finding my stride. 'What a fortunate man I am! Who else is granted this very fine privilege of getting to *see* the effects that their actions might, in some way, have helped to cause. You are all people of quite extraordinary decency, and I owe you a debt of thanks.'

This statement provoked some uncertain expressions, a few shaken heads.

I was silent awhile. I looked down at the lectern. The gravity of this situation was weighing on me.

'What a week it's been,' I eventually said. 'You can't imagine. The stress! Terrifying at times.' Briefly, a private reflection on the race over here this morning. 'Living on my wits. What a fine irony that in being thought dead, I've been more alive than I have been in over a quarter of a century.'

I pictured myself exactly a week ago. Yet to encounter a cold and ailing Barry Detmer at the door.

'I've been reminded of something,' I said. 'Something that I'd long forgotten.' I was improvising now, my most satisfying lessons were always given this way.

'Every single moment of our existence is spent at the very leading edge of time unfolding. We are eternally running head-long, blind, into the unknown. The *unknowable*. This past week, I've remembered what it's like to really *feel* that. And it's reminded me of the most thrilling times of life.' Instinctively, another glance towards Junie. 'I've been reminded what it's like to feel that great wonder of an existence where it's hard to know quite how one's world will look tomorrow, the day after that, the week after, the year.

'I'm embarrassed to admit that I've been most terribly afraid. For decades I have been. I've not dared to look ahead, not dared to march with that ever-advancing front into the future. I've lived gazing only backwards. Holding on tight to the fragments of things mostly lost. To the notion that all that is good has already happened. Struck down by *nostalgia*—that rotten disease that robs one of half their eyesight: able to see all that's got worse, blind to all that has improved.

'No more! That's what I say. You wondrous people have shown me there is so much good still to know.'

I'd been rambling, the words bubbling up from somewhere deep. I was lightheaded, a little exhausted.

'Thank you.' I said it not as one might when closing a speech, but emphatically. 'From the depths of my heart, *thank you*. Thank you every single . . . every sin . . . every . . .'

It was no good. I couldn't help it. I had begun to cry.

Reverend Tim rose from his seat and laid his palm on the back of my head.

'What a fool!' I said through sobs. My voice, amplified, sounded broken and absurd. 'I'm just so grateful . . . I don't deserve this. I really . . .'

There came a shout from the congregation. Somewhere near the back. 'Steady on, Spike!'

I searched the church, peering through my tears.

'Steady on, Spike!' came another voice, this time over on the left.

'Oh, gosh,' I mumbled.

A rumble of laughter.

Slowly, it spread through the place. Something like thirty or forty unique voices, each in turn. 'Steady on, Spike!' they shouted.

I leaned forward on the lectern. My tears became those of laughter. What a sound!

The vicar escorted me back to my seat, his arm tight around me. More wonderful laughter. More applause.

Junie held my hand as Steven took to the lectern and read Dylan Thomas's *Do Not Go Gentle into that Good Night*. A poem that had always rung with sadness, yet today it was filled with optimism and I nodded emphatically with each stanza. We sang our final hymn (a rousing rendition of 'Love Divine All Loves Excelling').

Minutes later, we were filing into the dazzling midday sun. Muddy Waters' 'Rollin' Stone' played us out. Junie and Steven to either side of me. My own funeral! And a sense that without question, something had been laid to rest.

41

DENNY PATTED ME ON THE BACK. 'I'VE GOT YOU A BEER,' HE SAID. 'THEY BREW their own here.' He took a swig of his and considered it with great concentration. He was standing with his legs well apart and his belly straining at his striped shirt. It was a stance that had been serving him well for nigh on seventy years. 'Citrussy, quite hoppy,' was his eventual verdict.

'Moreish,' I offered, sipping mine.

'I'm glad you're all right,' my brother said, slapping my back again. 'Really made up.'

He'd never been one for sentimentalism; I fancied these would be his last words on the matter. I apologised for the great inconvenience I'd caused, and thanked him for his part in arranging this *wake*.

We were at The Marquis, a rather swanky pub a stone's throw from Allonby House. The large glass sun lounge attached to the rear (the establishment call it an *orangery*) was reserved for us. It seemed everyone from the church had continued on here.

Smiling, I looked out to the car park where the MG was stationed. A lady sat in the driver's seat and pulled switches. Two gents leaned on the open roof, smoking and drinking. Someone else inspected the engine bay. It'd had taken no more than a glance under the bonnet after the church to rectify the earlier running issue (a simple matter of a loose distributor cap). I'd

REPORTS OF HIS DEATH HAVE BEEN GREATLY EXAGGERATED

given a lift over here to a former student of mine by the name of McDade: he'd been heavily involved in the car's restoration in the late seventies. He was now in the field of medical engineering, I was enthralled to hear as we'd negotiated the South London traffic.

I'd left the keys in and was heartened to see another of my charges from the after-school club taking the old girl for a spin up the road.

I meandered over to the buffet (a quite remarkable spread) where I found Charles Sethi in conversation with a lady in a trouser suit.

'Raymond, my dear boy,' Sethi said, setting his white wine to one side and shaking my hand. 'You've no idea. I can't *tell* you how great it is to see you alive and well.'

'Likewise, sir,' I said. I'd never have recognised this stooped old man at a glance, but those eyes still glowed with the same charm they always had.

'Have you met Harriet Plumpton?' he said. '*Doctor* Plumpton?'

'Harriet will do just fine,' the woman said with a handshake. 'Honoured . . .'

'You're the present head . . . *teacher*,' I said, suddenly placing the name. 'Thank you for the card. Very thoughtful.' No sooner had I said it than I panicked: Was it just a formality sent by the office without her knowledge?

'Least we could do,' she said, laughing. 'Though I've never been happier to discover I've sent something in error!'

I blushed. 'It's a jolly nice card. Beautiful picture. Beautiful place.'

'Isn't it just? It's a pleasure to finally meet you, Raymond. You may not know me, but I assure you I know *you*. You are something of an Allonby legend.'

'Oh, don't talk such . . .'

'It's a very great shame we've not seen you for so long,' Charles Sethi said. 'You've had invitations to teacher reunions, yes?'

I nodded, embarrassed. There'd been a couple turn up over the past twenty years. 'I rather felt no longer welcome, after I retired,' I said.

'Unwelcome?' Doctor Plumpton spat. 'Not a chance!'

'Perhaps un*worthy* is a better term.'

Sethi shuddered at the suggestion. 'You were always very much missed.'

'I hadn't realised till that card arrived that Ceawlin Brown, *Mister* Brown rather, was no longer head,' I said.

Doctor Plumpton and Sethi shared a glance, a private thought about the man who'd been in office between each of their tenures.

'What's the expression?' Doctor Plumpton mused.

'Left under a cloud?' Sethi offered, learnedly.

'Oh really?' I asked.

Doctor Plumpton leaned in close. 'Made some *inappropriate advances*. To the elder sister of one of the boys.'

'You're kidding?' I banished the gossip's smile that was forming. 'You're kidding,' I said again, this time with appropriate gravity.

'Text messages. Notes,' Doctor Plumpton said. She grimaced. '*Pictures.*'

Wasn't this the man who'd said *my* conduct was improper? 'He seemed so . . . *strait-laced*,' I said.

'They always do,' said Sethi.

My mind flew back to old Rhind-Jones in the sixties and I smirked at my naivety.

'The young lady was *of age*, at least,' Sethi added.

'Really, Charles!' Doctor Plumpton said. 'Is that supposed to be a defence? Next you'll be telling us she was a *bit of a looker.*'

Sethi rolled his eyes. 'Point taken, Harriet.'

'Charles and I meet for breakfast once a month,' Doctor Plumpton said to me. 'With a few other old Allonby faces. Per-

REPORTS OF HIS DEATH HAVE BEEN GREATLY EXAGGERATED 317

haps you'd care to start joining us? Early start, mind. Six thirty. Last Wednesday of every month. There's a chair with your name on it.'

The pair of them looked at me. They seemed genuinely keen.

'Well, yes, of course. I'll be there early too. You wait and see.'

'There's that legendary enthusiasm I told you about,' Sethi said to Plumpton.

'I never doubted it,' she said. 'There are few people's opinions that I take as gospel. But yours, Charles . . .'

Doctor Plumpton turned to me. 'So the two of us have been talking. How busy are you keeping yourself, Raymond?'

'Well I . . . I . . .'

'You see, we're rather in need of a little assistance up at the school. Nothing too strenuous, someone who knows their way round a ride-on lawnmower. Someone who can line a football field. A couple of days a week, perhaps?'

Absurdly, I began mentally assembling my schedule: the long walk to get the bread twice weekly, litter picking on the common, tending to Mum, charity shop visits.

'We have a summer term production too,' Doctor Plumpton continued. 'We're doing *Guys and Dolls*. We could well use some help with building the set. Thirties New York—reckon you'd have some ideas?'

I banished all thoughts of routine from my mind. 'I think I could be a very great help. I suppose I'll need to come in for an interview . . .'

Doctor Plumpton shook her head. 'The guru has vouched for you,' she said, nudging Sethi. 'He, and a hundred others. So, we might see you after the Easter break, yes?'

'That would be . . . yes. Yes please.'

'My assistant will be in touch,' she said, in a *that's that then* fashion.

'A brandy to celebrate?' Sethi said, peering around to locate the bar.

I nodded, in something of a daze.

'Welcome back, Mister Thorns,' he said, with that wise smile of his.

42

'STOP APOLOGISING, UNCLE RAY, FOR FUCK'S SAKE!' STEVEN SAID, NEGOTIAT-ing my hallway in the low light. 'It's a damn sight less of a mess than it *was.*'

'Steady on, steady on,' I said to Junie, my hands hovering to either side of her hips.

'You two oldies put your feet up,' Steven called from the kitchen. 'I'll make the tea.' This was almost immediately followed by the sound of a cupboard being opened and its contents tumbling floorwards.

'Much still to do,' I mused to Junie, directing her to my armchair and clearing another for myself. 'But do it I shall. You'll see.'

The sky was indigo outside: one of those fragrant, damp evenings that follow a perfect early spring day. I'd spent some six hours becoming reacquainted with former students, my pockets bulging with business cards and hastily scrawled numbers and email addresses. Junie and Steven had insisted on following me home, making sure the old MG delivered me safely.

'Only too happy to help with the sort-out,' Junie said, unlacing her pink Doc Martens. 'You just holler.' She put her stockinged feet on the box marked *Best China* and emitted a loud sigh.

'You've done quite enough.'

'You might find me needing to move in anyway. Denny's probably hoofed me out already.'

'What's up with Denny?'

'I'm kidding about. It's more than his life's worth to throw me out of my own house.' She shook her head. 'The atmosphere is . . . *uneasy*, though.'

'You've had a . . . barny?'

Junie sniggered. 'That's one way of putting it.'

'Since I saw you yesterday?'

'Last night.'

'Not because of . . . me and you going . . .'

She waved the suggestion away. 'No . . . no . . . Kept that one to myself, didn't I?'

I grinned, enjoying the fact too much. 'What's his problem, then?'

'Oh, nothing out of the ordinary. He was just being his usual charming self. Grumping about everything—me being too noisy, making too much mess, daring to *breathe*—that sort of thing. A pretty standard evening round at ours.'

'I see. That all sounds rather depressing. I hope it didn't ruin the day. Yesterday was . . .'

'Yesterday was the best day in a very, very long time.'

This provoked a private thrill. 'I very much agree,' I rather weakly replied. 'But to end it on an argument at home, that's a shame.'

'I wasn't in the mood for it, Ray. For his . . . *crap*.' Junie's expression was nonchalant. 'I'm not really sure how it all came about. One minute we're in the kitchen and he's cursing and rearranging the dishwasher, and the next, well . . .'

'Do tell.'

'I find myself laying bare the evidence. Of all those . . . misadventures of his.'

'You're kidding me?'

'His *infidelities*—let's call a spade a spade here.'

'And Denny? How did he . . . react?'

Junie rolled her eyes. 'Anger. Denial. Some more anger.

Then some good old-fashioned gaslighting. All straight from the narcissist's playbook.'

'Gosh, I'm so sorry.'

She waved this away. 'And then this morning, it's as though nothing happened. Denny acting all *business as usual*. A little extra charm, perhaps. A cup of tea in bed, would you believe?'

'But it isn't . . . *business as usual*?' I asked uncertainly.

'Oh no. No sodding fear!'

'Haven't you been sitting on this . . . knowledge for *years*?'

'Decades.'

'It must have been killing you.'

'Yes. Yes, I think that's exactly what it was doing.' She spoke like this was the last word on the matter.

The question on my lips was *Why yesterday?*, but I thought better of asking. In any case, we were interrupted by Steven's entrance with a tea tray. A brace of digestive biscuits projected from his mouth.

It was fast getting dark and I wandered to the window to draw the curtains. Across the street, the lights were on round at Barry's. I caught sight of a figure moving about beyond the net curtains. The poor family, I thought.

'I left a note,' I told Steven and Junie. 'About his beautiful budgerigar. If nobody else is willing to, I said I'd be happy to take him on. That's not . . . opportunist of me, is it?'

'Hardly,' Junie said. 'You're a sweetheart. They'll be glad of the offer.'

Steven was crouched over the gas fire, clanking the ignitor, where he began chuckling, spraying crumbs about the place. 'And of course more *stuff* is just what you need.'

'I'll make the space, and then some,' I reassured him.

'Looks like you've gone and nabbed yourself an old bird, then.' He chuckled, winking at his mother as he walked by.

'Oh, do piss off,' she replied.

'What's it to be?' he asked, thumbing through the top row of records.

'Anything but *my* one, thanks very much,' Junie said.

'I'm easy,' I said, pouring two mugs of tea from the pot.

His choice was perfect: that otherworldly voice of Howlin' Wolf bathed the room.

'I wonder if a brandy chaser might be the thing?' I said, once Steven had left the room. Tea alone seemed geriatric. Bloody hell, we're not even *eighty*!

'Abso-fucking-lutely, babe,' Junie replied.

I dusted off a bottle of Courvoisier that dated back to Mum's era from behind the bureau. A couple of mismatched crystal glasses still bearing their Oxfam price tags were dug out, and generous tots poured.

'Don't suppose you've got a chessboard to hand?' Junie said, having taken a decent gulp.

'Would it surprise you to know that I have?' We both laughed as I unsteadily climbed the furniture and extracted a folding board from the clutter on the top shelf. I set it down on the box between us.

'We'll be needing this,' Junie said, producing the black rook from her handbag.

I was meanwhile transporting the other thirty-one of her father's ivory pieces from the mantelpiece.

'I noticed that had gone,' I said.

'How silly of me! What was I playing at? A little bit of the past to hang on to, I suppose.'

'Don't get into that habit!' I made a show of looking around the room. 'Things can get out of control.'

She put a pawn in each hand and held her balled fists over the board. I tapped the left: black.

Junie took a sharp breath and looked at me intently. 'I'd like us to spend some time together,' she said. 'I'd really like us to . . . do that.'

'Yes. I quite agree.' I swilled my drink around the glass.

Her gaze dipped down to the board. 'I've missed you most dreadfully, Ray. And I won't waste another moment.'

The game began: her king's pawn to king's pawn four.

Junie took a swig of brandy and smiled at me. 'Your move,' she said.

ACKNOWLEDGEMENTS

With heartfelt thanks:

To Harry Illingworth and Helen Edwards, who I am exceptionally fortunate to have championing my work.

To Meredith Clark—as smart and meticulous an editor as any writer could wish to work with.

To those many talented people at MIRA Books, not least Sean Kapitain, who has produced a knockout piece of cover art.

To my brothers, Will and Sam, to whose wisdom I turn with irritating regularity.

To my wife, Vikki, always my first reader and the person who continues to make everything (my books included) better.

To the kindness of strangers: the booksellers, bloggers, and reviewers who I will likely never meet but whose generosity means I can—four books in—keep on calling myself an author.

Last but never least: to you, the reader. You picked this book up instead of a million others, and have stayed to the last page. I am forever in your debt.